Perpetual

Search

BRIAN HUEY

ISBN: 978-1-9493-7900-6 (sc)
ISBN: 978-1-9493-7901-3 (hc)
ISBN: 978-1-9493-7902-0 (e)

Lulu Publishing Services rev. date: 10/03/2018

BRIAN HUEY

PERPETUAL

BOOK 1

SEARCH

A PERPETUAL SERIES NOVEL

First in the Series

Second Edition

Praise for PERPETUAL

Perpetual **delivers**. From the intricate opening sequence to the cleverly crafted details, the reader is taken on a delicious journey ... enough twists to keep even the most ardent reader of high-octane fiction entertained.
—Dr. Michael G. Meacher, COO, Front Sight Firearms Training Institute, Las Vegas, NV

A great story ... could not put it down ... riveting. **Filled with action, suspense and complex relationships**. *Perpetual* is a terrific book.
—Linda Kesler/Author and Speaker/ Palm Beach, FL

You are **drawn into this book** without realizing it ... captivating ...
—Roz Morton/CEO/Media Mark/ Rock Hill, SC

A thrilling ride across the Eastern Seaboard of the USA. I could not put it down!
—Robin Banks/ Proprietor/ Coruisk House/ Elgol, Scotland, UK

The new Robert Ludlam. *Perpetual* is **a plot-twisting, time-shifting, fascinating read**. Detailed ... and treats you as a sophisticated reader.
—Linda Franco/CFO/Lakeside Education North Wales, PA

Filled with **interesting characters and plot twists** ... will have you thinking about the future of energy and our natural resources, and the difference one person with a vision can make ...
—Jerry McGuire/Charlotte NC

Perpetual is a **fast paced intricate, suspenseful, intelligent read**—all wrapped around a love story born in the North Woods of Maine. As Brian says, "Enjoy the ride."
—Shirley Reading/ Literary Agent/ The Scotland Agency, retired/ Charlotte, NC

"*Perpetual* is well researched with **intricate subplots** and interesting snippets of information. What bothers me the most is differentiating what is real and what is fiction."
—Dr. Steven Jaynes

Perpetual ... speaks to the last cell in the "who done it" cortex of your brain ... exceptional **mind teasing plots and possibilities** ... with more gut wrenching adventures and convoluted plots than the last presidential election.
—Rodger Harrison
Guatemalan Consul General (Honorario) to the USA

I took this book on vacation and could not put it down ... **engaging characters** and a story with enough plot twists to **keep you wanting more**.
—Mark Black/ Senior Vice Pres/Corporate Development/ Charlotte Pipe

Explosive beginning maintained throughout this thriller. I'm looking forward to Brian Huey's next novel.
—Phillip P. Joyce, Mars, Inc. Senior Exec/retired. Chicago, IL

This exciting story is a wild ride but one which could happen. Mixing the U.S. government's various intelligence agencies, big oil interests and Middle East terrorists, *Perpetual* **leaves you wondering who the good or bad guys really are!** Combine all of this with the developing tale of relationships between families and friends on a personal level and you have a narrative with many intriguing characters and very engaging plot twists.
—Lee Jim Fleischer, Ill, retired/Downers Grove, IL

An intensely gripping novel that throws you immediately into the battle of energy development while interesting **twists and turns accellerate you towards the climax**. Where is book #2?
—Carolyn Souther/Engineer & Photographer/Atlanta, GA

A run-away train ... People and places seem familiar at first, then like passing through a dark tunnel, the reader emerges into a brightly lit world of **intrigue and suspense**.
—John J. Rego/Phunny Pharm Entertainment/ Cincinnati, OH

This is an adventure to read. It is a story that, while **extraordinarily entertaining**, will stay with you. Every time you see another gas price spike, or open your utility bill, you'll remember Brian's **wonderful characters**, and hope that somewhere, somehow, a real-life Matthew is at work in his research lab.
—Barry Reitman/Author Memory Shock & Public Speaker/NY,NY

Cleverly crafted, *Perpetual* is an appropriately titled novel that produces a perpetual stream of twists and turns and takes the reader on **a memorable journey chock full of historical facts, current topics and engaging characters**. Readers will be left wanting to get on the next rollercoaster ride in this engaging series.
—Devin Steele/Steele Media Group/Greenville, S.C.

The PERPETUAL Trilogy

BOOK 1—Search

BOOK 2—Assassins

BOOK 3—Abducted

BOOK ONE

TIMELINE

Chapter	Title	Characters	Timeline	Location
Prologue	Revelation	Matthew & Maria	March 17, 1995	Miami
PART I	**PERPETUAL**	*Sun*		
1	Invent	Dr. Cameron Jackson	1955-1973	Indiana Dunes
2	Threat	Omar bin Taliffan	1973	Vienna
3	Anguish	Matthew & Maria	1983	Maine
4	Resolve	Tremont	1989	Indiana Dunes
PART II	**PERPETUAL**	*Journey*		
5	Spirit	Sean	1994	Maine
6	Bond	Tremont & Sean	1981	Yale
7	Ramble	M&M	March 15, 1995	UMaine
8	Patriot	Tremont	1981	Yale
9	Security	Dr. Jackson		Indiana Dunes
10	Quest	M&M	March 16, 1995	I-95 S
11	Remember	Dr. Jackson	1981	Indianapolis
12	Genius	The Eaton's		Maine
13	Honor	Tremont & Sean	1982	Afghanistan
14	Terror	Omar bin Taliffan	1983	Vienna
15	Transfer	M&M	March 17, 1995	Miami
PART III	**PERPETUAL**	*Tragedy*		
16	Tutor	Matthew	1987	Maine
17	Suspect	Fazio	1988	
18	Declare	Dr. Jackson	1989	DC
19	Free	Tremont		The Atlantic
20	Chill	Tremont		The Gulf
21	Breach	The Jackson's		DC
22	Face	Tremont		DC

23	Destroy	Tremont		Indiana Dunes
PART IV	**PERPETUAL**	*Convergence*		
24	Purpose	Flannigan		DC
25	Converge	M&M	March 17, 1995	Miami
26	Flee			
27	Arrive			Homestead, FL
28	Chase			I-95 N
29	Corner	March 18, 1995		
30	Target	March 19, 1995		
31	Fail	Flannigan		DC
32	Hide	M&M		I-95 N NC
33	Escape			NY
34	Safety		March 20, 1995	Maine
35	Riddle		June 2, 1995	
36	Lost		June 3, 1995	
37	Search		June 6, 1995	
38	Storm			
Epilogue	Genesis		The Summer of 1995	
Acknowledgement				
I	Introduction to Book II – *Assassins*			

Contents

Prologue xxi

Part I   **PERPETUAL Sun**
Chapter 1   Invent... 1
Chapter 2   Threat 6
Chapter 3   Anguish 13
Chapter 4   Resolve..19

Part II   **PERPETUAL Journey**
Chapter 5   Spirit 23
Chapter 6   Bond...37
Chapter 7   Ramble...41
Chapter 8   Patriot..50
Chapter 9   Security..54
Chapter 10   Quest 62
Chapter 11   Remember 71
Chapter 12   Genius..74
Chapter 13   Honor 78
Chapter 14   Terror...83
Chapter 15   Transfer 88

Part III   **PERPETUAL Tragedy**
Chapter 16   Tutor 99
Chapter 17   Suspect... 114
Chapter 18   Declare 120
Chapter 19   Free 131
Chapter 20   Chill...141
Chapter 21   Breach 146
Chapter 22   Face 149
Chapter 23   Destroy 152

Part IV   **PERPETUAL Convergence**

Chapter 24   Purpose..161

Chapter 25   Converge 166

Chapter 26   Flee 178

Chapter 27   Arrive..183

Chapter 28   Chase 193

Chapter 29   Cornered...201

Chapter 30   Target..210

Chapter 31   Fail 217

Chapter 32   Hide 222

Chapter 33   Escape 227

Chapter 34   Safety 232

Chapter 35   Riddle..239

Chapter 36   Lost 248

Chapter 37   Search 255

Chapter 38   Storm 267

Epilogue...273

Excerpt from Book II...285

Acknowledgments..289

About Brian 291

Dedicated to

The Entrepreneurial Spirit

When bad men combine, the good must associate;
else they will fall one by one,
an unpitied sacrifice in a contemptible struggle.
– Edmund Burke

All of us failed to match our dreams of perfection.
So I rate us on the basis of our splendid failure
to do the impossible.
– William Faulkner

When I see a man on a bicycle,
I do not despair for the future of the human race.
– H. G. Wells

What is the use of a house,
if you haven't got a tolerable planet to put it on?
– Henry David Thoreau

Prologue

Revelations
March 17, 1995

MATTHEW THADDEUS EATON sat in the tow truck beside Marcos, the manager of the Miami Beach Shell station. The VW bus hung off the back of the truck.

It was after midnight, and they could hear the faint sound of the South Beach entertainment coming to life a few blocks away.

He helped Maria into the cab and turned his attention to a man standing down the street, *Cracker Jack*. He was a head taller than the two FBI agents. They talked in front of the Cuban diner where Matthew and Maria had spent the last hour mesmerized by Cracker Jack's tale of intrigue.

Marcos maneuvered the wrecker out of the parking lot with the VW bus in tow. Gunfire erupted.

"*Bajar!*" Marcos yelled for them to get down. Matthew pushed Maria toward the floor as a bullet tore through the door. The gears ground from first to second, and more cracks of gunfire sounded.

"We're being shot at!" Maria screamed. "Marcos, *¿Qué diablos?*"

In Spanish, Marcos cursed the wrecker's slowness, and said, "You kids keep your heads down. We'll be out of here in no time." Marcos forced the stick into third gear, hit the gas, and the huge wrecker jerked forward.

Matthew looked out the window, and his eyes met Cracker Jack's.

He saw everything, absorbed every detail. He had a recent dream of a plane flying overhead, shooting at the VW bus—but he assumed it was because he read too many Jason Bourne novels.

There was no plane, but someone was shooting. Cracker Jack's last words in the diner came back to him: *I need your help; you might be my last chance.*

An FBI agent put his back to Cracker Jack in the corner of the building. The other was firing across the street. Their only protection: a palm tree.

Matthew glanced at the two men taking cover behind a U.S. postal box on the other side of the street. He had assumed they were FBI. Cracker Jack had said he was expecting replacements for his current chaperones, the G-Men that had him under protective custody.

"Stop the truck!" Matthew yelled. "We have to help!"

"Cracker Jack told me to get you kids out of here no matter what."

"I don't care what he said. He's out in the open."

With that, Marcos brought the rig to a skidding stop a dozen feet past the shootout. Matthew reached over Maria to open the door. He saw one of the agents go down. Cracker Jack jerked and fell against the wall, landing in the dirt. A patch of red bloomed on his white shirt. The two G-Men lay sprawled in the sand. "They shot them. They shot Cracker Jack!" Matthew heard someone scream—and then realized it was his own voice. Under the street lamp, the bodies lay still, covered in blood.

"I have to help him," Matthew said, opening the door.

Maria put her hands on his chest. "No! You'll be shot!"

Marcos ground the vehicle into gear. The pungent smell of gasoline and exhaust filled the cab. With a tremor in his voice, Marcos said, "It's too late, *amigo*, it's too late."

He barely missed a parked car on the narrow street before he got the rig under control.

They drove two or three blocks before a bullet shattered the rear window inches above Matthew's head.

"We have to go back, Marcos! There's a chance he's alive."

He grimaced and said, "My job is to get you kids out of here, and that's what I'm going to do."

"Your job?"

The rig was pushing forty as bullets twanged off the back. Before Matthew could yell, the truck barely missed hitting a grizzly man holding a bottle to his lips in one hand and gripping his fully-stacked shopping cart with the other. He froze in suspended animation a second before diving like an Olympic athlete out of their path. Marcos swerved and smashed two large garbage cans before regaining control.

Matthew looked out the shattered rear window at the green sedan that was catching up to the VW bus, bouncing around like a tetherball behind the wrecker. A man who Cracker Jack had called Cue Ball, leaned out of the passenger window. He smiled and leveled his gun. Matthew grabbed the wheel, and Marcos objected as they veered left, barely missing a group of pedestrians. They careened into an Ocean Drive park area knocking over iron cast benches.

Marcos regained control, and Matthew let go of the wheel.

"*¡Hijos de puta!*" Marcos yelled.

"*¡Que locura!* There's no seat belts!" Maria said, waving her hands.

"Bring it up to my boss," Marcos shot back, "if we live!"

He muttered something Matthew could not understand and swung the wheel into the path of the approaching sedan.

Maria screamed, "What are you doing?!"

Matthew looked into Cue Ball's glaring eyes and then at the gun. He tensed, expecting a bullet. Before Cue Ball could shoot, the wrecker careened into the sedan with such force, Matthew thought the four-ton wrecker would flip. Instead, the impact thrust the car upward, and it fell back on its top, crushing the passengers like potato chips in a bag. Sparks flew with the sound of metal scraping the pavement. The sedan looked like a Fourth of July sparkler before hitting a short stone wall, rolling two, three, four times, before landing right side up in the sand.

"*¡Madre Santa de Dios!*" Marcos whispered, crossing himself.

"That was close. Damn good gamble, Marcos," Matthew said. Maria also drew the sign of the cross, then held tighter to Matthew. The trio traveled west on Fifth Street, north on Alton and over the MacArthur Causeway, then headed south on Route 1.

PART I

PERPETUAL Sun

Chapter One

Invent
1955-1973

CAMERON T. JACKSON, a world-renowned quantum physicist and alternative energy pioneer, expanded on the concept that energy emanating from the sun, captured by solar or photovoltaic cells, would one day run all household lights, appliances and more. In his book *Capturing the Sun*, published in 1955, he warned of the inevitable depletion of our natural resources and the imminent dependence on foreign oil leading to geopolitical strife and imbalances. Dr. Jackson was an environmentalist long before the term became popular. He wrote:

> My mission is to advance the theory, development, and application
> of naturally emulating energy sources such as solar, water or wind,
> and through quantum action combine emerging nanoscience
> and other available technology with the distillation of atoms and
> neutrons, to create clean, cost-effective renewable energy.

Although Jackson received international critical acclaim for his forward-thinking theories, investors showed little interest in capturing energy from the sun while oil and coal were plentiful. He personally funded his own research, relying on limited government grants.

After the inexplicable death of his wife Karen Carson in 1959, Jackson led a reclusive lifestyle. He focused on his son and his work, pausing only for a bottle of cognac. Meanwhile, the public attitude around energy shifted. The oil embargo of 1973 forced global consumers to accept the reality of limited and depleting resources, inspiring an interest in renewable energy.

The public often misunderstands and even fears genius. Later, long after Jackson's death, they would say, he was a man before his time. But while he lived, he spent decades in a lab below his home. They lived on a forty-acre lakeside ranch

1

his wife dubbed *Jackson's Place*. For ten years after Karen's death, the only visitors to the compound were Cameron's in-laws, the Carsons; a mysterious friend who lived on a sailboat off the panhandle of Florida; an unkempt FBI agent; and the occasional deliveryman.

Fourteen years after the first publishing of the then obscure *Capturing the Sun*, Jackson's publisher asked for an update. The second edition sold well to libraries, universities, and researchers.

A magazine article compared Jackson's theories to the science fiction of Jules Verne's novel *From the Earth to the Moon*, which caused a fanatical anticipation of space flight in 1865. Jackson found himself with a small cult-like following of scientists, students, and laymen. His detractors, mostly large companies, alleged that he was an alarmist, a troublemaker, a gadfly, a mad scientist with unrealistic ideas.

The *Indianapolis Star* printed,

> Dr. Cameron Jackson's revolutionary studies and sharp criticisms have received mixed reactions throughout the scientific and political world. He attempts to stir up despair equaled to the fear of nuclear destruction in the 50's and the melting polar icecaps of the 90's. Imagine a reaction like the 1938 *War of the Worlds* hysteria.

The *New York Times* reported on October 31, 1938,

> A wave of mass hysteria seized thousands of radio listeners between 8:15 and 9:30 o'clock last night when a broadcast of a dramatization of H. G. Wells' fantasy *The War of the Worlds* led thousands to believe an interplanetary conflict had started, with invading Martians spreading death and destruction in New Jersey and New York.

Dr. Jackson chuckled as he read the article while sipping on a Hennessey's cognac.

"Dad, they wrote about you again in the paper."

"Let me see that, son."

He stepped over to the security system and flipped between monitors. He said to the ten-year-old, "H.G. Wells, huh? This reporter has quite an imagination."

Tremont replied, "He also said you might be like Galileo, Isaac Newton, Max Planck, and the man who gave you that flask."

Dr. Jackson took a sip from the flask, gave Karen an apologetic glance, and whispered, "To the bastard Wolfgang Pauli who sent me on this perilous mission."

Yale University
1969

Cameron Jackson enjoyed the criticism and embraced the comparisons to science fiction. He was aware of the political and economic tension he caused. Still, that didn't curb his own sharp critiques of Congress, who were sitting on their hands with environment-friendly forms of energy in reach.

In May of 1969, his first appearance in years, Cameron presented the next phase of his research. His work in solar energy led him to his most amazing discovery: energy *could* replicate itself, saving as much as ninety-eight percent of the current energy with no adverse effects on the environment.

Two months before Apollo 11 landed two men on the moon, the marquee at the door of Davies Auditorium read,

Dr. Cameron Jackson
The Jules Verne of Energy
Presenting: The Alternative Energy Revolution
Featuring updates to his groundbreaking book, *Capturing the Sun*

The Yale Dean of the School of Physics stood at the podium and said, "It's no coincidence that we chose Dr. Jackson for this occasion, just weeks before Americans land on the moon. As a man before his time, Jules Verne predicted submarines, flying machines, skyscrapers, and the most preposterous—a landing on the moon. Dr. Jackson has the audacity to suggest we will one day derive all energy from limitless sources. Perhaps another dean will stand here one day and compare a new visionary with Dr. Jackson."

Jackson looked out into the crowd. He knew his shadows were here. They're always here, he thought. They were willing to kill to get his research. Though he had proof, he was hesitant to risk his family's safety. He had taken precautions for his son to carry on the work if something should happen to him, but Tremont was still young, and there was so much more to accomplish.

"Ladies and gentlemen," the dean continued, "please join me in welcoming the Jules Verne of energy with PhDs from Harvard and MIT, and most important, an honorary doctorate from Yale University. You know we don't give those to Harvard boys lightly." A chuckle spread through the crowd with a few student cheers. "I give you Dr. Cameron Jackson." The ovation lasted several minutes.

Jackson stepped onto the podium. He strained to see the back of the hall where stood two stern-faced men wearing sunglasses and dark suits. The only relief from his shadows was at home, Jackson's Place.

A slide presentation ran on a huge screen behind him. He presented a forty-year overview of the history of alternative and renewable energy sources; the failures, the challenges and the risks. He closed with this: "As you know, there are rumors that I'm a mad reclusive scientist." That incited a chuckle from the crowd. "Maybe they are right. What have I been up to? Even some of you might ask." He paused for effect. "Here's the thing. Before the end of this century, I will introduce an entirely new, potentially limitless energy source." "If I should live so long." He bowed his head slightly and took his seat.

Total silence.

Scattered applause.

"Within thirty years? Impossible," whispered the Dean of Mechanical Engineering.

"It appears the good Dr. Jackson is well ahead of his time," the Yale President, Kingman Brewster Jr. whispered.

"By a few centuries," said Paul Hessen with disgust in his voice.

Dr. Randall Parez ignored Hessen and said to Brewster, "Of course this comes from the man who introduced coeducation to Yale, this very year."

President Brewster grinned. Though many alumni objected, he had pushed the idea since becoming president in 1963. If Yale was to attract the best minds in the country, it was imperative to open the school to women.[1]

"This is science fiction indeed," Hessen whispered. Hessen—a former classmate of Jackson, and a current MIT professor of Mathematics—was Jackson's greatest detractor. "Where will he get the funding?"

"Perhaps from NASA," said an academic sitting next to him. They both laughed.

As Dean Santos closed out the night at the podium, Dr. Jackson determined to ignore the obvious skepticism from his colleagues. He was happy to let them think he was speaking of solar-based energy and not a new form of clean energy emulation; something he dubbed nanotechnology.

But the hour was now, not ten, thirty or a hundred years away. But how? What should the first applications be? Perhaps home heating and cooling? Electronic power sources? Automobiles? He frowned. The bigger question was whether to reveal his research at all. Before Karen died, he swore that no corporation or government would control CJ Energy Cells. It will be available to the entire world equally, or to no one at all.

Cameron felt dizzy; sweat collected under his collar. He pulled out his flask from his coat pocket. Smiling sheepishly at a slack-jawed professor in the front row, Cameron took a long pull.

While the dean rambled on, he thought of his brilliant son. Other than his research, the only reason for living was Tremont. Dr. Jackson had done all he could to keep him safe at his lakefront high-security compound. But he had buckled to his

---

[1] Since becoming president in 1963 President Brewster championed coeducation against intense alumni resistance. If Yale is to attract the best minds in the country, he wrote, it was imperative to open the school to women.

strong-willed in-laws who insisted Tremont attend school in Indianapolis, where he was top of his class and exceled in basketball. Cameron worried throughout the school year, even though his in-laws, the high-profile Carson family, had security fit for a senator.

With each public appearance, he risked the chance that they would follow through their threats. He had letters and chilling videotapes that said if he offered his research to anyone but *them,* his son would be next. He didn't even know who *them* was. Government? The oil cartels? Independent parties? There were many factions threatened by his research. If *they* knew what he had really discovered, there's no telling to what lengths they would go. The letters and tapes came by express mail, and he could not risk turning them over to the authorities.

He rubbed his forehead. The headaches worsened over time, first starting as a child. He ended up in the hospital after his book made headlines. The real pain started when he lost Karen.

Why had he accepted this engagement? He stood up from his chair without looking at the dean or the crowd and stumbled off the stage. He needed to call the Carson's and check on his son. He needed another drink.

Chapter Two

Threat
1973

TWELVE MEN ROBED IN WHITE occupied the extravagant conference room in the basement of a Vienna, Austria office complex. They inhaled khubz, pita bread, hummus, kataifi, baba ghanoush, and Um Ali. They chased the mezze or appetizers, with dark Arabic coffee and Shai tea.

The men were in good spirits—except for one. The only one in black robes, he sat rigid at the far end of the table. The founders in the early sixties called their organization Hafiz Islam Bitrūl Saumba Shokran, meaning, Protectors of Islam's Petroleum Stability and Longevity.

Sheik Mohammed bin Bandar, a robust man of fifty-some years, stood at the head of the table, raised his hand, and smiled. "I would first like to welcome our two new members to this important meeting at this critical juncture in our history: Sheik Hassan Al-Fawza of Saudi Arabia, representing the royal family—" He indicated an equally robust man to the center left who gave a slight nod. Sheik Bandar then turned toward the man in black and said, "Please welcome Omar bin Taliffan, representing the newly formed United Arab Emirates.

"As you know, I have been asked to be a spokesperson to the world for OPEC. I come here today to emphasize to you how important it is that we all stand together for the sake of each of our countries and Islam. We will turn the world upside down with the upcoming announcement."

They knew what was coming next. Nonetheless, they were eager to hear the announcement.

"OPEC member countries will not ship petroleum to countries that support Israel." He paused and said, "Insha'Allah," *if Allah wills.*

The room erupted in chatter. Bin Bandar raised his hands. "Our target countries are the United States and their allies. Your importance, the significance of this group, will multiply exponentially, my friends."

The representative from Syria, an elder statesman, said, "The U.S. and the U.K. will not sit idly by."

"There is not much they can do, Mustafa," countered the representative from Iran.

"I disagree, General Daneshvar. Once we make this announcement, we will set in motion what has been on the table for over a hundred years. America and many European countries will increase their efforts to lessen their child-like dependency that fuels our economic growth."

The General nodded in understanding. "Yes, the U.S. will step up exploration in the Gulf and Alaska ... but this will take many decades."

Their leader interrupted. "You are correct, which leads to the purpose of our meeting today. We now have a quorum of member states and propitious timing. For twelve years, OPEC has created continuity between each member state. The mission of Hafiz has been covert to maintain OPEC's stability while protecting our interests worldwide. Over the last years, we have gained control of thirty percent of the world's oil reserves." The room echoed with boisterous affirmations. "Much of OPEC's success can be attributed to efforts put forth by this small group and your associates. Our mission will not change with the future embargoes against the West."

General Daneshvar lifted a page from a stack of newspapers. "We indeed met the challenges of the past and have much to be proud of. If we allow our brothers to fall asleep at the feet of prosperity, then, in the end, we will have failed. With the efforts towards alternative and renewable energy sources, our responsibility grows. In 1960, most of the world said OPEC would not last, that they would control our oil fields. They now pay for their skepticism."

Sheik Bandar took over. "OPEC has made a strategic move this very month toward a substantial increase in the base barrel price." He grinned. "Today, the world is paying a premium for our natural resource. The Seven Sisters, they now call themselves P7, and western leaders will learn to give us respect.[2] They will recognize us as a formidable force—for generations." The group rewarded him with nods of approval and praises to Allah.

"This aggressive move does not come without a cost," he continued. "They have convened their various energy councils and attempt to gain control of their addiction. Expect retaliation with our upcoming embargo announcement. Regardless of our sectarian differences, it is our mandate to secure the longevity of our lands and our peoples. We must now increase our defensive measures."

---

[2] The Seven Sisters refers to the western alliance of petroleum companies. P7 splintered off from this group, forming a secret society allegedly linked to the ancient order of the Illuminati and the Knights Templar.

The man in black stood, his tall frame stretched over his counterparts. A deep growl quelled the room's festive mood.

As was their custom, the leader took his seat, and their newest member had the floor. "You are wise not to deceive yourselves with a false sense of security, my friends." He was the youngest in the room by ten years. He dressed as a scholar, his garb blacks and grays, from his turban to his sandals.

Omar bin Taliffan, represented the UAE, formed in 1972. Once the Emirates had learned of Hafiz, they pressed the native Yemeni bin Taliffan family to join the tight group and protect their interests. Omar's father, Mohammed—before his death in a plane crash with Mohammed bin Laden—required his son to attend. The UAE leadership could not have been more pleased on hearing that the eldest son and patriarch of the family would be their man. Omar bin Taliffan's father, a self-educated man, had been one of the most powerful and wealthiest Middle Eastern businessmen in memory. He was also a close friend and ally of the Saudi royal family. Omar had four principal business interests: the UAE members who contracted with the bin Taliffan Construction Group to build their cities; his company and family; his partnership with the bin Laden family; and his contracts with the Saudi royal family. He accepted this challenge with reservations as his responsibilities to Hafiz conflicted with his much larger purpose.

After several formalities, thanking the leadership for inviting the UAE and himself to the meeting, Omar bin Taliffan folded his hands against his chest and said, "We sit in our lavish estates and palaces living sheltered lives while millions of Muslim people remain in poverty and ignorance. We open our kingdoms and businesses to the western ideology and lose our identity.

"Do you think the heathen Christians and their sheep will wait for us to bankrupt their economies while we gain economic and political strength? If so, then you are what many have claimed: foolish old men who have lost their way." He quoted the Koran, then closed his eyes to recite a prayer.

A few of the men in the room grumbled. Abdullah bin Sultan, the only other Saudi present, fumed and moved to stand. Sheik Bandar raised his hand—and the Saudi sat. The representatives from Iran and Iraq, no love lost, seemed to enjoy the moment.

Bin Taliffan opened his eyes and waited for silence before continuing. "You—and even the old men of my father's adopted country—have become fat and happy on your wealth while Western ideas and capitalism creep into our cities, schools, and homes." He glared around the table. "You claim to protect our people and our future. At the same time, you discuss contracts with AT&T, IBM, and McDonald's. Make no mistake, Western capitalism and ideals represent the devil's doorways into Islam." He pointed at the representative from Saudi Arabia and said, "You allow cancers to lodge themselves in greedy bellies. You give your Western infidel partners sanctuary, letting them devour our way of living."

Abdullah's clenched fists left imprints in his palm. The young dark bin Taliffan heir wielded power he was not ready to challenge, even as a Saudi prince himself. The bin Taliffan's were one of two families that had bailed the Saudi government out of its mid-sixties bankruptcy in return for multiple billion-dollar construction contracts.

Bin Taliffan allowed a slight pull on the corner of his mouth. "Let us not be lulled by the opium of wealth. The infidels' principal objective has always been to convert those who reject their Christ and their democracy. They will not let us be. To this day, they lead crusades into our lands and murdered millions of our people in the name of their God."

He walked to a picture of an oil well in Saudi Arabia. "The raw crude under our feet is not our greatest asset. As out family has benefited by building the governments and civilizations above these rich wells, we are humbled by the strength we gain from these resources which Allah provides to our people." He clapped his hands. "This blessing can also become our greatest curse. We have been in a holy war with the West for a millennium. It won't be long, maybe a century, perhaps two, before we are lost."

Their leader interrupted. "Thank you, Omar. As always, your passion is commendable. Your family is one of the most respected in the world. As a young engineer only a few years out of George Washington University, I worked with your father and Mohamed bin Laden to design bridges, buildings, mosques, and much of the infrastructure in Saudi Arabia, Syria, and Kuwait. We were all saddened by the loss of your father and uncle in that tragic aircraft accident."

Omar simply nodded.

Middle Eastern historians would later suggest that the unsubstantiated belief that Western intelligence agencies, in collusion with Mossad, were responsible for the loss of their father. That this even sparked that ignited Islamist extremism.

Prince Hammad Outed of Qatar, whose country sat upon one of the richest veins of oil in the Middle East, stood to say, "I agree. Though I would like to suggest that we move today's meeting along. Several members have flights this afternoon." Omar sat down.

Outed, heir-apparent, and his five younger brothers would inherit the majority share of his country's oil deposit. He looked at the head of the table and said, "The bylaws of Hafiz were drafted in 1960 by my grandfather, King Shaikh Ahmad bin Ali bin Abdullah Al-Thani, Sheik Bandar, and OPEC. Once we have most of OPEC as members of this organization, we will elect officers to protect ourselves. OPEC cannot be associated with what we do from this room to protect our region of the world."

He continued, "As Sheik Bandar and Omar bin Taliffan have pointed out in several ways, we have awakened a divisive force—a sleeping giant. If we do not begin to take evasive action, our grandchildren may find themselves selling rugs in a desert market. I have counted your votes, and Sheik Bandar will act as our Secretary General. I shall serve as his assistant."

The representative from Iran, General Velayatollah Daneshvar, stood to address the assembly. The General was a dutiful soldier of Mohammad Reza Shah Pahlavi, the Shah of Iran, the pro-Western Iranian Monarchy. He asked, "And who is your sleeping giant, Hamaad? The USA? They are awake and have meddled in our affairs since 1948. Perhaps you refer to my good friend Richard Nixon?" A few of the men chuckled.

"Nixon is busy with East Asia and Russia and his own internal strife in Washington; he is the least of our worries. As with much of the invention and ingenuity of the twentieth century, the U.S. is the main harbor for this threat."

"You leave us in suspense," said Sheik Bandar.

The Iraqi representative, Ibrahim al-Maliki, a Baghdad-born Sunni Minister of Oil under Saddam Hussein, agreed. "We are at your mercy."

Prince Outed smiled. He was about to speak when there was a light knock on the door. A teenage boy rolled in a cart. He first handed a note to Sheik Bandar and, with a nervous hitch in his voice, said in Arabic, "Sweet and spicy black bread and the finest Yemen green mocha coffee—for your pleasure." He backed out of the door. The rich aroma of the oldest known cultivated coffee in the world, grown at high altitudes, filled the room.

Sheik Bandar read the note and said, "It seems Dr. Jean-Paul Esquirol, the leading physicist in fuel cell research, has had an unfortunate accident. He received a medication overdose while in the hospital in France and is not expected to survive."

"How tragic," Omar bin Taliffan commented. "Without Esquirol, western fuel cell development could be set back a decade. Insha'Allah." All eyes were on bin Taliffan when he said, "Allah smiles upon us this day."

Prince Outed walked to the far wall as a large white screen was lowering from the ceiling. The first slide showed a California-style home with four large rectangular objects on the roof. The next slide revealed hundreds of windmills lining a desert backdrop. Another displayed a familiar face; Dick Gertenberg stood next to an unusual automobile. Typeset on a sign above the car were the words: *GM Electric Car (1973) - Prototype of the Future.* The next slide revealed a quote in bold white letters on a pitch-black background: *Big Three, General Motors, Ford, and Chrysler agree to work together to reduce the cost of driving for the average American.* Followed by a quote from an unnamed industry leader:

> We will combat rising oil prices and the increasing threat of the
> Middle East holding America hostage. We will do this by producing
> more energy-efficient automobiles and by engineering new forms
> of energy to power the future. Our combined efforts will lead to

less dependence on foreign natural resources and ensure affordable transportation for generations to come.

Prince Outed left the damning quote on the screen for a few minutes and then followed with a dozen more frames depicting other experimental forms of energy in action around the world. Without saying a word, he had driven the point home. The sleeping giant, Outed said, was not a country but a concept they all understood: inexpensive forms of energy. The next slide had a black and white picture revealing a tall ruddy man behind a podium. A sign on the podium read *Yale University*. Prince Hamaad poured a cup of the green mocha coffee. The group took their cue to stand and refill their drinks. They waited for an explanation for the picture on the screen.

Omar asked, "You are a master of the cliff-hanger. But we are not at your monthly book club. Who is this man?"

Once everyone had taken a seat, Outed said, "That man is one of the most respected modern fathers of energy science—a physicist without peer. Since his days at MIT, he has been researching and developing practical uses of solar energy. Though Ericsson and Kemp experimented with and implemented many successful solar products, it was this man who proposed the extensive use of solar cells, photovoltaic cells, in the late fifties."

The Iranian general responded, "Solar energy is not our primary concern. It will take two hundred years for it to be competitive with fossil fuels. We should be more concerned with the expansion of nuclear energy."

Sheik Bandar looked to Outed and then over to bin Taliffan. "As it is, solar is not our challenge. You are correct. Fuel cell advances could be a more pervasive technology, but like the quest for cost-effective solar energy, scientists have been trying to develop a marketable fuel cell for over one hundred and fifty years." Bandar put his finger on the line of light from the projector behind him and pointed to the man on the podium.

"While other scientists toil over solar and fuel technology, Cameron Jackson has been researching and perhaps already developing something of far greater consequence. P7—"

"P7?" Someone interrupted.

"Our competition in the US is reluctant to allow us to fail. Middle East losses equate to long term Western instability."

"So, they support our embargo?" another asked.

"They encourage it. They tell us that Jackson is developing a new form of alternative energy that could replace nuclear energy. A powerful solution that you can hold in the palm of your hand."

The room erupted with questions.

"There must be quite a bit of his research already published," said the Iraqi.

"That is the quandary. After his wife died in childbirth, Dr. Jackson retreated to his home and lab in a secured compound near Chicago."

Omar bin Taliffan growled, "If your suspicions can be verified, insha'Allah, then, like Esquirol, we should pray for misfortune to befall Mr. Jackson as well, don't you agree?"

Sheik Bandar blanched.

Prince Outed placed his hands on the table and leaned forward. "Whatever it takes, Dr. Jackson must be stopped. Insha'Allah."

Chapter Three

Anguish
1983

AS THE PRIEST SPOKE in Latin, Matthew looked to the thick dark clouds covering the sky from the northern mountains to the southern pine tree-lined horizon. Even for Maine, it was a miserable, unseasonably cold spring night. Lightning spread across the sky, illuminating the hill for a moment. He took a deep breath through his nose and recognized the sweet scent of ozone, produced, he knew, each time lightning flashed and split two parts of oxygen into three atoms of unstable oxygen, O_2 into O_3. He also knew people were destroying this natural occurrence, and he wanted to do something about it, when he grew up, of course. He also knew kids his age didn't typically know that kind of stuff, much less understand the chemistry. He loved that smell.

He looked back to Maria Valdeorras and didn't move his eyes from her again until the priest began the graveside service. He remembered one of his vivid dreams; there was this gravesite, there was Maria, and there were bats, Pamola, zoo animals, a Lynx trying to claw him and a man in a sombrero. Strange.

The service started, and lightning followed the crack of distant thunder to the south over the sprawling Great Northern Paper Mill. Many people on this hill, alive and dead, had worked at the mill.

The lightning outlined Mount Katahdin to the northeast. For a second, he thought he saw the outline of a moose with wings—the Penobscot Indian Spirit! His heart raced. His brother's Micmac friend, Pete Marks, told Matthew and Pete's cousin, Kyle Gespasian, stories about the angry spirit. They said this spirit devoured entire hunting parties for simply climbing the forbidden mountain. They called the angry god, Pamola. Most of the tribes believed Pamola lived at the top of Mount Katahdin.

Matthew counted the seconds between the thunder and the lightning: *one one thousand, two one thousand, three one thousand.* The heart of the storm was getting closer.

His father would brag that at barely seven, Matthew knew more about meteorology than the weatherman on Channel Five. He could hear his father's bass voice as he said Matthew knew "a hell-of-a-lot more than that damn cheese-head trying to pretend he's a Patriot!" He had no idea what that meant, but it made him happy.

The crowd assembled at the Willow Run Cemetery in a semicircle under a huge oak tree. There were no willow trees in sight. Maybe they meant Widow Run and someone wrote it down wrong.

In the Eaton family, boys could identify the traits and uses of fifty species of trees before they knew the difference between a noun and a verb. Matthew's father owned one of the most successful timber and logging businesses in North America.

Most of Millinocket came to the wake held earlier at St. Martin of Tours Parish, the only Catholic church in town. Salina Valdeorras was Mr. Eaton's executive administrator for two decades, and Maria's mother.

Matthew stood holding the hands of his parents. His older brother was behind him, standing tall in Marine dress uniform with one hand on Matthew's shoulder and the other holding a large black umbrella over the entire family. He was home on leave from a special assignment in the Middle East. No one knew what Sean did for the Marines; everything was top-secret.

Matthew glanced over at two men who stood away from the circle. One he knew was Dennis Weaver, the strange lanky Katahdin Sporting Lodge innkeeper. His mother always said not to pay him any attention. The other, a mysterious newcomer to the small mill town, was Mr. Estebanez, who was staying at the lodge. The townsfolk whispered about the flatlander and his peculiar interest in Millinocket.[3]

Matthew had heard the old-timers grumbling about flatlanders that wanted to take over their backyard, to make changes too quickly, to line their pockets with greenbacks. Whatever that meant. In the end, the women were fond of Mr. Estebanez, and the men remained suspicious. Whatever their opinion, they realized the development brought jobs to the area. The newspaper was mostly positive about his generous donation toward Maine's first science center, devoted strictly to the environment and renewable energy. Matthew felt like there was a new Disney in his backyard!

The only other funeral Matthew had been to in his short life was the

---

[3] Mainer (Mainah) jargon includes flatlanders (flatlandahs), those that are from elsewhere. You might be a flatlander if the first question you ask is, "Where can I see a moose?" Or, "Where can we see a lighthouse? You might be a flatlander. Or, you are wearing one of those tourist t-shirts. Or, if you look cold. Or if you overdress for the North Woods, or your low riding BMW got stuck on the rocks.

unceremonious burial of Mr. Pibbs on a hill behind the family ranch. Mr. Pibbs was his father's old lumber mill dog. That darn dog didn't like anyone except Matthew. Shot twice by hunters, he nearly died each time. He once took on a lynx. The veterinarian said he had nine lives. Dr. Yates said, "I'd hate to see the other guy." Matthew had replied, "But, there wasn't another guy." Mr. Pibbs met his final demise when hit by a company vehicle up at the old saw mill off Fire Road 13, near the Micmac burial grounds. He shivered. In that case, he thought, there was another guy.

Matthew was curious that Maria didn't look sad. He heard one woman say, "Maria is still in shock." Mrs. Valdeorras was Matthew's second mother. He stayed with her whenever his mother traveled, and she had been teaching him Spanish, which she said he picked up rather easily. The Valdeorras family were unique as the French Canadians settled Northern Maine, and the Italians built the mills. A cluster of Italians still live on the southwest corner of town—Little Italy.

He looked around at all the people with dark shadows across their faces, donned in black and holding black umbrellas over their heads. Of the thousand—nearly one-fifth of the town's population—who signed the register at the wake, about a hundred had braved the weather. Matthew had heard his father say that the priest and some wealthy family members had flown in from Northern Spain. Two towns had lost somebody special.

Everyone looked like the zombies he saw in a black and white movie.

He caught his breath. This time, she was staring back at him. It was dusk and quite a distance to the other side of the large semicircle around the gravesite. He felt a dull pain in his chest. It was hard to take his eyes away from her. He noted the huge hand on her shoulder pressing her against the leg of a large man. When he looked back at Maria, she was still staring at him. He decided she didn't look like a zombie at all. She was a princess caught in a rainstorm. The rain soaked her, though covered by three umbrellas. Her black veil could not contain tight curls cascading halfway down her little body. In her hands, she held close to her chest, a bouquet of colorful flowers.

He wondered if you could die from a broken heart as his mother said his great-grandfather had after her husband died. He remembered feeling a little like this when he pet Mr. Pibbs for the last time. If he felt that way, Maria and her father must be feeling worse.

They watched each other as the Friar Tuck priest conducted the sermon in three languages.

As the men lowered the casket into the muddy gravesite, the Valdeorras aunts from Spain wailed.

Still, Maria did not cry. Matthew felt a welling in his chest. With Maria watching, he wanted to be as strong as an oak tree.

The rain died down. The priest concluded by crossing himself, and people milled around to speak to the family. Matthew's father shook Mr. V's hand with both of his and walked with his mother and brother to their cars. Matthew didn't follow. Instead, he drifted toward the blazing eyes of the Great Northern Paper Mill. It dominated the view south of the river like an old monster waiting to consume the small town and its residents. A streak of lightning brightened the sky to the northwest of the factory, revealing Mount Katahdin overshadowing the monstrous mill and everything else in the region. He tried to shake off the strange ominous feeling and knelt next to the ancient oak tree.

"Hello, Matthew."

Matthew jumped when he saw the newcomer, Mr. Estebanez.

He knelt next to Matthew. "Do you know who I am?"

Matthew nodded.

"I found some neat games put out by Scientific America. Thought you might like them. My particular favorites are the crossword puzzles and riddles." He handed a plastic bag to Matthew and landed a soft punch on his chin. "Nice weather you have up here. Reminds me of spring in Moscow." Mr. Estebanez stood up and walked down the hill. Moscow? Matthew considered. From that day forward, Matthew thought of the stranger as 007.

Matthew took out the pocketknife his brother had brought from Kuwait. He smiled. *The knife that was never to leave the house.* He carved into the tree.

A few minutes later, someone touched his shoulder, and he thought he was in big trouble, either for cutting into the big oak or for keeping the family from leaving. He was still kneeling, frozen with his pocketknife half embedded in the tree when Maria leaned in, kissed him lightly on the cheek, handed him a yellow rose, then ran down the cobblestone path toward her father.

Matthew turned to finish his carving when he heard his father yell his name. He surveyed his work. Satisfied, he took the bag full of magazines and ran. His brother gave him a swat on the back of his head as he sprang into the back seat of his father's GMC Jimmy.

"Here."

Sean handed Matthew a package.

"A book my friend Tree thought you would like."

"Tree?" Matthew tore off the paper and gasped. It would be safe to say that no other child his age could have understood the value of what he held in his hands.

Capturing the Sun, by Cameron T. Jackson.

Over the next few years, Matthew spotted Maria around the town and at her father's restaurant. He never forgot the memory of Willow Run or the dreams he had before the funeral, and the ones he had since. His more vivid dreams involved bats, Kung Fu type monks, fire, storms—and Pamola, the Micmac God of Thunder, but Maria was always there, too. When they passed each other on the street, they stopped and stared, until his parents and her doting aunts shuffled them off to one place or another, breaking the spell. When he was ten, he rode his bike past her house and caught her watching him out of an upstairs window. He clipped her mailbox with the handle of his bike and tumbled into the grass. Besides a small dent in his pride, he was uninjured and grinned wildly as her laugh followed him all the way down the next block.

She attended the Catholic school, and he went to a private prep school. They did not see each other much, but he thought of her often. Her piercing black eyes unnerved him. One night, he and his parents were having dinner at her father's restaurant. Mr. V mentioned that Maria would begin classes at the public middle school in the fall.

After weeks of incessant begging, he finally talked his mother into allowing him to transfer schools. His father was too preoccupied with ELF to put up much of a fight.[4]

Matthew walked into Mrs. Pulaski's sixth and seventh grade combined English class. Maria's smile struck him. He was lightheaded and thought he should retreat and come back another day.

Mrs. Pulaski guided him to his chair two rows away from Maria, who stared at him boldly. His face felt sunburned, and a frog jumped around in his stomach.

Mrs. Pulaski looked at a card she held in her hand and with concern in her voice said, "Matthew, did you bring your pills?"

Matthew reached into his pocket and produced a small silver container. "Yes, ma'am."

During lunch, while a breeze spun leaves in small tornados around their feet, they sat on a bench together without saying a word. In a few weeks, they hardly stopped talking. Maria went on and on about one thing after another, which didn't bother Matthew. He was intrigued when he learned her full name, Maria Teresa Bierzo Valdeorras.

"My father's name is Felipe Juan Carlos Bierzo Valdeorras, but everyone in town just calls him Phil. My father's family owned hundreds of acres of vineyards, and my mother, a Bierzo, was the only daughter of the governor of the region. They left Spain in a hurry because of a family feud between the Bierzos and the Valdeorras. Isn't that romantic?" She smiled, and Matthew was speechless again. They stopped at a park bench, and Matthew set down the two stacks of books he insisted on carrying.

"So, they first came to Boston when they were eighteen, got married, and had their honeymoon at the Katahdin Lodge. The mountains reminded them of home, so they opened Godello's Spanish Cuisine Restaurant." Godello's had become a popular landmark in north central Maine. "The name Godello's comes from the area where my extended family still lives. I can't wait to go visit. It's also the name

---

[4] ELF: Eaton Land and Forestry.

of the type of grapes my father's family grows." She took a breath and looked over at Matthew. "What?"

Matthew leaned against a tree. He shrugged and smiled sheepishly.

She threw her hands up. "I'm sorry. My father says I can be overwhelming," she said.

As for the newcomer, Mr. Estebanez, he became Matthew's tutor. They met at the library or in the Eaton's kitchen. The Eaton estate was five miles west of town, a mile off the Golden Road which cut through one hundred miles of Maine's north woods from Millinocket to the Canadian border. They also spent an increasing amount of time studying at the Katahdin Sporting Lodge where Mr. Estebanez stayed when in Maine.

Mr. Eaton was not too keen on the unusual relationship and hired a family friend, private investigator Joe Fazio, to keep an eye on the flatlander, the interloper. His mother, Kate, seemed intrigued by the mysterious philanthropist. After all, she would say, Mr. Estebanez appears to be the only person in the region able to challenge their son academically.

While Matthew came of age in the remote mill town, powers beyond his wildest imagination were converging on his world.

Chapter Four

Resolve
August 1989

TWELVE HUNDRED MILES away from northern Maine on the shores of Lake Michigan, a father and son were working together on calculations at the Charleston style home, complete with a wraparound porch, decorative trim, and stained-glass windows, they called Jackson's Place. They were together for the first time in nearly a decade in a basement lab more elaborate and equipped than MIT's finest.

"Dad, I was going over these figures, and if I'm calculating correctly, the tests have come out with less than a .003 margin of error? You've come a long way while I was overseas."

His father didn't look up from the microscope, but he could not hide his excitement. "And I have been able to stabilize the metals, oxidation, and atomic exchange down to the same margin. The little molecule buggers are still renegades, but if they are contained, they never dissipate." He looked up and said, "I think this calls for a drink."

Once back on the ground floor, Tremont studied a wall full of family pictures while his father fixed cocktails at the wet bar. Some of the portrait sketches dated back to the American Revolution, with Andrew Jackson, the 9th president, on his father's side, and Lindsey Carson on his mother's side. Carson was the father of twelve children, including the frontiersman, Kit Carson. Another photo showed Tremont's grandfather, the Honorable Senator Stephen John Carson. But to Tremont, the most mythical were pictures of his own father.

Cameron and Tremont spent the last few weeks of July 1989 in the lab or on the beach with the dogs, Popeye and Brutus. They shared cognac in the evenings. Life was easy—like it was before Tremont left Indiana for graduate school at Yale nearly nine years earlier, then joined the Marines.

The day that father and son were anticipating was fast approaching. In DC his father would present his research to WCASE, the governing body of alternative and renewable energy. His father convinced him to book separate flights. Tremont took the opportunity to spend a few days with his grandparents while his father flew off to meet a friend in New York City.

After checking the settings on the extensive security system and putting the cover on his new Mustang GLX, they put the dogs in the GMC Jimmy SUV and headed out for the city three hours south of their Indiana Dunes compound. Tremont dropped his father at the airport and reminded him that they would meet at the Washington International baggage claim in DC on Tuesday. "The Senate Travel Department already has a limo set up for us, so I guess we'll be arriving in style."

"As it should be," his father said.

Two days later, Tremont left the sprawling Carson estate and drove to the Indianapolis International Airport. He was excited and nervous. After years of ridicule and a lifetime of research, his dad would finally reveal and shock the government and the world with the biggest game changer since spectacles, the printing press, or the computer. He knew it was dangerous, but with the high security around the Senate and seeing that now he could keep a close eye on his father ... all should be well. He hoped.

So why did I let him go to New York without me?

Something made him uneasy. Throughout the morning, he called to verify that he had backup in DC. First, to Agent Flannigan, a pain-in-the-ass FBI agent who visited Jackson's Place a few times a year. Then to his godfather. Then to his grandfather, who would be in the Capitol Building when they arrived. All the calls went to voicemail.

His next call was to his best old ex-friend, Sean. He left a message, "I don't know where you are, or if we are on speaking terms. Kabul and Peshawar were firestorms—I should not have left before we straightened things out." He dropped the phone to his side, then back to his ear and said, "So, if they have you back in DC, I'll be there with Dad tomorrow. Meet me at 9 a.m. in front of the Capitol Building. Wear your sidearm. I could use your help." He paused again, was going to say more, but ended with, "Thanks. Ooh Rah."

He checked his locked handgun case into baggage and received his ticket. On his way through security, he could not shake off the trepidation that something was amiss. What was he overlooking?

He tried to focus on the day. His father would be unveiling the greatest energy miracle since electricity.

The status quo was about to come unhinged.

PART II

PERPETUAL Journey

Chapter Five

Spirit
Summer 1994

THE SUMMER BEFORE COLLEGE, Matthew purchased a 1967 Volkswagen bus for the price of moving it off deceased Mr. Pelletier's mountainside place. The family had an estate auction and planned to convert the quaint turn-of-the-century home into yet another bed and breakfast. There were already six B&Bs in the Katahdin region, three in Millinocket.[5]

Sean was home on leave between missions in eastern Asia. Off the record, he told Matthew, he was working undercover in North Korea. Something about acting as a businessman to get coordinates on a target. Matthew asked what kind of target, and Sean changed the subject.

"I looked for you last night," Matthew said as Sean drove his blue Jeep Grand Cherokee northeast on Millinocket Road.

"You can blame it on Pete Marks. Excuse me, the new Ranger Marks. The Sailor Son Saloon is the best thing that happened to that dead-end of Maine."

So, Sean and Pete were out drinking all night. He didn't look the worse for wear, he thought. It must be part of the military training. "Ayuh, but the owner and his English barmaid are a trip, right?"

"Wicked strange. They aren't the first or the last flatlanders to hide out in Millinocket."

"Hide out?"

"Just a figure of speech."

---

[5] Millinocket is a town with less than 5,000 residents. A shadow of what it was during the peak of timber cultivation, pulp and saw mills. Even so, it is the base to an outdoor playground. Close to Interstate 95 the area boasts dozens of campgrounds, the best hunting in the north, a fisherman's heaven and adventurous sporting camps. Baxter Peak, the tallest peak on Mount Katahdin, is the northern terminus of the Appalachian Trail.

"They've been open just a year, but the place looks and feels like it's been there forever. I was over there before eight, knocking down Molson Goldens. The place was empty, 'cept for Nick St. Adam trying to decide which hat to put on the moose head. By nine, you'd have thought Ben & Jerry came into town again. Everyone was buying me beers. After we had worn the old timers out, Pete, John, and me—we sat there, trading old Micmac stories. Pete started going on and on about Pamola—"

"Pamola! I can recite all Chief Tanner's stories."

"Right, anyway, nobody knows folklore better than Pete—he spent his life at the feet of the old Micmac chiefs—"

"And Bouchard. That medicine man messed me up, I swear."

"He did the same thing to Pete and me when we were kids. Do you get those dreams?"

"More like nightmares!"

They both laughed. "I'll tell you one thing. If we ever did get into a pinch with Pamola, all we would have to do is sic Pete on him—he would talk the great moose bird spirit to death."

The Pelletiers' place looked abandoned. They pulled up to the garage. Matthew jumped out and opened the door. They loaded the once pastel green classic VW bus onto the ELF fixed bed truck. Sean adjusted the controls on an 8,000-pound super-winch.

Since Maine did not have titles on vehicles until the mid-eighties they drove away from the future B&B with Matthew's new toy bouncing along behind. Sean steered west on Fire Road 13, turned right on Fire Road 15, and then right past the old burial grounds onto a dirt road carved into a dense wall of trees. When they came out into the open, there stood five neglected buildings. On the front of an enormous barn that seemed to meld into the hill behind it, was a weathered sign: Eaton Land and Forestry, est. 1937. They drove up to the mammoth barn and Sean backed the rig up to the doors. Following Sean's signal, Matthew jumped out and opened the two barn doors.

"I remember Dad saying something about this old place," Matthew said. They walked along the late model cars and touched them with reverence. A metallic blue '64 Corvette, two '64 Mustangs, and a red '66 Corvair.

"It's good to see that Mr. Johnson is still coming up here—"

"To get away from Mrs. Johnson," Matthew said with a chuckle.

"He took me to the shop to help him with the company vehicles and skid-steers when our old man kicked my ass about one thing or another."

"I've worked with Mr. Johnson in the East Millinocket shop since I was ten," Matthew said. "He never mentioned there were cars in the barn, not once."

Sean unchained the VW and lowered it to the gravel and stone floor.

They ripped the engine apart, cleaning each piece meticulously and filing down rough edges.

They drove to Bangor the next day in search of parts and a set of new tires. Over the next week, they worked long hours. Soon, the bus was ready for a test drive.

"Do you still have the crazy dreams?" Matthew asked.

"Do you?"

"Sometimes. Well, all the time."

"Bouchard says the dreams are a foreshadow of things to come."

"What do you think?"

"They are just dreams."

"When do you have to leave?" Matthew asked as he rolled out from under the bus on the six-wheeled mechanic's creeper.

"I'm sorry, bro. I got a change of plans this morning. I fly to Bangkok tomorrow. We'll have to put our hiking trip on hold until next time." He tightened the nuts on the battery and chuckled for the first time since he had been home. "I would love to see the look on the old man's face when he sees this peace and love wagon." Their father served during both the Korean and Vietnam Wars and strong feelings about the protestors.

Matthew wiped his greasy hands on his overalls. He crouched down and stared into the little engine.

Sean handed him an ice-cold Sea Dog Old Gollywobbler Ale. They sipped the tart brew, and Sean asked, "Where did Johnson get these?"

"They just opened another brewery in Bangor." Matthew grinned. "Just in time. You know how pop only drinks Bud? I think I'll only stock Gollywobbler at school." They clicked the glass bottles.

Sean pointed his beer at Matthew. "You go down there and study your ass off, little brother. Don't be drinking yourself under the table every night like Tree and I did down at Yale. You hear me?"

"Tree? The one who visited just before you enlisted. So, you guys ended up serving together?"

Sean avoided Matthew's eyes and poured gas into the tank. "Never mind," he said. "He and I grew apart years ago."

"But—"

"I said never mind," Sean snapped.

"All right, all right," Matthew said. After a childhood of watching his older brother butt heads with his father, Matthew knew when to stay quiet. Unlike Matthew, of course, Parker never let Sean off with a short answer. They would both push until someone walked out.

"Okay, here goes." Sean turned the key. Nothing. He pumped the gas twice and turned the key again. There was a quiet little rumble; the VW bus shook. The engine sputtered and held. Sean jumped out of the front seat, whooped, and slapped the windshield. He grabbed Matthew by the shoulders and gave him a bear hug. Somehow, Matthew knew, this memory with his brother would be one of his best.

Sean left for Asia, and Matthew worked on the VW's interior adding authentic parts, like wooden beaded seat covers that arrived from San Diego. Before he sprang it on his father, he wanted it to look and smell as good as it ran.

The next day, Maria met him at the barn. "So, this is where you have been hiding all these weeks." She opened the doors, sat in the seat, and then crawled into the back.

Matthew lifted the hatchback and looked at her with anticipation. "Well?"

"All we need back here is a blanket."

"Vixen."

She grabbed the front of his gray coveralls to pull him into the vehicle. "I think your little van is so, so, so cute." She kissed him on the lips.

He pulled away. It might not have been so bad if she hadn't used that high-pitched, cartoon voice. "Cute? That's all you can say, cute? It's a work of art, a piece of American history. And it's a bus. Not a van. A bus."

"Okay, I love your cute little civil rights and love-not-war bus."

Not amused, Matthew went around to the front of the shop to open the large double doors. "It's D-day. Time to lay this one on Dad."

Maria pouted but drove her Mazda back to her father's restaurant, leaving Matthew to head home. "He's not going to like it," he admitted aloud. He pulled up to his parent's estate, and as he shifted into park, it backfired.

His mother met him in the driveway, smiling. "It reminds me of a van my sister's boyfriend had when we were in college. They were the oldest hippies at the Cape. In '69, they drove it to Woodstock filled with a dozen free spirits. Two got pregnant that weekend, and nobody got arrested."

His father, on the other hand, was predictable. Mr. Eaton was standing on the porch with a grizzled, leather-skinned man. It was Mr. Johnson. He taught Sean and Matthew everything they knew about engines.

His father said, "What are you going to do with this piece of junk? Go to Oregon to join a commune? And how safe is a vehicle with one thin piece of metal between you and the guy coming at you?" Matthew had hoped he would at least open a door or kick a tire.

"It's a classic, Dad. Not a piece of junk." And after his father went into the house, he said, "And I thought I would put off joining the commune until after college."

Mr. Johnson shrugged as if to say, *I tried*, and walked down the steps toward them. He whispered, "I stopped at the shop in the old barn last week. I'm one of the few who remembers the place exists." He dropped the butt of his cigarette to the dirt, but not before he used it to light a new one. "It will be our secret. Capisce?" He went to the back of the VW and raised the engine lid. He said, "You and Sean did a fine job, Matt."

Matthew beamed. "We had a good teacher."

Kate returned to the VW. She said, "I'm sorry, honey. You must understand that while your father was on his second tour of Vietnam all the anti-war demonstrations were going on, and this," she ran her hand across the side of the bus, "represented everything he detested. So, perhaps you could just let it go?"

His father snorted, "If every cop from here to Bangor stops you to search for wacky-tobacky, don't come crying to me to pay your tickets."

"If I drove up in a four-wheel drive pickup, he would still find something wrong with it."

Mr. Johnson said, "Some say that the VW bus is still one of the top ten worst vehicles ever, right up there with the PACER, Gremlin, Pinto, Chevette, and all time no contest winner—"

"The Vega," Matthew said.

"Ayuh. My brother had him a '72 Pinto with the faulty fuel system."

"They put the tank behind the rear axle instead of above it. Ford's cost-benefit analysis judged that it was cheaper to pay the damages than to fix an $11.00 engineering mistake."

"Right. How'd you know that? Anyhow, my brother nearly fried like chicken when that logging truck hit him in the back! Damn thing bursts into flames. So, you be careful there, Matty. You be careful. Don't get shot by any veterans or nothing." Mr. Johnson got into his company truck and drove out the long Eaton drive.

A few weeks later, Matthew loaded up the bus and left to begin his college career. Maria stayed in Millinocket to finish school, then joined Matthew at the University of Maine the next fall.

Spring Break
March 15, 1995

March delivered record cold temperatures, and the students at UMaine were looking forward to the prospects of spring break— preferably somewhere hot.

Matthew replaced the phone on the hook outside his dorm room and shook his head. The call was from an uncle who lived in Homestead, south of Miami. Uncle Carl was his father's estranged youngest brother whom Matthew had not seen since he was a boy.

Matthew was so busy with finals and training on the rowing team, he hadn't considered what to do for break. He finished two term papers, turned them in that morning, and focused his attention on addressing an express mail. He reached for the envelope on the shelf above him and bumped a row of books. They all came crashing down.

His eyes caught a well-worn title, *Capturing the Sun*. He opened the jacket and read the handwritten inscription in blue ink on the inside cover: *Matthew, the answers surround you in every atom and neutron. Look to your environment, and deep within.*

Signed, Cameron T. Jackson, Ph.D.

He remembered that moment after Mrs. Valdeorras's funeral when his brother gave him the book. Sean never said how he got personal signature.

When someone murdered Dr. Jackson, Matthew felt like he lost a family member.

Matthew held the sacred text for a moment. He flipped to the middle and removed a folded sheet of paper. It was a note from his mentor, Mr. Estebanez.

Matthew;

I wish you well at UMaine and your MIT correspondence work. Never lose focus. Remember, you can achieve whatever you can imagine is possible. Dreamers become poets, but inventors change the world. Think long term. You are unique and in an advantageous position to help solve the impending energy crisis. And you will have all the assistance you need in your endeavor. If you need anything, leave a message with Weaver at the lodge.

E

Matthew replaced the note in the jacket of the book. The stack of papers in front of him held the results of his nine-month-long independent energy science lab, which he entitled *Solar Energy: Advances in the Nineties.* The term paper was part of maintaining a full six-year UMaine and MIT combined scholarship grant he had won his senior year of high school.

He had considered going out of state, however UMaine made it easy to stay close to Maria by offering him a full swimming and scholastic scholarship, plus complete access to labs and technology at MIT. He would wind up with an undergraduate degree in applied sciences from UMaine and a second degree from MIT in quantum physics.

The first semester flew by, and Matthew had returned to Millinocket for Thanksgiving and Christmas. Though they usually exchanged less than five words together, Matthew's father said he wanted him to come home on the weekends to work in the ELF office. Since Sean was dedicating his life to the military, the burden of taking over the family business might fall to him. He frowned at the thought.

Matthew felt like he needed a break to concentrate on this huge project and his other studies. But along with grueling swimming workouts, he splashed into the Penobscot and Stillwater Rivers before dawn, five days a week, usually circling the sixty-two-acre Ayers Island. When they had time, they would travel ten miles northwest on Pushaw Lake.

Stuffing the solar energy study in the express envelope, he rushed out of the dorm, down its granite steps, two at a time and then slid across ice-encrusted puddles. While he ran, he looked toward the Memorial Union post office across campus and then at the clock on a nearby building. He had ten minutes. With one eye closed against the pain in his head, he sprinted. Once inside the bustling student union, he reread the address on his package and dropped it in the mail chute.

Outside, he began jogging back up the hill. He stopped suddenly, bent over, and put his hands on his knees. Not again, he thought with a grimace. After a moment, he shook his head, took a deep breath, looked at the clock tower, and started up the hill. If anyone saw him, they would have thought he was drunk. Not expecting Maria until that evening, he could take his time, get some ice and rest.

"Matthew!" A voice hailed him from behind.

He turned to see Chase and Corkey, two of his pals from the swim team, running to catch up. They greeted each other with fist bumps.

Chase was a business-minded fast talker and went on about a new concept for delivering snacks to students, about a girl he had met, how hard his midterms were, and how sore he was from the hard week of training. "So, what are you doing for break?"

"I've just now been able to think about it. Maybe Florida."

"With your hot tamale from back home?" Corkey said. "Does she have a sister?"

Matthew chuckled, "No, she's an only child. My uncle has been bugging me to fly to Miami and visit. It's kind of weird because we've not been close. He's cool though, even adventurous." Matthew was thinking about the last call from his uncle that morning. He had sounded close to pleading when he asked Matthew to visit. He said he had some things to show him from his years of flying cargo to Central America. What could possibly be so important that he couldn't tell me what it was over the phone? He wondered. Besides, I've only seen his uncle twice, maybe three times in the last nineteen years. "He's sort of the black sheep on my father's side of the family."

"So why not go?"

"Ayuh, we'll go with you!" Corkey said.

Matthew had a snap image of an 1,800 mile trip with these two and said, "I'll let you know. If you don't hear from me, I'll see you guys on the water when I get back."

Matthew began to jog up the hill toward his dorm when a wave of dizziness overtook him. He stopped and leaned up against a lamppost, then bent over and vomited. His phone buzzed, and he answered. It was Mr. E.

"You don't sound good, kid. You all right?"

Matthew said he would live and asked where Mr. E was this time. He avoided the question, as usual, giving credence to Matthew's spy theory. When Matthew mentioned the idea of Miami, Mr. E was uncharacteristically excited. He said Matthew and Maria should go and asked if Matthew would drop off something to a friend when he got down there.

Matthew hung up, looked around, put his back to the post and slid down to the ground. He closed his eyes and reached into his pocket for another pill.

Maria was in the last semester of her senior year in Millinocket and made frequent weekend trips south to UMaine to see Matthew. She packed two large suitcases, a backpack, and a cosmetic bag. In her mind, she would not be coming home until after UMaine's spring break. This meant missing a week of school.

As she drove her old Mazda south, she thought about her growing affection for Matthew. She decided it would be best not to leave Matthew alone for long stretches of time with a candy store of college girls. "They might take advantage of his naive good nature," she told her friends.

She remembered Matthew with *that, that, other girl*. The blood in her body heated up with the thought. She looked at the little stuffed black bear Matthew had given her at Christmas. It stared back at her from the dashboard. "I mean, it's up to me to keep him out of harm's way. Isn't it?" She took his silence as an affirmation. "Thank God I was able to shake him loose from that Boston floozy. There was nothing *real* about that girl except maybe her money. What was he thinking? *¿Dios mio que es lo que estaba pensando este hombre?*" The UMaine mascot remained silent. Maybe he didn't understand Castilian Spanish, she mused.

"I mean, no commitments have been made, but the idea of him with any other girl, *me vuelve loca!*

She drove down Highway 95, deep in her thoughts. They had both been so busy with school, sports, and work that they had only spoken a few times on the phone and had last seen each other over the Christmas vacation.

But when she saw the signs for Orono, her insides felt like there were butterflies bursting out of their cocoons by the thousands. "He's really an amazing, isn't he?" She scooped up the bear and kissed it.

The door was open. I know I closed that door, didn't I? Matthew asked himself, worried about the stereo system his brother sent him from wherever he was the past winter. Matthew stepped into his dorm room to find Maria sitting on the bed with her back up against a large stack of pillows, legs crossed, drinking from a bottle of French spring water. She couldn't be more beautiful. She appeared completely absorbed in *The Mind of the Serial Killer.*

"There you are, handsome." She bounced off the bed and gave him a big hug. "I parked up on the hill and saw Erich on the way down to the dorm. He wanted to know what your plans were for spring break; for that matter, so do I."

"Chase and Corkey asked the same thing. You met them the last time you were here."

"Right, Chase, the future wolf of Wall Street and Corkey, the future Saturday Night Live host."

"You do remember." He chuckled. "They want to go wherever we go. I told them you would love that."

She gave him a knuckle punch to the shoulder. He winced and said, "Okay, okay, I'm kidding. So, do you remember me telling you how Uncle Carl has been bugging me to go to his place in Miami?" Matthew lay back on the bed and adjusted the ice behind his neck.

"Bad?"

"It'll be fine. I took a second pill a little while ago."

She sat beside him. "You are only supposed to take one."

"Okay, Mom."

She went to the bathroom and returned with a cold compress and laid it across his eyes. "You were saying about Uncle Carl? I remember. You thought it was kind of strange after all these years."

"I still do, but heck, what do you think? We can stop at beaches all along the way. It'll be fun." Matthew's voice was rising. He wasn't sure if it was the closeness of her body or the possibility of a week alone with her. Both, he decided.

"Florida! I'm all packed, ready for anything except I need to go shopping for a suit, maybe in Boston?" She sat back on the bed with wide eyes, biting down on her bottom lip.

"Great." He had decided to go even before he'd seen Maria. But was it his decision? It was as if he was supposed to be in Florida. A slew of vivid dreams rushed past his closed eyelids. He couldn't shake off the feeling of something surreal, even spiritual, about this trip. He thought aloud, "Going with no sleep for three days can sure make a guy wacky."

Maria said, "No, it's not wacky at all. Florida sounds great! When can we leave? Do you want to drive my car?"

"I was thinking of taking the bus. It was made for this type of road trip."

"I think it fits best in Woodstock, or L.A., not Miami." Maria perched on the edge of the bed.

That was what his father would have said. When Maria chided him, it made him smile.

He pressed a thumb and finger on the bridge of his nose and closed his eyes. As soon as he wasn't seeing prisms, he would pack.

She leaned over him and kissed him hard on the lips. Matthew grinned, put the washcloth and ice pack aside, and stared at her.

She studied his face. "What?"

"Nothing, it's all good. So, you're packed, huh? What did you tell your father?"

"Oh, he'll be okay."

Matthew wasn't so sure.

"You know what I love about you?" Maria asked.

"And what is that?" He asked and sat up.

"Never mind. Your ego is big enough."

He attempted to grab her for a dose of tickling, which she hated more than anything.

"Go ahead, say it, you want to say it, you do." When he just grinned in reply, she reached back to smack him, and he caught her wrist. "Why don't you say it?" she asked pouting.

He tossed an imaginary line of a fishing rod out in front of him and pretended to reel it in.

"You're darn right I am." She poked him in the chest. "Where's the romantic guy I know that is hiding in there?" She pursed her lips.

"You're going to miss home, aren't you?"

"Not on your life, mister. Especially without you there."

Matthew looked into her eyes. "Oh, I don't know, I have missed being home. Man, we've had some extreme times. Do you realize we've known each other most of our lives? I appreciate you always being there for me." There, he thought wryly. That's kind of like saying it.

Maria had a satisfied look on her face and walked to the other end of the room. "I always said I would go where you go just so it was out of the Katahdin region. I mean, I love it up there, and I love my papa, but there's so much to see."

He also felt a strong attachment to his hometown of Millinocket and the mountainous Katahdin region of northern Maine. He had enjoyed a lifetime of adventures with Maria, his best friends, Johnny Fazio, the local detective's son, and Kyle Gespasian, his Micmac pal that loved the woods and a rock for a pillow more than anything, and Sean. Much to her father's chagrin, Sean had often taken all the youngsters hiking and camping into the Katahdin wild. Maria could shoot a pinecone out of a tree at fifty yards.

He got up and went to the bathroom sink. "You would miss Millinocket and the region. What about the weekends we spent sitting together on the rocks above Little Niagara Falls? There's nowhere else in the world like that." He splashed icy water on his face.

Matthew looked at the book she had brought. "I see you are still reading the same gruesome stuff."

"You got a problem with that?"

"You are a strange bird, Clarice."

"Scaredy-cat."

"You really need to meet Stephen King one of these days. You two have a lot in common."

"We should go visit, Hermon is near Bangor."

Matthew knew that most of the books Maria read, were not just horror stories but also about criminal psychology or forensic medicine. Forensics hooked her after she dragged him into *Silence of the Lambs*. The whole idea gave him the willies.

Matthew remembered how he would go on and on about his dreams, inventions, and aspirations while she read. He could see her on the moss near a stream, sitting cross-legged, eating an apple, and without looking up from her engrossing book (emphasis on gross) and say, "That sounds good to me too, Matthew." She said he was the dreamer and was perfectly content to be a part of his dreams. She had told him many times that, along with following him to the ends of the earth, she had her heart set on becoming a forensic medical examiner or crime scene investigator and solving the world's worst crimes. Meanwhile, he had no problem with biology or anatomy, not even with dissecting. It was the gory stuff people could do to other people that made Matthew's stomach churn. He went to a horror movie only if Maria insisted, and only because he would not let her go alone.

Maria hugged herself. "Do you remember when we were on Millinocket Lake after I finished reading about the Savannah serial killer who drowned all his victims?"

"Sure," he said and grabbed an afghan his grandmother Joyce knit. He put it around her shoulders. "It was the first time you got faint when we crossed the dike between the two lakes."

"You rowed back, like the Loch Ness Monster was behind us."

"The vision of drowning. And Pamola."

"It's so real; I see it in the day and then again in my dreams. We are thrown from the boat, and I can't find you." She closed her eyes.

Matthew thought of how Maria would become physically ill each time they cross the dike area. It was truly inexplicable.[6]

"The vision of you and me on the lake in a storm was so real, I could feel the water and then see that damn Pamola that the Chief and Kyle put into our heads. We were thrown over by a wave and then," she closed her eyes, "I drowned."

In truth, Matthew did understand. His dreams continued to become more vivid. He tried to lighten the moment. "Hey, I thought you psychologists all agree that you cannot die in a dream." He sat down next to her.

"That's a myth. It's the most stressful dream and the body releases adrenaline, so it's hard to go back to sleep. But mine are lucid dreams, maybe more like visions."

"Like the difference between a bus and a van?"

Maria threw a pillow at him.

"Do you want to go see *Seven* tonight?" He did not respond so she asked, "What are you thinking about?"

He was thinking about how he still could not get Hannibal Lecter out of his mind, and the last thing he wanted to do was go to another horror film, even if

---

[6] The dike is a manmade strip of land created at Spencer Cove by the Great Northern Paper Company to prevent water from flowing from Ambajejus Lake into Millinocket lake on the other side. It also served the evolution to trucking from transporting logs on water through the Pemadumcook Chain of lakes.

it did star Pitt and Freeman, with Spacey as the serial killer. But he said, "I was thinking about how you like to face your fears, and how much fun we've had; how you would suddenly throw caution to the wind; like sneaking us into the movie theater. And how about that night you opened the restaurant and cooked for me. Do you remember when we hiked Daicey Pond trail and then you suggested we cross through Little Niagara? Even my brother would think twice!"

She smiled. "It's true. I would never have considered doing that myself, but I knew you would protect me. I think that's why my dad didn't put up such a fuss today. He knows you'll keep us safe." She laughed.

He loved her laugh. "What?"

"I just remembered," she said, "three summers ago when you were working nights for the shopping center, and I had an insatiable craving for chocolate."

It was convenient that Matthew had keys to Mrs. McGregory's confectionary store. They still argued about whose idea it was to go in for chocolate. They had lost track of time while dipping their fingers in the churning mixing vat full of dark chocolate.

"Things sort of got out of hand when you smeared chocolate in my face," she said.

"Hey, you started it."

"Whatever," she said.

Within minutes, the playful chocolate smearing had turned into an all-out fight. They found themselves covered from head to foot. Laughing like hyenas, they cleaned up and drove up to the southern edge of Millinocket Lake.

"I can still feel that ice-cold water," Maria said. "I think that was the last time we skinny dipped together. Why was that?"

Matthew smiled sheepishly. It was different when they were pre-teens. That night the realization set in that his best friend had developed a woman's body. After they had swum, he stayed in the water until she went to dress. Then he rushed to the bank and pulled his jeans on without first toweling off.

He said, "We were careless, eh? We should've taken our clothes in the water and removed all the evidence. We were caught with the contraband."

"That was so embarrassing." Maria put her hands on her face. "I barely had my bra on when," she paused to salute and change to a deep voice, "Deputy Dubois appeared out of the woods. I still wonder how long he was standing there."

"At his age, you could have given him a heart attack, which would have saved us a lot of trouble."

"I think it was more excitement than he's had since McGrath stole the hat right off his head at the Homecoming game. He sure spent a lot of time looking for evidence when it really wasn't hard to find."

There had been just enough chocolate behind their ears and plenty on their clothes for irrefutable evidence. Their punishment, besides having to deal with the consternation of their parents, was to work over at Mrs. McGregory's for a month without pay.

"The punishment wasn't all that bad, but it took me a while to lose the extra pounds," said Maria. "Now hurry up and pack your two pairs of jeans and all four of your t-shirts."

While he packed and changed, she talked on and on about the things they would do in Florida. Eventually, he interrupted to say, "You know, I really appreciate how you always encourage me."

"Cariño? How do you mean?" she asked with a wink.

"I mean about my inventions," he said with a chuckle. "But, yeah, that too." I would've never entered the MIT scholarship program had it not been for you." She always listened intently regarding one energy invention or another, even when most of the details had to be boring to her.

"But speaking of visions, I have an idea this trip is going to change our lives."

"How so?"

"I'm not sure," she said.

"Well, in any event, you, my dear, are my secret weapon."

"I don't know what you're talking about," she said but was grinning.

"Right. How about when you entered me into the Smithsonian Science contest?"

"You mean for the national competition? You know that I didn't do that on my own. Mr. E used me to get you and your parents to fill out the entry forms. You won, I might add, and then won how many times since? Five?"

"Six actually," he said, and then by the look on her face, realized that she knew that. "Mr. E has really been there for me, that's for sure. He can be quite persuasive."

"Have you heard from him lately? He left Millinocket when you left for school in September and hasn't been back."

"Only once since, and then, ironically, today. He thinks we should go to Florida."

Matthew reached up to the set of books that had fallen on his head earlier. "He sent me some interesting studies on fuel cells conducted in Germany. He thinks they're flawed and wanted me to look them over and send him my suggestions. He said they'd pay me for my time. Imagine that."

"He's an eccentric man, isn't he?"

Matthew laughed. "I guess you could say that."

"Secretive even."

"I overheard Mr. Fazio telling my father he thought Mr. E was working for the government. That it was odd that he took such an interest in you and your studies. But I think he's harmless. That was the night I went home early from work at the restaurant, and you met me at my house. My father shouldn't have been home for at least another hour. Oh my God, he nearly caught us. What were we thinking?"

"Thinking had nothing to do with it," Matthew said.

"Father would have killed us!" Maria said.

"No, he would have killed me. You, he would have locked in the wine cellar until you were thirty. It's your fault for being so damn irresistible," he said, snapping a wet towel in her direction. She reached out and grabbed it and tackled him onto the bed. He put his hands up in surrender, laughed, and pushed off the bed. He balled up the towel then put it in his bag. She was about to scold him for that when he jumped back onto the bed, grabbed her around her tiny waist, and pulled her to him. "Do you remember the day we met?" Just as soon as he said it, he regretted it. Maria's face turned dark.

Matthew drew her tighter to his chest. "I'm sorry. I was just thinking about how we connected that day."

"I know. It's still hard for me to talk about it."

He took her hand, picked up his two bags, and locked the door. As they went down the steps, he said, "Sorry to bum you out. Once we get on the road, you'll feel better."

She put on a smile and said, "Hey, once we get in the bug, it's all about finding a bathing suit and getting a tan."

Bus, he thought, but knew she was baiting him. It's not a bug, not a van. It's a bus. They hiked up the hill to Matthew's four-wheel treasure.

Chapter Six

Bond
1981

TREMONT SAT ON THE BENCH lacing up his shoes. He contemplated his future after graduation. Though joining his father at Jackson's Place was certain, he had at least one detour to make, one obligation to complete, before he settled into the sedate scientist's lifestyle.

Ever since he could remember, he had held the solemn ideal that it was his duty to serve his country in the military. In time, he formulated the objective of working on national security. He knew the micro technology was available to protect every vulnerable area of the country, like commercial airlines, border security, and public utilities. But few in business or government were taking steps to make changes. He also knew it was a vast bureaucracy and the cogs in the wheel of change encompassed complicated issues. But that didn't mean that he could sit back and do nothing about it. *It is every patriotic, healthy man's God-given responsibility.* Those aren't my words, Tremont thought with a grin. He could hear his grandfather's baritone voice reverberating through his brain. *Not only a patriot's responsibility, but a Carson imperative.* And the Jacksons, he mused, going all the way back to Andrew Jackson.

His post-graduate work in applied physics and computer science at Yale dominated his time; that and rugby. He was still gung-ho to enter the military in two years and would probably enter officer training next year.

His thoughts evaporated as he hit the ground. As he lay in two inches of mud, gasping, he found himself looking up into the familiar, sparkling blue eyes of his muddy attacker. He was not surprised to see Sean Eaton, from Mill-something, Maine, standing over him with a triumphant grin. Sean took Tremont's hand and jerked him to his feet. When he could finally gulp in a breath, Tremont squeaked out, "That was a cheap shot, Eaton. You better watch your back."

"I always do, Tree." He laughed and ran back to the huddle with his team.

Club rugby was a sadistic alternative to an NCAA sanctioned collegiate sport.

Hard-hitting, unpadded, screaming, scrambling students came together to rattle each other's brains outside of the classroom at the one-hundred-year-old Yale University Rugby Football Club. Today, Sean, six inches shorter but twenty pounds heavier, put Tremont in the mud twice. Tremont retaliated with two borderline illegal tackles. After the last tackle that ended the game, Sean could have gotten mad. Instead, he began to laugh with Tremont following suit. Soon both teams were guffawing like drunks at a bachelor party.

For the next two years, they were inseparable. Every weekend, they executed an adventure—including the Ironman Canada competition, scuba diving off the Florida Keys, and mountain climbing wherever they could find a mountain. Their Legal Ethics professor grew frustrated with them missing almost every Monday morning class or sleeping through it when they graced him with their presence. He nicknamed the delinquent pair Huck and Tom, after Mark Twain's famed adventurers.

They had met when Sean was working toward a degree in law with a specialization in criminal justice, criminology, and law enforcement. Though Sean had a rough time in high school, mostly getting into fights, he went on to excel at the University of Maine and when he was accepted into Yale's Law School, everyone was surprised back home; everyone except perhaps Matthew's tutor, Mr. Estebanez. Like his father and grandfathers, Sean intended on going into the military with the hopes of working his way into military intelligence. Unlike his friend, Tremont, his motivator was not a grand idea of patriotism but the opportunity for nonstop excitement, danger, and intrigue. Sean revealed to Tremont his long-term plan to work for the CIA or another branch of the secret service once discharged from the military, as a hero, of course.

Just months before graduation, they were navigating their kayaks down a full days journey on the Gauley River, infamous for some of the wildest rapids in the Eastern United States. Half way through what some river guides call "The Marathon," Tremont and Sean stopped to rest before taking on the challenging Pillow Rock between two level five rapids. The pair sat on top of a large boulder that jutted out over the river, suspended mid-air.

Tremont had come to a decision. "I'll go with you."

Sean took a ravenous bite out of a baloney sandwich on white bread, void of condiments. "What the hell are you talking about? You *are* with me."

"I'll go with you," Tremont said between scarfing down a sandwich while unwrapping another.

"Where?"

"The Marines, brainless. Someone's got to keep an eye on you."

Sean uttered a few choice curse words and laughed. "You can't do that. All you've talked about for two years is getting back to research with your old man. What kind of crap are you shoveling?"

"I talked it over with my dad last night, and he supports my decision." Though thinking back to his conversation with his father, he could not help feeling a sharp pain in his heart. The things his father didn't say revealed the most. "I'm sure he's worried about all the unrest in the Middle East," he said, referring to an escalation in terrorist activities overseas and the taking of Western hostages by Iranian extremists. "And he won't say it, but he's disappointed that I won't be at Jackson's Place this summer. But he's okay with my decision," he offered unconvincingly. "Like he said, saving the world from a catastrophic energy crisis can wait."

"Wicked!" Sean laughed and almost choked on his baloney. "You two believe you're onto something, don't you? Matthew would love that shit."

"I look forward to meeting him one day. Anyway, it's all theory," he said though he knew that was not true. As far as the military is concerned, ironically, the hard sell will be my mother's family, but the Senator won't argue."

"Ayuh, that's right. Like me, you come from a long line of warriors, only you also have a bunch of sleazy politicians," Sean mocked.

"You're twisted." Tremont stood and reached high over his head to stretch his long body from fingers to sandals. "Those rapids aren't going to wait all day, and there's still Sweet's Falls. Shoot, there might not be anything left of either one of us to deliver to the Marines."

Sean asked, "Would you join anyhow?" He finished pulling on his neoprene wetsuit, picked up his kayak over his shoulder, and walked down to the water's edge. "I mean, if I wasn't joining?"

"Yeah, I would. I want to do a lot of things, but this is an experience I need to have. My whole life I've been doing what everyone else wants. Don't get me wrong, I love basketball; the scouts are still calling me to go pro, which just isn't in the cards for me. And I miss working with my father." He changed the subject. "I can't wait for you to meet him."

"Maybe I will—someday. Say, don't take this wrong, but he sounds a bit obsessive, compulsive, and reclusive to me."

"Obsessive yes, but not compulsive. All great inventors in history were obsessed about their product. If they weren't, they couldn't take the hundreds of failures it took before reaching success." Tremont was tempted to reveal more about his father's work but decided against it. "It's safe to say he's on the verge of more surprising discoveries."

"You don't say a lot about the nature of his work. I mean, I know what I've read, but what's he working on now?"

Tremont set his kayak into the water. "All I can tell you is that solar energy panels will pale in comparison." He hoped Sean would change the subject.

Sean didn't pursue it. He said, "You remind me of my brother—or he reminds me of you."

Tremont looked away and smiled.

"It would have made more sense for him to be born in your family rather than with a bunch of loggers. Matthew constantly talks about solar power, electricity, fission, and everything science. A year ago, I was home during break and went with him to the Stearns High School science show; he was just in kindergarten. It was all we could do to get him out of the gym, hours after it ended. I remember him giving suggestions to one teacher who he felt was incorrectly helping a student. I think it was a hydro-energy experiment. I'm sure the teacher thought he was humoring my brother as they debated for a while, and it turned out Matthew was right.

"Call it silly or a sense of fate, but I don't think it's an accident that you and I met. Next week, we'll run up to Maine, so you can meet Matthew, my mom, and of course my old man." He shook his head and then spit. "That will be an experience. For my mom's sake, I should tell him about joining the service in person. He'll probably lose it, especially when he hears I'm not going to practice law and coming back to ELF."

"You don't talk about him much," Tremont said.

"Not much to tell. He's like an old bear caught in a steel trap."

"You two don't get along."

"We have our good days. Like when we are at least two hundred miles apart."

"I look forward to meeting him, your mother, and your little brother. Maybe someday he can come out to Indiana and play in my father's lab. You'll get a kick out of the security; it's tighter than Fort Knox. Until then, looks like it will be my job to keep you from getting your lily-white ass shot off."

Sean shook his head as he finished locking himself into his kayak. "It will be the other way around, chump. There's not a tank big enough to hide your hulking frame. We'll have to keep you in camouflage twenty-four-seven."

They pushed their kayaks into the gushing river. Seconds later, the current drew them up ten feet above the water level, sideways along the smooth surface of Pillow Rock where the water converged from all sides. A surge of water tossed the fiberglass shells and human cargo so fast and so hard against the rock that they hung in suspended animation, nearly upside down for a moment, before the force of the water slammed them forward and down into the roaring river. Though they could not hear anything above the thundering waves, they screamed like madmen, wide-eyed with ear-to-ear smiles.

Chapter Seven

Ramble
March 15, 1995
10:00 A.M.

MATTHEW PUT MARIA'S BAGS inside the bus. He held his tongue, but she caught him rolling his eyes.

"What? I didn't want to forget anything." She stood back to look at the VW bus. "It'll be fun going down the highway in this old thing."

"Like I told my dad last summer—"

"I know. It's a classic."

"Right. Remember the bus in the Harvard movie *With Honors?* They used my bus."

"They didn't use your bus."

"They might as well have used my bus."

They drove down the hill toward Memorial student union.

She tugged on his shirt sleeve. "Hey, mister, and where were you just now?"

Matthew hadn't realized he'd phased out—he hated when that happened.

"I should write a paper on the male attention span, but," she laughed, "it would be a blank page."

"Forget forensics, you should be a stand-up comic."

In the back of the student union parking lot, a man lurked in an idling large gray sedan. After Matthew walked past, a man exited the car and ambled over to a payphone.

"So far, so good," he said into the receiver. "It appears it's going according to plan." He listened. "They won't see me unless I want them to see me. I'll keep in touch."

He returned to his car and smiled as he watched Maria get out of the van, open the back hatch, and begin rearranging the luggage. He stuck a piece of gum in his mouth, got into the sedan, and laid his head back on the rest.

Matthew jogged into the student union and up to the postal desk. "Sandy, did express mail pick up on time? My package has to be in Boston in the morning."

While Sandy went to check on the packages he turned to the commotion behind him. "Hey, Donna. Darma. What's up?" He looked over their shoulders at the bulletin board covered with advertisements for roommates, furniture, and books. One of those notes had phone numbers written on the bottom to tear off. None were missing. The note said: URGENT! NEED RIDE TO FLORIDA! WILL PAY FOR GAS! Darma Swenson and Donna Fisher.

He observed the designer luggage. Donna was from upscale Greenwich, Connecticut, and the daughter of a prominent Wall Street attorney and a podiatrist. Darma was from Los Angeles and daughter of a movie industry executive who was famous for ... something.

"Where are you going?" Donna asked.

"Florida." Right when he said it, he realized his blunder. Maria would kill him. Please, don't say it, he prayed.

Matthew's eardrums nearly fractured. They threw their arms around his neck and kissed him on both cheeks.

"Matthew, you're a doll!" Darma exclaimed.

I'm toast, Matthew thought.

Sandy frowned when she saw the girls and confirmed the package was safely on the way to Boston. Relieved to have that burden behind him, Matthew focused on the new challenge. He carried one bag under each arm, and one in each hand as Donna and Darma followed. What was it that Erich called them? Ah, yes, he remembered, the Doublemint twins.

As they approached the VW bus, Matthew smiled at Maria but knew, judging by her body language, he was toast. Afraid to put the bags down and give Maria an open target, he made the introductions and explanations.

Darma and Donna seemed oblivious to Maria's anger. They focused their attention on the mode of transportation, and their faces twisted.

"Will this thing make it to Florida and back? I'm not sure it'll make it to Greenwich," Donna complained.

"We have these vans all over LA," Darma added. "But in better shape."

Maria beat Matthew to his little speech. "It's a bus, not a van. And hey, it's a classic, and Matthew rebuilt the engine himself. This will take us to hell and back, if Matthew asks it to."

"That's what I'm afraid of," Donna quipped.

Matthew grinned, surprised at Maria's defense of the bus. He arranged their suitcases in the back, covering everything with moving blankets. He froze—something from one of his dreams projected into the moment. He studied the contents and shook his head. He turned, fully expecting to see his Uncle Carl, and a man wearing a sombrero. But that was ridiculous. He did see a man leaning against a gray Cadillac, reading a newspaper, and smoking a cigarette.

Matthew closed the side doors and heard Darma whisper to Donna to humor the lumberjack and when they got to Daytona, maybe her aunt could fly them back. He shot them an angry look, and they shrugged.

Matthew tried to give Maria a hug. She pushed him away and said, "Who the hell are these *Baywatch* chicks? I'm not happy sharing you or the trip with anyone." She put her arms around his neck and said, "But they are not going to ruin our road trip, so let's go."

He decided he wouldn't push his luck, as there was already enough high-test estrogen in the vicinity to fuel the space shuttle. After lifting the hidden back seats and storing their luggage behind, he was about to get in the VW bus when he saw Erich standing at the curb with a huge sports bag slung over his shoulder. He knew Erich would be waiting for the team bus to take him and the track team to Boston to catch a flight to the elite Olympic training camp in Colorado Springs. He caught sight of Matthew and hustled over to the bus. "You look like you're heading to Woodstock." Through the window, he could see Darma and Donna roll their eyes.

Maria smiled and lifted on her toes to give Erich a big hug.

"You know, dude, of all the things you could do this week, you choose Florida with three beautiful ladies. What were you thinking?"

"Bus," Matthew corrected and raised his eyebrows. "Training trip?"

"Yep, Colorado to lift weights and train with fifty skinny, sweaty athletes. I like your idea better. Any extra room?"

"We'll be thinking of you when we hit the beaches, and I'll still get in my swimming and running."

"Just be sure to bring me back something interesting, like a southern belle from Savannah." With that, he spun around and walked back to the curb to meet the Athletic Department bus.

Maria stepped up into the front passenger seat, the valley girls fastened the seatbelts Matthew had installed last summer, and they headed for the highway.

On the way out of the parking lot, Matthew caught the eye of the man leaning up against the Caddy.

March 15, 1995 11:00 a.m.

The four travelers left Orono and drove down Interstate 95 past Bangor. The tension was palpable. He tried to break the ice. Maria had never ventured farther than the Maine coast and one or two school trips to Boston. So, when Matthew asked his other passengers about their travel experiences, they dominated the conversation talking nonstop. Darma and Donna took them around the world, twice, before the VW bus reached New York City. As they passed Greenwich, Matthew thought about asking them why they did not stop and pick up the Lincoln Navigator from the Swenson fleet. He had a feeling Donna's parents were not aware of the Florida trip.

When they stopped for gas, he noticed a gray Cadillac.

They all went to the Stuckey's store. When they came out, the Cadillac had disappeared. "Coincidence," Matthew wondered aloud.

"What's that?" Maria asked.

"Nothing."

By New Jersey, the blondes had tired of the aria of themselves and began an inquisition about Maria.

Matthew was surprised to hear Maria elaborate, especially about her mother. Maybe talking about the loss would be good for her, he thought.

"My father didn't venture far from home. After my mother died, he lost heart in anything but taking care of me and *Restaurante de Godello's.*"

"Godello, like the wine?" asked Donna.

"My father named the restaurant after the grape his family harvested for generations in Ourense in Galicia, the northwestern region of Spain."

"Godello's is a very traditional Spanish restaurant," Matthew said. "People come in from New Hampshire, Vermont, and Boston."

Darma said, "My father filmed in Spain one summer, and Mummy and I spent an entire month traveling and eating. I don't think we got to Glacier."

Maria overlooked the mispronunciation. "You would love the dishes at my restaurant: Mariscos, which is a shellfish dish, and *Mecoras*, a delicious spider crab entrée ... the *santisguinnos* is what they call crayfish here. And of course, what Northwestern Spain has in common with Maine is our many lobster dishes."

"Do you think that's why your father picked Maine?" Matthew asked.

"I think being close to the ocean was vital for him. There were too many restaurants on the coast, so he picked a small town that would not have an upscale Spanish restaurant. That was many years ago when the town was three times the size it is now. If we didn't lose my mother—" Maria paused, then said more quietly, "Papa had talked about moving to Boston and opening a restaurant."

Matthew lightened the mood. "Maria, tell them about your favorite dish—other than me."

"Oh, my favorites are wine-marinated scallops and stewed octopus."

Matthew was not a fan of octopus. He said, "In Galicia, some restaurants specialize in octopus."

"They're called *Pulperiias*. While *we* go to a steakhouse, the locals go to an octopus-house restaurant." They all laughed at this peculiarity.

They passed signs for Baltimore and Washington. Matthew was having hunger pains. He'd already finished two packages of Fig Newtons and was working on a box of Nilla Wafers. "We also serve classic Spanish dishes like *Paella*—a thick gumbo-like chicken and tomato-based soup accompanied by *Tortilla de Patatas, Gazpacho,* and *Horchata de Chufa.*"

"'The drink of the gods,'" Matthew quoted from the menu.

"What is it?" Donna asked.

"A thick, creamy substitute for milk, coffee, or other dinner drinks prepared with *Chufa,* the rare tiger nut from Spain, which my father had his cousins ship because it's too expensive through normal channels." Her father would get very dark if he had to substitute *Horchata de Almendra* when he ran out of Chufa. "Then we top off the night with sweet flan."

"Oh," Darma exhaled, "I've had that in Spain. It's sinfully delicious cake. I love the caramel."

"Try to control yourself, darling. Save it for the boys in Florida," Donna chided.

"When you come to visit, you can have all the flan you desire, or you might want Matthew's favorite, *churros.*"

"What's that?"

"Keep talking and I'm turning around and heading back to Millinocket," Matthew said. He knew one thing for sure. Listening to three girls discuss food, like they were talking about something else entirely was why guys loved watching food channels.

"*Churros* are fried dough sprinkled with sugar and served with a cup of thick hot chocolate. But even better than the desserts, are the bread."

"I'm way sorry, but bread over dessert?" said Donna.

"Yes, ma'am," Matthew said, "people come to Maria's restaurant just for the authentic *Pan de Horno* bread. My uncle had him ship it all the way to Miami for the holidays. It's tough to make and impossible to reproduce without a good recipe, which, *en la cabeza de Señor Valledoras.*"

"Muy bien, cariño. It's true. The recipes go back many generations. My father took to cooking with his mother very early in life."

Matthew couldn't help thinking this trip would be good for both Maria and her father.

9:00 p.m.

While in training, Matthew ate four times a day. His first experience with a Cracker Barrel restaurant was a scene fit for a commercial. He ordered a full breakfast of hickory-smoked country ham, eggs over easy, grits, biscuits and gravy, hashbrowns, and, since it was on the menu, Maine blueberry pancakes! Matthew was about as happy as he had ever been. The girls ate light and shook their heads in amazement that anyone could eat that much food in one sitting. But they got even.

Matthew turned to the challenging task of getting the girls out of the gift shop.

He had hoped to make Miami before tomorrow afternoon, but they had lost a lot of time. The girls were finally in the bus when he noticed the Cadillac. It must be the same car, he thought. He was halfway to the car when the driver began pulling away. Matthew picked up his speed, and the driver took off. What the hell, he thought. He had heard about a college girl abducted on spring break. He'd tell the girls to be more careful, at the next stop.

Matthew slept while Maria drove through the night, down through Virginia, and into the Carolinas. Matthew took over in Fayetteville, home of Fort Bragg. He thought of his brother who, last he heard, was in Afghanistan. They crossed the South Carolina border and passed dozens of colorful billboards covered in sombreros and a cartoon named Pedro. The sombrero? He wondered. Eighteen hours after leaving the University, they approached a gaudy tourist attraction in South Carolina, "South of the Border."

Maria awoke, rubbed her eyes, and said, "Matthew! I think you made a wrong turn. How did we get to Mexico?" They stared up at an eclectically painted cartoon wearing a sombrero and holding a South of the Border sign. Painted in bright colors, all the buildings had high false fronts. Along the highway and flanking the buildings on all sides were sky-high billboards advertising peanuts, fireworks, sunglasses, and sandals. All the signs used poorly-constructed English, such as *Pedro ver' glad you come* and *Pedro got 112 meelion Amigos who stay weeth heem.*

"How, like, not PC," Darma commented. "Reminds me of Tijuana, shopping with Mummy."

"Someone really needs a lesson in color coordination," Donna said.

The three girls got out to stretch their legs and went into the store. Matthew made sure they were within sight. Maria called to him from the changing rooms.

"So, what do you think, handsome?" Maria said with one hand on her hip, brandishing her new bikini.

"I have to admit, that beats all the fireworks in the store—*and* in China."

Maria smiled. "Right answer, mister."

While Maria changed, Matthew walked over to look at sunglasses. Someone grabbed him just above the elbow.

"Come with me, Matthew."

Matthew tried to pull his arm away, but the man had him in a vice-like grip. He pushed Matthew out the side door and toward the back of the building. With one quick move, Matthew pressed back on the man and forced him against the stucco wall. Matthew turned, ready to defend himself, and looked into familiar eyes. He was speechless.

"Hello, Matthew. Sorry about the strong arm, but I didn't want Maria to see me. Let's go behind the building."

When they turned the corner, Matthew exclaimed, "Mr. E! What are you doing here?"

"I thought I would catch you before you left." He handed Matthew an express mail envelope. "Keep this hidden." He went on to give Matthew detailed instructions about where and when to deliver the package.

After a handshake and a side shoulder hug, Estebanez walked away. "Wait, what's in the—" but Mr. E was gone. Matthew, worried about the girls, and rushed back to the souvenir store. Still baffled, he started thinking. How did he get here? If he was willing to come all this way, why didn't he handle the situation himself or send it express mail? And why me?

Feeling the ghostly weight of conspiracy in light of his dreams, he returned to the back of the store, ran down the length of the building, swept his eyes across parking lot. But he was gone.

Inside the store, the girls were gone. He ran up and down the aisles and out to the VW bus. He leaned over and put his hands on his knees, bile bubbling up to his throat. What about the Caddy? If the guy was with Mr. E, then why didn't one of them give him the package earlier? Why play cat and mouse all up and down the highway?

In the VW bus, the girls were comparing items from their shopping spree. Matthew opened the doors at the side of the bus and removed the thick moving blankets. He then lifted a few suitcases and placed the large envelope underneath. After replacing the bags and the moving blankets, he climbed in next to Maria and started the engine.

"Hey, did you buy fireworks?" Maria asked. Matthew didn't respond. She tapped him on the arm. "What's the matter?"

"Nothing. I decided we could get the fireworks on the way back." He feigned a laugh. "This way I won't be tempted to shoot them off. I wouldn't want to get arrested in Georgia or Florida." Matthew felt dizzy and blinked at the prisms that appeared in front of his eyes. Not again, he thought.

Maria reached for her purse and took out a silver case.

"Then what did you put in the back?" Darma asked.

"A pair of sunglasses in one of my bags," he lied, putting the pill in his mouth and taking a quick gulp.

"Won't you need them to drive?" Darma persisted.

Matthew drove around the huge parking lot of South of the Border looking for the gray sedan. Nothing. And no sign of Mr. E.

Maria stared at him, curious.

They drove through Georgia until Matthew saw blue lights in his mirror. He cursed. The girls looked behind to see the police approaching fast.

Matthew pulled over and, from his side mirror, watched in amazement as the officer approached. This was just like in one of his dreams.

"This trip is getting more interesting by the minute," he said with a sigh.

Belly bulging over his belt and a mustard stain on his gray shirt, the officer stood behind the bus, wrote down the license plate number, put his large nose up against the back window, and then leaned on Matthew's windowsill. His face was close enough for Matthew to smell his chewing tobacco.

"You know how fast you was goin', boy?"

"I'm sure it was within the speed limit, officer."

"Don't you go gettin' smart with me. Where did you get this hippie mobile anyways?" he said as he wrote out the ticket on what looked to be a spiral notepad instead of the usual citation on a clipboard.

"I found it on a farm near my home in Maine. My brother and I, he's serving overseas now, rebuilt the engine and fixed it up."

"You serve?"

"No sir, I'm in college."

"Should do your duty, like yor' brother."

"Yes, sir."

"Try paintin' it a normal color." He handed Matthew the paper, which simply showed the name of the county, a charge of going twenty over the speed limit, and one hundred dollars next to the amount due. Matthew was about to argue that his VW bus could not go twenty over the speed limit, but he sensed that it would be futile. "Can I write you a check?"

"Sure thang," he drawled. "Just make out the check to Buster Pawley."

"Who is he?"

"You Yankee college kids ask too many questions. He's the local Brunswick Magistrate. Course, you could just come down with me to the county jail and see Magistrate Pawley in the morning to state your case." He reached to take back the makeshift ticket, but Matthew pulled it away, took out a pen and began to write.

Matthew handed him the check. He figured since he wasn't speeding, Boss Hog saw the Maine plates, and that was justification enough to issue a ticket. He had read about Sherriff Tom Poppell, from McIntosh County. Matthew was pretty sure it was not far from Brunswick. The author noted that Poppell was the last of the high sheriffs. The majority black community had called him Robin Hood. For thirty years, until his death, he stopped the Yankee truckers, relieved them of a portion of their goods and passed the ill-gotten gains around to the poor. He would also walk into your house, Matthew remembered, and sit down to supper unannounced, anywhere in the county.[7]

"Smart, young man. You pick up on things real quick. But you have to remember one thing."

"What's that, sir?"

"There is two types of Yankees. There is regulah Yankees, and there is damn

---

[7] *Praying for Sheetrock*, by Melissa Faye Greene (1991), Da Capo Press, tells about Sheriff Poppell, one of many real characters who helped to create the southern sheriff stereotype.

Yankees. Now, a Yankee comes to the South and passes through without too much of a fuss. Far as I'm concerned, Floreeda is part of the North."

Boss Hog seemed to have forgotten where he was going with this, so Matthew helped. "And a damn Yankee?"

"A damn Yankee, well, he comes to the South and stays."

Darma laughed. Donna hit her so hard, she yelped.

Boss Hog furrowed his brow and leaned in close to Matthew. The rancid smell of the chewing tobacco was making Matthew nauseous. Out of the corner of his eye, he could see it begin to drip down Hog's chin.

"Now which are you, boy? A regulah Yankee or a damn Yankee?"

"Today we're just regular Yankees, sir."

"Good, good. Now y'all get your Yankee tails out of my county and slow this mule down while you go."

Matthew drove away and didn't start breathing normally till he saw Boss Hog's blue lights disappear in his rearview mirror.

"So, it's not a van. It's not a bus. It's a mule," Maria said.

"I totally didn't think people like him existed," Darma said. "My father actually reviewed the script to do a remake of *Dukes of Hazzard*. He turned it down."

Donna snorted and mimicked Boss Hog.

Maria shushed Donna with a wave. Then whispered, "I really do feel like we've been transported back to 1967."

Matthew chewed two antacid pills. A few movie clips ran through his mind about the old south. He feigned a lackadaisical smile. The responsibility for the safety of Maria and the Bobbsey twins weighed on him. His stomach pitched and rolled: first the gray Cadillac, then Estebanez, now this. Things come in threes, he thought. He frowned. Who the hell were the Bobbsey twins anyway?

He decided he would focus his attention on getting to Miami without another incident, enjoy the beach, visit his uncle, drop off Mr. E's package, and then return to Maine. That sounded like a simple plan.

Little did he know a firestorm was brewing in Miami Beach.

Chapter Eight

Patriot
1981

UPON GRADUATING FROM YALE with a master's in physics and computer science and an associate Ph.D. in energy engineering from MIT, Tremont joined the Marines with Sean Eaton. First came boot camp, and then per their Sergeant Major, assignment to a special operations unit based in California. The Carson family went into shock. The Senator took pride in his grandson's decision, but under pressure from his wife back in Indiana, he had to get involved. Cameron Jackson on the other hand, though disappointed in not having his son's companionship, remained supportive.

Though he was the majority leader with the Senate in session, Tremont's grandfather arranged to fly to Hartford's Bradley Airport from DC. He called a friend in the State Department from the plane.

"I need you to head off Tremont's officer training papers before administration logs my grandson permanently into the system." He listened. "Thank you, Jack. I owe you one."

Once at Bradley, a limo met him. He directed the driver to make double time to New Haven. The double resulted in a ticket passing through New Britain, the billboard-slated home of Stanley Tools. The disingenuous highway patrolman became belligerent when the Senator referenced his friendship to Connecticut Governor William O'Neill.

Once they were back on the road, he returned his thoughts to his grandson, the living memory of his beloved daughter, Karen. Though he was a staunch supporter of the military and sat on the Senate Armed Services Committee, he never considered the military an option for Tremont. He felt certain he could talk him out of this whim, this temporary insanity.

Little did he know that his own repetitive monologs about the Carson military history contributed to create Tremont's patriotic character.

Tremont met his grandfather at the McDougal Graduate Student Center, and they embraced. They had always been close. Over coffee—Tremont with an extra-large white mocha latte and the Senator, just coffee, strong and black—they talked about everything from politics to basketball: the Hoosiers were in a slump due in part to last year's championship team going pro.

"I think they should make a rule that players have to finish four years before they can be drafted," Tremont said.

"Bobby Knight said you were the best sixth man he'd ever coached."[8]

"Someone had to warm the bench," Tremont said, and they both laughed. "So … the elephant in the room …"

Tremont rattled off his rationale for joining the military. Senator Carson offered an "I see" or "uh huh" without interrupting. The evening waned.

They switched to decaf, and Senator Stephen John Carson resigned himself to his grandson's decision, though returning to Grandma Carson with the news was a daunting thought. "You know, you truly are your mother's son. She was, and you are, more stubborn than me. When I talk to you, I think of Karen, and my heart wells up with pride." The Senator stared at his coffee grounds. He said, "The past twenty years seem like a day."

"Not a day goes by that I don't wish I had even one day to know her. That's not to say I don't appreciate how you and Dad have kept her memory alive."

"Your mother knew what I thought before I thought it, and she always called me out. Do you know how much she loved to argue with me? I always said she would have made a good legislator up on the Hill. I suppose a military career wouldn't hurt if you should ever have a desire to enter politics."

"I'll keep that in mind," Tremont said with a grin. "I hope to qualify for special operations, I'll be busy trying to use my computer science and engineering skills against terrorist plots."

"It's a noble ideal. Terrorism is a problem that will only get worse, I'm afraid."

"It's only a matter of time before the fanaticism gets to our shores. Someone is going to attack our infrastructure, or, maybe even our airports. We need to take some lessons from Isreal."

"You've given this a lot of thought."

"Yes, sir. When I get out, I'll work with my father to devise security equipment to help ensure our country's safety. I can already see that along with Dad's work—" Tremont paused. "Along with his work on energy solutions, we can start a company focused on advanced detection and assessment technology."

The senator said, "It's obvious you've developed a passion for our country's

---

[8] In basketball the sixth man refers to a player who does not start but fills in off the bench with more playing time than the rest of the bench. The NBA award was first given in 1983 to Charlotte, NC native and UNC Tar Heel, Bobby Jones of the Philadelphia 76ers.

security, and by God, if I didn't know better, I would think you were tapping into our closed-door sessions."

Tremont chuckled. "Maybe I have, Grandpa. Maybe I have."

"All the issues you raised are on our plate every month, but I'll be damned if I can get the other side of the aisle to move the necessary funds from social programs to defense and security. I'm afraid it will take a major breach before everyone wakes up."

"I wrote a paper on that my senior year. Did you read it?"

The Senator smiled and nodded.

"Our apathy regarding terrorist and their organizations today mirrors the general sentiments before the bombing of Pearl Harbor. What will it take—" Tremont leaned forward and said, "I think I just had an epiphany." He took a notebook from his backpack and began to write and talk at the same time. "When it comes down to it, Grandpa, everything Dad has dedicated his life to, is directly correlated to our national security."

"How do you figure?"

"It's about money and oil, about power. Successful, cost-effective energy sources would lessen our dependence on foreign oil and put us into an even stronger economic and strategic position in the world."

"Each year, we shelve energy for more immediate and tangible priorities." He sipped his decaf. "So, how do you see all these energy issues directly affecting our national security, or more precisely, how is it intertwined with a potential terrorist threat?"

Tremont was too engrossed in his writing to reply.

Senator Carson left Yale and returned to Hartford. When he arrived at the Carson estate, he walked into a full house of concerned family members. He lumbered into the great room and announced, "As usual, Tremont is going to do what Tremont wants to do. If he wants to use his talents and brains to help protect the future of our country, how can I or anyone else fault him for that?" The Senator hoped to close the matter without delving into too many details.

"It's not enough, Stephen. Did you try to talk some sense into him?" his wife asked.

He sat down in his soft black leather chair, took a deep breath, and said, "How on earth could I argue with him? Nearly every Carson man has served our country in the armed forces. Many sacrificed life or limb during one war or another."

Mrs. Carson shook her head. "I'd better call Cameron. He so looked forward to having Tremont back with him. He'll be extremely disappointed." She walked out of the room.

Six grandchildren converged on their grandfather like bees on honey. One by one he pulled them onto his knee. "John," the senator said, "could you grab the bag next to my coat?" He asked. "I just might have something in there for these rascals."

John, his youngest son, city manager for Indianapolis, retrieved the bag full of goodies and handed it to his father. He stood swirling his drink and said, "You know, Mother always favored Cameron and seems to be the only one who understands his quirky and eccentric ways."

"I think what bothers you, John, is that you don't have a clue as to what's so important that it must be kept behind a shroud of secrecy?"

"Maybe, Father. But she dotes on him and Tremont more than any of us."

The Senator handed out the toys he had picked up at the airport. He looked up at his expectant son. "I know you don't understand Cameron. None of us really do but let me tell you, son, one day that eccentric scientist's work is going to change this world. Mark my words."

Senator Carson considered disturbing conversations he had with Senator Green, chairman of the Energy and Natural Resources Committee. He always asks leading and peculiar questions about Cameron and Tremont; not casual curiosity, more like he was investigating. Then James Seebert came to mind. He knew Green and Seebert were tight. Senator Carson determined that he would contact Deputy Director Harrington over at the FBI and ask him to investigate a possible connection between the two men.

Chapter Nine

Security
1981

THE DELIVERY VAN pulled up to the solid steel gate. The driver reviewed his delivery manifest. He was new on this route that included no more than five stops, with the first being over sixty miles from his hub location. His ten-hour day included dropping packages here, the state park ranger office to the east, and some sparse residential areas inland. The driver leaned out of his truck and pressed the button below the speaker.

While he waited for a response, he reread his route notes: *Be careful dealing with the security system and the owner.* He looked to the right and left, impressed with the heavy-gauge steel fence that disappeared into the pine forest. He took note of three rows of barbed wire, gracing the top of the fence, ten feet off the ground. He noted that the gate in front of him had heavier reinforcement than the White House gates. He would know. The compound only lacked armed marines and executive service officers, though he got the feeling they might appear at any time.

The computerized soft female voice on the speaker surprised him. "Please state your name and your business."

"John Lomax, Government Express. I have a package for Mr. Jackson that requires his signature." He clicked his tongue and watched a blue heron flap toward Lake Michigan.

"Please type in your security code."

John typed in the code listed on the manifest that he knew changed with each delivery.

"Thank you, Government Express. Please retype your security code."

He typed it again.

"Thank you, Government Express. Please type in the package airbill number."

Lomax was not expecting this, and he was a man that didn't like surprises. He typed, and after a long pause the latch clicked, and the gate began to open. The voice stated, "You may drive forward, Mr. Lomax. Your vehicle will be under constant surveillance. Please wait until you receive further instruction." Lomax thought that command a little strange.

While briefing for this assignment, he learned that he would deliver envelopes and boxes, and occasionally highly-insured wooden crates. He heard about the crates that would arrive, marked fragile, that each had a fifty-thousand-dollar insurance policy. Lomax grinned, thinking he might drop the box just to see if the insurance would pay that ridiculous amount, and get a look at what was so damn valuable.

He drove down the blacktop driveway, taking in the lay of the land. The gate closed behind him. Tall pines eventually opened to a clearing bordering the drive. There stood a magnificent white Charleston-style home with beautifully detailed moldings and trim. On the wraparound porch were four Red Oak Brumby Rockers, planters empty of foliage, and two statues that reminded him of beasts in *The Omen*. John Lomax opened his door and approached. He heard a muffled rumbling on his right and then his left. He cursed and began to back up. His eyes darted to the sign on the landing: *Beware of Dogs. They don't bite. They masticate.*

When the statues stood and stretched, he blanched.

"Please remain in your vehicle until further instruction. Thank you for your cooperation."

Lomax cursed, still retreating as the beasts lumbered down the steps. He had military working dog training and knew it was important to remain calm. He had confronted the enemy in war and was willing to throw his body in front of a bullet for the president but getting gnarled by a dog was not the way he wanted to go.

His back touched the delivery truck. He dropped the package, opened the door, and jumped in. Slamming the door, he gasped as two beasts bounded, their front legs pressed to the window. He leaned over to the passenger seat with one hand on the power-window switch. He could feel their hot breath as they barked, and the window closed. He had seen what he needed to see. For now. He needed to keep this job. For now.

He didn't wait to see what the next instruction would have been. He'd finish his deliveries, find out what he could from the park rangers who managed most of the dunes and property along the lake and then endure the long drive back to the station. No wonder it was so easy to request this route when he moved to the Chicago station. They had not been able to keep a driver on this delivery. He would report in and meet the owner of this secret hideaway next time. Lomax knew this was a long-term assignment. He was tired of the daily pressures in Washington, and this paid five time as much. He'd do this, and then back to Dallas to retire and use his season tickets.

Back at the porch, the two dogs, one with the large package clenched in his mouth, returned to their posts. One dog placed the package on one of the Brumby rocking chairs; the other was already lying down, eyes closed, satisfied with the nice stretch.

The two wide-jawed Rottweilers were an obvious deterrent to any visitor who might not heed the clear message to stay in the vehicle.

Above the dogs and the stained-glass windows accenting the mahogany door, a carefully carved and delicately painted sign creaked. On the sign, were the words, "Jackson's Place."

About one hundred yards to the right of the house stood a large electrical transformer, more commonly seen in a city than in rural farmland with sandy beaches. Multiple cables ran a few hundred feet across the width of the property and threaded through three telephone poles before hooking into this out-of-place house. On both sides of the house, were six-by-ten feet freestanding solar panels, with more adorning the roof. Despite his quick exit, Lomax could not have missed a dozen windmills, at least three hundred feet in height lining the length of the property. Surrounded by a thick green coniferous forest on the south, west, and east, with Lake Michigan on the north. Close to the back porch of the house, visible above the roofline, a forty-foot ancient oak waterwheel turned slowly in a stream which cut across the property before emptying into Lake Michigan.

Within a few yards of the northeast corner of Jackson's Place, a park ranger guided a tour of nature enthusiasts. With his back to the tall fence, he said, "Ladies and gentlemen, you have seen half of the Dunes that have marveled naturalists for nearly a century. A most diverse area, this 15,000-acre sanctuary is described as the land where prairie, marsh, and forest meet."[9]

A woman walked down to the water to take pictures of the windmills.

"I wouldn't go down there, ma'am," the ranger said.

One man asked, "Is it true a famous scientist lives behind that fence?"

"Yes, his name is Dr. Cameron Jackson. They say he is the great, great, great grandson of Andrew Jackson, that Jackson received a thousand-year lease on this land. One of President Jackson's descendants donated most of the land back to the government but kept this prime real estate."

The tourist said, "He prefers his tranquility and privacy."

"As a scientist, he certainly has a place where he can submerge himself completely in his research."

The woman with the large zoom lens on her camera continued to wade into

---

[9] Indiana Dunes National Lakeshore is on the southern shore of Lake Michigan in Indiana. Replete with birch and jack pine trees, wetlands, dunes, and trails, the Chicago skyline can be seen from the beaches. Other than Jackson's Place, more inland on the Calumet River, the park system has restored the Bailly Homestead, the Chellberg Farm and an 1822 fur-trading post. –The Jackson Diaries (1950 – 1989).

the water as the ranger went on to tell about how another ranger had climbed the high rock wall that stretched a dozen yards out into the lake. He ended his story by saying, "An air-raid siren blasted out a sound so loud, he could not hear for hours. Then a commanding voice stated, 'You are trespassing on private property protected by watchdogs, electric fencing, motion sensors and video surveillance. Enter at your own risk.'"

"What do you think he's hiding?" another naturalist asked.

"My guess is that he works on government projects. He's a physicist, so maybe it's nuclear-related? Who knows, but it would have to be something important." He turned around and yelled, "Ma'am! Hey!"

When the woman began to climb the rocks, the siren split the air, ending the conversation, sending the group into full retreat, with hands covering their ears.

Dr. Jackson was sitting in the den of the house his wife had designed, contracted, and decorated three decades before—when the northern property siren went off. That was the third time this month. He spun his chair around and pointed a remote control toward the large wall of monitors. He chuckled as he saw the young woman splash into the water, though he felt bad about her camera flying into the air and splintering on the rocks. He recognized the young ranger holding his ears and running to save her.

He rolled back around to the scrapbook that held his attention and took another sip of cognac. His current page depicted the house that had inspired Jackson's Place. The Market Inn, in historic Charleston, South Carolina, was the bed and breakfast where he and his Karen had honeymooned.

He closed the book and placed it gingerly on the mahogany shelves to the right of the monitors and security system control center. Since everything in the house reminded him of Karen, he stayed busy with his work in the lab. He spent most of his time developing his proprietary solutions to the inevitable depletion of natural fossil energy resources.

On rare occasions, he traveled to universities and government agencies to raise grant money. He preached about the necessity of accelerating the development of renewable and alternative energy sources. From those necessary fund-raising tours, curiosity percolated from advocates and detractors alike. Supporters joined in his mantra, calling for change. Opponents feared disruption of the status quo. Jackson had proved he could deliver with advanced solar technologies, but what if he could come up with a better source that was compact and cost-effective. It could cost the oil and automotive industries billions and potentially render them obsolete.

Jackson swirled his drink and shook his head. The world was making progress but at a snail's pace. If they could not help themselves, he would have to give them a push. He just had a little more work to do in the most sophisticated energy lab on the planet, right there, below ground at Jackson's Place.

He nursed another glass of Hennessy cognac. He swirled, deep in thought, after a disturbing phone conversation with his son, Tremont. He was aware that another delivery van had braved the compound and that Popeye and Brutus were keeping watch over the package. As with the tour of would-be naturalists, he had watched it on one of the screens on the wall of plasma monitors across the room. He had screens placed throughout the house, so he would be able to look at any part of the property from the labs, the kitchen, or his bedroom. Each monitor displayed eight views of the expansive compound in the rotation. Motion and sound sensors triggered alarms if anything over the weight of a large raccoon came within sixty feet of the electrified fencing surrounding the property. Often a deer or a black bear sounded the alarm at night, but that was all right. He was glad to wake up and review the projections from the infrared night video cameras. Proof of the system's effectiveness gave him comfort. He fell asleep in his chair.

The alarm went off at 5:00 a.m. On a monitor, he saw a family of deer feeding close to the western fence. He decided to head down to the lab. The coffee maker turned on at six. While he dressed, he pictured, instead of a family of deer, a well-trained team of Iranian terrorists crossing over from Canada, storming Jackson's Place to kill him and steal his work. A few years ago, he might have expected the Russians, but now the threat could come from many a nemesis.

He owned quite a few weapons, but his favorite was a custom-made .45 caliber handgun, engraved with the initials "CJ" on both sides of the grip. His father had given him the pistol when he retired from the Marines, just after Karen died. Cameron always kept the gun near him, whether in the basement lab, drinking himself silly in the den, or walking the compound with the dogs.

After Karen's funeral, his closest friend and Tremont's godfather had helped him obtain much of the compound's security equipment. He also had the help of an FBI agent, Patrick Flannigan. Both his friend and the agent had also suggested that Cameron keep a gun close. Both had agreed that it was at least possible that what happened to Karen was a warning with fatal consequences.

He poured another glass of cognac and cursed. Agent Flannigan was a rookie, but he could have prevented it, if he had only listened and convinced his boss, Harrington. Cameron tossed down the shot, trying to erase the black thoughts from his mind.

He stared at a picture on the wall, of himself on a large sailboat, arm in arm with a handsome dark, shorter man. What was it he called himself now? The man was a mystery to most. Cameron had laughed when he received the last wooden case holding a bottle of expensive rare wine, with it a note from his old friend bearing just the initial, Z. Over the past three decades, there had been times when had his friend not intervened, Cameron would not be here to continue his work. But even his friend could not stop them when it counted the most. Even he had not been able to save Karen.

The next morning, Cameron made a pitcher of Bloody Mary's and pushed a large red button next to an oversized dumbwaiter. "Down you go, Mary." He was in the lab before 7:00 a.m.

Ten hours later, he wrote in a leather journal that it had been a good day in the lab. Cameron made a habit of denoting the day's progress and any thoughts or clues about where to start the next day in one of his many journals. No matter how sure he was that he would remember the next day, the notes were essential. Scientific creativity came and went like waking from a dream. The vision could be gone in moments.

He considered going back up in the dumbwaiter. Both he and Tremont had done it more than once over the years. Instead, he stood, stretched, and climbed many flights of stairs, stopping to set the security system at each level. He was out of breath when he reached the main floor.

Cameron walked to the kitchen bay window overlooking the back of the property, the beautiful water wheel, windmills, and Lake Michigan off in the distance. Twelve posts topped with halogen lamps lit up the compound like an evening Cubs game. The giant windmill guardians cascaded toward the sandy beaches. He opened the door to the deck and stepped into the night air. Cameron thought of how he enjoyed his daily walks with his son along the untouched beaches, throwing sticks into the lake for Brutus and Popeye to retrieve. But not since Tremont went to Yale. Besides his nightly cognac, his son and the oversized Rottweilers were sources of joy outside of work. He whistled for the boys, and though stiff and tired, he walked down the steps and off toward the shoreline.

Brutus and Popeye darted past him, then ran back to him and took up sides. "You miss our walks too, don't you, boys?" They responded with boisterous yelps, tumbled over each other as he said "Go," and they sped to the lake. Cameron joined them at the water's edge and picked up sticks to begin their old ritual. Though the boys could keep this up all night, Cameron became tired and settled on a shelf of thousand-year-old Bedford limestone—or a million years—depending on whether you were talking to an evolutionist or a creationist. Off to the west, he could see the Chicago skyline sitting north of the obtrusive Gary, Indiana steel mills. To the east, he could see the lights of Michigan City. Brutus jumped on the rocks and rubbed against his leg. Cameron smiled and scratched behind his ears. Jealous, Popeye appeared on the other side for his share. "It's not such a bad life. I have you guys, and I have my Jackson's Place."[10]

Revitalized by the fresh lake air, Cameron and his four-legged companions

---

[10] In 1816, two years before Indiana became a state, Andrew Jackson, the seventh president of the United States, a Tennessean, purchased Indiana Dunes from the French-Canadian farming family that owned the entire 15,000 acres. The property spanned twenty-five miles along the Lake Michigan shore.

climbed the grade to the house. This was another of many nights he did not want to save the world. Once inside, he allowed himself more drunk than usual and one of the Cuban cigars given to him by his friend Z. He reminisced about what could have been.

It was sinking in that his son said he would not be back this summer. Of all the crazy patriotic things to do, Tremont had entered the Marines officer training program. He knew it was part of his son's long-term plans, but he secretly hoped he would return home after graduate school.

He sat down at his desk and looked at a picture of Karen, and said, "Sometimes there's too much of your father—and my father—to that boy," and then as if she had replied, "I know, honey, just one more sip, and I'm off to bed. I'll cut back. I promise." He made that pledge nearly every night.

After a few hours, Brutus and Popeye slipped in through the door as he stumbled to the front porch. He leaned onto the porch railing and noticed a familiar red and yellow, slightly gnarled, express mail package left the day before by yet another deliveryman who could not follow simple directions.

Cameron fell into one of the Brumby Rockers and tore the package open. He pulled out an unmarked video tape and a letter typed on plain white paper.

> We are still watching and expect right of first refusal on your research. Our offer remains the same. Half paid when you deliver and half when prototypes are operational. The bonus is that you and your son get to live. Time is running out. We are not impressed with your security system. It's a minor inconvenience. If we wanted to be in your house drinking cognac and smoking your expensive cigars, we would be. But who can work efficiently with a gun to their head? Let's be practical, Cameron. The FBI and that bumbling Flannigan cannot protect you. And the Marines will not be able to protect Tremont. Time is wasting. When you are finished, remove the Jackson's Place sign from the porch, and we will be in contact.

Cameron knew that for the last twenty years the same person had typed these letters. They had the same tone and tenor, and were typed on the same old Smith and Corona typewriter, displaying a weakness with the "n" and "t" keys. After Karen's sudden death, he had presented the letters to Homicide detectives with the Indianapolis Police Department and then to Agent Flannigan. He wanted revenge, but against whom? He had to protect his son. As the letters and videos continued to arrive, he kept them to himself. Not even Tremont was aware of their content. He had planned to reveal it all to him this summer. That would have to wait.

He perspired though the night air was cool. As usual, the return address was a Washington DC post office box—a false address, when Flannigan had traced it down. The videotapes were generic and untraceable. He, his friend Z, and Flannigan, had tried. Cameron's vision blurred as he stared toward the front of the property. He knew they could not know the depth or even the premise of his research. One day it would be easy to replicate CJ Energy Cells—as soon as he solved the final combination. He was close. Any day now.

They guessed that what he was working on would have a significant impact on the world. They were right. Ten million dollars was a lot of money, but that was chump change compared to the financial impact CJ Energy would have on industry, government, and the world economy. If they hoped to obtain anything from him with intimidation and threats, they were sorely mistaken. Either the entire world would benefit equally, or they could bury a life's work with him. No single government, industry, or monopoly would control the future of energy.

He wobbled back into the house to a cozy, acoustically perfect room where he and Tremont had installed their audio and video systems. He inserted the tape and sat back on the corner of a chair. The video revealed soundless scenes of him playing with the dogs on the beach, Tremont walking on the Yale campus, Senator Carson on the steps of the Capitol, nieces, and nephews at play on their school campuses, and other family members shopping at the mall or working in their offices. A veiled threat to hurt those closest to him if he did not comply.

He pulled out the VHS tape, wrapped the letter around it with a rubber band, and set it on the desk. Then he grabbed it and threw it against the wall. "It's been twenty years, you bastards." The dogs came into the room and sat at the foot of his leather armchair. He rubbed their ears. Before he fell asleep, he thought of his son, his wife Karen, and his life's work.

He grumbled, "I'll outsmart them, or I'll die trying."

Chapter Ten

Quest
March 16, 1995
Noon

IT WAS LATE MORNING when they saw the signs for Jacksonville, Florida. Matthew looked at the odometer. It had been thirteen hundred miles since they had left Maine.

They all cheered, under the illusion that they were almost there. Matthew missed the sign that read 357 miles to Miami. The girls slept at least half of the trip, and he was running on what was at the bottom of his adrenalin tank. He had planned to stop in Daytona, so they could see the Speedway and drive on the beach. When he saw that it was fifty miles off the highway, he changed his mind.

The next stop was to drop off Darma and Donna just south of Daytona, in Port Orange. After a few wrong turns, Matthew pulled up to the gated community. What a difference GPS will make one day, he thought. Getting through the gate was tough. Matthew was sure the security guard questioned seeing disheveled teenagers in late model VW's.

"You just get back from Woodstock?" the guard asked.

I had not heard that one before, Matthew thought.

The guard opened the gate, and they drove down the long, lush drive, flanked by majestic palm trees. Impressed, Matthew pulled into the driveway of a lovely Spanish-style home with a perfectly manicured Florida-style lawn and a premium ocean view.

Once Matthew unloaded their bags, he expected them to chip in again for gas. No such luck. He shook his head.

Matthew and Maria were leaning up against the VW, soaking up the sun, when Donna came prancing down the front steps.

"My aunt isn't home, Matt." She smiled and batted her eyes. "See you on Friday?"

Donna pranced back to the porch and into the house without looking back. He and Maria got in the VW and headed out of the neighborhood.

Maria said, "Next time maybe you won't—"

Matthew glared over his sun glasses.

"Just saying."

Matthew stopped at a Publix and drew money from the ATM before stopping at Waffle House.

After the All Star Special, they felt revived and pushed south. And that's when he first heard a strange rattle in the back.

When they filled up in Fort Lauderdale, Maria said, "Do you hear that noise in the back?"

"You look exhausted. Want me to drive?"

"There's a lot of traffic."

"You didn't imply that I can't drive as well as you."

"I, um—"

She growled, folded her arms around her legs, and fell asleep.

They drove the next few miles with the only sound being the cling-clang growing louder in the engine.

Carl Eaton stepped out of his quiet suburban home, stared down the well-lit street, and looked at his watch. The Eaton's lived in the Homestead area just south of Miami. Carl was a pilot for a cargo airline and once had the distinction of logging the most hours, without incident, while transporting cargo to and from Central and South American countries. That is until mountain-based guerillas shot his plane out of the sky over El Salvador. His copilot died on impact, and he spent the next few years in rehabilitation.

If anyone knew about his side occupation, his life and the lives of his family would be at risk.

After months of rehab, Carl recovered but had to give up flying. He made a small fortune in real estate and continued with his import-export business. As an additional sideline, he collected and worked on vintage cars.

His wife, Carol, came out of the house and said, "You look worried."

He looked at his watch again and muttered a few curses.

"It's too early to worry, honey. They probably got tired and stopped to rest."

"I guess."

Carol went inside, and his phone buzzed. He answered and listened. He cursed. "You said the kids weren't in any danger. Anything happens to them, I'll hold you responsible." He listened. "Is that a threat? You know where I am. I know where you are."

"I'm on my second wind. But the bus is getting worse." When she didn't respond, Matthew said, "I'm sorry. You can drive whenever you want. You're a great driver."

She gave him an extra-evil look, then smiled, and said, "There's a little of your father in you."

"I'll work on that," Matthew said seriously.

She punched his shoulder. "Hey, lighten up. It's a small thing."

A small thing, he considered. Matthew thought of the express mail envelope. He wanted to deliver it but was torn between his promise to Mr. E, and getting to his uncle's house before the engine blew. I'll take it tomorrow he decided. He had also told his uncle he would be there by dinnertime. With less confidence than he felt, he said, "We'll sleep on the Biscayne beaches all day tomorrow."

"Wonderful. Hey, you know it's so nice just to have you all to myself." Maria slid over and gave him a kiss, then crawled into the back and again fell fast asleep.

The VW bus sounded like a steam engine—it even whistled every few minutes. Matthew was beyond tired. Come on, just a few miles farther. The mechanic's bill would kill his budget for the semester.

He decided to gamble that the engine would hold up at least until they reached his uncle's house. He said, "Did I forget to tell you, I have to drop something off in Miami Beach."

"Drop something off? No, you didn't mention it."

"I didn't? It's nothing, just a package."

"Something from your father?" Maria asked skeptically.

"Something like that."

She frowned at him. Then she saw the sign again. "There's the Miami Beach exit! Don't miss it. Let's run down to the ocean while we're there, just for a few minutes. I'm still mad at you for missing Daytona. Hey, do you know who lives in Miami Beach?"

"A whole lot of people from New York?"

"Yes, and one of them is Thomas Harris."

Matthew raised his eyebrows.

"You know, he wrote the Hannibal Lecter books. Maybe we'll run into him."

"Sure, Clarice, perhaps he'll be walking down the beach in the middle of the night," he said, and then flinched as she punched him in the shoulder.

He would not mention Mr. E's unexpected visit to South of the Border, until he sorted out what he's up to. "I think it's a good idea to let the engine rest a bit. We'll deliver the letter, and we can sleep on the bus for a few hours. It's really too late to drive on to my uncle's house, anyway." As if on cue, the engine whistled and sighed.

Maria leaned her head out the window. "I can smell the ocean and hear the waves. Let's go walk on the beach before dropping off your mysterious package."

He followed the signs from 1-95 to 195 East onto Arthur Godfrey, which dead-ended on Collins. He turned onto a side road between two condominium complexes, thinking the beach must be somewhere in that direction. The bus sounded worse. It was pitch dark, about midnight. Suddenly, a terrible grinding sound came from the back of the bus like lug nuts rattling in a coffee can. Then there was a loud bang, and the whole bus shook like they'd hit a roadside bomb.

Smoke billowed out from the rear of the bus. Matthew laid his head on the steering wheel and then got out to investigate. When he dropped the door to the engine, steam bowled him backward.

"Bad, huh?"

"Yeah, pretty bad. I don't get it. Sean and I overhauled the whole engine."

Matthew slammed the hood and stormed down the alley toward the beach. He ran down the boardwalk steps and out onto the beach.

Maria caught up with him. She stood at the top of the boardwalk stairs and watched, as he kicked the sand and waved his arms.

"You're going to bring on an episode, Matthew," she yelled.

Matthew sat down on the sand and stared out at the luminous waves.

He took a deep breath and turned to see Maria, sitting at the top of the boardwalk, looking adorable with her knees pulled up to her chest. The look on her face was one of amusement.

Matthew liked to be in control of his emotions as well as the situation. At least that way, when things went wrong, there was only himself to blame.

It was late in the evening, and the chance of finding a mechanics shop was slim. He walked back up to the boardwalk.

"Matthew, Matthew," she said with a tsk tsk. "Feel better?"

All but the breakdown in a dark alley where we don't know anyone. No worries, he thought. They walked hand in hand to the boardwalk and back onto the street. The bus looked to Matthew like one of those dead-car-cartoons, with large Xs for eyes on the headlights, smoke still rising from the rear.

Matthew squinted as a lanky man, well over 6 feet tall, dressed as a character from Miami Vice, emerged from the smoke. A halo surrounded him in the lamplight and incited a sense of potential danger. Matthew looked around for a weapon, but there wasn't anything there except concrete, the side of the building, and a large green dumpster. He started playing out fight scenarios in his mind.

Maria seemed curious but not scared. She whispered, "This tall fellow reminds me of someone. A singer."

The man leaned in the shadows against the driver's side door of the bus, his head above the roof of the VW. As they drew closer, they noticed he held a box of Cracker Jack.

A guess would put him somewhere in his early to mid-thirties. He was clean-shaven with khaki pants and an untucked white, silk shirt, with unruly hair and tight, reddish curls. His prominent nose reminded Matthew of the Boston Celtics center. When he saw them coming, he pushed off the bus and into the moonlight with his face brightening into a broad smile. The height, the ruddy complexion, and the smile, all seemed familiar to Matthew.

"That's it," Maria said.

"That's what?" Matthew said, not taking his eyes off the man, and preparing himself to dive in punching and kicking.

"Barry Manilow."

"What?"

"That's who he looks like. Barry Manilow, except a lot taller."

"Larry Bird."

"Who?"

"Larry Bird. You know the Celtics center. He's now a coach."

The man interrupted. "I don't know about that, but they call me Cracker Jack," he said with an even broader smile. "Looks like you kids have some major problems with this classic."

"Cracker Jack?" Maria whispered.

Well, Matthew thought, he's the first person this trip to recognize the VW bus as a classic. He kept his guard up all the same. For all he knew, this guy could be a psycho killer. Still, something about him seemed familiar. To hide his tension, he laughed. "Is that the first name you could come up with? The tag on the box?"

"Well, young fella, it's the handle I go by these days. Long story. But I have time, and it looks like you have time."

The stranger shook Matthew's hand and nodded with a bow toward Maria. Matthew thought that he appeared to be harmless, but Sean had often said, beware of the friendly raccoon that shows up during daylight. Well, it was nighttime.

Matthew followed behind as they walked to the back of the VW, while Maria explained how they had ended up there. She finished by saying, "I was insistent that we stop and see the ocean."

"Well, I'm glad you broke down here rather than the highway." The stranger sauntered to the back and opened the engine flap. The steam had settled down. He reached behind his back and under his shirt.

Matthew said, "Why would you carry a Mag-Lite tucked under your belt?"

"Listen, kid. Do you know where you are? This is a suitable instrument to deter criminals. If you're going to make a habit of breaking down in dark, crime-ridden alleys, you should have one—or a gun."

He had a point, Matthew thought. Guns in Maine were akin to carrying a wallet. His father made him promise he would not carry a weapon on this trip. State by state firearm reciprocity was complicated. On this trip, Virginia to Florida was not an issue, but the troopers in the five states between Maine and Virginia might lock him up and throw away the keys.

Shining the light on the engine, he cursed under his breath when he burned his hand.

Matthew leaned in beside him, still wary and ready to block if the stranger swung the heavy flashlight. Somehow it reminded him of standing with Sean, while they studied an engine problem together.

"Hmm, I'm afraid we are going to need a mechanics bay, lift, and parts." Cracker Jack listed the parts required. All Matthew heard was expensive and more expensive.

"That's what I was thinking," Matthew said defensively. "These air-cooled engines are rare. We'd have to find a junkyard."

Maria stood quietly behind, but Matthew knew she was already profiling the man as a potential gentleman criminal: *pretty much harmless, but possibly into the high-end theft of diamonds and furs, or perhaps securities fraud.*

"Any suggestions, Mister—" he paused, "Jack?" Matthew laughed. He could not bring himself to say the outlandish name. Cracker Jack looked over Matthew's shoulder at Maria and smiled. The light from a street lamp shone on his face. So familiar, Matthew thought, when a spurious thought came to mind. He dispelled it as impossible.

Matthew had turned to the engine and was not paying close attention when Cracker Jack suggested that they go over to see his friend at the Shell station and see if he could give them a tow.

Matthew was about to ask him to repeat the gas station attendant's name when Maria nudged in between them.

"My name is Maria." She offered her hand and shook his firmly. "It's a pleasure to meet you, Mr. Cracker Jack."

Maria could charm the rattle off a snake, Matthew thought. Cracker Jack seemed to be under her spell, or was it something more?

"So, you are Maria. It's a pleasure to meet you."

Why would he say it that way? Matthew wondered, repeating it in his head, So, you are Maria? Cracker Jack was charismatic and charming, as he told one story after another.

"Look, you two kids go over there and tell Marcos that it would be a favor to me, and he will do whatever he can. Let's just say he owes me."

"What did you say his last name was?"

Cracker Jack did not miss a beat, "I don't think I did say, but it's Estefon."

"Oh, right."

Maria looked at Matthew with an inquisitive expression.

"I could have sworn he started to say Esteb, not Estef." Matthew whispered.

"What are you talking about," Maria whispered. "You mean like Estebanez?"

"I have to make a call from the diner," Cracker Jack said, "and I'll ring Marcos at the Shell. I'll be right back." And he sauntered around the corner.

"He asked me an awful lot of questions," Matthew said, "and I can't believe how we've rattled on about ourselves. There's something really familiar about this Jack."

"His name is Cracker Jack," Maria said with a smile. "I think he's delightful. How old do you think he is?"

"I was figuring around Sean's age," he said. "I've read that people tend to talk easily about themselves if you just ask them a lot of open-ended questions."

"Open-ended?"

"The kind you can't answer with a 'no' or 'yes'. I think that's what he was doing to me."

"In my criminal psych class, I learned a great interviewing technique," Maria said. "By changing every sentence of the conversation into a question, people will tell a perfect stranger their middle name, social security number, and bra size."

"Thank goodness he left before you could reveal that."

"Very funny. I also felt like he was analyzing us."

"Or interviewing," Matthew agreed.

"I think you two might have a lot in common."

Cracker Jack came back around the corner. "Sorry, guys. I had to check in with my G-Men. You two look famished. After you talk to Marcos, come over to the diner." He turned and pointed. "It's around the corner at the end of this building. My apartment, compliments of the U.S. government, is right above the diner. Juanita will take care of you. I'll meet you there in a bit." He spun around and disappeared around the corner.

Matthew and Maria looked at each other quizzically. "G-Men," Matthew said. "Doesn't that mean the FBI?"

"Yeah, that's what they used to call them, but maybe he meant something else. I don't like the sounds of any of this, Maria."

"I think it's exciting, and I believe that you are misjudging Cracker Jack. He's a character, but harmless, at least, to us."

"You're the psychologist."

"Not quite yet."

"Okay, let's go over and meet Marcos before we get some food."

They walked out of the alley, across the street to the Shell station. His mother had said that Uncle Carl warned that Miami Beach could be dangerous at night. The Shell station's backlit sign was in the shape of a shell, an antique, and the cement building, white at one time, was all different shades of grime and dirt. Two gas pumps stood out in front, like a couple of tin soldiers with red bodies and round yellow heads.

Sitting in the office with his legs on a desk reading a racing magazine was a short man, wearing a freshly-pressed gray shirt with red pinstripes and a Shell patch just below the embroidered name, George.

"Hi, I'm Matthew, and this is Maria. This guy told us to see Marcos, is he—" Matthew said pointing back in the direction of the bus.

Startled, George dropped his legs off the desk and stood up. In Spanish, he said,

"My name is Marcos, and Cracker Jack called me. He may seem loco, but he's okay. He has helped many in this community. What can I do for you, niños?"

Matthew didn't have too much trouble following the Spanish. He spent the first six years of his life around Maria's mother and these many years with her two doting aunts. While noting Marcos' neat appearance and lack of grease, or even a little dirt on his hands and under his fingernails, something else occurred to Matthew. "Maria, ask him if he thinks Jack has ever been in Maine? I have this nagging feeling I know him or have seen him before."

Maria translated, and Marcos replied, "I do not know about that, Mr. Eaton. Cracker Jack has been around the world, but here in Miami for a few weeks."

Matthew cocked his head and tried to think if he had told Cracker Jack his last name. He didn't think so. And why would Marcos have a shirt that says, George? He was about to ask, but Marcos spoke first. The conversation continued in Spanish.

"My mechanic, he is not here today, and since it's Sunday, we would not be able to get parts from Miami until Monday. So, Cracker Jack, he says you have family in Homestead?"

"Yes, his uncle," Maria said.

Marcos walked to the gray metal desk and punched some keys on a worn-out adding machine. "Then for *cuarenta dólares*, I take you *esta noche*."

Matthew turned to go, and in passable Spanish asked, "Marcos, what is your last name?"

Marcos turned, smiled and said, "Estefan. *¿Porque?*"

"I just misunderstood what your friend said. That's all. Thanks." Matthew did an about face and did what he called his Columbo impersonation. He asked, "So, how is Mr. Estebanez?"

"Who? Estebanez? I think there was a conquistador that ruled Cuba after discovery by Christopher Columbus in 1500."

A Shell manager that studies history, Matthew considered.

While they waited for Marcos to get off work or finish reading his racing magazine, they walked back to the VW bus. Maria laughed when she opened her door. On her seat was a large box of Cracker Jack.

"Is this guy for real, cariño?" Maria asked.

"My guess is that he's a little bit crazy."

"He's right. There was a conquistador named Estebanez that took over Cuba. They tried to tame the Aboriginal people, but in the end, European viruses like strep killed all three tribes. Estebanez was the governor of Havana, I believe."

Mr. E has more *splainin* to do, Matthew thought. But that's nothing new. There were so many inconsistencies over the years. For instance, it occurred to him that he didn't know Mr. E's first name. He always wondered if Estebanez was his real name. When he was about ten, he opened a passport that Mr. E had on the dashboard of his rental car. It had a different name, Antonio Brey, but with Mr. E's picture. He never asked him about it as he would have to admit that he looked at it. Perhaps Mr. E borrowed his name from the conquistador?

He locked the bus, the smoldering casualty of their long journey. They walked away from the Shell, toward the all-night Cuban diner, first passing some busy bars.

Two men were walking toward them, taking up the whole sidewalk. Matthew stepped aside and pulled Maria with him. But the larger of the two moved their way and bumped into Matthew. One of the two well-dressed men that Matthew assumed were leaving the upscale strip bar scowled and the other smiled. With a Middle Eastern accent, the smiling man said, "Please excuse my brother and me." With a slight bow, he put a hand on his brother's shoulder and directed him across the street. Matthew took Maria's arm and held her close.

They entered the dimly-lit diner.

Chapter Eleven

Remember
1981

STILL FEELING THE EFFECTS of the Hennessy Cognac, Cameron arrived at the Carson family cemetery in Indianapolis. He sat in the spring rain next to his wife's grave on a well-worn stool. The journey was nearly a three-hundred-mile round-trip, but he visited at least twice a month. Under duress from her suspiciously sudden death and pressure from her father, the Senator, he had succumbed to burying Karen in the Carson family cemetery. He regretted that decision as he would have preferred her being closer to him at Jackson's Place.

Wet and chilled, he took a long, warming swig of Hennessy. He stared blurry-eyed at the beautifully-designed Moravian, ceramic flask, given to him over thirty years ago, by the German physicist Wolfgang Pauli.

"Sweetheart, do you remember the story about this bottle?" he asked. "Well, I'll tell you again if you won't be too bored by the details. This great man, Pauli, won a Nobel Prize for the Exclusion Principle, the *Pauli* Exclusion Principle. It sounds a bit dicey to the layman, but simply put, electrons, neutrons, and protons can possess the same energy or quantum state in an atom." Wouldn't Pauli have been impressed, he thought, to see how far we've come. "Anyhow, Pauli gave the flask to me in 1956 while he was attending the International Energy Conference. I suppose he was listening to some cocky college student present a halfway credible case for the potential of cost-effectively harnessing energy from the sun." He chuckled, thinking how idealistic he was up on that stage.

"You know, Pauli was ailing and died only two years later, at the age I am now," he said. "He walked up to me and Craigo and handed me this flask." Cameron scrunched up his face and said in his best German accent, 'Young man, if you intend to go against the establishment, you are going to need this.' Then, he walked away."

"'Do you know who that was?' Craigo said. I told him he looked like someone I saw in a textbook. Michael said, 'He's Wolfgang Pauli—perhaps this century's greatest mind in quantum physics.' I just stared at this exquisite multicolored bottle, screwed off the top, and sniffed. My head reeled backward, and my eyes watered—what an intoxicating aroma. My apologies, Karen, Hennessey hooked me ever since.

"I had one problem after another in the lab this week, and something occurred to me. Pauli was also infamous for The Pauli Effect. I cause the same thing every time I'm in a lab—catastrophe! Old Wolfgang Pauli had the reputation of walking into a lab only to watch the experiment in process, self-destruct." He sat quietly.

"That FBI agent, Flannigan, he came by the house again. I'm rough on him. I suppose … I suppose I blame him." He stared off into the dark. "And your good friend, Tremont's godfather, yeah, the one I was so jealous of when we met … he continues to stay in touch with us both. There's not much he can do—but if we need him, he'll be there." He took another drink.

"Where was I, dear? Oh yes, I stood there looking at my new trophy—this flask. It was full to the top with cognac. When Pauli died, the entire department met on the roof of the Hayden Barker Science Library and toasted his passing. We sent our glasses and bottles crashing to the alley below."

Cameron pushed himself off his stool and toasted Wolfgang Pauli. His eyes filled with more tears. He told her about their son. Tremont had ten times the potential he ever had. "I know you're proud of him, too. He joined the Marines, but I don't have to worry, because Tremont has his own guardian angel.

"It's tough to work without him here. I didn't tell him that. What he doesn't know is that CJ Energy is ready. I could have revealed the results a few years ago, but I was waiting for Tremont to finish his studies. I don't know, maybe I'll never release it—if I'd only done what they asked, you'd still be here with me." He sat and buried his head in his hands. "Tell me what to do, Kay." He wiped his nose.

"You're right, I have plenty of corporate work to do on solar cells and whatnot. When Tremont gets home for good, then we'll see what the world thinks of CJ Energy. Once it's made public, P7, Hafiz and the other criminals should have no reason to hurt Tremont."

Unless their motive is then revenge, he thought. He stood and folded the chair. "Keep an eye on him, Kay. You know how he is. He's bullheaded like your father, impetuous like me, and an idealist like you."

"God, I miss you, Kay. I'm keeping the place up nice. Not much has changed except the lab and all the security shit. Sorry." She hated profanity. "But I'm still a lonely son of a bitch. Sorry again, honey. But I'll be seeing you when my work is finished here." He kissed her tombstone, promised to quit drinking, and brushed away some dirt from the glistening white marble. The inscription read:

Perfect Wife, Daughter, and Friend

Karen "Kay" Carson Jackson

Born March 3, 1935

Gone to help God organize heaven, August 17, 1959

Cameron dropped the stool. He tripped trying to reach it and saw a movement. He withdrew his .45. "Who's there? By God, I'll—"

When he stumbled into the parking lot, tires screeched, and he watched the taillights of an SUV disappear around the corner.

Chapter Twelve

Genius
1981

MATTHEW WAS A CHILD when Sean brought his best friend, Tremont, to Millinocket. Tremont stepped out on the porch where Matthew sat with a pencil and paper. A scruffy, longhaired collie mix lay next to him. The dog's eyes followed Tremont's every move. They were both quiet, and Matthew pretended not to notice the skinny, redhead giant. Tremont stood on the opposite end of the porch, leaning against one of six oak posts, supporting a massive overhang, which surrounded the front of the colonial-style home. He observed Matthew.

Several minutes passed before Tremont spoke. "I've heard a lot about you from your brother. Can I help?"

Sean Eaton was inside the house, discussing joining the Marines with his father. By now, both voices were bellowing accusations and insults. Matthew didn't flinch, but it bothered Tremont. He could not remember a cross word exchanged between him and his father, though he had witnessed many altercations between his father and his grandfather, Senator Carson.

Young Matthew continued to focus on the task in front of him. Tremont edged closer.

Something crashed inside. They both heard Mrs. Eaton. "Please don't fight, and please be careful, that's my great-grandmother's china. They have made it through four generations, but how they made it twenty years with the two of you, I'll never know! Now sit down and have some cobbler."

She stepped up to the door and said, "Tremont, would you like some apple cobbler and coffee or tea?" The dog's ears rose when he heard the word cobbler. Her eyes followed Mrs. Eaton.

"No, ma'am, but thank you just the same," Tremont said.

"Matthew?"

"Do you have any cake left? German chocolate?"

"No, you know I only make that on your birthday. But I made carrot cake on Sunday, and I believe there's a piece with your name on it."

Matthew frowned, not looking up from his paper. "No, thank you, Mom."

She brought him out a glass of milk and a pill before returning inside.

Matthew ignored the shouting. Tremont noted his focus. Since Matthew had not acknowledged his presence on the porch, Tremont sat down next to the boy and pretended not to look over his shoulder.

Someone pounded on a table. Sean's father said, "You never think of anyone, but yourself. What if something should happen to me? Who would oversee things at the mills? When my father died, I—"

"I know! I was with grandad that day! Nothing is going to happen to you, old man. You're too damn ornery to die before your time. Besides, if we worked together, we'd kill each other inside of a year."

Over Matthew's shoulder, Tremont studied a drawing of what appeared to be a windmill, much like the ones his father had installed at Jackson's Place. Except, Matthew's picture included auxiliary solar panels indicated by an arrow pointing at large rectangles running vertically down each side of the pole, with the words scribbled "solar panels." This justified Tremont's suspicions that, just as Sean had said, Matthew was a young Cameron Jackson.

"Do you always sit around and invent—drawing like this?"

Matthew looked up and smiled. "Every day."

"What are you trying to solve here? I see solar panels. What do you know about solar energy?" He worried that he might intimidate the boy, but on the contrary, Matthew looked at him directly, analyzing.

"You're the science guy, my brother told me about. I've wanted to talk to you for a long time," Matthew said.

Tremont nearly chuckled aloud. He thought, what could be a long time in a child's life?

"I heard him call you Tree," Matthew said and turned back to his drawing.

"You should hear what my father and grandfather call me—"

Matthew interjected, "Well, I was thinking that all those windmills in California don't work all the time, but they have the sun all the time. So, if we can get energy from the sun, the windmills would run all day and then have enough power to continue through the night."

Though surrounded by intelligent people, this kid was more than he had expected. He was not only smart, but he also had a natural affinity for science and energy science at that. Tremont couldn't wait to tell his father about Matthew.

"How did you get interested in windmills and solar panels?" Tremont asked.

Matthew shrugged.

Having forgotten that he was talking to a child barely out of kindergarten,

Tremont changed the subject. "I noticed when I walked out on the porch, that you seemed to be perplexed—"

"Perplexed?"

"Confused. You seemed to be confused about something."

Matthew gave him an incredulous look.

"I mean, when I walked out, you were working on some part of your design."

"I know what you meant. I just needed context."

Tremont covered his grin with his hand. "And?"

"There must be a way to make the same power with something a whole lot smaller. Kind of like my dad's computer. Did you know they used to fill up a whole building, and now it sits on his desk?"

"You use your dad's computer?"

"I mean if someone can shrink—Did you see that black and white movie where the guy had this big machine, and he shrunk everything and everyone around him? I love that movie. Sometimes I imagine that's how they shrunk the computer."

The path of this child's logic enthralled Tremont. "My father has spent his entire life trying to do just what you've described, Matthew. Take the power of the sun or the wind or the chemical action in water and capture it into a small vessel."

"Vessel?"

"A cabinet like what houses the computer, like a battery, but with the ability to regenerate itself and not wear out," Tremont continued. They talked for a while longer, and then he asked Matthew what books he had on alternative energy.

"I have some kids' books, and I've asked my teachers for some real books—"

"Real books," Tremont said, amused.

"I asked her for specific books on solar panels. She never got them for me."

"I bet she didn't think you would be able to understand the concepts. I'll send you a few books that I think you'll enjoy and some others you can keep for when you get older."

I have a feeling, Tremont considered, in a couple of years, you'll be able to comprehend most of *Capturing the Sun*.

As the evening waned on, Tremont found it easy to talk to Matthew about world events, archeology, geography, politics, and their mutual favorite subject of science and inventions. Matthew was patient as Tremont explained various concepts.

The sun was setting over the forest, and the two boys faced the northern mountain ranges of Maine, toward the border of Canada. Sean and his father were still arguing, drowning out Kate. Tremont told Matthew briefly of Cameron Jackson's work. He glimpsed a rudimentary conceptual understanding in Matthew's eyes. A few minutes later, Sean came barreling out and nearly threw the screen door off its hinges.

"Let's go, Tree. He's an ass and always will be." Sean reached down and put his

hand on Matthew's head. "I'll see you later, little brother. Keep sending copies of your drawings, okay?"

Matthew blinked hard against tears.

Sean knelt. "Sorry we can't go hiking. Next time, I promise. And we'll shoot that .22 Verminator. Deal?" When Sean tried to ruffle his hair, Matthew ducked. Sean stormed down the steps and out to the Land Cruiser.

Tremont turned to Matthew, who was now drawing imaginary lines on the pine floorboards. "Listen, kid, your brother talks about you constantly. You two have a special bond. Hey, I'll be back. We'll both be back soon with lots of good stories." Matthew still didn't look up, and Tremont caught a glimpse of Mrs. Eaton, standing in the doorway, listening. "You and I are going to be great friends. I guarantee it. And I'll write to you and send you some ideas for your class science projects. Would you like that?"

Matthew rubbed his eyes with a knuckled fist and nodded. Tremont grinned, and Matthew did not duck when Tremont ruffled his hair.

"Watch over my son, Tremont," Kate said.

"I will, ma'am."

As Tremont stepped off the porch, Matthew said, "I'll draw a picture of my rain-catching machine for you. I think it will work, but I don't know.

"I'll bet it will."

"I'm only six, you know ..."

Tremont walked away, shaking his head. He muttered, "Yeah, only six—a genius kid who loves quantum energy projects. What's the chance of that?"

Matthew watched the SUV plow down the long driveway. Parker came out of the house, crossed his arms, and stared after the SUV, not saying a word. He walked back into the house, rubbing one hand across his forehead.

Kate edged past Parker and stepped out on the porch. "He's angry, Matthew, but you have to know, he is also proud of Sean and maybe a little scared for him. She patted his shoulder, then retreated into the house.

Matthew patted Nuke's head, and said, "You know, I think Tree really liked my drawings and ideas."

Matthew didn't see Tree for another fourteen years.

Chapter Thirteen

Honor
1982

AFTER LEAVING MILLINOCKET, Sean and Tremont returned to New Haven, where they loaded up Tremont's safari-style Land Cruiser with a rack on top and a black iron grill in front built to deflect a charging rhino. They bade their final goodbyes to Yale and traveled the seven hundred miles south to Camp Lejeune in Jacksonville, North Carolina.

Neither Sean or Tremont had any trouble with boot camp. Almost. Sean and Sergeant Schmolz butted heads.

Tremont split his leave time between Jackson's Place and Indianapolis with the Carson's. Sean got to know the ladies and bartenders in North Myrtle Beach. The local sheriff's department provided Sean accommodations on two separate nights.

They received their orders and shipped out to Miramar, California, attached to the Third Marine Aircraft Wing. In Miramar, they were promoted and joined a newly-formed, secret Marine Antiterrorist Intelligence group. Along with two dozen other Marines, they spent a month in the desert, training with seasoned military intelligence professionals and civilian CIA personnel. They were now officially Marine military intelligence officers. Within the Marines, they were known as Badgers for the way they infiltrated terrorist camps and flushed them out into the open.

Within weeks of completing their training, the Badgers shipped to Kuwait to deal with an upsurge in the taking of U.S. and NATO hostages in Iran and Syria by Islamic extremists. They arrived in the most dangerous part of the world, as Iran and Iraq fought another war. In Kuwait, they learned Arabic and Farsi, recruited informants, and trained Islamic moderates to infiltrate terrorist cells. They were part of, and soon led, covert missions throughout the region.

After their tour in Iraq, the Badgers arrived in Pakistan to advise the Mujahedeen, made up of the Taliban and al-Qaeda insurgents, on the war against the Soviet Union supported Democratic Republic of Afghanistan (the DR).

Tremont thought it ironic that their mission was to work with an extreme Islamic fundamentalist group to undermine the Soviet occupation of Afghanistan. He told Sean, "If the Mujahedeen are successful in overthrowing the DR and the Russians, we'll be back to fight the Taliban and al-Qaeda a few years later.

Months after arriving in Islamabad, Tremont sat alone, next to a small fire outside of Jalalabad, the capital of the Nangarhar province of Afghanistan. He used to love to study the history of this ancient place near the Khyber Pass. Now, he just wondered how he got here.

He positioned himself in the shadows, with his back to the fire, not wanting to blind his night vision or to be a target for a communist sniper. Sitting around the fire, at least four to five feet from the flames, were a dozen Mujahedeen freedom fighters. Tremont did not like their company. In his opinion, the Taliban would be a far worse regime. If human rights, particularly for women, were not already horrendous, the Taliban would set Afghanistan back to the Stone Age. He sent weekly reports to his superiors, never expecting them to get any traction. His grandfather later confided that his committee received Tremont's observations from the Pentagon. Tremont's review also reached the chairman of the Joint Chief of Staff and POTUS's briefing agenda. Senator Carson said President Reagan was looking forward to meeting Tremont—not ironically, it was shortly thereafter that Sean and Tremont were introduced to national security aide, Oliver North.

Meanwhile, the current U.S. Executive branch covertly placed domestic and military secret service agents around the world. The long-term goal was to spread the ideal of freedom and democracy, taking the fight to the terrorists before they brought it to the U.S.

Tremont struggled in the firelight to write his weekly letter to his father. He wrote that it would take a couple hundred years after planting these seeds to see results, to affect centuries of tribal and hard-line religious societies of the Middle East. "We are seed planters," Tremont said aloud, pleased with himself.

"What was that?"

Sean was trying to sleep with his head on his pack.

"I was thinking about whether what we are doing has any value, or if we're spinning our wheels for nothing. If these zealots take over Kabul as planned, they'll throw the country five centuries behind."

"That's not our decision to make. The White House wants the Soviets out. They would rather fight the Taliban, ten or twenty years from now, than have to try to beat the Soviets in this part of the world alone."

"So, it's the Soviets out and anyone in."

"Exactly.

Tremont laughed. "We're pawns."

"Damn dangerous pawns, my friend. What are you writing?"

"Letter to my dad. I'm letting him know I'll be home soon."

"You're signed on for a few more tours."

"Ah, that's where you're wrong. I added an addendum to my last commission. I'm month-to-month, brother. As soon as this mission is over, I'll be heading home and trading in my rifle for a soldering gun."

Sean sat up and stared at Tremont for a long moment. "You never mentioned that."

"Wasn't sure until now."

Sean lay back down and said, "Not me, man. Death or retirement, I'm getting kind of used to these rocks and my anti-American buddies."

Tremont knew where he was heading, so he let it rest and returned to his letter.

"Hey, is your father still working on the same project you told me about back at Yale?"

"Same project."

"You still a believer?"

"Still a believer."

"That's great. I gave my brother your father's books, and you would have thought I brought him a motorcycle."

"I'm glad he liked them," Tremont said and held his breath until he could hear Sean's heavy breathing. Once again, he was pleased that the conversation hadn't gone any further. He was tired of lying to Sean about how much he knew about Matthew. The last he had heard, Matthew had come up with a new form of hydro energy conversion system. Matthew's concept was unique though MIT had similar projects on the books, and his father had worked with a team of hydro energy researchers back in the fifties. For a child to consider the possibilities of hydroelectric power on his own and develop a prototype, was astounding. If Matthew could do that before he was in middle school, what could he accomplish in college?

Tremont couldn't have picked a better protégé. Is that what he was? A protégé? Or something more? Insurance—perhaps. And what possessed Uncle Felix to make Millinocket a second home? He thought he knew. He felt a little guilty about working behind the scenes in the boy's life without Kate and Parker's knowledge. Considering the weight of his father's work and the impact on the future of civilization, he could live with a little guilt.

His father was nearing the completion of his experiments and would soon be ready to develop a prototype. He would ask for a discharge from the Marines when that time came and perhaps maintain his active status with the National Guard. Tremont was committed to throwing himself into his father's work, full time. Imagine, he thought as he folded the letter and addressed the envelope, if the U.S. and other developed countries were no longer dependent on foreign oil but could be independently secure in their energy consumption without depleting another iota of the planet's natural resources.

Tremont had not been asleep for more than a few minutes when bullets began to fly overhead and then chink off the rocks around him. He dove for his M-249 rifle. Sean was already throwing dirt on the fire, and they retreated to the rocks as bullets ricocheted around them. He could hear the screams of the hard-fighting Pakistani Taliban, as the enemy, shooting American-made M-16s, and the distinctive Russian Kalashnikov Assault Rifles, the AK-47s, picked his allies off, on the west side of the fire.

Trapped behind a boulder, he cursed the politicians on the hill for allowing US weapons to get into the hands of their enemies. He peered over the rocks. The moon brightly lit the area, an advantage for the shooter.

Their last mission, after Iraq and before Afghanistan, included participating in a highly classified guard detail. Tremont and Sean met Lt. Col. Oliver North in Geneva, Switzerland. Ollie said everything they did not know was on a need to know basis.

In full Marine dress uniform, they stood guard, outside of the penthouse presidential suite in the Hotel President Wilson. Ollie suggested they carry two extra clips of ammo. The bell rang on the elevator, the door opened. Two secret service agents stepped out, looked up and down the hallway, and nodded. They both said, "All Clear," and three high-ranking officials stepped out of the elevator: CIA Director William Casey, Vice President and former CIA Director George H. W. Bush, National Security Advisor Vice Admiral, John Poindexter, and Secretary of Defense Casper Weinberger.

The men went into the presidential suite where Iranian Prime Minister Banisadr and his entourage were waiting.

The deal struck in the Wilson was a mystery, but as the years passed, he learned that it was an arrangement to trade weapons for the return of hostages. Ollie told them that US arms had been filtering through Iran since Carter's inability to free fifty-two American hostages before the end of his administration. Reagan gained their release only a few months later. Tremont had learned from Senator Carson that the meetings had continued after their covert night in the Wilson. More deals. Since they had no hostages, the Iranian's were allegedly trading oil.

A shot ricocheted off the rock above Tremont's head. Five Taliban men lay dead or wounded near the smoldering fire.

"Spot for me," Sean whispered, "hurry."

Tremont went to a canvas supply bag and grabbed an M121 spotting scope. He crawled to the top of the boulder. *Twang*. The snipers bullet ricocheted inches from Sean's shoulder.

Sean adjusted his rifle scope. "I've got him in the crosshairs. I need elevation. I'll only get one shot, and he'll be gone.

"Where."

"Top of that ridge, right of the hawthorn bushes and left of the rock that looks like it has fox ears."

Tremont set the scope on its tripod. He lined it up to the fox ears and then shifted the scope left an inch. "Got him. 863 meters. Tremont whispered the elevation and tilt angles. He listened as Sean adjusted for holdoff and clicked a sight correction on the Barrett M82 .50 scope. Sean took in three deep breaths and exhaled the last.

Tremont whispered, "Send it."

Sean pressed, and it was gone.

Tremont saw the Russian sniper jerk and disappear. He took his eyes away from the scope. "That—"

Sean had disappeared.

Tremont hurried out to the fire and helped to drag the survivors to cover. Over the next hours, four shots were fired out in the dark.

Tremont and a surviving medic worked on the wounded. They traded off on sentry duty. Tremont was on duty an hour later when he heard someone coming from the hill behind him. He pulled his SIG P226 from its holster and pressed himself against a boulder.

A hawkish chirrup sounded, which gave him the creeps. It always did. Sean had said it was the sound of Pamola, the god of thunder, an infamous man-moose-eagle that caused significant storms, deaths, and disappearances. The funny thing was, Sean said it like he believed it.

Sean slid from the top of the boulder and landed next to Tremont.

"How many?"

"There were four," Sean said. "Two Russians."

Tremont had no doubt that amidst the camel thorn, locoweed, and wormwood, there were four more men ready for body bags.

In the morning, they checked and tagged their dead. The opposing force had lost eleven, including the four that Sean hunted down in the night.

Tremont changed blood-sopped bandages with the help of a tall, quiet man, they knew as Usama bin Mohammed bin Awad bin Laden[11], the youngest son of his billionaire father's eleventh wife.

Tremont did not like the way bin Laden looked at him—with a hateful glare. It was, however, impressive, almost cultish how even the older Mujahedeen soldiers followed his commands.

Tremont decided that this is getting old. It's time to go home.

---

[11] Osama bin Laden's given name. The founder of al-Qaeda.

Chapter Fourteen

Terror
1983

"A UNIVERSITY STUDENT, a mother, and her small child, dead in an explosion! Hundreds have been hospitalized with injuries," reported the dark-eyed Austrian News Network anchor. The car bomb in Israel was the third bombing in a civilian area this month. She stopped mid-sentence as she was handed a piece of paper. She told the camera, "Sheik Mohammed bin Bandar, the assistant secretary general of OPEC has been assassinated in Egypt. According to a source, Mohammed bin Bandar had been in a heated battle with other OPEC members over what some considered his pro-Western positions. Here at ANN, we have been covering this controversy and—" She put her hand to her ear. "We now have a live feed outside the Hotel El Houssain, at the Khan El-Khalili bazaar. Sudir?"

Two blocks from the ANN headquarters, twenty men sat around an ornate marble table. The room displayed a colorful Middle Eastern silk tapestry, enormous Persian carpets, and hand-carved marble furniture. Original oil paintings hung on two walls. One depicted desert landscapes, and another showed three medieval Islamic empires. Dozens of photographs hung on another wall, showing oil fields and refineries. Affixed to the bottom of each framed and matted picture, was a silver-engraved label listing the locations; Bahrain, Kuwait, Qatar, Iran, Iraq, Saudi Arabia, Egypt, Syria, and various states or emirates of the United Arab Emirates.

Hafiz Islam Bitrūl Saumba Shokran met in a conference room on an underground floor of a building in the marble OPEC complex at Donaustrasse 93 in downtown Vienna. IBM's Austrian headquarters were to the left and Bank Austria to the right.

Outside, more than a dozen Austrian GEK Cobra military police soldiers stood guard, all carrying automatic rifles. The Cobra special forces were developed in 1972 to protect Jewish immigrants after the attack on athletes at the Munich Olympics. The Cobras also helped end a siege led by the infamous assassin, the Jackal in 1975.

Two Cobra soldiers stood guard outside the conference room. Although Austrian citizens, their features were distinctly different than their comrade Cobras. Earlier, each Hafiz board member exited the elevator and greeted the soldiers, "As-salāmu 'alaykum, Ahmed, As-salāmu 'alaykum, Saleh. The Jobrani Maher brothers were well known.

Inside the conference room, the seat at the head of the table was vacant. The two screens on the wall transfixed the men. One screen featured the local Austrian news with subtitles in Arabic. The other screen blared with the Al-Jazeera news report.

"It is a great tragedy," said one board member, as he touched his forehead, lips, and his chest before bowing his head. "He was a great man—a very great man, with the hand of Allah on his shoulder. May he find his peace and guide us through these difficult times."

Most of the men nodded in agreement. One man—tall, dark-robed with a medium-length graying beard, long black and gray robes, sandals, and turban—did not seem disturbed by the news.

Before the reporter concluded, the tall figure turned off the screens. All eyes were on him, as he first went to the head of the table, stood still for a while, and then paced around the room.

Omar bin Taliffan said, "Most of us agree that Mohammed bin Bandar was weak when it came to making crucial policy decisions that affected our profits, our stability, and our very existence.

"We have been playing right into the hands of the West," the self-appointed new President of Hafiz said. "All that I had predicted has come about. OPEC is weakening as development in the Gulf of Mexico, and the North Sea continues. Exploration in Alaska, Siberia, and China is on the horizon. Fossil fuel faces extinction in the nuclear age. Since my father and uncles helped form these councils, this group's mission has been to provide stability, protection, and balance. Is this not what Hafiz Islam Bitrūl Saumba Shokran means in its most pure interpretation?"

Bin Taliffan growled. "What have we done in the past decade to assure our corporate future? Since the formation of Hafiz, what have we accomplished?" A few of the members shuffled through papers. *"La shayy!* Nothing, my friends. Nothing!"

Since 1973 and the oil embargo, the group had doubled in size from its original twelve-country membership. Assistant Secretary General bin Bandar had led its political and commercial activities while ignoring suspected illicit deals, assassinations, and sponsored terrorism. With bin Bandar out of the picture, there was only one elder statesman left to object. The bin Taliffan's successfully replaced the older Sheiks, Ministers of Oil, and princes of this secret society. The younger family members looked up to the strangely charismatic Omar bin Taliffan, an outspoken Islamic leader calling for Jihad against the West. Many in the West believed that the only difference between Omar and his extremist cousin, Osama bin Laden, was that he directed his network from boardrooms rather than from desert terrorist training camps and caves.

Wringing his hands was Sheik Hassan Al-Fawza of Saudi Arabia, the last of the old guard, a founder of Hafiz.

There was a knock on the door. Taliffan signaled Nafed, a servant, and the Cobra guard who led in two men. The Anglo men looked out of place. The first man, just short of 6', had sandy-brown hair, striking blue eyes, and a prominent cleft chin. He wore long Docker shorts, a Dallas Cowboys cap, flip-flop sandals, and a wrinkled short-sleeve button-down shirt. He removed three thick manila folders from a worn canvas satchel.

The second man, dressed in a pinstriped suit, carried a leather briefcase. They took their seats as their host stalked around the room.

Sheik Hassan Al-Fawza stood up. "I demand to know what is going on!" he said to Omar bin Taliffan. "Did you and these American's have anything to do with Bandar's murder?"

"We are Canadians," John Lomax said, with a wry grin and clicked his tongue.

The room became silent. Al-Fawza cleared his throat. "You cannot take Sheik Mohammed bin Bandar's position without a vote. We will not stand for it." He looked around the room and found no support. "And what are these men doing here? This is a closed session. I will take this up with the OPEC membership later today."

"Please sit down, my dear uncle. How long have you and my father been business partners and friends? Forty years? Please drink and eat. All will unfold within the hour, I promise you." Taliffan now stood behind the old Sheik. "You are not looking well, Uncle. Can I have Nafed get you something from the infirmary?"

Though the room was quite cool, the Sheik mopped sweat from his head. He replied with a cracking voice, "I am feeling fine, but why are you—"

Taliffan spread his fingers over the man's shoulders. "Everything will be revealed in time, insha'Allah."

"Canada?" Taliffan returned to the head of the table. "Let me introduce Senator Wayne Green from Texas, and his associate—" he paused while his and the other man's eyes locked— "Mr. Smith. They represent those in the United States, who share our objectives. To continue to increase our dominance in the world market, we must avoid the mistakes of the past, such as the failed embargo of the early seventies. The unexpected result was the empowerment of nuclear energy proponents and renewable energy conservationists, creating a quiet but deadly enemy to our way of life—"

All eyes turned to Al-Fawza the elder as he stood, grabbed his chest, and fell chest forward on the marble table, his head bouncing in his soup.

Unfazed, the man next to the sheik, looked at Taliffan for direction. The Senator stood, knocked his chair over, and backed up against the wall. Lomax took something from his pocket, leaned back in his chair, and started chewing a stick of gum. He fiddled with the wrapper.

"Yes, of course, Cousin Mahmoud, check on our uncle."

Mahmoud, a former al-Qaeda lieutenant—and first cousin to Omar, Ahmed, and Saleh—had joined the secret society to replace General Daneshvar, who had taken ill and then died in Vienna the previous year. For Al-Qaeda, Mahmoud had developed a long-term plan to infiltrate the US with teenagers, where they trained in aviation, energy sciences, security, and business. While that program percolated, bin Laden wanted regular briefings on the progress with disrupting efforts to circumvent the Middle Eastern fossil fuel industry which would indirectly cut off Al-Qaeda's funding. With no love lost between the Iranians and the Yemenites, General Daneshvar threatened to expose bin Laden and bin Taliffan one too many times. As with Secretary General bin Bandar, the media had alluded to foul play regarding Daneshvar's death, but an investigation by the Vienna police and the Iranian government had been inconclusive. When welcoming Mahmoud as Daneshvar's replacement, Omar had said, "One more trusted cousin and one less Shiite to worry about."

Mahmoud felt for a pulse. He announced, "He is dead."

The door opened and the two Cobras, Ahmed and Saleh, entered the room. Taliffan shook his head. "Our uncle will be missed. Please, help Nafed take him to the infirmary until we have time to take him to the hospital." They lifted the Sheik's body and carried him out of the room.

Taliffan motioned to the Americans.

The Senator stood up, sat down, wrung his hands, took a deep breath, and replaced his glasses. He pressed his shaking hands over his yellow pad as if he were forcing wrinkles out of a shirt. "Gentlemen, as Prince Taliffan said, we have much in common. Our goals are like yours." He launched a diatribe against the current global, political, and economic situation, as it related to the oil industry. "If we sit back and allow men like Dr. Jackson to succeed, you may be looking at only fifty years before the United States and Europe are energy source independent. Already, France has initiated construction of the largest nuclear plant in Europe and hopes to be fossil fuel free in a few years. I am concerned about global economic instability. To summarize, we must work together to assure our constituents—"

"The Seven Sisters, P7?" Taliffan interrupted to clarify.

"I'm not familiar with that." He cleared his throat, and Omar harrumphed.

The Senator continued, "For the record, many leaders within the industry, most governors of oil-producing states like Texas, Louisiana, and Alaska, disagree with me—with us. But our constituents include hundreds of other companies and many governments who depend on the stability of the oil sector." The Senator flipped a page and said, "We must keep competing supplies of crude oil from gaining availability to make sure our demand for oil remains a constant—"

"Our oil," Omar said.

"In part."

"A large part."

"It's important that our demand for oil stays constant. We can do that through legislative and economic means. As I chair the Committee on Energy and Commerce, we have managed to slow their growth by not appropriating funds to research and development.

Your fathers," he motioned around the room, "your fathers and I long ago agreed that we must further hinder the growth of other forms of energy. With," he cleared his throat, "with nonviolent methods. You'll note that Doctor Jean-Paul Dominique Esquirol is now a permanent resident of Hôpital Pitié-Psychiatrique. His foundation's advances in micro-hydro energy have been set back by more than a decade."

"And, Senator, how do you think he got there? Luck?" Omar said.

The senator did not look his direction and stuttered.

Omar continued, "The threat we are curious about, is in your own country."

Smith's head nodded, and he opened his eyes. He looked around the chamber. "Don't worry, folks. I have dear Cameron Jackson under round-the-clock surveillance." He chuckled. "I must say, I'm becoming quite the Tchaikovsky and Mendelssohn fan." He studied their blank stares and said, "If he leaves his compound with his mysterious little energy experiment and heads to Washington, we'll know it. You boys hold up your end of keeping a juicy supply of oil available, and we'll keep your competition in line, including Dr. Jackson and his pals … What do they call themselves, Senator?"

"The Fraternal Order of Alternative Energy," the Senator said, with a grumble. "A bunch of MIT eggheads."

"Jackson is the smartest egghead of all," Smith said.

Chapter Fifteen

Transfer
March 17, 1995
1:00 a.m.

JUST AS MARIA SAID, "I wonder if Cracker Jack will be coming back," he walked in through the door. They heard his melodic voice say, *"Juanita, hola guapa.* They look famished. Fix them up with whatever their hearts desire."

Juanita was a compact Latin girl in her mid-twenties. *"Si, mi querido, enseguida.* It will be my pleasure," she said.

"Gracias, mi amor. Tan bella y amable como siempre. Put it on my tab, or better yet, put it on you-know-who's tab. They can afford it."

Juanita smiled slyly at Cracker Jack, and Maria whispered to Matthew, "Something is going on between those two, and it's not just bacon and eggs."

Cracker Jack came over and sat down next to Matthew. He stretched his long legs out and gave them a radiant smile.

When Juanita took their large order, Cracker Jack chuckled. "I thought you two looked famished."

"One can't live on Cracker Jack alone," Maria said, "but it sure looks like Juanita could."

"Seriously," he said, and his smile disappeared. He leaned toward Matthew and Maria. "I'm going to tell you the most incredible story. What I say, you can't repeat to anyone—ever. Just having met me, it's too late to turn back. Knowing what I'm about to tell you may put you at risk." He had their undivided attention.

Though intrigued, Matthew was feeling a bit sarcastic. "I think to some extent, you're kidding around with us. Tell you what, the least we can do is listen."

Cracker Jack smiled. "It's been my pleasure. I know it's hard to conceive, but you may be my last chance to save decades of research."

"You said earlier that you had to check in with your G-Men? That's the FBI, right?" Maria asked.

"That's right."

"Have they formally arrested you?"

"No, they are holding me under an obscure national security risk law. Flannigan thinks he's helping."

"Flannigan?"

"They have me under apartment arrest. I haven't been charged."

Matthew was intrigued but skeptical. "It hardly seems legal or American for that matter."

"My lawyers are doing all they can, but this is the first chance I've had to talk to anyone but Marcos in weeks. The most important thing is to get my father's life work into safe hands—in a safe place."

"Why not entrust it to the FBI?" Maria asked.

"The government is half the problem. No, it has to be you."

"You don't even know me."

"If you agree to help me, Marcos will know what to do, and he'll see to it that you're compensated. Money is no object."

Maria raised her hands. "I'm confused, Cracker Jack. Why would you want two college kids to help you? Why would you think we even could?"

Cracker Jack told them about his father's nearly obsessive need for the highest of security. "He feared that one day someone or some institution would either steal or destroy his life's work, either to satisfy their greed or for fear that Dad's success would threaten their business or government."

Matthew thought everything Cracker Jack said was plausible and feasible. His skepticism waned. The man was either crazy or the son of a genius or maybe both, Matthew thought. It's funny, he thought. If he were talking about—Matthew's mind was spinning. It couldn't be! He thought. Could it?

"How long have they been holding you?" Maria asked.

"For the last three months. Until I break loose or—" Cracker Jack paused and took a deep breath. "Or I have a convenient accident." He put his hands behind his head and looked up at the ceiling.

It occurred to Matthew that anyone around Cracker Jack might be in jeopardy.

They dug into a second helping of scrambled eggs while Cracker Jack continued, "I grew up working with my father. The lab in our house was my playground. He has over a hundred patents on energy innovations, including some of the first active solar panels."

"Solar panels!" Matthew exclaimed with a full mouth of eggs. "What's his name?"

Cracker Jack put up a hand. "All in good time, Watson, all in good time."

Matthew sputtered, and Maria pounded his back.

He could barely contain his excitement. "I've read a lot of your father's research." Looking back to Maria, he continued, "Cameron Jackson cut the path for every other alternative energy scientist. He gained very little credit for being the first to develop an efficient solar panel. Then, after writing *Capturing the Sun*, tragedy struck, and he disappeared off the grid. My MIT advisor, Dr. Hessen, said that Dr. Jackson had gone crazy." Matthew wondered why Dr. Hessen disliked Dr. Jackson so much.

"Hessen, hmm, yes," Cracker Jack said, then smiled, and nodded. "Oh, and Russel Ohl actually patented the first solar cells in 1946, and my father went on to patent specific improvements in new generations of photo-electrochemical, polymer, and most recently nanocrystal cells. Behind the scenes, with a crazy bunch of guys called the Fraternity—"

"The Fraternity?" Maria said.

With a chuckle, Cracker Jack added, "Yes, his closest friends, Dimitri, Sergio, and Randall. I'll introduce you to them one day. So, Dad had been involved in research and development of nearly every type of alternative energy source you can imagine, and some that no ordinary person could imagine. He was one of the pioneers of fuel cells, but when those he consulted would not listen, and spent billions of taxpayers' money, he left to concentrate on something with greater impact than the invention of electricity."

Maria was shaking her head. "You're talking to the right guy. He dreams of inventing something—Ow!" She kicked him back and hit him in the shoulder. They exchanged a look.

Cracker Jack chuckled.

Maria continued, "Matthew wants to do something that would change the world for the better—like solar panels, windmills, electricity, hydroelectricity, and fuel cells. He even won a national Smithsonian—"

"Maria," Matthew implored.

"I'm just saying."

"I know." Cracker Jack paused. "I mean, I assumed that would be the case earlier as you spoke about your major at UMaine and your course selection."

Matthew looked quizzically at Cracker Jack. Something wasn't quite right, he thought, but plowed forward. "I've considered working in some form of energy engineering and quantum physics. That's how my scholarships are designated."

Matthew looked over at Maria, who studied Cracker Jack. Matthew knew what she was doing. She may have found the perfect subject to study, Matthew thought, besides me. "So, Mr. Cracker Jack Jackson, what is your first name? I think I read it somewhere once, but I cannot recall. Terry or Trevor?" Matthew noticed a slight hesitation.

"I'm actually named after my father."

"You were right about perceptions. To some people, my father was the mad scientist of Indiana, the son-in-law to the rich Carson political heritage."

"Senator Carson. I think he had more tenure in the Senate than Strom Thurmond?" Maria said.

"Almost. You know your American government," Cracker Jack observed.

"Not really. I just remember that he and Thurmond wielded a lot of power and helped defeat a lot of progressive legislation. Who's that Senator that championed the elderly?"

"Pepper. Claude Pepper."

"You mean liberal legislation," Matthew interjected and received a kick.

He then said to Cracker Jack, "Hence the inheritance."

Cracker Jack nodded, "He passed away only a few years ago. As for my father, anyone who knew science knew he was not crazy …"

"He's an icon," Matthew agreed.

Cracker Jack nodded, clearly pleased with the compliment. "Think about the many forms of energy we depend upon today: electrical power reformation, solar, wind, hydro, and nuclear. My father made contributions in all these areas."

"Along with … the Fraternity," Maria said.

Cracker Jack chuckled. "Yes, and his focus was on harnessing natural forms of energy. It's clean, neat, and potentially less costly if critical mass can be reached."

"Critical mass?" Maria asked.

Matthew chimed in, "That's the point at the top of a bell curve or where two axes cross on a graph where the benefit equals the cost or demand equals supply, and the product takes off like it has a mind of its own. Kind of like, one day there were no personal computers, and it seemed like the next day they were on almost every desk in the world."

"Critical mass," Matthew said.

"I think I'll stick to psychology," Maria said.

"Excellent," Cracker Jack exclaimed. "The problem is, critical mass could take decades in any one of the clean alternative energy sources, maybe longer. My father is partly responsible for hundreds of government-subsidized projects around the world. Before I was born, he built a compound on a large piece of land, left to him by his father. After my mother had died, he spent his life researching and developing energy systems, most of which have never been seen by the public."

"You lost your mother," Maria said. "I'm sorry."

Cracker Jack looked at her with knowing eyes. "She died in childbirth."

"I lost my mother."

"I know, I'm sorry," he said.

"You know?" Matthew queried.

Cracker Jack sat up straight and said, "But all this is another part of a very long story. We might not have a lot of time. His experimentations covered our compound on Lake Michigan. He installed a dozen wind turbines in our backyard. We had enough solar panels to illuminate New York City, and, my favorite, Dad built an old time Danish-style water mill. That was a sight to see."

Maria was about to comment, probably on the water mill, when Matthew jumped in. "You mentioned fuel cells?"

"Dad rebuilt an old tractor that ran entirely on a twenty-kilowatt hydrogen and oxygen fuel cell. It was as reliable as the sunrise. The concept and first working models have been around since the mid-1840s. My father developed the modern variations now used in space, prototype cars, and hundreds of other test markets. But he concluded that the cost was prohibitive, and there was a slim chance of making a final product that was stable and marketable. And the battery waste is an environmental hazard. He began telling people to save their money."

"That must have ticked off the investors," Maria said.

"Indeed. Since then, government and private industries have invested billions. The very people he helped put into business ostracized him."

"They have a lot to lose," Maria observed.

Juanita placed on the table three small cups of a molten white brew.

"Yes. After discarding fuel cells as an inevitable dead end, Dad turned his attention back to using the same concept of capturing energy from the most natural source. The reaction between neutrons and protons in a stable environment agitated by the perfect set of solids, which—" Cracker Jack leaned forward, folded his hands together and pointed his two index fingers toward Matthew, "—which causes energy that reproduces itself."

Matthew's heart was pounding. "A self-replenishing energy source."

Cracker Jack sat back in his seat and drummed on the table. "That is exactly what he proposed: energy that does not depend upon refueling—ever. My father spent decades creating near perpetual energy."

Matthew took a breath. "I knew it. I just knew it." He couldn't think of another scientist in the world that could match Cameron Jackson's brilliance.

While this information settled into a prolonged silence, Juanita served espresso in small colorful cups. Matthew sipped his café con leche and said, "Wow, that's sweet."

"Whatever happened to Popeye and Brutus?" Maria asked.

"I left them with my uncle up in the Florida Panhandle when I left for Europe." He looked down as he stirred his cortadito espresso. "Both have passed since then."

"I'm sorry," Maria said.

"Rotts only live eight to ten years. They were the second generation. Dad brought Popeye and Olive Oil home when I was four. They lived until I was thirteen. We were both sick when we lost them, so he went to St. Louis and brought home Popeye and Brutus."

"What have you been doing since your father's death?" Matthew asked, hoping this would bring the discussion back to Cracker Jack's interest in him.

Maria was startled and said, "I'm sorry. I didn't realize ..."

"Thank you. It's been difficult." Cracker Jack sighed and continued, "These last few years, I've picked up where my father left off. I spent time in the military with the intention of coming home and helping my dad with his research. I lost a lot of time with him.

"Anyhow, they watch me too closely to get anything accomplished, and I have something that needs finishing—" his voice trailed off.

"Who are they?" Maria asked.

He considered before answering. "I need to focus my attention on taking care of some dangerous people."

"The ones who are trying to steal your father's research and inventions?" Maria asked.

Cracker Jack nodded somberly. "I won't let my father's death be in vain."

Maria tried to lighten the moment and said, "My father often said that if he could bottle my energy, he could make millions."

Cracker Jack displayed the most disarming smile. "My father said the same thing. And then he did. Bottled energy, I mean. My dad liked to watch our windmills. He would say, 'I can bottle that energy, son, and use it whenever I wish.'"

"There are batteries, of course," Maria said.

"Yes, the battery was the first step, placing finite chemical energy into a cylinder which can only be maximized when combined with electricity. What has been the obvious problem since batteries were introduced in Baghdad over two thousand years ago?"

"Consistent and quick energy loss."

"Right, which leads to the disposable waste of billions of batteries," Maria said. "What about rechargeable?"

"That was the logical next step if consumers were willing to take the time to recharge. But, like fuel cells, it's still a band-aid, not a cure."

"Right. Rechargeable batteries, like our discussion about fuel cells, have a finite life," Matthew said.

"True, and people throw things away. So instead of trying to change consumer perception and habits, industry must come up with more disposable solutions. For instance, every two years, the entire supply of the world's computers becomes obsolete. Our own innovation creates a need for recycling solutions."

Maria interjected, "Even so, less than one percent of waste is recycled."

"You can work on that problem next." Cracker Jack laughed.

Matthew frowned. "Next?"

"Listen, my father dedicated his life to finding solutions to the depletion of our natural energy resources."

"But can a cost-effective solution be achieved in our lifetime? It's my dream, but—"

"My father thought so. And he found the solution."

"Perpetual energy." Matthew had been dying say it. He had years of vivid dreams about the possibilities. If what Cracker Jack said was true—

"Near perpetual." Cracker Jack sat back in the booth with a satisfied smile.

Maria broke the extended silence. "You know, I suspect you have more in common than just your love for renewable energy. Have you never heard of the theory of Five Degrees of Separation?"

"I think it's six degrees," Matthew corrected and flinched, expecting another punch in the shoulder. Instead, Cracker Jack mediated.

"Well, actually, you are both right. Everyone on earth connects through a chain of acquaintances, with no more than five intermediaries. It was later changed to six degrees—"

"To include the subject," Matthew said.

"Fascinating," Maria said while giving Matthew *the look*. She changed the subject. "You're saying your father came up with the invention of the century, possibly slowing or solving global warming, something that could help millions around the world. What could anyone possibly gain from stopping you?"

Matthew frowned, and Maria said, "Matthew has decided to take on Al Gore and Kyoto by publishing his own theory, that the warming cycle is normal, and it will reverse naturally."[12]

"Either way," Cracker Jack said, "that would be quite a leap, but to answer your question, many companies and industries have a lot to lose. People will kill over what's in your wallet. Imagine what they are willing to do when billions of dollars are at stake."

Matthew reached his hand to the pulsating scar on the back of his neck, and then to the lanyard. A sign? He looked around. Everything was quiet—peaceful even. "Did you work with your father on the research?"

"Until I went into the service. Like I said earlier, I could have been working with him."

Cracker Jack rubbed the tears from his eyes and said, "The next stage was to make a working prototype and begin a beta test project. I was ready to do that a few years ago when my uncle—"

His brief hesitation was not lost on Matthew

"—when I was informed that I was under surveillance. A few weeks later, someone ransacked my apartment."

"FBI?" queried Maria.

"Perhaps, but companies, governments, and criminals are interested in obtaining

---

[12] Al Gore worked with scientists and politicians around the world to create a climate change treaty. In 1997 they named the accord the Kyoto Protocol. Tied to the UN Framework Convention on Climate Change, Kyoto established international emission targets.

my father's work. Whoever *they* were … are … they kept him under surveillance all those years, but they had a tough time keeping up with Dad's extensive security system."

"I found out the hard way that even the delivery driver was a spy."

There were two break-ins, past some serious security."

"So, you got them on camera?" Maria asked.

Cracker Jack nodded. "But they wore black stealth gear."

"They even neutralized my dad's dogs."

"Killed them?" Maria's voice hit a higher octave.

"No, thank God, just knocked 'em out. But both times they were walking sideways for weeks. They would have to have known that Popeye and Brutus were there."

"Perhaps the delivery man?"

"Their names are Popeye and Brutus?" Maria asked with a laugh. Matthew and Cracker Jack laughed, too.

"Did they get all of your research?" Matthew asked.

"They thought they did, but my father outsmarted them.

It would take a consortium of quantum physicists a decade to piece together my father's work. Even then, they would have to get lucky. Much of my dad's research was in his head."

"And now in yours?" Matthew concluded.

Cracker Jack smiled.

"Where have you been? I mean before you came to Miami?" Maria asked.

"They followed me here to Miami, from where I barely escaped. From there, I've lived in London, San Francisco, and most recently Scotland."

"Really, where?" Matthew asked.

"The ends of the earth," he said with a grin. "I'll tell you about that enchanting place another time. I'd still be there, but they put the screws to my mother's family, knowing that would smoke me out. My uncle found tracking devices in all their cars and even on my grandfather's yacht. The FBI cornered me, and I've been stuck here. A sitting duck, no less."

"Who else do you suspect, besides the FBI?" Maria asked. "I have a mind to contact a few civil rights groups."

"I wish my illegal detainment was the worst part of my problems. There are major conglomerates with endless resources and corrupt governments, that would do just about anything to be first on the market with the answer to the impending energy crisis."

"And, like you said, those that might prefer to destroy your product before it destroyed them."

"Precisely. Some rogue members of the oil industry, part of a group called P7, are in a twist, and they are not even sure what we have. My lawyers deter companies, individuals, and governments. They want first right of refusal and have offered seven digits as a signing bonus. I've told them I don't have the research. Once the formulae are active, one country or group could hold the rest of the world hostage."

"In a way, fossil fuel does that now," Matthew interjected. "Gas prices will triple in the next decade, and oil company profits to skyrocket. The oil conglomerates, especially OPEC, use fear and demand shortages, like the embargo and the Gulf War, to jack prices up."

Maria queried, "I don't understand. If they don't know what your product is, why all the attention?"

"They just know that Dad made significant advances in energy technology. They know that Dad was the first to accelerate to market solar and fuel cell energy, and they want what is next."

"¡Esos ladrones avariciosos!" Maria exclaimed, pounding her fist on the table.

Matthew reached out to catch a glass before it hit the floor, then said, "Greedy thieves is right."

Maria barely noticed as Matthew cleaned up the water. She said, "Something like this belongs to the entire world, don't you think? Not any one single company, government, or person?"

"Precisely, my dear Maria. Precisely."

PART III

PERPETUAL Tragedy

Chapter Sixteen

Tutor
Spring 1987

MATTHEW WAS IN THE FOURTH GRADE when his mother dragged his father to a parent-teacher conference. As Parker put the large dual-rear-wheeled pickup truck they called the mule into gear, he grumbled, "I don't see why we have to hear what we already know. The boy has never had anything but the top scores."

Kate said, "Parker, honey, at least everything is positive. The only trips to school when Sean was growing up, were when he was in trouble."

"Damn right," Parker grumbled, "Sean might as well have had a permanent seat in detention. At least he's using that energy to give our enemies hell."

Matthew sat quietly in the back and listened to them argue. Matthew tried one more pitch, "You know, I don't have to be there. She sees me every day. I'd be glad to stay home and do chores.

"How many ways do I need to say no? If you ask again, little man, you will not be able to sit down for a week."

"Don't be so hard on him, Parker." She turned to Matthew and said, "Maybe next time, dear."

Once they arrived at the school, he sat on a cold metal chair outside his classroom, while his parents talked to his teacher, Shirley Reading. He amused himself by putting various last names with her first. Shirley Arithmetic, Shirley Writing, Shirley Quantum.

Out of his back pocket, he retrieved a rolled and torn Scientific America puzzle magazine given to him by Mr. Estebanez. On the front was a picture of the latest Nobel Prize winners in Physics. Georg Bednorz and Alexander Muller had won the prestigious prize for their breakthrough in ceramic superconductivity. Bednorz appeared so young. I'd like to win that, he determined. He looked at a riddle that Mr. E had sent him. *What eight letter word can have one letter in it?* Matthew answered it in a few seconds. He then devised one that would stump Mr. E. *What eight letter word is still a word while taking away one letter at a time, until you end up with one letter, and it's still a word?* Then he worked on a *New York Times* crossword puzzle entitled "Great Scientists." It was a Saturday puzzle, the most difficult.[13]

On the way home, Matthew was curious as to why his mother and father were arguing about Mr. Estebanez. His mother didn't see why his father had a problem with a man that was providing so much for the schools in the area. His father said that he had no problem with any of his philanthropy but did have an issue with a strange man showing interest in his family, particularly his impressionable son.

Matthew decided he was not impressionable and that his mother was right on this one.

A deer leaped across the path of the truck. Parker barely missed it. He cursed. "And what do you think about him living up there at the sporting lodge with that eccentric old kook, Weaver? I hear all they do is smoke cigars and drink wine all day long."

"You're listening to Joe Fazio too much." his mother said. "Not everything is a conspiracy, dear."

"Matthew's teacher sure thinks he walks on water. I thought the conference was about Matthew. The two of you talked more about that Cuban than—"

"As does every other woman in town," Kate said, igniting another grumble from his father.

Matthew said, "I like him. He gave me a stack of great magazines last time he was at school. He looked at my drawings and ideas. And he's the only person I know that is interested in alternative and renewable energy science."

"What's wrong with nuclear energy and oil?" Parker Eaton asked.

"Well, nuclear is alternative energy. It's not renewable. And it's dangerous. Wind and solar are renewable. Oil is non-renewable, and we will run out of it—one day." Matthew sat forward until his head and shoulders were nearly in the front seat. Oil pollutes, and we are going to run out of it soon," he paused, "and we have no solution for the waste byproduct. I want to design the next generation of solar panels using wind—and water, as a backup source. It's all been done before, but my models are smaller, more energy efficient, and will cost less."

"All this makes perfect sense to you, doesn't it, honey?" his mother asked.

When Matthew didn't reply, Parker said, "So how do you figure this Cuban fits into your plans?" He was still annoyed, but curious.

His mother chimed in, "When Mr. Estebanez finishes his project, Matthew will have quite a place to study until he goes off to college. He's been underwriting and obtaining grants for the region's first environmental science center. There won't be anything like it this side of Boston. It will add some life to this dying town."

Parker grumbled about a waste of taxpayers' money.

---

[13] Epolevne. Gnitrats.

They arrived back at the Eaton estate just before nine. Matthew ran straight to the freezer, pulled out a pint of Ben & Jerry's, Cherry Amour ice cream, and sat at the table before his father could demand that he go to bed.

"Were you old enough to remember when we went to see the largest ice cream sundae in the world, over in St. Albans?" His mother asked.

"I remember. And then Mr. Fazio got them to drive the Cowmobile, here, right?"

"Right. I can't believe you remember that. Ben and Jerry drove it here after Boston and Bangor. What you might not know is that they drove it to Cleveland—"

"That's out west."

"Yes," she chuckled, "way out in Ohio. It caught on fire!"

"I wonder what the Cowmobile looked like on fire?" Matthew imagined Godello's fried ice cream.[14] I think I'll make a tiny solar-powered windmill to generate the electricity to freeze the ice cream, he determined.

His mother settled at the table and began writing on a lined pad. Parker returned to the kitchen, took a beer from the fridge, and leaned against the counter. His mother started asking questions about their annual company picnic. His father said to keep the cost down, and that she could cancel it for all he cared. He said he had enough to worry about with lumber sales and pulp volume at an all-time low.

"I could sure use Sean's help. Do you think he will reup his commission?"

"You should tell him that you need him," Kate said.

"He knows."

"You hardly ever talk to him when he calls." When Parker didn't respond, she said, "I've noticed Sean is changing and not for the better. He snaps about everything, and other times he is despondent and distant."

Matthew was about three-quarters through the Cherry Amour. He tried to be invisible. He missed Sean and hoped that he would come home for good, so they could spend more time backpacking and working on engines.

His father turned and sat down. "He's always had a chip on his shoulder," his father said without his usual edge. "The kind of work he's doing either makes you tougher or spits you out. When I was in-country," he said, referring to Korea and Vietnam, "we knew our enemy, though it was tough to fish them out of dense jungles. Searching the desert and caves for terrorists is a whole new ball game. It takes men like Sean."

Not long ago, Matthew had opened the cedar chest in his parent's bedroom and found his father's Purple Heart and Silver Star. He could not ask his father about

---

[14] Under a photo of the Cowmobile, the Cleveland Plain Dealer headline read: "Ben & Jerry's Fried Ice Cream". It's thought that the press from this, and a lawsuit against Häagen-Dazs owner Pillsbury, for limiting their distribution, and a "What's the doughboy afraid of," campaign, gave the regional company national attention and their sales skyrocketed.

them as mentioning them would reveal how he knew about them. His mother said that his father was a full bird colonel when the Marines discharged him. Sean had later explained that full bird differentiated a higher-ranking colonel from a lieutenant colonel, and said their father was in the DOD DIA with a brief explanation. So, Matthew concluded; his father was a hero who honorably left the Marines when grandfather died of a massive heart attack.

Matthew jumped when his father barked, "Shouldn't you be in bed?" Matthew looked down into the empty pint and wondered where it went.

His father finished his beer and stood at the sink glaring out at the bright waning gibbous moon hanging over the Katahdin Mountains. "I'll talk to him next time he calls. Like I said, I could use his help around here. I don't see getting any use out of Matthew for a few years," he said, "and as usual I can't depend on my brothers. Jim's busy with his furniture and cabinetry. Darrell will probably retire from teaching soon, but I don't see him coming back." Darrell had tenure at Springfield College, where he taught forestry. "And damn that Carl, he hasn't had the decency to come visit. Who the hell even knows what he does. I wouldn't be surprised to find out he works for the CIA."

"Wow. Seriously?" Matthew said.

"Are you still up?" Parker barked.

Matthew's mother reminded his father that they had paid to put his older brothers through college and grad school, bought the equipment for the cabinetry shop, and helped Darrell obtain the teaching position. She also reminded him that it was his own stubbornness that had kept Carl at a distance. According to his mother, Carl, a former Air Force pilot, flew cargo between Miami and Central America. Just as he imagined Mr. Estebanez as 007, he could see Uncle Carl busting the drug cartels, dodging bullets, and jumping out of a crashing plane.

His father seemed not to be listening. "I see the pulp industry getting a lot worse before it gets better, and if anything ever happens to me … you can sell everything, and that should be enough to take care of you and Matthew for life."

Still silent, Matthew pretended to scoop ice cream from the empty carton. It was a lot more comfortable sitting here and listening to the latest family news than at the top of the stairs, he thought.

"I don't know about Matthew coming into the business," his mom said. "I wouldn't be surprised if he went on to study on a full scholarship."

"He's a bright boy, I'll give him that. I guess you're saying I shouldn't wait around for him to take over ELF?"

As he often did, Matthew imagined the Seven Dwarfs running through the kitchen, and he stifled a chuckle. Matthew wanted to say that he was sitting right here but thought better of it.

"It's because of your hard work, dear, that he'll have the opportunity to follow his dreams."

"Dreams? He's just a kid, Kate. How could he know what he wants to do with his life? I was working ten hours a day, sweeping the saw mill floors when I was his age."

I just told you in the truck what I planned to do, Matthew thought.

Parker went to the bar and poured a tall Scotch whiskey.

"One look at his library of books and his many tablets of drawings of windmills and other contraptions will tell you all you need to know about your son."

His father pointed first to Matthew and then to the stairs.

"Yes, sir," Matthew said, jumping off the chair and throwing the beat-up carton in the trash. When his father was out of earshot, he said to his mother, "Do you really think I have a chance of getting a scholarship to MIT?"

"Of course, dear. You'll be able to choose wherever you would like to go. Though I dare say, you could not do better than MIT. And you would be close to home."

"What about Mr. Estebanez. What do you think of him?"

Matthew thought she got a strange look on her face, like when she opened a present on her birthday or when she took a bite of dark chocolate. "He's harmless and a blessing. My goodness, he could charm the jewels off the Queen."

She turned quickly and took her teacup to the sink. He headed to the stairs, past the sound of sawing wood from the living room.

He brushed his teeth and then he and Nuke jumped on the bed, and he got under the covers. He turned a switch he had rigged, and a thousand tiny stars illuminated on the ceiling. He was glad Mr. E and his mother got along so well. His mother grew up in an affluent family on Martha's Vineyard and attended the best prep schools. And all he knew about Mr. E was that he lived on a boat, when he was not here, somewhere between Florida and Alabama. Well, Mr. E had single-handedly gotten the community fired up, that's for sure.

Matthew picked out a few constellations in alphabetical order, Andromeda, Antlia, Apus, Aquarius—by the time he got to Coma Berenices, he was dreaming about building wells in faraway places with villages powered by Matthew Eaton's solar-windmills.

Johnny Fazio was one of Matthew's best friends. Johnny's father, Joe, was a local private investigator, and he aimed to find out who this mysterious carpet bagger was that slipped into town. The man did not seem to have a job, he did not have relatives in the area, and he asked way too many questions about the Eaton's.

Joe Fazio, with dark olive Sicilian features, standing half as wide as he was tall, walked into the foyer of the Katahdin Sporting Lodge, with a nervous-looking county deputy following close behind. Looking like a pallbearer in a Mafia funeral, Fazio approached Estebanez and the proprietor, Dennis Weaver, as they played chess in the library. Fazio asked Weaver if he and the deputy could have a few minutes with Mr. Estebanez.

Weaver, older than Methuselah, over six foot and skinny, studied the board, pointed a long bony finger at Estebanez, smiled, and retreated to the front desk.

Fazio turned a darkly-stained solid oak chair around backward and settled his bulk into it. His deputy walked around the extensive library pretending to study the titles of the old books.

The chair complained under Fazio's weight. Estebanez lit up a long cigar and extended one toward his visitor, who waved it off.

"Those legal?" Fazio said.

"Wine?" Estebanez offered. "This is an excellent Cabernet Sauvignon you should appreciate; it's a 1968 Tuscan Sassicaia, the first vintage available to the public. It will warm the Italian cockles of your soul."

"My cockles are dandy, and I'm a beer and whiskey man."

"An Italian who doesn't drink wine?"

"I didn't say I don't drink wine, but it has to be accompanied by antipasti and a plate full of risotto, or lasagna, or eggplant parmigiana."

"Suit yourself," Estebanez said.

"You know, when I came to town, I was considered a carpetbagger just like you, except over in Little Italy of course," he chuckled, "and many people looked at me cross-eyed. Hell, they still do. What's your story?"

"I feel quite welcome," he said. "It must make you miss the fun in Chicago—murders, robberies—family ties?"

"I see you have been doing your homework on me."

"People talk."

"Well, therein lies the mystery, Mr. Estebanez. People do talk, but they don't seem to know anything about you, except that you have adopted the town—and its favorite son."

"What can I say, Mr. Fazio. Science is my life."

"Perhaps. It seems more like wine, women, and cigars."

Estebanez smiled. "I like a good song too."

Fazio returned his smile. "Do me a favor. Keep your distance from Kate. She's a good woman but not your type."

"What's my type?"

Fazio ignored the bait and said, "The Eatons are my good friends. Any improper advances toward Kate—"

Estebanez leaned in toward Fazio, but just puffed on his cigar. "I hold all of the Eatons in the highest regard; you are way off base, paisan."

Fazio stared at Estebanez for one uncomfortable moment, reached into his back pocket, and took out a notebook. He asked him another twenty questions, receiving obtuse answers. He finally motioned to the deputy, who was flipping through a first edition copy of *A Connecticut Yankee in King Arthur's Court*, that it was time to go.

"Crazy Weaver let you down in his wine cellar yet?" Fazio asked, in a hushed voice.

"Let me ask you, Fazio; why is everyone so contentious? Weaver is the chief strawman."[15]

Fazio grunted as he pushed out of the chair. "I thought we were bad in Chicago. These people will debate over the direction of the sunrise. And let me tell you, as an outsider, a flatlander, if you, your father, and your grandfather can't prove roots in the area, your opinion is not worth crap."

Estebanez blew smoke rings toward the ceiling. "No. He hasn't taken me into the secret cellar yet, but I'm working on him."

"Don't hold your breath. Some say he's got gold bullion buried down there."

The innkeeper, after grabbing the book and chastising the deputy, made a chess move, queen to bishop. Estebanez moved his bishop putting Weaver in check.

"Check and mate," Estebanez said. Weaver cursed Fazio and his deputy for messing with his concentration.

Outside, Fazio said to the young deputy, "I can see why people like the guy, but he's a player. I've seen his kind, too many times. A guy with a lot to hide, and certainly not someone that would be here unless he had an ulterior motive, like that bartender, St. Adams."

"What is that? I mean what do they have to hide?"

"I did a background check on both … they barely exist. Nobody is that far under the radar, unless you're Ted Kaczynski."

"Forensic handwriting."

"How's that?"

"That's how they nabbed the Unabomber. They published his style of writing and his brother recognized it. Turned him in. They always make a mistake."

"Okay, Quincy."

"We could book him and get some fingerprints."

"I already did that. Tell you what, if you can catch him doing anything more than jaywalking, then, by all means, take him in; but until then, I think we'll just have to keep an eye on Mister Smooth."

A week later Fazio decided it was time to discuss his informal "lack of findings" with the Eatons.

His son and Matthew had just finished playing in an American Legion little league baseball game. The adults were setting out the hot dogs and fries while

---

[15] Estebanez may be referring to the technique of using a false argument to win a debate. The first recording of this tactic goes back to Aristotle, Plato, and Aquinas. The intensity of the debate is like attacking a straw man by misrepresenting the position of your opponent.

Matthew and Johnny Fazio were leaning up against the concession stand talking to Maria and another girl. Joe Fazio wasted no time digging into two foot-long ballpark franks and a large box of fries. He was sitting across from Parker and Kate Eaton at a picnic table, who both watched in amazement.

Mrs. Eaton called for Matthew.

She whispered in his ear.

"Not right now, they make me drowsy," he said, looking over his shoulder.

"You let me know."

"Yes, ma'am."

"You want to get back to Maria."

"Naw. It's not like that, Mom."

She smiled and kissed him on the cheek. He ran back to his friends.

Fazio said, "So, what do you know about this Estebanez?"

Parker grumbled.

"Doesn't it strike you as funny," Fazio continued, "that a guy not from around here would invest so much money into an off-the-map mill town?"

"I never really thought about it," Kate said, "but I will say, everyone in town has nothing else to talk about than the charming Mr. Estebanez."

Parker frowned and said, "What are you getting at, Joe? When you came to Millinocket, there wasn't anything normal about a cop picking up his family and moving here from clear across the country."

Fazio laughed, "This is true." He added a pickle spear and tomato slice to his ballpark dog, dipped it into a pool of mustard, and took a large dripping bite. "Reminds me of White Castle back in the Windy City." He licked his fingers and took a long swallow of AJ Stephan's Creme Soda, not suppressing a burp. "Parker. People come here for a lot of reasons." He pulled out a spiral notepad. "Outdoor sports, retirement, escaping the city," avoiding my father, he considered, "but scholastic philanthropy is not one of them, and then there's Matthew—"

Kate craned her neck toward the little notebook. "What is it about Estebanez and Matthew that bothers you?"

"Isn't it peculiar that this philanthropist, for lack of a better title, would choose Millinocket to be a benefactor? Why wouldn't he pick Miami, Jacksonville, Atlanta, or his own Gulf Coast region? While I was checking up on him, I could not find much in a background check, but following his flight manifest, I did conclude that he resided in a small town in the Florida panhandle called Destin." He paused for emphasis. "On a sailboat."

The Eaton couple looked surprised. Mrs. Eaton smiled and said, "How mysterious and romantic."

Her husband grunted his disapproval and spat.

"So, what else did you uncover?" Mr. Eaton asked while wiping mustard from his mouth.

"Nothing. Absolutely nothing. The man has no history."

"So, why is that a problem? I know a half a dozen people here at the park that would fit that description. Folks like their privacy."

"A man like him doesn't live half a century without a measurable trail unless he has something to hide. Why is it that no one in the world of science has ever heard of him? There're too many holes in his story, that's all I'm saying."

"It seems to me that someone who is running away from something would keep a low profile," Kate said. "And Matthew?"

Fazio closed the notebook. "Someone has gone to a lot of trouble to eliminate his past, and that can only mean one of two things: government or criminal—or maybe both."

Kate repeated, "And Matthew?"

They all looked toward a commotion. The boys were trying to impress the girls with their French fry food fight skills. "I wouldn't want to see anything happen to Matthew."

"You think Matthew might be in danger?" Kate asked.

"Unni c'è focu, pri lu fumu pari"

"And that means?"

"Where there's smoke, there's fire. My grandfather had a saying, *L'occhio del Siracusano fa uscire i serpenti dalle loro fosse.*"

"Meaning?" Kate asked.

"The eye of the Syracusan makes the snakes come out of their pits." Fazio said, with a chuckle.

"Meaning?" Parker asked.

Fazio had to think about it. Finally, he said, "When there's a snake in the grass, someone has to smoke him out."

"You're incorrigible!"

Fazio raised his eyebrows and cocked his head. "My mother used to say the same thing."

"Are you saying Estebanez has an ulterior motive that somehow involves my son?" Parker asked.

"I'm making no accusation, Parker. What I'm saying is that from the day he arrived at the Lodge he began asking questions about your son. Since he seems to have an unusual interest in the sciences, he might have read about Matthew's intelligence, and that led to curiosity, but one might also say everything has been orchestrated for a purpose."

"I'm sure you have a proverb for that," Kate said.

"Not today," Fazio said as he turned his attention to the apple pie.

Mr. Eaton got up from the table shaking his head. "Well, if you get something solid, you know where I'll be." Parker got up and whistled between his teeth. "Let's go, Spaceman," Parker said.

"Spaceman?" Fazio queried.

"Bill Lee's nickname," Kate said. "He's a friend of the family, a former Red Sox pitcher who retired in Vermont, due west of Millinocket. He came to Millinocket to buy slow growing ash, maple, and yellow birch from ELF."

They watched Matthew jump up to follow his father.

"Matthew," his father boomed, "don't forget your bat. You lose it, I'll tan your hide."

Kate stared at Fazio as if she was trying to make up her mind. "Thank you, Joe. I appreciate you keeping an eye on Mr. Estebanez. I'll talk to him as well. He's supposed to come over for tea sometime next week with some books for Matthew. What do you suggest we do in the meantime?" She fumbled through her purse.

"They really need to leave more room between the bench and the tabletop," he grumbled. "Maybe it's nothing, Kate, but there are too many holes to be plugged before trusting this ship in deep water."

Fazio watched Kate walk off in the direction of her husband and son. "Fine looking woman," he whispered. He pulled out the notebook again and flipped half way through. "Oh, and Kate?" He yelled. When she turned, he said, "Have you heard of a scientist by the name of Cameron Jackson?"

She paused. "The name sounds familiar. Yes, Matthew has the book in his library."

"He has a library?"

She chuckled. "A huge library. Why?"

"I'm not sure. It's just like a name that came up in conjunction with Estebanez, and he mailed a few packages out to the scientist's place in Indiana. Another name that came up was that old Indiana Senator," he looked at his notes, "Carson." He could see that didn't ring any bells. "I'll let you know what I come up with."

Fazio made a notation and walked over to Johnny who was showing the girls how he could spin the baseball on his index finger. "Ok, Casanova, your mom had sauce and snails simmering all day. Let's go get some dinner."

"We just had hot dogs, Dad."

"Appetizers, son, and don't you dare tell your mom."

Estebanez settled into a leather chair in the lobby of the lodge and flipped through a copy of *Field and Stream*. He loved the mountains and outdoor sports nearly as much as he did the freedom of living on a yacht. Can't have it both ways. He chuckled. Then again, maybe you can.

He tried to convince himself that extending his stay had nothing to do with Matthew's mother. But he knew better. She reminded him of Karen. The thing that bothered him—no, intrigued him—was that she was closer to his age than any woman he had courted—since Karen. over the last twenty years.

He had stuck to a principle. As soon as they cleaned his cabin or baked a casserole and left it in his fridge, they were history. There was something about this sophisticated woman, hidden up here in logging country, which he could not shake.

As for all the attention he was attracting from the local authorities, he would take his chances. He kicked his feet up on a slab of oak. He had many assignments in his life of espionage: extracting political prisoners from third world countries; eliminating threats to democracy; developing sleeper agents and moles. And his covers: teaching criminal justice at Georgetown under the pseudonym Alberto Estefan; a few years out at Front Site just west of Vegas, as a firearms trainer; and most recently as a wine and sailboat broker. When bored, he would hire out as a private contractor, slipping in and out of a country—leaving one less terrorist. This gig? Keeping an eye on a genius kid. Well, that was a twist, and Kate, well, she was an unexpected bonus, the icing on the cake. When he first arrived in Millinocket, the night of Maria's mother's funeral, it was a quick-in and quick-out task. He owed it to his old friend. He owed it to the only woman he thought he would ever love … then he met Kate.

The greatest benefit was perhaps how the low-key atmosphere ironed out his hard lines inside and out. He now felt like he was taking a vacation every few months. He rather liked the people of this region, and Kate was a bonus. Though from a family of deep Catholic convictions, which he embraced when it suited him, he didn't look at it as adulterous thinking.

His mentoring mission was simple. It helped that everyone, save Fazio, was so accommodating. All of Matthew's teachers, friends, and even strangers were quick to brag about their young science genius.

"Are you quite comfortable, Mr. Estebanez? Is there anything I can get you?"

Estebanez looked up to see the proprietor. Though sometimes the long-limbed gray-haired innkeeper could get on his nerves, he kept to himself for the most part, respecting his patron's privacy. When Estebanez first arrived, he got the overview, like the prelude to *War and Peace*. The proprietor took him everywhere except where Estebanez wanted to go the most—the wine cellar. Weaver had told Estebanez that he was the fourth-generation owner of the pre-Revolutionary War establishment. Each owner bore the same name, Dennis Weaver.

"Not to be confused with the actor," he had said more than once. "Though I've been told that I look and sound a lot like him."

The lodge was peppered with the actor's memorabilia and collections of Northeastern American and Native American history. Dennis Weaver shared his lifelong dream: one day soon, his actor friend would be staying at this lodge, and they would get a picture together. He was quick to point out that they corresponded regularly and that he had visited the actor's homes in L.A., Jackson Hole, and Santa Fe. Estebanez learned from the townsfolk that the lodge owner was on a short list of stalkers and had at least one restraining order against him.

"Everything is impressive, Mr. Weaver, just splendid," Estebanez had said. "I was wondering if you would be kind enough to take me on a tour of your wine reserves." Weaver had refused. So, today Estebanez decided to ask again.

The proprietor feigned a look of shock and said, "You know those cellars have had few visitors over the years. I'll consider it. You have been the most frequent visitor to the lodge since Milton Bradley, one of Maine's favorite sons. In 1860, he developed *The Checkered Game of Life* while sitting in this very library!"

"You don't say."

"My great-grandfather gave Bradley a similar game that was left in the library by a Brit. The next thing he knew, Bradley had changed his lithography shop into a game board company. The rest is history. I'm sorry, there I go again, where were we?"

"The wine cellar."

"Ah, yes." He made a partial bow and said, "If you will follow me, monsieur."

Estebanez put the magazine on the coffee table and followed his host. This wasn't his first trip to the hallowed cellar, as Estebanez had found the false wall the night of his first visit to Millinocket and had been enjoying exquisite bottles of wine ever since. To date, he had shipped more than two dozen priceless bottles out to Indiana.

With their shared extensive knowledge about the fermented grape elixir, the two unlikely friends spent many hours late into the evening playing chess, smoking cigars, and drinking. Estebanez found Weaver, though schizophrenic, intelligent with an encyclopedic knowledge. As a spy, you learn that people love to talk about themselves. A pro lets them.

Weaver reached into a four-foot section of the large library bookcases. He retrieved an original first-run *Tom Sawyer*, handed it to Estebanez, reached in, and pulled a lever that released the bookshelf, which rolled out on ball bearings. A glistening black rock wall was revealed. In the center of the wall was a black oval-topped steel door, like what you might see in the hull of an ocean tanker. He lifted a silver necklace over his head and inserted the skeleton key into the keyhole. He spun a large four-prong dial and pulled on the door. They walked down a steep set of steps to a natural rock-walled cellar. At the bottom of the steps, Weaver pulled on a massive oak door comparable to one leading into a medieval dungeon.

Endorphins spiked as Estebanez stepped into the familiar presence of perhaps the largest wine cellar in the country. Though he now knew his way around with his eyes closed, he pretended to grope along the cold slate shelves lit only by the light from the library behind them.

Weaver took pleasure in lighting the oil lamps positioned throughout the cellar. Estebanez didn't disappoint and gave a wide-eyed show of amazement as the huge cellar unfolded before him.

"You know, I ascertained that you were a professional, a true wine connoisseur." As they walked, Weaver began his oration like a docent. "In 1774, General Gage, the antagonistic leader of the British Army, built this magnificent cellar and the original lodge. Gage claimed King George had granted him the entire Katahdin region. He imported hundreds of cases of the most expensive wines of the day into this cellar. Many of the bottles are still on the shelves. Though called back to England in 1775, Gage continued to finance construction of the lodge. The northwest cornerstone was engraved on July 4, 1776."

Weaver pulled a bottle out of the mahogany shelving and presented it, holding the neck with one hand and laying the body of the bottle across his palm.

Estebanez's eyes widened as he observed the dusty 1770 bottle of Chablis from a famous Bousquette vineyard in the south of France. How could he have missed that one? The spirit may have long ago turned to vinegar, though that did not affect its priceless value.

Weaver grinned, looked a bit ominous in the flickering light, and didn't miss a beat. "This bottle was already in Boston when the Revolutionary War began on April 18, 1775; rung in by the famous midnight ride of Paul Revere." He quoted Longfellow:

A hurry of hoofs in a village street,
A shape in the moonlight, a bulk in the dark,
And beneath, from the pebbles, in passing, a spark
Stuck out by a steed flying fearless, and fleet:
That was all! And yet, through the gloom and the light,
the fate of a nation was riding that night.

"Fascinating," Estebanez said, truly intrigued by the story behind any bottle he purchased from Sotheby or absconded with a spoil of war. He almost corrected the proprietor regarding the facts of the story, particularly the part where Paul Revere was in prison at midnight. Instead, noticing that Weaver was counting bottles in the same rack from which he had pilfered a rare bottle to sell at Sotheby's, he said, "May I offer to purchase this bottle, Mr. Weaver? Please, name your price."

Weaver could not hide his immense pleasure. "Why, Mr. Estebanez, we rarely sell bottles from this area of the cellar. We would soon lose the museum quality preserved by my family for many generations."

That's ironic, he thought. Though he was an expert in the art of negotiation developed through many years of bargaining for hostages or negotiating his way out of a mess, Estebanez decided to quit while he was ahead and returned the bottle to Weaver.

Weaver soon found his vocal cords. "I dare say, even the few bottles that have been sold," he said, while looking up at the slate ceiling for theatrical emphasis, "to my ancestors' holy indignation, sold at Sotheby's."

Damn, Estebanez thought, I should have known Weaver had been selling at Sotheby's. He's not getting any younger, and he's always talking about buying a ranch in Wyoming next to his actor idol. So far, the Sotheby auctioneer staff had not questioned him as to where Estebanez obtained his rare bottles, assuming they were from his private collection.

Weaver nearly dropped the priceless bottle as he added, "Oh, how they brought a pretty price!"

Recognizing a familiar glint of greed in Weaver's eyes, Estebanez raised one eyebrow.

And Weaver took the bait. "However, I think an exception could be made. Let me make some inquiries into the bottle's market value."

Estebanez hid his disappointment. Stealing the bottle would have been a lot more fun, and less costly. He noted that Weaver started counting the bottles on a rack of 1974 Château Lafleur burgundy, Estebanez said, "I'm feeling ill," he said a bit louder than he intended.

"Excuse me?" Weaver asked.

"I think I may need to lie down. Perhaps the cool air and excitement have gotten the best of me." As he turned, he noticed in the far-left corner, a stack of barrels and 17th-century wine-making equipment. He wandered in that direction and felt a breeze coming from between the cracks of the neat stacks. "What is behind here?"

Weaver stuttered and said, "Just the back wall. We really should be going, I have to tend to the other guests." He turned and walked away while muttering that he needed to do an inventory.

Estebanez stared a bit longer at the wall. He felt a strange sensation and then a shiver. A foreboding? Unlike Matthew and his Micmac friends, he did not believe in the ethereal. He found that things either were, or they were not. He turned and followed Weaver up the stairs.

Once they went through the process of extinguishing the lamps, locking up the cellar doors, and closing the false bookshelves, Estebanez put *Tom Sawyer* back and followed Weaver through the library where, instead of pricey wines, there were walls of vintage poetry and prose. In an adjacent room, Weaver placed the bottle into a wooden box surrounded by enough straw and bubble wrap to secure nitroglycerin.

"I need to make a few calls," Weaver said. He left the room. Estebanez reasoned that he was off pretending to be researching the bottle's value. He knew Weaver knew what he wanted for the rich jewel of the vine.

Weaver returned with an apology, wrote a number on a lodge postcard, and handed it to Estebanez, who looked at it, frowned, wrote another number, and handed it back. This process went on until Weaver finally said, "You, sir, drive a hard bargain. Congratulations. This lovely bottle of Chablis is yours."

I'll have to sell four of Weaver's bottles at Sotheby's to make up for this one, he thought wryly.

Weaver asked, "Have you ever been to Sotheby's?"

"Never. Why?"

"I was just on the phone with Pierre from New York, he handles the wine opportunities, though wine auctions are only held in London."

Well, damn. The crafty old bat, Estebanez thought, amused.

"He says Andrew Lloyd Webber's collection should go for over five million. Pierre hopes to auction the entire Weaver cellar one day. They can dream on," he said without conviction. "Pierre said that Serena in London called recently and asked why I was not selling individual bottles directly through Sotheby's, yet they were showing up through a broker."

"That *is* strange."

"That's what I told him. I asked him to describe the broker—"

Estebanez gave Weaver a quizzical look.

"He then said he had already spoken out of turn and went on to point out the confidentiality that protects all buyers and sellers."

Weaver sealed the crate. He studied the obscure Indiana address Estebanez had written on the bill-of-lading envelope. Weaver strained to read what his eccentric guest had jotted down on a Millinocket postcard before stuffing it in the envelope.

C—*For your safe keeping. M.E. continues to excel – better than expected. Send my best to T. See you soon. –Z*

Chapter Seventeen

Suspect
Summer 1988

FAZIO, HUFFING AND WHEEZING, climbed up the back stairwell to his office above Danny's Nook, a small café in the center of town. He walked down the dark hallway to a single door at the end. He entered a dark, damp office, not much more than a couple of walk-in closets. He switched on a brass and green attorney's lamp at the desk and sat down to turn on his new computer.

He pulled a couple of faxes from the tray behind him. Even with fingerprints, neither his pals at the CPD or the FBI could find anything more than basic identification on Estebanez. He shook his head and reached into his desk drawer for a pound bag of peanut M&Ms.

It was one of the shortest civilian and veteran background checks he'd seen, more in line with someone who grew up and died in a West Virginia mountain cabin. Or, he thought, someone who went through the federal witness protection program. He had some experience in that area, having worked with many mob informants while on the Chicago police force. Back then, being Sicilian on a mostly Irish police force was no picnic, and worst of all, pitted him against his own family and friends. Today, things were different. Organized crime was shifting to other ethnic groups that had much less honor and scruples than the Italians. The Russian mob would kill their own and their families, with a mere accusation. When the Mafia decided to kill another Italian, they made sure the rest of the household was cared for. Chinese human trafficking was becoming a big business, and the Central and South American drug trades were expanding faster than the DEA could calculate. Joe thought of his father, shot and killed by members of a competing family while eating at his favorite restaurant. Joe's two older brothers took their revenge on the family and ended up in prison.

He tapped a pen against the green light shade while he stared at the faxes. Or, Estebanez could be with the government. Joe had worked with the CIA on a few cases, and the agents were nothing like Estebanez. But he had come across a few CIA spooks when he was in Nam, and they were always a bit crazy. Estebanez was smooth, too smooth. He always sat with his back against the wall, his eyes were always scanning the room from left to right, and he answered questions with a question. Fazio faxed his suspicions to his contacts in DC and Chicago, shut everything down, and turned out the light.

After Fazio had turned the corner, a dark figure stepped out of the shadows and climbed the stairs to Fazio's office. He picked the lock and turned on the computer, putting his gun on the desk, sifted through drawers and files, and snapped pictures of each fax. He sat behind the desk, ate M&M's, and leaned back at ease as he waited for the computer to reboot. After downloading files, he uploaded a virus and let it loose on the operating system. He then shut down the computer and left the office.

Turning at the bottom of the stairs, the intruder yelled, "You!" He reached behind his back for his gun as the attacker swung an object into his gut. He doubled over and fell. A foot on his back held him down.

The assailant grabbed the hard drive and the intruders gun.

"Tell your family that this is my town. Next time I won't go so easy on you or them. Estebanez picked up Matthew's bat and slipped out into the night.

That same evening Matthew and his mother answered the ringing phone at the same time.

"Parker. It's Sean," his mother yelled up the steps. Matthew was supposed to be asleep hours ago. He sat on the floor in the dark hallway hoping his father did not wake up.

Kate gave Sean all the details about the new art gallery in town run by a woman who grew up in the region but moved to DC when she was young. She bragged about how Uncle Ken sold his bookbindery business in Boston and then bought a B&B in Gatlinburg, Tennessee.

Matthew yawned. He wanted to talk but was about to hang up when his mother asked, "Sean, do you know anything about Estebanez, the man that gave Matthew the magazines at Salina's funeral?" All she got in return was a brooding silence—his new default. "He's donated a lot of time and money to the school system. And he's taken quite an interest in your little brother."

"How so?"

His mother told Sean about the Smithsonian and the tutoring.

"What do you know about him?" Sean asked.

"Just that he's a philanthropist and energy consultant."

"Did you say energy?"

"Like me, he's an environmentalist. Millinocket is a perfect place to build a world-class research lab while he studies wildlife in the North Woods. Most everyone likes him, and you know these folks. They usually hate strangers, but the only other idea anyone had was to add a moose zoo near the entrance to town."

Matthew stifled a laugh, and Sean chuckled. "Not that again," he said. "You can't cage a moose." He asked how Matthew was doing with his studies, then said, "Don't push him too hard, Mom. He should enjoy his childhood. Where's the old man?"

"The floorboards are shaking, and my china is rattling, so he's asleep. He's had a long week at the mills, and the economic downturn is putting the pulp industry into a tailspin."

"He'll pull through, Mom, even if he has to make wooden nickels and sell them on the corner." There was no humor in his tone. "I'll call again. Keep an eye on that Spanish guy." Before his mother could respond, he raised his voice and said, "Goodnight, Matt, we'll hike around Sandy Stream Pond when I get home. Don't you let Pop catch you—he'll tan your hide."

"What makes you think he's on the phone, he went to bed hours ago?"

"He's always listening in on the upstairs phone, Mom."

Matthew slipped the phone on the receiver. As he closed his door, he could hear his father's heavy footsteps. A moose zoo!

He peered out a crack in the door until he was sure the coast was clear. He wished his father and Sean got along better. Love and hate, his mother said, were two explosive emotions easily confused.

She talked a lot about Mr. Estebanez. Whenever he was in town, she dressed up and looked in the mirror an awful lot, and then they would run into him at places like the AT Café or the library.

He crept back into the hallway and sat on the first step.

Parker followed her into the kitchen. "What did Sean have to say?"

"Why didn't you talk to him?"

"There's no use getting into another argument. Remember when I told him not to reenlist, and we got into a brawl."

"Tell him how much you need him here. It would make a difference."

"Sean will do what he wants to do. It doesn't matter what I say."

"Keep your voice down."

"Matthew was sitting in the hallway listening on the extension."

Matthew held his breath.

"I want you and Matthew to stay away from that smooth-talking *gusano*."

"Parker," she whispered heatedly, "that's a horrible thing to say. Castro killed thousands, and that's what he called those who escaped." She turned to the sink. "What makes you think he's Cuban?"

He sat at the table and sighed. "I spent three months undercover in Havana. He's Cuban."

"I didn't know you were in Cuba."

Undercover, Matthew thought. He whistled, then covered his mouth.

"Nobody knew, except my CO. I worked as a Mobile Oil executive."

She put a bowl of cobbler and ice cream on the table. "I remember. Sean was six and you said you would not be in touch for a few weeks. I was really upset as the weeks turned into months. I called the Pentagon a dozen times. I'll never forget his name, Colonel Oglethorpe."

"My CO."

"He called me and told me not to worry. That the work you were doing was keeping our country safe. And, he said, you were not in any danger."

Parker chuckled. Yeah, Castro and his commie buddies were boy scouts.

Matthew grasped the spindles of the hallway railing. Undercover, Castro, commies. Wow.

"Anyhow, if Mr. Estebanez's parents escaped Cuba," she said, "then really it's no different than your grandfather or mine emigrating from England and Ireland."

He waved his hand like he was swatting a fly. "Me and Fazio will figure him out."

"I wish Joe would leave him alone, and don't you dare get involved. What if Estebanez finds out? I will not have you and Joe running him out of town like you did those nice boys who had the knick-knack shop."

"Knick-knack, my ass," he said with a chuckle as he took a bite of cobbler. "It was a head shop. They were drug dealers."

Matthew tried to process that. He would ask Sean.

Kate took the empty bowl and put it in the sink. She said, "You're impossible." She poured him a cup of tea.

At the bar, under the stairwell, Parker poured a large shot of scotch into his hot tea. "Hey, Clouseau. Get your butt back into bed."

Matthew lay in bed until Johnny Carson delivered his monolog. He tiptoed down the steps and into the kitchen. "Everything okay, Mom?"

"Oh sure, honey."

"Sean sounds okay."

"He's so quiet these days. Next time, let me know you are listening in, and you can talk. He misses you."

"Don't worry about Mr. Estebanez and me. He likes my ideas on solar panels in windmills, and I think he was a secret agent or something."

His mother dropped the empty cobbler bowl into the sink. "What would make you say that?"

"He reminds me of James Bond." Matthew had read all the Ian Fleming novels. "He also knows a lot about science, and knows Dr. Jackson, which is cool."

"Dr. Jackson?"

"You know, the book Sean gave me after the funeral." Matthew thought of the funeral, and of Maria. His tongue twisted into knots.

"What are you thinking about?"

"N-nothing. Goodnight, Mom."

She leaned in to give him a hug and a kiss. "You are getting so tall, Matthew. I'll be looking up at you in no time. I love you, sweetheart. Now get some sleep." She looked up at the clock. "School starts in eight hours." Matthew opened his mouth, and she said, "And no, you cannot sit up and read. Goodnight."

Matthew wanted to ask her about Cuba, and more about his father's life as a spy. Maybe tomorrow. He lay in bed with a penlight shining on *Capturing the Sun*. He wondered how Sean got a signed copy.

Soon he was fighting side-by-side with four robed men against leather armored warriors on a cliff in front of a temple and a dozen pagodas. Dozens of bats swooped down from the trees.

He woke swatting left and right, a little afraid to go back to sleep.

The dreams were becoming more frequent.

He opened the book.

His mother came into the room to find Matthew fast asleep with the book across his chest, and the penlight dimming from low batteries. She thought of how he planned to make a battery that would last longer. She put her hand on his forehead and said a prayer. "You'll make a difference, Matthew." She picked up the book and set it on his shelf next to a dog-eared *Atlas Shrugged*. "Sleep and dream of windmills, my sweet boy."

Back in town, Fazio returned to his office. As he came around the corner, he bumped into a man. He grabbed the man's arm. "Hey, fella, are you okay?"

The man muttered that he was okay; he had a strong Middle-Eastern accent. Fazio stared after him as he disappeared into the night.

"Joe, is that you? What the heck ya doing out here this late at night?"

Fazio turned to see Officer Franklin Dubois walking his usual beat. Though crime was rare in Millinocket, he checked all the retailers' doors each night.

"I was working late and forgot something. How have you been, Frank?"

"Good, Joe, you?"

"Good, thanks. Hey, did you see a guy stumble through here, black shirt, holding his head?"

"Nope, nobody like that, just the usual flatlanders. Bunch of Japanese are staying at the AT. Pete Marks is taking them to the terminus tomorrow.

"How far they going?"

"All the way."

"How many actually make it to Georgia?"

"Less than a quarter."

They heard the engine start and Fazio looked in the direction the man had gone. A large vehicle screeched out from an alley two blocks down and sped out of town. "You're not going after him?" Fazio asked.

"Yeah, I'll chase him down." He grunted. "You have a good night, Joe. Give my best to your wife."

Fazio climbed to his office and turned on the light at his desk. Everything looked normal. He thought about firing up the computer and decided against it. He picked up a bag filled with bagels that were on the windowsill. I could have sworn I left those on the desk, he thought. He reached for the M&M's. That's lighter.

Chapter Eighteen

Declare
1989

THE GLARING SUN STARED BACK AT TREMONT as he sat on a canvas covered folding stool. The desert shimmered ten thousand miles away from Jackson's Place. Imagining the cool wind coming off the lake, he pictured Brutus and Popeye running along the beach. He dialed up his father on the satellite phone and looked at his watch. It was dinner time back home.

"So, you decided to announce your plans to change the world?" Tremont asked.

"I don't know, son. Some days yes, some days no. I could have launched a prototype product years ago, but you understand my reservations better than anyone. Sergio, Randall, and Dimitri believe—"

"The fraternity! Tell them I said hello."

"They always ask about you."

"Dad, I was thinking how when I was a boy, we were at the family reunion, and Grandfather Carson said, 'If you could only bottle that energy you could run a city on it.' Do you remember what you told him?"

"I said, that's exactly what I intend to do."

"I remember everyone laughed, and you smiled. You knew what you had even then."

"Yes, I did. But I wondered then and still wonder if anyone in that room will be alive when CJ Energy powers entire cities. It's one thing to have the technology. It's another to implement it in this culture of fossil fuel dependence."

Tremont said, "I guess I've always known this day would come." He wiped his forehead with the handkerchief that hung around his neck. "I could use one here to power a few high-velocity fans."

"I could use the miniature fan design we made for the computer industry, make it pocket size, and plug in a CJ Energy chip."

"You would."

"Indeed." They both laughed. "You always cheer me up, son."

"How do you think you'll launch the first chip? Computers? One of my technicians showed me a design for a new computer. He could make it smaller than a briefcase if only there were a battery that could power it. I had to hold my tongue."

"You should meet Stephen Jobs and his partner. What's his name, Wozniak? When you get home, perhaps the two of you can work something out. It's funny how things change. It seems like yesterday that I imagined we would launch our product in transistor radios. Who could imagine that a mainframe computer that took up a New York block would be the size of a breadbox?

"But I'm concerned about someone abusing CJ Energy. Greed is the enemy to progress. I'm not sure the world is ready for us to let the cat out of the bag."

"Have you had more threats?"

"There's no need to worry, son. Wait until you see some of the security additions to Jackson's Place, infrared motion detectors, with visual surveillance." He laughed. "The den looks like a television studio control room. Sometimes I'll sit in there with a glass of cognac and watch the deer and the rangers."

"So, you have had more threats."

"I'm not worried … just being careful over there."

"I'll be home soon, and you'll have your own government trained Special Forces security guard. Then we'll give them a real Jackson in-your-face run for their money—just like we always planned, Dad."

"Are you sure they're going to let you out?" Cameron asked. The last time Tremont thought he was coming home, the Marines extended his tour when the Lebanese Civil War escalated.

"I didn't give them a choice this time, Dad. Lebanon was a disaster. The lines are fuzzy here in Afghan hell. The Russians are out, but I have a feeling we'll be back. I've served my country, and I think it will take years for me to process all that we've done—good and bad. I survived, but many of my guys have not been as lucky. We lost little John and a dozen Mujahedeen last month. They have this leader—he's Saudi—and he sends his men in on suicide missions like their lives are no more important than wormwood." Tremont got quiet as he thought about the guys he left California with eight years ago. Most went home in caskets, others maimed for life. "We take three steps forward and two backward."

His father said, "Speaking of holding things back, what else is on your mind?"

"It's Sean … I'll tell you more about it when I'm home."

"Did he find out what you're doing?"

"I don't think so … it's not that. It can wait."

"I'm proud of you, son," Cameron said. "I'll see you soon."

Washington National Airport
March 1989

One intimidating man stood at the top of the escalator; another at the bottom. A third man, decked out like he was going to a Dallas football game, stood by the sliding glass doors leading to ground transportation. He cocked his head and spoke into a mic on his collar. "Dom, here he comes."

The fourth man sat in the car outside baggage claim. When a ramp agent knocked on his window, he showed his Secret Service credentials.

Cameron carried an overnight bag and a briefcase. The limo driver waved a white sign with his name in black letters. Too noticeable, he thought, looking around nervously.

As they drove, he prepared himself. After years of turning down requests from around the world, Cameron agreed to speak in Washington. The Georgetown Physics Department molded the symposium around Dr. Jackson's schedule. Cameron reasoned that if he got in and out of Washington in twenty-four hours, *they* ... those bastards ... *they* would not even know he was there.

A black SUV followed closely behind Cameron's limo.

"Damn it, Klaus, you are too close!" DelGercio added a few choice Brooklyn flavored curses. "Follow three cars behind. We know where Jackson is staying, and we know where he'll be tomorrow, so there's no need to rush."

The driver spoke with a thick Eastern European accent. "I still don't understand how that old man can be such a threat that they pay us so much to babysit."

"You are not paid to think—or talk," the man with the baseball cap said.

"Still, what does he have in that briefcase, a nuclear bomb?"

"Just drive," the cowboy said.

It had been nearly twenty years since Cameron last made bold claims to a skeptical crowd. Since then, he had toned down, and when the subject of near perpetual energy came up, he brushed it aside as a topic for the future. Now that Tremont was coming home, his fellow fraternity brothers convinced him that it was time. Feeling a deeper sense of his mortality, he didn't want to leave the burden and danger to Tremont. He thought about Matthew Eaton and smiled. The invention of the century was too big for them to handle alone; they would need help.

If he could gain unilateral support from the members of the World Council on Alternative Sources of Energy (WCASE), he could place CJ Energy Cells in their protective custody. There would be one stipulation: CJ Energy Cells would have to be available equally to all. Without that, he would rather destroy it all. Perhaps the animals, the murderers who had been hounding him for thirty years, would have no choice but to leave him and Tremont alone. Or they might finish him off out of spite. Either way, he was tired of hiding.

After checking into the Georgetown Inn—he chose to overnight away from the crowds—he retired to his room for a short nap. Later he walked two blocks along Reservoir Road, then into the Georgetown University Conference Center.

In the auditorium he stopped and stared at the large crowd. He took a swig from his ceramic flask.

How things had changed since his last visit here and at Yale, more than twenty years ago. Much of the then current technology had a small space in the Smithsonian. All the while, he had been developing the power source that would run the technological revolution into the next century.

But today's oration was different. Cameron was weeks away from making theories fact. Only he, Tremont, and his old friend knew—though *they* suspected— that all the years of hibernation would produce something significant. He wondered where Estebanez was this week: Istanbul, Millinocket, Bangkok?

If all went well, they would obtain enough grant money to develop prototypes.

Of course, he thought, it was probable that those who had proven they were willing to go as far as murder to obtain his research would only step up their efforts. Or *they* would lock him up in the loony bin like they did Dr. Jean-Paul Dominique Esquirol, just before releasing his new form of fuel cell technology. Mysteriously, the French physicist's work burned up in an electrical fire.

Or *they* would kill him.

It had been years since he was out in public at all, let alone in front of a crowd of academics and media. As he waited for the ovation to die down, his knuckles turned white from gripping the podium.

He put his hand up to shield his eyes from the lights. Ominous men were standing at each exit door. Or, were they just ushers that happened to all look like trained mercenaries.

They took her from him. *They* had to pay. It had been twenty-six years, yet it seemed like days. The authorities had long since ignored his calls, passing him off as a conspiracy theorist. Only one lone agent had taken him seriously when Cameron insisted their lives were in danger, but he got there too late. When Flannigan bucked his superiors, they threatened his job.

Cameron knew that Flannigan would be in the audience tonight.

He spoke for two hours. Drawing on the blackboard behind him, he became animated. "Ladies and gentlemen, if given the funds, we will all see the result of my life's work in action: the world's first source of near perpetual energy." He had not meant to use the damning word *perpetual*. It just came out.

The crowd took a breath and then the applause was thunderous.

Reporters called in the news, while others pushed their way to the stage. The Washington Post reported, "Cameron 'Jules Verne' Jackson is at it again."

Cameron noticed the doormen depart from the hall—his shadows. There was no holding back now. They could try and stop him, or they could get on board.

Dr. Jackson was soon drowning with congratulatory praise and questions. Seeing that their friend was in distress, a few of the Fraternal Brothers led him out of the building.

Once they had him safely back in his hotel room, he agreed to meet and greet at the black-tie event that evening at the chancellor's home.

That evening, at the reception attended by senators, congressmen, business leaders, and academics from around the world, his friends once again surrounded him.

"Still uncomfortable at parties, Cameron?" The deep voice resonated over his shoulder.

"Brewster! I thought you'd retired to London, and we'd never see your liberal face again," Cameron said. He took Kingman Brewster, former President of Yale, by the arm.

Brewster took Cameron's hand. "We have all missed you. The President asked about you."

"Please give him my best."

"So, Cameron, where is that genius son? I expected him to be right by your side. He's missed at Yale. There was never a dull moment with him and that lumberjack."

"Sean Eaton. The boys have been raising Cain somewhere in the Middle East. My son is due home this summer. I must say I've missed him. He was my right-hand man in the lab."[16]

"How about those monster dogs, what were their names?"

"Popeye and Brutus. They are getting old and a bit slow," he chuckled, "like me." They have been hopeless without him as well."

"I'm not saying this because you're my friend, Cameron. God knows I wouldn't do that." Many in the group laughed. "But your son was the brightest student in his class, and most accomplished. Yale and MIT—and I don't know how many other universities—are still using the software program he developed to track experiment progress and analyze data. We don't offer an energy science degree," he said for the benefit of others in the group, "so he crafted his own. Why he went into the military, I'll never know."

There was a chorus of agreement. Cameron downed another gin and tonic and was clearly enjoying the discussion about his son.

"Patriotism, impulsiveness, and maybe a sense of adventure. Some kids go to Italy for a semester; my son had to see the world from a helicopter."

"What area did he specialize in?" Randall Parez, asked.

---

[16] Raising Cain. This idiom refers to raising hell, and similarly that idiom refers to acting in a rowdy or troublesome way. As a threat, someone might raise Cain if they don't get what they want.

"He's a Marine but attached to the Department of Defense as an intelligence officer—"

Brewster interrupted, "I saw that Tremont's work is detailed in an Antiterrorism Act before Congress this year."

"After all the failed involvement in the Middle East and South-East Asia, do you think the boys regret joining?" asked Sergio, an Italian nuclear physicist.

"He said he sometimes wishes he didn't have such integral knowledge about the terrorist threat to our nation, but he will never regret the opportunity to protect his country from this imminent threat.

"Tremont was able to stay immersed in research ... learning things that will accelerate our work when he returns." He paused, fearing that he might reveal too much about his son's sensitive position. "His plate's been full."

"So, Dr. Jackson, your son is a military spook," blurted out a short young man with wiry hair exploding out of a black yarmulke. So, he's in the DIA?"

Cameron Jackson laughed. "I don't know about that. What I do know is that he's a soldier working with thousands of other young men and women to keep our country free."

The man pushed forward and persisted. "Maybe we'll never have to worry about terrorists here in our country, but there's always going to be dissension against the U.S. in the third world and Arab nations. We need to understand their culture and not kindle their anger against Americans. I mean, look at our audacity in the West Bank, Afghanistan, Lebanon, Syria ..."

"I'm a scientist, not a politician, Mr. um—"

"Kip Ackerman, *New York Times*," he said.

At last, face to face, he thought. Ackerman had contacted Cameron many times since publishing his NYU thesis which featured Wolfgang Pauli's and Cameron' research. Following in the footsteps of his father, Irving Ackerman, *the King of Crime Reporting*, to the *New York Times*, Kip continued to write under a pseudonym, covering subjects from the idea of big industry conspiring against alternative and renewable energy, a deep state in D.C. run by billionaires like James Seebert, and a possible connection to the mysterious deaths of scientists throughout the world.

Cameron continued "Mr. Ackerman, we thought the same thing before Pearl Harbor. I think that if we don't step up our efforts to protect against terrorism, the battle will come here. Security should be our nation's number one priority."

Two men stood off to the side. Cameron nodded to Felix Estebanez and Israel Samuels. They both smiled and lifted their beers in his direction. Cameron wanted to tell Ackerman to talk to Samuels, who could give him a blueprint to print in the *Times*: How to build an impregnable shield of security. Israel, who was a former Mossad intelligence agent, was responsible for much of the security systems in his native country.

Ackerman surely knew the answer to his next question, but he baited Cameron anyway. "You Don't you think it looks to your colleagues like a bit of paranoia living on a compound more secure than Fort Knox?"

Randall Parez broke in, "Here's to national security and renewable energy."

Cameron caught Randall's eye and nodded. Ackerman turned his attention to Parez.

"Mr. Parez, are you still focused on security issues with the overburdened electricity grids?"

Cameron squinted at a man standing on the other side of the room. He was out of place with his casual attire … and he looked familiar. The man took off his baseball cap and put on a pair of dark glasses. Cameron said, "Excuse me," and walked over to Samuels and Estebanez who were heading back to the open bar.

"I'm so glad you are here. Do you know the man over there—" he turned, to point toward the man who he thought looked just like his delivery driver, but he was gone.

"What did he look like," Estebanez asked and Cameron gave a general description including his Cowboys cap, cleft chin and sandy hair.

Estebanez looked at Samuels and said, "You thinking what I'm thinking?"

"I'm never thinking what you are thinking," Samuels replied.

"I'll take a look around," Estebanez said. "We probably should not be seen together. We'll see you tonight at the hotel bar—around eleven."

Cameron returned to his group who did not seem to miss a beat; though Ackerman looked at Cameron and then off toward Estebanez and Samuels and back to Cameron. He was about to ask something when Parez interrupted. "Yes, indeed, Ralph Nadar and I have consulted Congress on many occasions emphasizing that the interlocking grids with Canada and Mexico are facing an inevitable overload. Worse yet, the system is still vulnerable to terrorist tampering, including our water sources—and that goes for all our natural resources."

"And how do you find the support from government and industry?"

"Apathetic," said the old fraternity brother. A Russian defector, Dimitri Yanovsky had leather-like skin, and eyebrows that rivaled the fur of a black bear. He was known for advancing nuclear energy component modifications and was once Russian Deputy Energy Minister. "Until citizens realize the enormity of the danger," he continued, "it will remain a minor issue bouncing around the halls of the legislature."

Padma Shri, a scientist from Supaul, wrapped in a purple silk sari, said, "Isn't it an economic issue? Throughout India we must spend billions to upgrade the infrastructure."

Parez nodded. "But we cannot afford to stand still, especially in sensitive markets like Washington, and New York. And we must protect our exposed borders."

Brewster interjected, "This political gridlock, on all of these interlocking issues, will stand until a catastrophic event forces change."

"I hope that day never comes," chimed in Francesca, an energy researcher from France.

Ackerman said, "That sounds like a cop out. I look around the room filled with some of the greatest scientific minds of our century. There must be something that can be done."

"Ah," Parez said with a chuckle, "Dr. Jackson and physicists like him give us all hope. He has focused all of his resources, indeed his entire life, toward the solution."

Cameron knew more than anyone in this circle about the dangers America was facing. He was not able to say much since Tremont was in a sensitive area dealing with classified information. He knew his son's missions were top secret but also knew part of it had to do with infiltrating terrorist groups like al-Qaeda. Cameron would not be happy until his son was back in Indiana.

Ackerman asked, "Dr. Jackson, I could have sworn you were intimating that perpetual energy was a fact rather than just a possibility."

"Near perpetual," Cameron corrected.

"Okay. Near perpetual. So, when will we get something more than speculation?" asked a tall white-haired man wearing a white suit and a peach bowtie.

Cameron viewed the expanding audience. A lot of new faces. *They are here,* he thought. He looked at the man and thought he recognized him. "When I know, you will know. Do I know you, sir?"

"James Seebert," the man said, brandishing an ivory smile.

The scientists all leaned away from the wealthy power broker, like he had a contagious disease. This was the man that allegedly ran P7, a group steeped in mysticism, claiming to be members of the ancient order of the Illuminati. A group of men with money and power who allededly moved DC, the stock market, and banking like pawns on a chessboard.

Cameron was feeling the effects of his third double shot drink. Could this be the leader of the stalkers? The killers? He said, "What if I told you that all of your investments will soon be worth zilch. And what if I told you—"

Sergio grabbed Cameron's arm, and in a thick Italian accent whispered, "Jules, I know what you're thinking, and you'd better keep it to yourself. We all have much to lose if you are right. And, nobody more than Seebert and the people he represents."

Cameron sensed more than friendly advice from Sergio. Maybe it was the liquor, but there was a tone of warning in Sergio's reprimand, perhaps bordering on a threat. Is he one of them? Is he with Seebert?

Zaffar Abdula, a geologist and consultant in the oil industry said, "If what you are proposing is possible—and for the record, I'm not saying that it is—" Zaffar looked around nervously. "You'll only make yourself a target if you are proposing simple cost effective solar energy."

Cameron noticed Zaffar wink at Seebert. He's one of them. And Ackerman seemed to take it all in, jotting notes down like a madman. It was well past time to leave. Over Ackerman's shoulder, he noticed two of the men he'd seen in the auditorium earlier.

Dimitri said, "It is true, my friend. The oil industry has not been concerned with us. Were I to succeed in miniaturizing the nuclear process and reducing the cost to a nominal figure, I would be a target. No? It would be wise to surround myself with bodyguards and check my vehicles for explosive devices!"

Another warning? It sounded more like a threat. Cameron thought.

Then Yanovsky chuckled. "But of course, my friend, we are not even close. I will not have to change my name and ask for political asylum anytime soon." Everyone in the large group laughed and looked to Dr. Cameron Jackson for a reply.

"Amen, my Russian friend." He tossed down the balance of his drink and slipped away from the increasingly argumentative crowd. He turned around to see Seebert on his heels when Kip Ackerman cut the oil tycoon off. Kip turned and nodded to Cameron, a smile on his face.

A dubious ally? Cameron wondered.

Ackerman said, "Mr. Seebert, do you have a comment on the legislation you have lobbied to block oil exploration in the Gulf? Is it because higher supply would mean lower prices?"

On his way out the door, Cameron saw an unshaven man wearing a rumpled brown suit. He was leaning up against a lamppost smoking a cigarette.

"Agent Flannigan, it's not a surprise to see you again."

"It's good to see you too, Mr. Jackson."

"Still with the Bureau?"

"Much to Assistant Director Harrington's disappointment. Do you mind if I walk with you back to your hotel?"

"Actually, I would prefer that you did."

Flannigan coughed and offered Cameron a cigarette and said, "Sorry, I don't carry cigars with me."

"I quit years ago but thank you anyway. You should have that cough checked."

"Who were those two men you were talking to earlier?"

"I talked to a lot of people, I'm not sure who you mean."

"Hmm. Never mind." He smiled. "So, Dr. Jackson, did you notice a few serious looking men that were definitely not scientists wouldn't know the difference between a solar panel and a shingle?"

"I thought I was paranoid. They've been in Indianapolis, Tremont's basketball games, and I'm pretty sure one of them followed me into the cemetery a few months ago. Who are they?"

"I haven't been able to get a read on them. The way they carry themselves, I would say former military. You know Tremont called me, or I'd be oblivious, again."

Tremont must have called the senator, and Estebanez as well. "My son worries."

"For good reason. If you could afford it, I could place a man out at Jackson's place day and night."

Cameron scowled and waved the idea away.

"Also, I have access to new wireless surveillance technology I would be more than happy to let you test out at your compound."

"I might take you up on that and I want you to know that I appreciate the equipment you've installed over the years."

"If Colin Jester weren't taking classes at Georgetown, I would not have heard you would be here today."

"How is Colin?"

"He's studying to be a preacher."

"You don't say," Cameron said.

Colin was the first African American hired as an FBI agent and Patrick Flannigan's closest friend.

They talked about Tremont and the past for the rest of the walk.

"Well, it certainly was a pleasure seeing you again, Agent Flannigan. Thank you for your concern." Cameron had turned to walk up the stairs when Flannigan touched him on the shoulder. "Yes?"

"I believed you, even before the hospital. You know that, don't you?"

"Yes, I know, you were only following orders. You're the only one, Agent—"

"Call me Patrick. Please."

"Your concern for Tremont through the years—well, it's appreciated. I only wish you and the bureau had found out who was responsible for Karen's death, and who has kept me in fear for my son's life all these years."

Flannigan looked away. "They—we—didn't take your calls seriously enough."

"You weren't alone, Agent Flannigan," Cameron said. "But your help has kept Tremont and me alive."

"What do you know about James Seebert?"

"A low life billionaire lobbyist."

"So, you like him. Could he be the one?"

"Man, we've checked him out for so many reasons. He comes up as clean as those white suits he wears."

"Hmm."

"Are you sure about going public with your research?"

"As sure as I'll ever be, I suppose."

"Then let us help you. When is the WCASE presentation?"

"August. I'll fax you the details once they're set. Tremont will be coming with me."

"He's grown into a fine man, Mr. Jackson. I'd like to bring him into the Bureau, but I know you need him."

"I am very proud of him, Agent Flannigan. Thank you again."

When Cameron reached the bell captains desk at the top of the stairs, he looked at Flannigan's receding figure. He recalled Flannigan arriving at the hospital. But it had been too late. A few months later the videos and threatening letters began to arrive.

The message was always clear: finish the research or suffer the consequences.

Chapter Nineteen

Free
May 21, 1989

TREMONT LOOKED AT HIS WATCH and then at the Atlantic Ocean out the window of the C-130 Hercules military transport plane. He could barely believe nearly a decade had passed since he and Sean were battling the Gauley River.

He was excited to be heading back to help his father accelerate the launch of CJ Energy Cells but worried about his father's safety. His father's enemies had become desperate, and he wanted to know how far they were willing to go.

Many times, while serving his country in the Middle East, Tremont had wondered if he should have gone straight back to Jackson's Place after finishing his graduate studies. On the other hand, the things he had learned and the people he had met would be an asset once they were ready to go to market. And he was sure that he would not have the same sense of urgency that he did now. He and Sean entered Kabul moments after a teenage suicide bomber walked into a busy market and killed himself along with children, mothers, and fathers. There was no limit to the chaos and havoc that religious zealots and power-hungry leaders could create to eliminate Western infidel influence over their region and their people. Tremont would like to believe that they were freedom fighters, but the motivation was greed and power, and that was unacceptable.

He marveled at how the capitalist Arab oligopoly used supply and demand like the slide on a trombone, throwing western economies and stock markets into flux.

It was time to launch CJ Energy. To free the world from foreign oil and to make safe, low-cost energy available to developing countries.

The C-130 landed on the tarmac of the McCutcheon New River Marine Air Station, part of Camp Lejeune, North Carolina. His first task and last order was to attend a lengthy debriefing. Afterwards, he was invited to join the base commander and his family at an impressive Emerald Isle home. He spent two hours on a lunch of surf and turf thwarting one bribe after another. The Marines wanted him to reup for at least another two years. General Oglethorpe read him into Operation Just Cause. Panama was heating up and President Bush planned to take out the dictator Manuel Noriega and replace him with Guillermo Endara. The DIA wanted Sean and Tremont to lead the intelligence gathering prior to the invasion.[17]

How Tremont got out of that meeting in civilian clothes, he would always wonder.

Back on base, Tremont looked at his watch, threw his duffel bag over his shoulder, and jogged to the MP Station. He had an MP drop him off at the Ford dealer in Jacksonville. Tremont smiled all the way down Marine Boulevard as the MP chatted on about who knows what. He was a free man, and he had coveted one car for as long as he could remember.

He waved to the MP, set his duffel bag next to the reception desk inside the dealership, and walked over to a new black Mustang GLX convertible.[18]

"I'll take it," Tremont said, handing the man a check and a copy of his military ID.

"Umm, I'll have to check with … I'll be right back." A few minutes later, the salesman came back, accompanied by an older man wearing a starched white shirt and burgundy-striped tie. They both wore broad grins. The sales manager, identified by his nametag, Billy Ray, said "Mr. Jackson, I like to meet a man on a mission. Congratulations on your discharge today. When I got back from Korea, I bought a new Ford Fairlane. It wasn't until 1964 that the first Mustang came off the assembly line, or I *guaran-damn-tee* I would have bought that."

Tremont shook both men's hands.

A skinny man with Coke-bottle glasses came into the office and whispered into Billy Ray's ear. He dropped his file and left the office.

"Tell you what," Billy Ray said, "You've cut a fair deal here." He handed Tremont the keys. "Step over to Kent's office, and he'll get the title paperwork in order. Which way you headed, son?"

"Off to the Florida panhandle, then up to Indiana."

"You're going to enjoy the scenery much better now, I *guaran-damn-tee-it*."

"I don't doubt it one bit."

A half hour later, Tremont pulled out onto Highway 74 heading west. He had

---

[17] The US relinquished sovereignty of the canal to Panama. Ten years after the Torrijos-Carter treaties the US invaded Panama to thwart Noriega's efforts to align Panama with the USSR and his alleged ties to Columbian drug trafficking. On schedule, December 31, 1999, Panama became complete owner of the Canal. A judge swore in Guillermo Endara as president the night before the invasion. He is known for reestablishing democracy.

[18] Ford rolled Mustang number 10 million off the line in 2018. And, the first Mustang sold in April of 1964 was located in Chicago. The original owner, a new school teacher at the time, said that it sat in their garage for the last 27 years. It has now been restored and is worth over $350,000.00. –USA *Today*, Phoebe Wall Howard, *Detroit Free Press*, August 15, 2018.

studied a map while at the dealer and memorized the simple directions. He would take 1-95 south, connect to 1-20 west to Atlanta, and then it was all downhill to the Gulf Coast. He cruised through North Carolina, and South Carolina, through dozens of small towns.

His thoughts drifted to his protégé. The kid had become a major part of his long-term plan. He knew the chance of finding another person with Matthew's savant understanding of energy science engineering and physics was slim.

Until this morning, he had considered going north and checking in on the kid, but Sean was suspicious. He decided to wait to contact Matthew. Besides, he thought, his uncle had kept close tabs on Matthew's development. Smiling, he remembered Sean boasting about Matthew's accomplishments whenever postcards arrived from home. He didn't think Sean was wise to give Matthew his own surveillance program but could not be certain. There were those times when talking about his brother that Sean quipped, "But you knew that, didn't you?" or "Well, you probably have more intel on that than I do." Then he would laugh and change the subject, but Sean seldom laughed lately. Tremont attributed his cynicism to stress, and they were not as close as they had once been; one might say estranged.

Intelligence, Special Ops, and Special Forces soldiers had to undergo psychological evaluations at regular intervals. Though the doctors concluded that both he and Sean were suffering from post-traumatic stress disorder, their commanders found that their work was too valuable to pull them from the field. Tremont tried to let his CO know that Sean was getting out of control to no avail. For one thing, Sean was taking more than a little joy in what should be the undesirable part of their various assignments.

One night they had infiltrated the PLO and Jammal compound in Syria during the Lebanese Civil War. They took out fourteen combatants while extracting six hostages with no casualties. Something happened that Tremont decided he would never talk about and he strongly suggested that Sean get out of the service before he killed the wrong person, they killed him, or he lost it completely.

Sean said, "It's my life, and I would definitely rather die by the sword."

"Do you know who said that?"

"It's in the Bible," Sean said. "Though I suppose you're going to enlighten me."

"That was first spoken by Jesus. After Judas betrayed him, the Apostle Peter attacked a guard. Matthew 26:52—"

"You know the blasted verse." Sean threw a rock into the fire, scattering sparks in all directions.

"Jesus said to Peter, and I'm paraphrasing, to put his sword away, for all those who take up the sword perish by the sword."

"You missed your calling, Pastor," Sean grumbled. They retreated to their own thoughts.

The incident in Syria was the beginning of more frequent angry and even psychotic episodes. I have no desire to suffer twice, in reality and then in retrospect. Tremont sighed.[19]

Tremont cruised through Charlotte, Greenville, and Clemson, then it was autopilot to Atlanta where he stopped to see a former Navy Seal and his family. The Seal had alerted Sean and Tremont to evacuate a building in Kandahar seconds before an RPG obliterated the building. After a huge dinner, he continued on I-85 to Alabama where he turned south on 331 toward Destin, Florida.

He felt he had barely made a dent in his mission to accelerate implementation of advanced detection and assessment systems, to rewire America's energy and security systems in his deployed regions. Despite consulting politicians on antiterrorism mechanisms for domestic U.S. and international cities, few of his suggestions were executed. Their excuse? Budget constraints.

In their spare time, he and Sean eliminated terrorist cells—Tremont did not like that part—and helped Seal Team Six with extractions of political prisoners, abducted Americans, and enemies of the state. They set up a network of informants and spies to infiltrate terrorist cells and provide data leading to air strikes on terrorist training camps in Afghanistan, Libya, Syria, and Iraq. The Islamic extremists were gaining ground, and he knew why. It was impossible to convince poor and disenfranchised youth that there were other nonviolent paths to enlightenment. He couldn't hope to convince them that the leaders of terror, like bin Laden, were poisoning their religion and their people.

He pulled off for fuel near Columbus, Georgia. While filling the tank, he looked across the highway at the signs for Fort Benning. He thought of Little John, a soldier who died in his arms. It was last year, while they were on a routine fact-finding mission in the northeastern corner of Iraq, that everything detonated.

During the hottest part of the summer, two clicks from the Turkish border, Sean and Tremont sat with a Kurdish rebel company, having finished setting up a temporary camp on top of a ridge with low-profile camouflage tents. The group of eleven Kurds, six US Army GI's, and two military consultants took up positions a dozen feet away from the center of camp. Out of habit, one Kurd prepared a makeshift fire, though they all knew it could not be lit. The rest of the team ceremoniously cleaned their weapons. Instead of an easy fact-finding mission, orders came down to infiltrate an al-Qaeda camp.

Tremont threw a granola bar at Sean. He caught it without looking in Tremont's direction. Tremont said, "All that Kung Fu training."

"Kung Fu, ayuh, but Brazilian Jiu-Jitsu focusses on breathing which keeps you calm and your reactions sharper."

---

[19] —Sophocles, *Oedipus Rex*.

"So, hey, I know you don't want to hear it, but I think it's time for the both of us to go back to the States. We've done more in eight years than the CIA has in ten toward our mission. I think we're taking too many chances, and the statistics are going to catch up with us. Not to mention … our mission did not include assassinating public figures, which has been illegal since the Carter Administration."

"Carter! Half the reason we are in this predicament. The Gipper isn't afraid of Russia or God Almighty for that matter."[20]

"Hey, I didn't say I agreed, but it's the law of the land."

"Liberal bleeding hearts are delusional to think these religious fanatics care one bit about diplomacy. Tree, while politicians are trying to negotiate for oil, the lunatics, like Osama bin asshole, are working behind the scenes to undo any progress we have made."

The Kurds looked across the unlit stack of wood at their two American consultants. "We can't put our sword up on the mantle until every one of these freedom-hating whackos is wiped off the face of the earth!" Sean stood up and shot the Kurds a glare. One soldier made a comment, which brought on a chuckle from the group. Sean spit and said, "If they get in the way of me completing my mission and setting up my network, heaven help them."

Tremont couldn't help noticing how Sean now referred to the military-sanctioned missions in the first person. Marine psychologists call it a symptom of battle fatigue where the fight has become so personal that the soldier cannot differentiate between their egocentric need for power and their job. A Pentagon shrink usually debriefs the soldier and recommends long-term medical leave or orders a discharge from the service. Sean's time for debriefing had long come and gone. Tremont figured that their command wanted the results coming out of special-ops teams like theirs but also wanted to claim plausible deniability should things go wrong or become public. In that case, he thought, Sean and anyone within range, including Tremont, would become the designated scapegoats. That's exactly what happened to Ollie North, he thought.

"Hey!" Sean said, pointing his rifle in Tremont's direction, "are you listening to me?"

"Whoa, point that SAW elsewhere, man. I blanked for a second. What were you saying?"[21]

Sean set his gun against a rock. "You're losing it, Tree."

That's the pot calling the kettle black, Tremont thought.

"We have an obligation. If that includes sitting here burning my ass in the sand

---

[20] President Ronald Reagan portrayed George Gipp, "The Gipper," in the 1940 movie *Knute Rockne*.

[21] The M249 Squad Automatic Weapon light machine gun is affectionately called the SAW.

until we rid the world of all the cockroaches, so be it." He picked up his new ultra-light M249 rifle and laid it across his lap.

Soldiers kept their weapons close for obvious reasons, but they never let these state-of-the-art weapons out of their sight, as their camp comrades would replace them with some ancient trinket or a less accurate Russian AK-47 that dated back to WWII.

Tremont was determined not to go into a dialog that neither of them could win. He had been down that road with Sean too many times these past months. An uncomfortable silence had passed before Sean spoke again.

"I wish," Sean said, "that I could do something with the Saddam directive." The Kurds perked at the mention of Saddam Hussein's name. Sean spoke in Kurmanji, a Kurdish dialect, "I would get that bastard, and then I would bring his ugly head to the center of Mosul and mount it on a pole like the English kings did. That way everyone could see his skin bake and peel in the sun until only the skull remained."[22]

Though most of his Kurdish cohorts spoke Sorani, they got the gist of what Sean said and rewarded him with grunts of affirmation. Sean shattered this rare sense of fellowship by laughing and pointing his M249 SAW at the group of Kurds across the camp who were staring his way and cursing their American sponsors. Sean made the sound of bullets discharging. "Pow, pow, pow, pow." The Kurds turned away and ignored him.

Tremont considered what it might take to aggravate these war-seasoned guerrillas, especially since the Americans brought them weapons and provided intelligence support to Sunni, Islamic insurgents from neighboring Iran and other countries. Emotions still ran high among the Kurdish long after Saddam's death squads slaughtered dozens of men, women, and children in retaliation for an assassination attempt.

"The last Pentagon report noted that Saddam may use chemical weapons, or weapons of mass destruction."

"If he does, it will be the last thing he or his regime does."

"Let's be honest. This is not just about terrorism; it's about who will control oil in the region," Tremont said.

Sean clapped. "Sure, it's about oil," Sean replied. "It's always been about oil, and if two *amigos* like you and me are sitting around a campfire outside of Mosul—ten, twenty, or thirty years from now—it will still be about oil."

Not if my father has anything to say about it, Tremont thought.

"Bastards," Sean said, along with a few additional choice words.

---

[22] Kurmanji or Badinani is spoken by at least half of the world's estimated thirty million Kurdish-speaking people. The men with Sean more than likely spoke a centralized dialect called Sorani or Xushnaw.

"So maybe you can see how much more important it is that I finish my work with Dad," Tremont said, and Sean grumbled.

Sean spread out a map on a rock and signaled for Tremont to join him. "This is the Iraqi airport. Abdul Kali is to meet Hussain's guard here." He pointed on the map. "If we can position ourselves here, we could take him out."

"We are to observe."

"Call in for clearance. If I have a shot …"

"They are not going to give you a greenlight. We are consulting. If the Kurds take him out, and we are here, there will be hell to pay. It's a no-win situation. We observe."

"See. You're no fun anymore, Nancy."

Tremont returned to his position, legs crossed and elbows on his knees. Tremont rubbed his eyes, ran his fingers through his hair, and said, "One of these days we're going to be on the wrong side of the probabilities. I don't need you adding to the danger," he lifted his chin toward the Kurds, "with our freedom fighters."

"You worry too much."

Sean's increasing sarcasm and insults aggravated Tremont. Others seemed to pick up on Sean's changes first. The Kurdish and Afghan rebels had labels for Sean: *Chatichat metooraf* translated as *you piece of crazy*. And there was another assessment while assigned to Paris. Their mission was to locate a Palestinian leader allegedly responsible for masterminding the deaths of Israeli athletes at the 1972 Munich games. These terrorists were planning a repeat performance during the upcoming Olympics. Two Mossad agents accompanied Sean and Tremont. During their month together, the Mossad agents dubbed Sean *Halev Mistagya.*

One Mossad agent whispered to Tremont, "crazy heart."

Tremont thought back to that simple assessment and wondered if what was becoming so apparent to him now had been inherent in Sean all along. Probably, he thought sadly.

"You know," Tremont said. "Sometimes I wonder if I should have joined up at all."

"Damn, Tree. You and my brother Matthew were sure cut from the same root."

Tremont looked up and frowned.

"You both belong in a lab."

Tremont studied Sean's face and wondered. Tremont said, "I look forward to seeing him again. Maybe you can bring him out to the Indiana Dunes and introduce him to my father."

Sean chuckled. "You're so full of shit. You don't really believe that working on your dad's energy project is more important than protecting his freedom?"

"I'll be making a difference. While here, watching your back while you took unnecessary risks, I might add, I gained a deeper understanding of how Dad's inventions can solve even the most desperate situations. Providing clean, inexpensive, and accessible energy will change everything. And I'm proud to have joined a long lineage of Carsons and Jacksons in service to my homeland."

Sean clapped his hands together. "Bravo. Bravo. A real live American hero. I think I'm tearing up!"

"What seemed so clear back there on the Gauley River while we were preparing to go over Sweet's Falls, has become cloudy now."

"Hang in there, bro. We'll have the worst of them dead or in custody in no time."

"It seems that we take out one, and we get ten more," Tremont said with a sigh.

"We're making a dent. We can develop better security measures the more we know about their plans. Wiping out terrorist cells is just icing on the cake. I do the dirty work, and you write the reports, Nancy. What a team."

One more jab like that and I might have to teach him a lesson, Tremont thought. "I can still kick your Rambo butt."

"You," —he pointed his gun at the Kurds— "and ten of them, maybe."

Tremont asked, "What is your long-term plan, Sean? You've done more than your share."

"Back to ELF and cutting logs? Not on your life."

You could teach boxing and martial arts, or paint, or both?"

"I was good, eh? Twelve bouts and twelve knockouts." He kicked at a rock. "You really think my paintings are good?" Tremont nodded, and Sean said, "Naw, just continue doing what we're doing. The way I look at it each terrorist I take out removes one potential suicide bomber waiting to take out a school bus full of children."

At that moment on the rocks in northern Iraq, Tremont said to himself, "It's time to go home."

Bullets began to whiz overhead. A brigade of Saddam's elite Republican Guard attacked from all sides. The firefight lasted twenty minutes; the Guard diced their group down from fourteen to five; Sean and Tremont, two Kurds, and one Army infantry soldier, nineteen-year-old private first class, John Imbrognio, Little John.

The five remaining men retreated down a dry ravine while the Republican Guard swarmed the camp. Little John insisted on taking up the rear as the rest of the team crawled down the ravine. At the bottom, Tremont whispered for them to hold up and wait for Little John. A few minutes later the big kid stumbled right into Tremont knocking him, Sean, and one of the Kurds flat on the ground, Sean on the bottom.

"You big assed son of a—" Sean said with menace.

"Shut up," Tremont whispered feeling contempt for his friend. "Little John, are you hit?" Tremont felt for a pulse, it was weak, and when he took his hand away, it was dripping with blood. "Damn." He put his hand back on his neck and applied pressure.

"We can't sit here and wait for the Saddam'ites to catch up with us. Let's go."[23]

"You go ahead. I'll catch up."

"I'm not leaving you here, Tree. We're Huck and Tom, remember?" For a long moment, they stared at each other.

"Go! We'll have a better chance split up."

Tremont knew by the amount of blood that the bullet had hit the carotid artery. Even with access to a medical facility, there was little chance of survival. He wrapped the wound as tight as he could without cutting off his air and put Little John's hand on his neck. "Press down as tight as you can, right here." Tremont jumped to his feet and looked for somewhere to hide.

"Will ya—will ya, let ma and pa know I—that I—"

"They know. But, I'll tell them."

"Thank ya, suh."

Tremont found a hole to crawl into and knowing he could not carry Little John even on a good day, he forced him to get to his feet and put the other arm around his shoulders. They were near equal in height, and if anyone saw the two of them standing in the dark desert against the moonlit sky, they would have thought a couple of giants were passing through. Targets.

He got Little John in behind the huge boulder and down into the hole. A bit of moonlight glistened off his face. Little John was smiling. "Aw guess," he said, "aw guess, I got a ticket home, eh, Corporal."

"You okay, man?"

Tremont looked up to see that he was standing in front of the cashier inside the BP Station.

"We ain't got nobody named Little John around here man. Hey, you play for the Hawks?" the young cashier said looking up at Tremont.

"I'm alright, and no, I don't." He handed the boy a fifty and didn't bother with the change.

Tremont pulled out of the gas station and saluted the army base as he passed by.

Back on the highway, he crossed into Alabama and noted the Pensacola-192-miles" sign. he flipped through his collection of cassettes and put a new one in the player. He frowned as he thought about who gave him the tape. Another ghost, he thought sadly. Brad was a southern boy he served with in the Middle East. Brad's armored Jeep hit a roadside mine not fifty feet from the base gate where Tremont was waiting to greet him. When Tremont got to the smoldering mass of metal, none of the four soldiers were recognizable.

Tremont closed his eyes tight and said a quiet prayer. When he opened them, he sharply turned the wheel to avoid hitting a dump truck.

---

[23] Sean is referring to Saddam Hussein's Republican Guard (1964 – 2003), an elite fighting force, similar to US Special Forces, made up of Sunni Arabs or Kurds.

The likable kid was a former football player for the University of Georgia, no more than twenty, fresh out of boot camp, and had only been in Tremont's reconnaissance unit for a few weeks. He played a mean guitar and had plans to play out his remaining years of eligibility with the Bulldogs. He would not have been in the armed services had it not been for the financial pressures causing him to work two jobs to support his ailing mother and younger siblings. Tremont remembered how the kid had told him that this band would be an enormous success. He was right on the money. Athens, Georgia's R.E.M., had taken the charts by storm.

As a song from their second album, *Murmur,* played, the lyrics struck home. It rang true that one person couldn't or at least shouldn't carry the weight of the world on his shoulder. Tremont tried to focus on the road. That lasted about five minutes until, in his mind, he was back in another part of the Middle East and then another, and then another.

The next thing he knew the sun began to rise, and he was pulling up in front of the central Destin, Florida boat dock. He looked out on to his uncle's floating residence.

Chapter Twenty

Chill
May 22, 1989

"HE HAS MORE POTENTIAL than any kid I've ever met," Tremont said, sitting back in his chair, and sipping on a glass of Pinot Gris as they sailed west along the panhandle of Florida. His uncle went on about how the world was finally becoming post-Chardonnay and that while Chardonnay and Sauvignon Blanc go well with fish, a Pinot Gris *enhances* the taste and is less oaky, has less alcohol, less acidity, and creates a balance with the food.

That was fine, Tremont thought, but he would have enjoyed the moment even if they were drinking Coke's and eating burgers. Of course, he did not reveal that to his uncle, his godfather, the man who defined aficionado.

"We trained many young men twice his age in language, self-defense, weaponry, and," his uncle paused, put his nose deep in his glass and inhaled, "and fine wine. Besides you, I've never come across a lad who absorbed information quicker. The tutor has already become the student. I just won't let Matthew know it."

"But he will figure it out." Tremont chuckled. "So, the crash course in quantum physics my father put you through is running its course?"

"I've confounded KGB agents with less effort." They both laughed.

He and his uncle enjoyed a lunch of baked lime-dill wild salmon on spring greens with Sichuan cucumber salad, served by a young female chef fresh out of The Culinary Institute of America. When she was not serving, or pouring, she was massaging his uncle's shoulders. Tremont said, "When I first met Matthew, he was sharper than I was at twice his age."

After lunch, they walked around the expansive yacht, *The Karen,* which was the square footage of a good-sized house. Though his uncle had sent specs and pictures of the floating mansion to Tremont while he was overseas, he repeated the dimensions and weight again for good measure.

Tremont realized he was not paying attention and tuned back in as his uncle was saying, "The ship is over 400 tons and one hundred seventy-eight feet in length. *Pero jovencito*, where the ocean vessel Karen is so very much like your dear departed mother is in her beauty. *Tu madre era la mujer más hermosa que yo he conocido en toda mi vida.*" he said quietly while touching two fingers and his thumb to his lips, kissing them and opening his hand quickly to the air.[24]

"She *was* very beautiful, wasn't she?" Tremont said, as more of a statement than a question. He often wondered about the sadness his uncle displayed whenever they talked about Tremont's mother. There was more to the story than just being a close friend of the family. One day he would press for more answers, but not today.

They both sat quietly while Tremont wiped at a tear. "How—how is Marcos? Is he still in school at FSU?"

His uncle beamed. He had taken Marcos under his wing when he was only five, the only survivor of a botched escape from Cuba in 1964. Years ago, Marcos told Tremont that Zebo, his uncle, never forgave himself for not being there for his brother and his family. He was on a mission, five-thousand miles away, and his brother never indicated that he was planning to escape Cuba. The Coast Guard picked up the little boy miles from where the boat overturned in a storm. Marcos told them he was going to swim to Miami to find his uncle. Ironically, the Captain of the Coast Guard Cutter served with his uncle during The Bay of Pigs incident and could find Zebo through their mutual government connections.

"You know Marcos looks up to you like an older brother."

Tremont nodded.

"He asks about you often. Did you get his letters?"

"Yes, there were dozens, and as witty and dry humored as always. I know he wants to be a pilot, but he really should consider the stage." They both laughed.

"He's also finishing his degree in criminal justice. I fear he wishes to follow me—and now you."

"So, he wants to be a scientist, a sailor and wine connoisseur?"

"Exactly." He clicked glasses with Tremont. "To family."

"To family."

"I got him an interview with the CIA and the FBI. They both offered him a job when he finishes his masters. Marcos called them amateurs and said that maybe he would start his own agency. Smart-ass. The other option he investigated was Defense Intelligence. I was actually hoping you would talk him out of that."

"Will do. Will try."

"Anthony?" he called, and a man appeared from seemingly nowhere. "Would you please bring me the last bottle I shipped to you when I was up in Maine?" Anthony raised his eyebrows, nodded, and turned to retrieve the bottle.

The soldier was unfamiliar to Tremont, but he knew the type. Anthony was a

[24] Your mother was the most beautiful woman I have ever met.

hulk of a man, not much older than Tremont, with a neck like a medium-sized tree trunk and muscles bulging out of a navy-blue suit. He wore a shoulder holster under his left arm. He was special-forces military and probably, like himself, a trained intelligence professional.

His uncle always had competent men around him. When Tremont was a child visiting his one houseboat or another, men like Anthony taught the boys to fish and fight.

It was about fifteen years ago when Tremont first boarded *The Presidents*, a Valiant sailboat built by Texan Rich Worstell. The ship was much smaller than *The Karen*. His uncle named the vessel in 1974 when he joined the Presidential detail. Then Vice President Ford specifically requested his uncle when it was clear President Nixon was heading for impeachment in the face of Watergate. It was a short assignment. Ford replaced Nixon, Carter replaced Ford; and the Southern Democrat could not tolerate his uncle's outspoken positions. He was out. But the current CIA director had plans for him, and that's how his uncle got *The Karen*.

As boys, Tremont and Marcos often fished off the stern of *The Presidents*. First mate, Stephan, was making repairs on the rigging above the mainstay when a crosswind forced the beam against the waves in what sailors call a broach. Stephan all but fell from his perch twenty feet in the air. His nickel-plated .38-caliber revolver slid the entire length of the deck to land at Tremont and Marcos's feet. Though they were trying to hold onto the bulwark with one hand and their fishing rods with the other, Tremont gave his fishing pole to Marcos and dove for the gun. He caught it as the boat lurched up to right itself and threw Tremont onto his back.

He held up his prize in Marcos's direction only to feel a vice-grip on his wrist while a force pulled him to his feet. Stephan took the gun out of Tremont's grip, checked the load, and then holstered it behind his back. He said, "Never touch another man's gun unless he offers. Do you understand?" The boys both nodded. "The first rule of firearms," Stephan had said, "is never to point your weapon at anything you do not wish to kill." He returned to his work on the rigging.

"What about paper targets?" Marcos had asked rhetorically. "You don't kill targets."

"I heard that—smart-ass," Stephen had hollered back.

"What are you thinking about?" his uncle asked.

"The first time I held a gun," Tremont replied.

Tremont and his uncle smoked Cuban cigars, drank a priceless glass of Merlot from the cellars of the Katahdin Sporting Lodge, and talked about the future.

His uncle relit and puffed on his cigar. "Your father has layers and layers of sophisticated security—Flannigan and I have made sure of that—but some people can get in there if they want to. I think they are just waiting."

"Waiting for him to finish."

"Or indicate that he's finished."

"Uncle Zebo, you don't think they would hurt him? I mean without Dad, there is no research. No product. Nothing."

"I don't know," Zebo said thoughtfully. "I do know this: when your father completes his work, there is no end to the depths of power and money that will be thrown at him to buy, stop, or steal the research."

Tremont felt a familiar wave of anxiety flood over him.

"You know," Zebo said, "before I forget, I knew the northern Maine Eaton name sounded familiar, so I checked the Agency's records and found something uncanny." Zebo leaned on the forward bow railing as the two of them watched the huge triple mast yacht ride high and cut through the water. "I was on a mission to Nicaragua with his Uncle Carl; I was CIA but attached to Seal Team Six, and Carl was Air Force. Miraculously he got us out safely with three of four engines shot out. How he landed that huge cargo plane we used as cover, I'll never know."

Tremont whistled. "Six degrees of separation, huh."

"Anyhow, I thought it was too coincidental, but I looked him up, and he's living in Miami. I gave him a call, and it turns out Carl and his brother are somewhat estranged, something to do with him not being interested in the forestry business. I didn't tell him much, except that I came across his nephew while doing business up in Maine. He asked that I keep him informed, that besides an annual call and card from Kate—" He paused.

"What? Are you falling for Mrs. Eaton?"

He puffed on the cigar a few times. "There's something about that woman."

Tremont smiled to himself. Putting aside for the moment that she was a married woman, Kate Eaton was a little old for his uncle. In fact, they were probably close to the same age. Just as he thought it, his uncle's chef, a late twenty-something beauty, returned with hors d'oeuvres.

"Simone trained with some of the best in France." He put an arm around her thin waist and said, *Vous êtes un chef merveilleux.* And, if you keep this up, I think you are going to have to put me on a diet, *Mon Chéri.*"

In French, she replied, "The only time to eat diet food is while you're waiting for the steak to cook."

"Who said that?"

"Julia Child, also a French chef, I might add," she said.

As she refilled their wine and returned to the galley they spoke in depth about Matthew and Sean.

"How long has it been since Sean was stateside to get a psych evaluation, debriefing, and some R&R?"

"Not once since we shipped out. He's been on some very sensitive missions and—" Tremont stopped himself, realizing that his uncle may or may not be cleared for this particular information. And even if he was, there were only four people alive who were privy to their orders.

He changed the subject. "By the time Matthew is in college, he might know more about centrifuge and nuclear fission than ten of the best capable veteran energy scientists combined."

Zebo set a picture of Matthew Eaton on the table. It showed the boy standing at a podium with silver-haired, bearded men gracing chairs in the backdrop. The banner on the podium read "Regional Junior Science America Awards, Smithsonian Institute."

Tremont beamed with pride.

"He beat a field of eighty thousand students under nineteen. His theory, get this, shows that science has been going about the search for renewable and alternative energy all wrong these past forty years. How about that? And from a child. They loved it!"

"I knew it." Tremont tapped the picture. "There's the future, Uncle. There's the kid we can hand the baton to."

"Nothing will happen as long as I'm here. And you don't have to convince me about Matthew. We've become quite close."

"I appreciate you taking time out of your sailing schedule to keep an eye on him."

Estebanez took a swat at him. "I'm not out to pasture yet. The Gipper is keeping me busy."

"You don't say."

"I didn't say."

"As far as hanging out in the wilderness, it's growing on me. And of all places, I've found undoubtedly the finest stash of rare wines in the world."

"Owned by the senile, eccentric innkeeper, you wrote me about?"

They sat in silence for a while.

"What is it?" Zebo asked.

"If what you say is true, there's a lot of money and power stacking up against Dad. We're going to take CJ Energy to WCASE this summer. How worried should I be? How much danger is he in?"

Zebo put a hand on Tremont's arm and said, "Nothing is going to happen to you or your dad—not while I'm around. Your father has been waiting a long time for you to get done playing soldier—frankly, he's been ready to launch CJ Energy for years."

"I suspected as much."

Tremont stood and walked to the starboard side of the ship and looked out into the open sea. It was a safe bet that he and his father would soon navigate into stormy weather. Or, he thought, a hurricane.

Chapter Twenty-One

Breach
August 1, 1989
8:50 a.m.

TREMONT AND HIS FATHER spent the better part of the summer in the lab. Every morning and evening they hiked with Popeye and Brutus through the pine forest and along the Indiana Dunes State Park beach. Each Sunday they visited his mother's grave on a hill under the oldest oak in the area on the Indianapolis Carson estate. Tremont often went on his own to see the old Senator and the rest of the Carson clan.

Cameron had not taken a drink since Tremont arrived. By the end of July, they had completed, printed, and bound several thick manifestos to hand out to the members of WCASE.

The day had arrived.

Tremont paced from one baggage claim turnstile to another. He looked up at the departure and arrival monitors. He scanned the list: *Albany, Birmingham, Charlotte,* and down to *New York LaGuardia.* The blue blinking letters read *delayed.* He felt the knot in his stomach again. He wondered why he let his father talk him into their splitting up. An hour ago, he had picked up his bags and then met with security to retrieve his compact Glock 43 handgun. Due to his high-security with the DIA, he was one of the 40,000 agents who flew armed.

He looked up at the top of the escalator to see his father and inhaled deeply. Until they were in the safety of Jackson's Place, he would not let his father out of his sight again. The knot was still there. On the way out to the limo, he scanned every person and vehicle. Nothing seemed out of the ordinary.

A black limousine bearing the United States Senate emblem drove Cameron and Tremont from the airport to the Hart Senate Office Building. Through the mirror, Tremont noticed a sedan still following close behind. Tremont removed his firearm and checked the load.

"What?" His father asked.

"Just cautious. Who did you see in New York?"

"Long story. I'll tell you after the presentation."

"Fair enough," Tremont said and reholstered the gun.

The driver walked around the front of the limo and opened the door. Tremont and his father stepped out onto the sidewalk.

He heard a sharp snap, like breaking a large stick. Tremont looked up and to the left, while reaching for his gun. His father catapulted into his arms; blood spattering. A second bullet shattered a window inches from Tremont's head as he pressed against the vehicle.

Tremont pulled his father to the back of the car as a third bullet hit the driver, spinning him to the pavement. People screamed, cars pulled to a stop, and sirens approached from a distance. As a fourth bullet smashed into the limo, Tremont pulled his father away and settled him to the ground behind a large oak.

The limo exploded, and shrapnel hit the tree. Tremont peered to see flames and a smoking inferno. Tremont recognized the pattern, the art of a trained professional. As he turned back to attend to his father, a bullet careened off the tree where his face had been one second before. The sniper was toying with him. Was this personal?

Though he knew there was little hope, Tremont tore off his shirt and put pressure on the wound. He felt for a pulse. It was weak.

A bullet split the bark near Tremont's face. The sniper was still at his post with all of Washington's law enforcement converging on the scene.

Why? Who? "Hang in there, Dad," he whispered. He slid off his undershirt and pressed it on the wounds. His father only had moments to live.

Tears streamed down his cheek. His chest convulsed, and his throat constricted as he forced back the sobs. He kept his hands pressed against his father's wounds. This can't be happening, he thought.

"Hold it right there!" a voice shouted. "Drop it. Toss it away."

Tremont realized he had his gun in his hand. He looked up to see two DC cops flanking him, their service guns aimed at his head.

Tremont said in a raspy voice, "My, my, dad is dying."

The younger officer said, "Malone, I wouldn't—"

The graying sergeant said to Tremont, "It's okay, son, we'll take care of your father."

As two medical technicians raced toward them, Officer Malone took Tremont's forearm and helped him to his feet. His father's blood dripped down his cheek and neck.

"Are you hit?" Malone asked.

"I should have been." He heard a hollow voice resonate from his own mouth. The two EMTs bent over Cameron Jackson. The young woman looked into Tremont's eyes and mouthed the words "I'm sorry."

Tremont found himself standing and following the policeman toward dozens of squad cars with lights blinking red and blue. He turned back, knelt down, put a hand on his pale cheek, and made his pledge: "I will hunt them down." He choked on his breath. "Your work will not be in vain."

Cameron lurched and grabbed Tremont by the arm. The paramedic fell back. Cameron sucked in what must have been an excruciating breath of air. "They can't scare off a Jackson. You … Felix … and Matthew—" He coughed, his eyes glazed over, and blood seeped from his mouth. Tremont felt for a pulse, laid his hand across his father's forehead and moved it down to close his father's eyes.

The other EMT checked Cameron's pulse and said, "Time of death, eight fifty-three a.m." The EMT avoided Tremont's eyes.

Officer Malone knelt at Tremont's side and said, "Marine. I'm sorry. I know it's difficult, but do you have any idea what we are up against?"

"How did you—"

"Your CO asked me to meet you and your father. I was also a Raider with Oglethorpe—in Nam."[25]

Tremont nodded. As Malone went to his squad car, he got up and walked toward the frantic activity around the smoldering skeleton of the stretch limo. He covered his eyes from the glare and scanned the buildings. Malone returned and handed him a shirt. Tremont put it on and said, "The shots originated from there." As he pointed, he caught a glimmer of something out of place and then movement.

He broke into a sprint toward the buildings north of the Senate Building.

---

[25] The Raiders are an elite Marines Special Forces team within the Special Forces, thought to have been disbanded after WWII.

Chapter Twenty-Two

Face
August 1, 1989
9:04 a.m.

TREMONT LOOKED UP at the elevator number. It was on nine. He ran toward the exit sign and swung open the door to the stairwell.

Out of breath, Malone came through the front door radioing to have all exits blocked.

Tremont took the stairs two and three at a time, climbing the nine floors in minutes. He got to the door of the roof, only to find it locked. He pulled a fire extinguisher off the wall and began to smash it against the door handle.

His mind raced. Only a qualified marksman with sniper training using a high-powered rifle with a thermal or electro-optical site and ballistic computer would even consider trying at this distance, let alone be so accurate.

The door opened from the other side. He stumbled onto the white-pebbled roof, squinted at the light, and raised his gun.

"You?"

"Well, Nancy, you gonna shoot?"

Sean leaned against the short wall at the edge with an unlit cigarette hanging from his lips, his arms crossed, and one leg over the other as if he were taking a smoking break in an office courtyard.

Through a blinding hate and excruciating pain tearing at his heart and soul, Tremont still hesitated. Sweat burned his eyes. He knew on a modified hair trigger, only the pressure of a fly on paper stood between Sean living or dying. He would place a double tap to Sean's heart, and it would be over. Hatred, anguish, and years of training screamed at his brain not to hesitate, *take the shot*, as he squinted against the morning sun and watched Sean light a cigarette with indifference. And he would have pulled the trigger, except a smidgen of reason seeped through the red blur in front of his eyes. If he killed Sean, he would not know who hired him. There was something else, he thought. How could this crazed animal be so confident I wouldn't pull the trigger after he shot my father? He would kill him, sooner rather than later, but right now he needed information.

Sean put two fingers to the barely burned cigarette, taking drag before flicking it over the side. He blew out a long line of smoke and magically had a handgun pointed at Tremont. "I love a Mexican standoff, don't you? Why do you suppose they call it that? I mean, do you really think the Mexicans invented it? You're the Bible scholar. Don't you think it would've been Cain and Abel? I guess not, since one of them got himself killed."

Sweat dripped into Tremont's eyes. He let Sean talk but held his Glock steady, despite the hurricane raging within his body and the lightning flashing in his brain.

"Come on, Nancy. Just like the old west, a couple of buddies at the O.K. Corral— or the U.S. Senate. Close enough. How about you lower your gun?" He put his gun back into his shoulder holster. "We'll count to three, and the fastest draw wins."

"Why?"

"To see who's fastest."

"Why did you shoot my father? For who? What price could they have paid you worth killing my father?" Tremont's gun hand shook ever so slightly, now the only indication of his rage.

"Maybe you were right, you know. Maybe I'm as crazy as they say." He made motorboat sounds with his lips and rolled his eyes. "Did you know those sons-a-bitches at DIA wanted to let me go on a Section Eight?" His voice modulation increased. "After all I did for our country? But I had too much shit on them, so how about this: I'm still on the government payroll and working as an independent contractor on the side. Quite a gig, huh?"

So, that's it, Tremont thought. "What did you do that finally woke them up to rein you in?"

"It was you, Tree. In the end, you almost brought me down. Your final report detailing our last mission, and that damn Little John getting himself all shot to hell. Did you know his uncle was an Alabama US Senator? Who'd a thunk it?"

"This is about revenge?" He had heard on the radio that two days ago, a sniper shot Congressman Imbrognio while visiting veterans in Birmingham. The reporter called the incident *racially motivated*.

"Don't you wish it was that easy, bro?"

Tremont could feel his pulse like the beat of a bass drum through his finger on the trigger. But not yet. Not yet. "Who, Sean? Who's paying you?"

"You're a whole lot smarter than all of us. My money is on you."

Sean's use of the word, *us*, resonated. He's too confident, Tremont thought. Sean could have been long gone from here. There's something more he wanted to say.

"What's your game, Sean?"

"The game. Now you're on target, buddy. Now *you* are on target. You've been playing a game, and my little brother has been a playing piece for you. Don't look so surprised; do you think I'm an idiot? That's why they call us intelligence officers." He chuckled. "So now the game and rules have changed. Oh, and lest I forget, Matthew is off the playing board.

"If you don't play smart, they will take out the rest of your family, one by one. Am I clear so far? By the way, if you or the men in blue swarming this building take me out, the whole sequence will speed up like fast forward on a movie. Keeping me alive keeps the Senator and the rest of the Kit Carson clan alive. *Capisce?*"

The insane picture was clearer—but barely. Today's hit seemed to be about money, jealousy, and revenge, through the clouded reasoning of a militant psychopath assassin. Tremont lowered his Glock. He would pick a time and place when he knew his family was safe.

"It's your game, Sean. What's the next move?"

Sean picked up the rifle that Tremont recognized immediately: a Barrett M82, accurate to 1,800 meters with a margin of error less than twelve inches, with the right shooter. Still, at this distance, only a sniper with Sean's skill could have picked off his father and the hapless limo driver with one shot each. He could see how he destroyed the limo; the rifle fired a bullet that could pierce an inch and a half of armor plating.

Sean cradled the gun and smiled at Tremont. "I don't suppose a hug is in order?" He raised his eyebrows and shrugged. "No? I'm sorry I had to take out your dad. Truly. Let's hope we don't have to eliminate the rest of the Carsons and Jacksons … whoa, wait a minute, there are no more Jacksons, are there? You're the last of the Mohicans, man.

"I need you to do one thing for me," Sean said, "a favor between old friends. I'm sure your new pals in blue have all the entrances guarded. Remember, it doesn't matter who kills me, the result for you will be the same." He swung the thirty-pound Barrett to his shoulder and pointed toward the Senate office building. "Is your grandfather over there today? I think he is." He knelt and expertly disassembled the Barrett rifle.

"Do you really think you can get off this roof?"

Sean whistled while carefully placing each piece of the rifle in a plastic case. He then slid the case into a laundry bag.

"The rear entrance will be clear in five minutes," Tremont said as he opened the steel door. He faced his once friend. "This is not over, Sean."

"If it were over, Nancy, what kind of game would that be? Remember our rugby matches? You smashed my face in the mud, and then I smashed yours." He walked to the end of the building and turned around.

"I look forward to the next match," Sean said.

Chapter Twenty-Three

Destroy
August 7, 1989

TREMONT STOOD ALONE watching the grave-crew shovel black soil upon the hand-carved redwood casket. Grandmother and Grandfather Carson were the last to leave of hundreds who attended his father's funeral. They came from all over the world. He watched their limo pull out of the grassy makeshift parking area and leaned on a large black umbrella with both hands.

While the rest of the crew loaded equipment in the back of a pickup, a man navigated a small Bobcat loader, pushing the remaining dirt into the slough. He saluted Tremont with a tip of his soaked Indiana University cap and drove the Bobcat up a ramp onto a flatbed truck.

Tremont knelt between the gravestones of Karen and Cameron Jackson. He arranged the fresh cut flowers on his mother's grave and placed a handful on his fathers.

And he prayed.

Tremont checked the pulse on both Popeye and Brutus. He pulled out the tiny tranquilizer darts embedded in their necks. The front door stood ajar. He reached behind his back and pulled a Glock from his belt holster, releasing the safety. After a search of the main floor, he went to the charred remains of the basement lab door hanging half on the hinges. They must have used sophisticated explosives to blow the door; it was nearly impregnable. The hinges were still warm. Tremont looked at the residue on his fingers and grunted at the clay composite they used to centralize the C-4 explosive inward toward the bolt. With the Glock in position alongside his cheek, he flicked the light switch. The stairwell illumined. He stepped soundlessly to the basement floor.

The lab looked like a tornado had touched down. Most of the PCs were still in place, but the hard drives were missing. He looked in a few of the opened drawers—empty. The shelves along the perimeter of the three-thousand-square-foot room once filled with volumes of energy textbooks and research. Now, empty.

Stepping into the middle of the room, he shoved a lab table to the center. He pulled together three more tables and knelt beside an outlet. Pulling off a plastic cover, he revealed a handle. He twisted it, and a section of the floor lifted to reveal a set of steps.

The room below was identical to the one above, but this one buzzed with activity. "Hello, darlings. Did you miss me? I'm going to miss you." Tremont went to a footlocker and retrieved four green duffel bags. He began stripping the room.

"Ingenious, Dad." I used to think it was a bit paranoid, overboard, he thought. He tried not to imagine his father down here, eating snacks, sipping scotch, and quizzing him on science, history, even grammar. This was their lab, his school, their playroom.

Along with manuals, hard drives, and research papers he collected personal items. Leaving behind his trophies, he grabbed an empty box of Cracker Jack. He gathered pictures of him and his father and the dogs, around the Indiana Dunes State Park grounds, or on the Jackson's Place property. He stared long and hard at one cherished picture of his mother and father.

He came upon a row of locked cabinets that his father seemed to never open. He found the keys taped under one corner. In the first cabinet, he found stacks of videos, each bound with a page of writing. Pulling up a stool, he read the dated letters starting with 1958, the year before Tremont's birth. The last came just a few weeks ago. He could only imagine what was on the videos, but judging by the letters, they were proof that the writer could back up his threats. Could these bastards be the ones that hired Sean?

Confused and angry, Tremont put the videos in one of four duffel bags; he would delve into this new evidence when he reached one of his uncle's safe houses. He would find out who was behind all of this, then, he would kill Sean, and then finish his father's work. He stopped packing for a moment. Too presumptuous? Matthew might choose not to work with him.

Would a horse refuse water?

Could he kill Matthew's brother? If not, Sean would surely stand in the way. Something caught his eye. One train was still running on the G-Series H/O track, propelled by his dad's latest CJ Energy Cell. He hated to stop it, but he needed that cell. Tremont picked up his father's journal and read his last notes. After jotting down the statistics, he shut down the railroad. He took all five of the trains with him. He and his dad built the retro railway system. Genius.

He put the bags on the dumbwaiter, but he waited to send it up.

A metal on metal noise startled Tremont. "Uncle Z?"

"Well, I'll be damned."

A gun pointed at his chest before Tremont could reach his Glock. He cursed.

Either he'd missed something on the compound security system or the intruder was already inside when he got here. *How could I be so stupid?* he thought.

The man standing at the base of the steps had a handsome face with a cleft chin. He wore a wrinkled Government Express shirt, and Tremont didn't recognize him.

"I knew your old man had somewhere he'd escape to. One minute, I'm listening to him whistling and humming Bach and Brahms, and then nothing; I wouldn't hear him again for hours. He taught me a lot about classical music. I used to think he was passing code through the music, so I logged every album he played—gotta love that he still played vinyl—Mozart, Beethoven, Schubert."

The intruder held his gun loosely crossed over his left bicep with his body turned just enough to fire a fatal shot. *Professionally trained.* "So, Mr.—"

"Call me Smith—John Smith. I'm like family."

"You've been assigned to watch my father ... for how long?"

"Well, I don't know if you would call it assigned, but if you mean how long have I been staked out here at Jackson's Place, eight years—off and on."

"U.S. government paid. Private contractor. Secret Service or CIA-trained," Tremont guessed. He watched the man to see if his eyes gave away the truth, but it was not necessary.

"You got two out of three. I'm impressed. It's amazing what you can learn with a few years of DIA training and in-country experience. If I had not had the patience of Job, you would have gotten away clean. You had quite a few guests while you were gone. The last left Monday after ransacking the sub-floor lab." He paused.

"Two labs. A decoy. That was genius," Smith said. "I think everyone knew everyone else was here, except for me—nobody knows about me," he said with a grin. "Some of those guys fit your description: government contracted, but mostly mercenaries hiring out to the highest bidder. The Russians recruited one group. The Saudis contracted another. And the sons a bitches that got here first, came in from the water. They were top notch, perhaps Seal trained. They are the ones that left their C4 calling cards."

"And you?"

"You know what would have been fun?" He didn't wait for an answer. "If they came into the compound all at the same time, man, there would have been fireworks." His eyes roved around the room. "So, this is where the future of energy was developed." He looked past Tremont into the dumbwaiter. "I take it everything of importance is in those duffel bags?"

"Laundry. I've been putting if off since returning from overseas."

"Your last tour was Iraq on the Turkish border. You boys with DIA did some considerable damage over there, training the Kurds to infiltrate terrorist camps, coercing the Mujahedeen to turn on the Russians. You know, we'll be fighting them, and the Taliban now that the Russians are back in Moscow." He clicked his tongue. "Not to mention Iran Contra with Colonel North. How did you get mixed up in that mess?" He clicked his tongue. "But it was clever work, kid—and that's close enough," he warned.

Tremont inched closer.

He continued, "I was teaching hand-to-hand combat before you were playing middle school basketball. Even with that reach, I'd blow your head off before you began to press."

"Sean send you?"

"Who?"

Tremont decided Smith was probably not a suspect in his father's death. He stepped forward another few inches. "You have the upper hand, John Smith. So, you won't mind telling me a few things, like what's your real name, and who hired my father's killer?"

"If I knew, I would tell you. I rather liked your ol' man. It wasn't my employer—in comparison, we are the good guys. Not to say they don't have their shortcomings. They pay well and think they have America's best interest at heart." He paused, and his voice became almost inaudible. "They don't harm innocent mothers-to-be—"

"What did you say?"

"They wouldn't have considered taking out the mind behind the product, unless—"

"Unless they knew they had all of the research."

Smith raised his eyebrows and said, "That's right. The guy who shot your father had some other objective. Or he was going after you."

"No, if he wanted to hit me, I'd be dead."

"That is curious. If it were me, I'd have taken you out. Eliminate future threats—basic protocol."

As Smith shifted his weight, his gun lowered slightly. Tremont lunged for the basketball trophy and launched it; Smith was unconscious before he hit the floor. Tremont stepped over his body and picked up the gun, a New Hampshire made SIG-Sauer model designed for the military and law enforcement. He checked the man for identification and, as expected, found nothing but a Government Express Mail name tag stating his name was John Smith. He dragged Smith's body into the dumbwaiter.

There was a chance Smith was not alone, so Tremont saluted the lab one last time and vaulted up the stairwell past the dummy lab and out onto the main floor. He went to his father's office and checked the security system, puzzled as to why it did not activate with all the intruders. There were many fail-safes from the front gate, along the driveway, and around the fencing, as well as triggers all the way to the porch surrounding the ranch. The first team into the compound had to have triggered alarms that relayed to private security companies in Chicago and Indianapolis, as well as his uncle's private firm in Atlanta. That they had covered all those contingencies, meant they were better than good.

Tremont went to the kitchen and pulled the large freezer away from the wall, revealing the dumbwaiter. He punched 5-2-2-5 (J-A-C-K) in the keypad, and the machine came to the main floor. Readying the .45 SIG, Tremont opened the dumbwaiter. Smith sprung like a cheetah, pushing Tremont against the butcher-block table. He tried to roll free, but Smith had him in a bear hug. He kicked out Smith's feet, and they both crashed to the floor. Tremont brought a knee up into Smith's groin, who let out a howl and released his grip. Tremont dove for the .45 SIG just as Smith recovered and pounced on top of him. Tremont swung the butt of the handgun, striking Smith with a bone-crushing blow on his already bruised temple. Smith went slack once again. He turned on the cold water and splashed his face while keeping his body at an angle to ensure Smith was out for the count this time.

Surprised the man was still breathing, Tremont took out two extension cords from the utility closet and bound Smith's hands behind his back, then tied his legs to his hands. He dragged him out onto the porch where Brutus whined quietly. Popeye was still out cold. He surveyed the property before returning to the kitchen to retrieve the duffel bags. When he returned, Brutus was growling at Smith.

"Keep an eye on our friend here, will you?" He knelt and scratched behind Popeye's ears, and he stirred. "Time to wake up, boy."

He went back to his father's wall of security in the rich, mahogany-walled study. Picking up a business card on the desk, he thought of the disheveled agent who would visit Jackson's Place with three or four FBI security technicians. Tremont was glad Flannigan was at the funeral. He had a lot of questions to answer.

It took him twenty minutes or more to type his way into his father's encrypted computer. After entering his username, password, and answers to some random questions, he typed "Jules Verne Is Dead" and touched the enter key. The screen went black. Tremont thought he made a typographical error, but the server was still humming, so he waited. And waited. Finally, a pop-up screen opened, giving him instructions. Tremont stared at the screen, feeling a tightness in his throat. He opened another drawer which he knew held a few of his father's treasures. Right on top was the colorful ceramic flask.

Dad had this with him 24/7, he thought and wondered what it was doing here.

In the drawers, he discovered letters and keepsakes from his parents' wedding and the architectural drawings for Jackson's Place. He carefully placed it all in a black satchel. He held a picture with his father at the NCAA Final-Four basketball championship and then one of his grandparents. He smiled at the thought of all the happy summers with his father working on one invention or another, and afternoons on the beach with Popeye and Brutus. With one bullet, Sean ended all the plans he and his father had for CJ Energy. He pressed his face into his palms and took a deep breath. "I let you down, Dad. But I will finish this. I promise."

Tremont picked up the phone receiver in the hallway and touched one of three speed-dial numbers. It took a while to bounce from one exchange to another.

"Destin sailboats and wines."

"Zebo."

"I'm sorry, we don't have anyone here by that name."

"Leave the following message. All is secure. See you tomorrow."

He waited until the receptionist hung up and then he returned to the den, moved the computer mouse, and clicked the arrow over the word *YES*.

Outside Tremont went over to the Government Express truck. He searched all the obvious places and found nothing of value. Then he started checking the places he might hide something. "Voila," he said. Smith had cut the seat cover with his go-bag stuffed inside. Inside the black canvas bag were neat stacks of currency, two guns, and five passports with five identities—and a Dallas Cowboys season ticket holder card with the name John T. Lomax. Everything would come in handy and tomorrow he could have his uncle alter the IDs.

He stared at his prize Mustang and realized there was no way he could pack it with everything and the pups. For a long moment he stared sadly out back toward the National Seashore and thought of leaving Mr. Lomax. "Ha, leave no trace. Right?" He sighed and started loading everything into his father's burgundy SUV.

Tremont went back to his father's computer, logged into his secure DOD DIA site, and searched for John T. Lomax. Bingo. There was no shortage of information on the former Secret Service agent. In contrast to his uncle, a former CIA NOC, Mr. Lomax was a mercenary. A US government multi-million-dollar investment turned deadly gun for hire.[26]

Like Sean.

Out on the porch he knelt and stuffed the season ticket card in his pocket. "Hello, John Lomax." He pulled the body over to the edge of the deck stepped off and hefted the body over his shoulder, carried it to the back of the SUV, and loaded him inside.

Before he closed the sweet Mustang in the garage, he ran his hand over the black hood.

Back on the porch he reached up and unlatched the handmade sign, Jackson's Place. he gave a push to the two empty rocking chairs.

"Okay, let's go." He went down the steps and looked back. The dogs did not move. Tremont understood. "He's not coming back, boys. It's just you and me. Let's go." They whined but got up and trotted over to the SUV. Tremont slid into the driver's seat and sped out of the compound. He knew time was wasting, and every highway patrolman in Indiana would be scouring a two-hundred-mile radius beginning in—he looked at his watch—twenty-one minutes.

Once he was safely out of the gate, and fifteen miles south down I-65, he pulled

---

[26] Department of Defense (DOD). Defense Intelligence Agency (DIA). Non-Official Cover (NOC).

over onto the shoulder. He looked at his watch. *Twenty seconds.* He knew he should keep going, but—

He stood on the running board with his eyes drawn north. *Five seconds.* The sun had just set, and the sky to his north was dark save an orange hue bouncing off wisps of clouds … a white flash swept across the horizon. One, two, and three bursts before the sound of the explosions reached him.

Jackson's Place became history.

If only Matthew were ten years older.

"But there's plenty of time now, eh, boys?" he said to the dogs.

He walked to the back of the SUV and lifted Lomax out. He carried him into the woods next to the highway and laid him upright against an oak. He snapped open an army butterfly knife.

Driving past Indianapolis, he felt a wave of regret. He wanted to see his grandparents one more time, but Sean's threat burned in his consciousness. He determined to trace Lomax and Sean back to the source. Remove the threat. Then … He whispered, "I'll take care of you, old friend—then your brother and I will get to work."

Given his father's notes and journals, it was clear that the threats, perhaps by Sean's employers, started before his birth. His mother's death was in fact a murder. No wonder his father drank himself to sleep every night, Tremont thought bitterly. He must have felt helpless to avenge her death, especially with the threat constantly looming that his only son would be next.

He felt contempt for the FBI. No wonder Agent Flannigan offered to help over the years. Guilt. He slammed both hands on the steering wheel, waking the dogs. "It's okay, boys." But it wasn't okay. His father protected him from the facts, and he had been living in an illusion all his years.

Persuaded by Senator Carson, the police begrudgingly opened a file in homicide, though there was no proof and no motive that they would understand. After only a few months, without further evidence, her death fell into the cold case files. Evidence was accruing; whoever employed Sean was responsible for his parents' deaths.

He looked at his white knuckles on the steering wheel and took a deep breath, stretching out his fingers. Somehow, he had to keep a clear mind; there was much to do. Once he settled into a safe house here or abroad, he would contact anyone and everyone who had contact with his father, like Flannigan. There were quite a few unfamiliar names in the journals, like Tom Muncie, and an admiral living in Groton, Connecticut. There were a few that he was quite familiar with, like Paul Hessen at MIT and his father's Fraternal Brothers, Sergio, Randall and Dimitri. Perhaps they could help to fill in some of the blanks.

Tremont figured he had made this trip a dozen times. Tears welled up in his eyes as they sped due south, down I-65 toward Destin.

PART IV

PERPETUAL Convergence

Chapter Twenty-Four

Purpose

THINKING THE DAY would be like any other, Flannigan arrived before sunrise at the J. Edgar Hoover FBI Headquarters on Pennsylvania Avenue. He went through security checkpoints as he had thousands of times over his thirty-year Bureau career. Flannigan wore a frayed brown tweed coat, a faded white shirt, and thin black tie. His boss often said that he could have passed for a homeless man on the streets of DC.

He had the third highest position in the Intelligence Division which grandfathered him in as the most senior agent in the Bureau because he had been hired well before engagement of the 30-year mandatory retirement. Tenure was the only thing that saved him each time he went against the system, as he had done a dozen times since taking on the Jackson years past.

It was the only file he had not solved or closed.

In his corner office, a view of the Hard Rock Café was out one window, and the corner of 10th and E Street was out the other. He hung up his coat, flung his leather shoulder bag onto the chair, and went to start coffee in the break room.

When he got back to his office he studied a bear of a man dressed in what he knew to be black Sunday going-to-meeting attire. The man was sitting in Flannigan's chair flipping through a stack of his files. Flannigan didn't try to stop him. Instead, he stepped out of the office. When he returned, he had the whole coffee pot. "How the hell did you get in here?" Flannigan said with mocking anger. "I thought Harrington put a restraining order on you,".

"Nice to see you too." They both laughed and former Agent Colin Jester, continued, "He did get a restraining order, but I think that expired a few years back. Judging by the look he gave me this morning, he hasn't forgotten our last altercation after they shot Cameron, so I won't be here long. I'm sure he'll come up with a few new allegations to get my black ass thrown back in jail."

Flannigan took an extra coffee cup off the filing cabinet and blew into it to remove the dust. He put the steaming cup of coffee in front of his friend and took a seat. They caught up on family, friends, lost loves, and divorces. They reminisced about their tour together in Korea where they were both Marine intelligence recon and had barely survived the Chosin Reservoir battle in sub-zero temperatures. Their small force had overcome six brigades of Chinese soldiers.

A few years later as a rookie FBI agent, Flannigan had received his first call from a paranoid scientist in Indiana with a crazy conspiracy theory.

Flannigan looked at the clock. Harrington would be in soon. "What's on your mind, Colin?"

His friend leaned forward, gripping the files. "You haven't given up on the Jackson affair." Flannigan did not reply. "This obsession is going to burry you." He growled. "You haven't taken my advice in twenty years, so I don't know why you'd start now ..."

Flannigan sat back in his chair.

Colin went on. "Your boy is back in Miami and attracting a lot of attention." He passed over a piece of paper with an address. "I'm not the only one who knows his whereabouts. There's a good chance of a hit going down, sooner than later."

"Shit. That's what I was afraid of. I'll head down there. It's the least I can do for botching things here and letting his parents get killed." He waved off Colin's objection. "Someone needs to protect his skinny Hoosier back."

"Any progress on his house going Hiroshima?"

"Nothing new." Which was not entirely true. Against his advice, Cameron had the house wired for destruction, a failsafe should the worst happen. Well, the worst happened.

"You think Harrington will let you set up shop in Miami? Officially?"

"Hell, no." He lowered his voice. "Cerraro is leading a joint task force with DEA. He's already got Tremont on ice."

"I don't want to know."

"So how do you like being a preacher? In a million years, I ..."

Colin got up and stretched. "Yeah, I know, but God can work through the most broken vessels. It's my calling, Patrick. When are you going to come over and visit my church, or for that matter, any church?"

"I don't want the place getting hit by lightning on my account."

Colin cursed when he saw the Director of the FBI heading their way. "Oh, I almost forgot. It's just a hunch. If you go down there, keep an eye out for a college kid named Matthew."

Flannigan turned to see the Director bearing down on them. Flannigan looked at the notes that Colin gave him earlier. "So, what's the scoop on this kid?"

"I'm not sure, but I saw the name Eaton on one of your file tabs. The kid is some sort of energy savant, Jackson's protégé."

How the hell could I have not known that? Flannigan thought. "Did you say Eaton?" He went over to the desk and shuffled through a stack of files.

"Could be a coincidence. And there's one more thing—"

"What the hell are you still doing here, Preacher? How the hell did you get past security?" John Harrington yelled from across the lobby; his face red and eyes wide with fury.

They both ignored Harrington. Flannigan asked Colin, "What else?"

"It seems that someone who is connected to the Jacksons has come back from the grave. You know anything about a guy by the name of Estebanez?"

"Estebanez?" Flannigan wrinkled his brow and feigned ignorance.

"Yeah."

"Wasn't that the name of the undercover agent who was poisoned by the ghost—Mikhailovich, I think that was his name, the KGB operative." None of that was accurate, but he did not know how much his friend knew, and Harrington had big ears. He was not sure this was the same man that he had met at Jackson's Place. What a twist it would be if it was—

"Could it be the same?"

"Doubt it. The one I'm thinking of has been dead for years. How did you get this information?"

"Do you remember Kelly Clawson—CIA guy?"

"He's got a reputation as a scary dude. Good thing was on our side."

"That's the one. He's a preacher, like me!" Colin said with a chuckle. "Proof there is a God. We are developing an inner-city mission in Brentwood. He said leaking a former NOC's whereabouts could get him killed—for real this time."

"So, Clawson is verifying this Estebanez' identity?"

"Are you two just going to stand there and ignore me?" Harrington had picked up a phone. "Security! Get your asses up to the sixth floor to escort *Pastor* Jester." He raised his voice. "Or I'll have every one of you on pre-school crosswalk duty before the week is out!"

Flannigan looked at the Miami address again and turned over the paper. He read the notes Clawson made. Zebo. "Well, I'll be damned."

"That's probable." the pastor said. "So, this Estebanez or Zebo flew from Destin to DC on a government owned jet the same day the sniper took out Dr. Jackson."

That was news, for sure, Flannigan thought. "You leveled Harrington, Ali style."

"I shouldn't have done that," Colin said, trying to look contrite.

They threw a couple of shadow punches and laughed as Harrington marched over to them.

"Let me see that paper, Flannigan!" Harrington growled, and Flannigan stuffed it in his mouth. Colin doubled over laughing. "Sorry, boss. I didn't have my donuts yet," Flannigan mumbled. "Coffee?"

Two security guards came charging off the elevator in a panic. They stopped, looking nervously between the decorated war hero and the furious Assistant Director. Harrington cursed and stormed to his office, muttering about Patrick Flannigan being the death of him.

The pastor put his arms around the shoulders of the two guards. As they walked toward the elevator, he asked, "Have you boys accepted Jesus Christ as your personal Savior?"

Flannigan took the damp piece of paper out of his mouth and tossed it into the trash. He recalled a friend of Cameron's, the same one with that expensive taste in wine who helped with security. There was also Tom Muncie, Cameron's friend from the Navy, the computer security wizard working in the nuclear missile bunkers in Colorado. Muncie. There's another Muncie he'd come across who worked with Bernie Madoff. Hmm. It's a common name. Muncie, Indiana.

He went back into his office to plan his trip to visit Cameron's elusive son. He shook his head. He'd known Tremont since he was born. It all started, that day. Flannigan would now save Tremont from himself, even if he had to drag him to DC in cuffs.

He rang Juan Cerraro's office on the fifth floor. "Juan. Would you and your team meet me in the seventh-floor conference room at nine? Thanks. What? I'm going to attach myself to your detail."

His office manager, who also should have retired a decade ago, dropped the *Washington Post* on his desk.

"Mildred, could you set up a flight to Miami—book the San Juan Hotel."

"You look like hell, Patrick." She returned to her desk.

Flannigan organized the worn files that the Pastor had spread out on the bureau. He reviewed each one as he had many times before. The labels read:

> Tremont C. Jackson, Senator Carson, Cameron T. Jackson, Senate Office Building August 1, 1989, Sean Eaton, Domenick DelGercio, Hafiz something or other, Bin Taliffan, John Lomax, Solar & Fuel Cells, James Seebert/ P7 / Illuminati?, The Fraternal Brothers of Energy, Dr. Paul Hessen.

He made a new file and labeled it *Muncie*, and another with the name Zebo. He made a call. "Mildred, will you do a complete search through all agencies and operations?" He spelled both names. "And look up Sean Eaton's family in Maine. See if he has any siblings and print out anything you can find." He took out a few new manila files and wrote on one, *Miami Beach 94/95*, and on the other *Matthew Eaton?*

He leaned back in his chair and looked at the ceiling. He thought about Colin—glad that he found his calling. But Flannigan gave up faith after everything he prayed for went to hell in a hand basket. He thought he found God in a foxhole, fighting against the Chinese. But that didn't last long. When he got home, he began blaming God for Korea, his first of four divorces, and everything else. "If you're up there," he said to the ceiling fan, "let's work together this time to keep the last of the Jacksons alive, then I'll retire." Or, just die, he decided. He stood and poured a cup of cold coffee. "Same difference."

He wished Tremont trusted him more, though his reservations were understandable. Tremont blamed him for not doing enough to prevent his mother's and his father's deaths. He would be right.

The call light blinked. He turned and pushed the green button next to the word Merlin. Mildred said, "The Director would like to see you in his office."

Flannigan cursed and tucked all the files back in a corrugated file box. "Here we go."

Chapter Twenty-Five

Converge
March 17, 1995
1:15 a.m.

"WHAT CAN WE DO TO HELP? Maria asked. "Matthew can assist you with the research, and I can organize a grassroots campaign."

"Maria keeps herself busy with plans to save the world."

"What's wrong with that?" Maria challenged.

Matthew raised his hands in surrender.

"What does the FBI want you to do?" Maria asked as Juanita cleared their plates.

"I don't know—maybe they hope to convince me that it would be better for everyone if I gave the technology to the U.S. government," Cracker Jack said. "They think they can protect me even after they failed in the past. My father thought that if we could get it in front of WCASE—"

"The World Council on Alternative Sources of Energy," Matthew interrupted.

"Right." His smile faded for only a moment. "Anyway, to bring things up to date, after the *last time* someone ransacked my Miami apartment, my landlord called the cops who called the FBI, who then moved in and is holding me hostage under a national security statute. My lawyers are on it."

"Has someone tried to kill you?" Maria asked.

"Kidnap or kill. Staying here makes me a sitting duck. They almost got me, twice. Last month, they stuffed me in the back of a black limo. Frick and Frack—" He pointed with his thumb over his shoulder toward the two agents sitting in the booth by the door. "They followed the car and got me out before I suffocated."

"Who were they?"

"Not sure. But one of the agents got a good look at one of them. I found him in mugshot book. They call him Cue Ball, a well-known mob captain, Vinnie Corelli.

He does contract work for the Gambino family. The thugs said they were helping a friend of my father's, and that it was for my own good."

"The Mafia!?" Maria exclaimed.

"The point is, if the FBI had not detained me, I wouldn't have ended up in that trunk. A week later two guys dragged me out of bed and I wound up on the floor of a speedboat, on my way to who knows where. The Coast Guard tried to stop the boat—it was a random drug smuggling checkpoint. When they would not stop, the Coast Guard shot over their hull with an M2HB .50 caliber Browning. The idiots shot back and still didn't stop. I dove into the water, and the Coast Guard fished me out. Everyone else on the vessel was killed."

"Who were they?" Matthew asked.

"They were Russian. Ever hear of Leonid Pankiv?"

"Sure," Matthew said, "He was head of the KGB and is now running for office."

"He's been obsessed with my father's work for many years. It's all in my father's journals—"

"You must have nine lives," Maria said. "Who else is after the research?"

"Besides P7 there's—"

"P7?" Maria asked.

Matthew explained, "They are a group of wealthy guys who think they are decedents of the Illuminati."

"Seriously!" Maria said.

Matthew chuckled. "I know, right?"

"In Turkey, it's called derin devlet, the deep state. A group of powerful individuals and security professionals working to control the government from within. It is difficult to prove its existence in a republic with all of our checks and balances, but—"

"But P7 could be the heart of the state within a state?" Maria asked.

Cracker Jack shrugged, and said, "I would worry more about Hafiz."

"Hafiz Islam Bitrūl Saumba Shokran." Matthew wondered why he rememebered that. "They are suspected of terrorism, right?"

"They use OPEC as cover. The CIA believes their mission is to eradicate any threat to their destiny. Alternative energy sources are top on their list."

"I have quite a few friends from that part of the world," Maria said, "but they also worry about extremism and fanaticism reaching America."

Cracker Jack nodded and said, "February 26, 1993. I had a lot of friends in the World Trade Center. It could happen again. It will happen again. Maybe not in New York City, but we have thousands of vulnerable points of entry."

"Can they prove that this Hafiz group was involved?"

"The FBI and CIA followed the money back to an Austrian bank. The same bank used by the current leader of Hafiz: Bahir bin Taliffan. That's the best they could do.

The Taliffan's are experts in covering their tracks. More than thirty energy scientists since 1972 have died in peculiar ways without a shred of evidence."

"I've heard of Bahir bin Taliffan. I read that he's related to bin Laden," Matthew said.

"Their father's, now both dead, were first cousins and together built the Saudi infrastructure," Cracker Jack noted. "According to my father's journals, he first thought the culprits were related to the oil industry. It seems like now, every roach in the world is coming out of the woodwork. I don't know who—" He pursed his lips and said, "I'm getting ahead of my story."

Maria said, "You need help."

"Well, I've made it hard for the FBI to help me. Nobody knew where I was. I wanted it that way. My uncle told me—" He chose his words carefully. "Miami was safe. I don't know how they knew I was here."

"No offense, but you do stand out in a crowd," Maria said.

"I know, Barry Manilow, right?"

"Larry Bird," Matthew objected.

They laughed, and Maria asked, "Have you tried appealing to the press?"

Matthew said, "You're just advertising for trouble with the media."

Cracker Jack nodded. "The FBI kept close to my dad for years. A lot of good it did him."

Matthew's head hurt as images from his dreams flashed in his mind; glass shattering, bullets flying, zoo animals, bats, pagodas, a German Shepherd ... He blinked and tried to concentrate on the son of one of the greatest scientists of this century.

Maria said, "They can't do any of this. This is not North Korea, or Iran! I'll go to Washington for you. We'll ... we'll ... I'll stage a protest!"

Cracker Jack and Matthew made eye contact and smiled.

"They can't do this," she said, louder. Matthew tried to put a hand on her arm, but she shook it off.

"There are powerful factions of business and those within our government that are tough adversaries." Cracker sat up and leaned forward. "Lobbies run by power brokers like James Seebert, head of P7, attempt to force the direction of our economy by controlling banks, the stock market, fossil fuels, transportation, education, and technology

"All the key components that make up our economy," Matthew said. "When they interfere, they make a mess of free enterprise economics."

"People like Seebert and Senator Green think that low-cost energy is a threat."

"Green. He heads the Energy Committee," Matthew said.

"This sounds like a conspiracy," Maria grumbled.

"A conspiracy is covert. These people operate out in the open. We want to believe that our vote matters, meanwhile they close deals in secret sessions that shape policy and the economy. Look how our government slowed IBM's growth through monopolization legislation in the '70s. The next thing you know, they'll be trying to break up Microsoft and Apple."

"Attempting to legislate a free market economy," Matthew said.

"Business law?"

"Last semester."

"How can you be so calm?" Maria was struggling to compose herself; her dark eyes ablaze, her olive skin tinged red.

Matthew loved that look.

Cracker Jack asked, "Did you know that every two years technology advances more than the previous decade?"

"The technological revolution," Matthew replied. "Someday I want to help change our antiquated energy systems—to convert everything to renewable energy."

"I know … I mean, I can tell."

I know? Matthew repeated in his head. He studied Cracker Jack. What's he hiding? "I've been working in a lab where we incorporate biotech advances with natural energy."

"Nanotechnology," Cracker Jack said, and smiled.

"Yes, ultimately the miniaturization of technology to the point of atoms and neutrons. Maybe it'll be my focus through undergraduate and perhaps a Ph.D. What I propose is to miniaturize current formats like solar energy cells. And then, like your father wrote, capture and store the energy."

Cracker Jack beamed. "If you only knew how close you are. By the time you finish graduate school, technology will be advancing so fast that what you buy today will be obsolete in six months. Dell decided that if he could make the computer the same day the consumer ordered it, he could keep the user up to date. Before Dell, the customer usually received obsolete equipment."

"I wish I met your father," Matthew said.

Cracker Jack winced.

"When did your father die?" Maria asked.

"He probably does not want to talk about it," Matthew said.

"It's okay. He was shot and killed in D.C. in 1989."

Maria caught her breath and said to Cracker Jack, "I think I do remember Matthew telling me something like that, but I didn't know it was the same man. I'm so sorry."

"Thank you," Cracker Jack said, clearly uncomfortable.

"Who would do such a thing? Same guys that threw you in the trunk and on the boat, I'll bet!" Maria said.

Matthew said, "It was just before Dr. Jackson was to present a breakthrough to the Congress and the Senate. Isn't that right?"

Maria interrupted and asked, "Why would they do this? What could they gain?"

"Fear, jealousy, greed, hate. And what would they gain? It's all about power and money." Whoever—" he paused and took a deep breath "—whoever ordered the hit was afraid of my father's discoveries.

"But who?" Matthew asked.

"I will find out."

"Is he telling you his version of Dr. Strangelove meets Ethan Hunt?" Said a voice behind Cracker Jack. "It's amazing what can be started in a basement, eh?"

"Don't you have a cartel to break up, rather than breaking my balls?" Cracker Jack said to the FBI agent, without looking up.

"That's the DEA. And don't you think you've said enough to these kids?" the man asked. "They really should get back to their spring break."

Cracker Jack looked at Matthew and Maria. "Pay no attention to the man behind the curtain."

Maria and Matthew chuckled nervously.

Frick or Frack continued, "I got a call from Flannigan. He'll be here tomorrow, something about moving you to a secure location near DC, so he can keep a closer eye on you." The agent yawned. "That man should have retired years ago, and I should be doing anything but babysitting you." He turned to go, then turned back, "Seriously, keep your head down. I'm going to catch forty winks. Ricardo and Hector are watching the street."

"Okay Agent Stevens, thanks," Cracker Jack said. "What would I do without my babysitters?"

Stevens put on thick black-rimmed glasses, folded his newspaper, and walked out of the diner.

"That's ... that's intense," Maria said.

Cracker Jack shrugged and continued as if there had been no interruption. "Is it hard for you to believe that this stored energy technology is already possible?"

"I'm too tired to think straight," Matthew said rubbing his eyes.

"When Stephen Jobs talked about producing personal computers, do you think anyone believed him? At that time, one computer took up entire buildings. My father miniaturized energy instead of information. When the time comes, your best bet for quick market penetration might be linking my dad's invention with the computer industry."

"My best bet?" Matthew queried, followed by a nervous chuckle.

"And why would anyone want to stop your father? Stop you?" she asked. "Just the conservation benefits would make it worth our government giving you its full support. Not to mention the reduction in greenhouse gasses!"

"They're scared. The last thing you want is to have the government subsidizing even one penny of your private enterprise. If they do, they'll own you."

This winding serendipitous approach to the story reminded Matthew of the way Mr. E would concoct their weekly riddles. It was as if Cracker Jack was feeding him clues to a puzzle. Matthew was usually on the other end of the game as he enjoyed dumbfounding his teachers. His fourth-grade teacher, Mrs. Michaud, had once ushered him to the Principal's office. The accusation? Plagiarism. She threatened a failing grade.

It was true. The very same work, word for word, was printed in the *New England Journal of Science* under the name Professor Digory Kirke.[27]

Later, Principal Lamm informed Mrs. Michaud that Matthew had submitted work to dozens of magazines under various pseudonyms including Peter Venkman and Ludwig Von Drake. He didn't believe that they would take a fourth grader seriously.

That game of *stump the teacher* had cost him, he remembered and smiled.

"Knock, knock," Maria said to Matthew.

"Sorry. You know, OPEC accounts for forty-three percent of the total crude oil produced in the world with the U.S. and Russia at 9 percent each."

"But," Maria interjected, "the U.S. consumes more than a quarter of all production. We waste more than our fair share!" Maria interjected.

Cracker Jack smiled, "Spoken like a true environmentalist."

"I don't know if that is a compliment or a jab, sir." Maria said with her classic left eye squint and lip purse.

Cracker Jack winked. "They accused my father of the same thing, so you are in good company."

Matthew said, "If one company or country controlled the low-cost energy source, economic power could shift."

"For anyone else to compete, it would take years of reverse engineering to replicate the formula my father has developed," Cracker Jack said.

"What is the formula?" Matthew asked, and immediately felt he had stepped in it.

"It's a fair question. Especially considering what I'm asking of you—of you both."

"Asking of us?" Maria said.

"The formula is the final piece to the puzzle, the prize inside the Cracker Jack box." Cracker Jack said with a wry smile.

Matthew frowned. "Why do you assume we'll get involved in all of … this?"

"I don't believe any encounter is chance."

Maria asked, "What's your angle?"

"My father believed that, in the wrong hands, his invention could lead to world war. Let's just say, for argument's sake, he was right. This invention is that important. The potential chaos isn't too hard to imagine. Is it?"

"It would be like one person controlling the air," Matthew said.

---

[27] Digory Kirke is a fictional professor from C.S. Lewis' *Chronicles of Narnia*.

"We've created a world dependent on fossil fuels. And that reliance is destroying our planet. My father warned politicians about the environmental ramifications as far back as the fifties. We've strained our electrical grids far more than their capacity. One glitch in one spot could shut down a whole region. It would cause chaos."

"I never thought of that," Maria said. "Have they listened?"

"Oh, they listen, but it will take a major incident for them to shell out the money to fix the infrastructure. It's the same for the terrorist threat. I call it the stop light syndrome."

Juanita refilled their coffee cups and winked at Cracker Jack.

"What's that?" Maria asked.

"A city will not put in a stoplight until one of two things happens. Either the traffic reaches a certain volume, or there are a certain number of accidents. It's the same with our water infrastructure. The EPA has warned cities like Newark that they need to invest in fixing their water supply infrastructure because drinking water has reached such dangerous contamination levels that no amount of chlorine can overcome it. Because of monetary objections from the city and state, the EPA extended their deadline by twenty years. So, when do you think the stoplight will be put in?"

"When people get sick and die," Maria said.

"Exactly."

This caused a quiet sober moment while they stirred their coffee.

"Imagine, once we go public with CJ Energy cells …"

"CJ Energy?" Matthew queried, and followed Cracker Jack's eyes as someone out on the sidewalk distracted him. He stared at his coffee while two men walked into the diner.

Matthew recognized the men. One had bumped into him earlier out on the sidewalk. Matthew had noticed them get into a vintage red and white Ford Thunderbird. Why were they still here?

They stopped to survey the diner. One man smiled and nodded, and then kept going, sitting at a table on the other end of the diner. The first man stared at Matthew and then fired a shot with his thumb and index finger before joining his companion at the table.

"What was that all about?" Maria whispered.

One of the other FBI agents, Ricardo or Hector, approached the two new diner customers. The first man reached for his wallet and handed the agent something.

"Do you think they are following you?" Maria asked.

"Possibly," Cracker Jack affirmed.

"Is all of your father's work patented?"

"Hundreds of patents and patent pending."

"Perpetual energy," Matthew noted.

"Technically, it's near perpetual, and that is not only possible, but we've done it over and over in our labs. That's the magic, kids. That's what people will kill for."

Cracker Jack glanced at the antique Coca-Cola clock on the wall and then to the men at the far end of the diner. "We'd better get going." He stood and stretched; his hands nearly touching the ceiling. "Marcos should have the rig and your bus ready."

Matthew wasn't sure he would be able to stand. He kept repeating to himself: *perpetual energy, perpetual energy, near perpetual energy.* He said, "A new power source is one thing, but a near perpetual source is quite another."

"That is what everyone had been telling my father for a long time. Ridiculing him, in fact."

"Great inventors suffer for their ideas," Matthew said. "And then they are labeled genius after they're long dead."

"Why do they call you Cracker Jack?" Maria asked.

"It goes back long before there was a snack food. Though we kept a twelve pack of boxes around the kitchen and lab at all times." He chuckled. "Dad even named the cell—"

"Cracker Jack cells?" Maria interjected.

"Something like that. He didn't tell me much about what he was doing, at first. I guess he figured the less I knew, the safer I'd be. But I read his notebooks while he was out and gained a good working knowledge by the time I was eight or nine."

Cracker Jack stepped behind the bar to pay the bill. He slid his hand to the small of Juanita's back and lifted her off the ground. He kissed her long and hard.

She looked surprised. *"Se sentía como—"* That felt like— Then asked, *"¿Es eso un beso de despedida?"* Is that a kiss goodbye?

He brushed his hand along her flawless oval face.

"I wonder what the story is behind their relationship. It seemed like farewell, rather than I'll see ya later," she said rhetorically. Matthew looked at the men at the back of the diner. The shorter of the two men smiled and saluted. The other man's back was to him.

At the counter, Cracker Jack said, "I'm staking a lot on you kids. This may be the last time I'll be able to see you for a while."

"Where will you go?" Maria asked.

"Most likely, I'll return to an island where my uncle is partners in some ancient buildings they renovated into vacation villas and a restaurant. When I'm sure it's safe, I'll contact you with the location. Don't write this down but remember the name Robyn Law, Elgol, and Ends of the Earth."

Matthew made a mental note.

Cracker Jack glanced over his shoulder. A man was walking toward the diner but stopped and went across the street where he lit up a cigarette. Marcos looked through the window, tapped his wrist, then raised his hands impatiently.

Cracker Jack went to the restroom. Matthew struggled to interpret Juanita and Maria as they broke into a lively conversation. Apparently, Cracker Jack had intervened when gang members tried to rob the diner. She said there were four of them and that Cracker Jack stood right up to them and asked the *matones* to leave. "One swung a stiletto," Juanita said, "and my Jack, he took the knife away—like a child's toy. Another one pointed a gun at him and he did the same. They all ran. Everyone in Miami Beach loved him for it. Because of the FBI, they think he is a mafia boss, but he's a very good man," Juanita said. She hugged Maria and turned away.

As Matthew and Maria pushed the front door open, they returned and nodded at the stone-faced FBI agents. Matthew leaned up against a lamppost and watched Marcos pace.

Marcos looked at Matthew, grimly, and shook his head. He opened the diner door and yelled, *"Vamos!"*

One of the agents said, "Where do you think you are going?"

Cracker Jack showed up moments later, walking out the door with the same easy gait as in the alley at midnight. If anything was amiss, you wouldn't know it.

"Like I said, the FBI is keeping a tight hold on me. In their words, there is a verified and imminent threat to my life. After the last two attempts ... It's not right that I'm placing you in danger," Cracker Jack said, "so you go with Marcos. He'll get you to your Uncle Carl's house, and I'll catch up. Don't worry, our fate can't be taken from us."

"It is a gift," Matthew said, finishing the Dante line.

Marcos appeared next to them in the doorway. *"Si, fate,"* Marcos mimicked. *"Si Dios quiere."*

Matthew frowned. He whispered to Maria, "I never said my Uncle Carl's name."

She replied, "We might have—when we first met him."

Cracker Jack smiled and turned away. Is it possible that Cracker Jack knew he was coming south?

Matthew kicked a pebble down the sidewalk. Once he got some sleep he could sort through the puzzle, and heck, there was plenty of time, wasn't there? Matthew saw Cracker Jack hand a set of keys and an envelope to Marcos and in Spanish say, *"Poner todo en el autobus. Ahora.* Put everything in the bus. Now.

"¿Todo?" Marcos asked incredulously.

"Everything." Cracker Jack said sternly.

"Absolutamente, mi amigo. ¡Tenga cuidado!"

"Cariño, I feel like we're in a James Bond movie," Maria said.

"I was thinking *Casablanca,*" Matthew quipped.

Cracker Jack joined them.

"I hope you don't regret driving into Miami Beach with your van."

"Bus," said Maria and Matthew in unison.

"Look," Matthew said, "Maria and I will talk this over. If we can help you, we will, though I can't imagine how. Is there somewhere I can call you when we get back to Maine?"

"I'll call you," Cracker Jack said. They all turned to see Marcos yelling from the wrecker down by the Shell station with the bus in tow.

"¡Vamos! amigos!" Marcos shouted. Matthew thought he seemed … frantic.

They were walking toward the Shell station when Maria blurted out what Matthew had been thinking—trying to rationalize a crazy set of circumstances. "We came here by accident. A few days ago, we weren't even planning to come to Florida. How do you know us?"

Cracker Jack appeared nervous, keyed up, like he was expecting something to jump out at them all from behind the palm trees.

"You're going to have to trust me. Bottom line, Matthew, I want you to take the project forward."

Matthew felt like the sky fell.

"You'll have to finish what we started, but you have help, I assure you."

"I'm in college. I can't see how I can help." Matthew kicked at the sand.

Maria grabbed his arm. "Matthew, we have to do what we can."

"If these people can get to Cracker Jack, what makes you think they won't track us down?" Matthew realized again the gravity of the situation. Maria was his responsibility, at least in their parent's eyes. Of course, if he said that out loud, Maria might knuckle punch him.

Maria turned to Cracker Jack. "We'll help you of course, but you have to level with us."

"I know you two, and I trust you." Cracker Jack put a hand on Matthew's shoulder. He said, "I've read the studies you did on energy management and sources of energy. Your hypotheses, theories, postulates, and even your conclusions were visionary. If I hadn't known it was your work, I would've thought my father wrote the papers. There are few in the entire world that compare. More importantly, Matthew, we know your heart and your character and … we need to entrust CJ Energy to you."

"Who's we?"

Cracker Jack turned away and walked over to the agents.

Matthew never thought of himself as a genius. Science came easily to him like an artist who effortlessly puts on paper what he sees, while others struggle with stick figures.

When Cracker Jack returned, Maria said, "He's kind of modest." She tweaked Matthew in the side. They began walking toward the Shell station.

"Also, a good trait; I can see you have something in you, Matthew, enough moxie to go all the way with something you believe in. Hell, you packed up and drove 1,800 miles just for the heck of it, right?"

"About that—" Matthew began.

Maria interjected, "Yeah. Why do I think maybe we didn't get to this place on our own?" "I had no choice. I needed your help," Cracker Jack said absentmindedly. He was looking down the street.

Did he just admit it, Matthew wondered? But admit what?

"Trust no one. Everything could be lost, and you could put all those around you in mortal danger."

"That seems a bit Macabre," Maria said.

"Perhaps. I told the FBI your parents are old friends. I think they bought it. I don't want them or anyone else to start trailing you. The idea is that you will be able to move the project forward without Big Brother looking over your shoulder."

Someone yelled, "Jackson, come over here, quick!"

Matthew sat down hard on the curb. The excitement, the danger, and the potential for his future were intoxicating, but at the same time his calculating mind was screaming, *this does not compute!*

"*¡Vamos!*" Marcos yelled from the wrecker. He cursed in Spanish and laid his head on his arms over the steering wheel.

Matthew noticed the FBI agents and Cracker Jack were in a heated discussion, and then said, "Do you see those guys—the ones across the road?

From the shadows of an alley across the street between the buildings, two other men had appeared out of nowhere.

"Now *those* guys do not look like FBI agents," Maria said.

Matthew noted that the men were out of the FBI agents' line of sight. He thought the one man looked like a pool table with a cue ball on top, while the other man had a full head of black oily hair and a skeletal face. They seemed nervous and agitated.

An eerie silence filled the night, broken by an occasional drunk, or a group of men stumbling out of one of the strip bars.

Cracker Jack hurried back to Matthew and Maria.

"What was that all about?" Matthew asked.

"They want me and you to wait for the agent I was telling you about. Flannigan. Look,"—he sat down on the curb— "one day you'll be ready to bring in your own mastermind group of techies and management, but until then, I or someone close to me will let you know when it's safe to go to market. Everything you do has to remain confidential. You'll have to be able to avoid direct questions from other scientists, the media, and,"—he pointed a long, bony finger back in the direction of the diner— "especially avoid government types."

Cracker Jack stood up and reaching for Matthew's hand, pulled him to his feet. He put one hand on each of their shoulders. "We'll talk soon, kid; everything will clear up, I promise."

He walked back toward the diner leaving Maria and Matthew dumfounded.

"A few hours ago," Maria said, "all I had to worry about was where I was going to buy a new bathing suit."

Marcos slammed the door of the wrecker and joined them on the corner.

Matthew noticed one of the men in the alley across the street reach under his coat behind his back and produce something in his hand. Matthew started to yell to Cracker Jack when Marcos pulled him by his arm.

"¡Por favor, Matthew!"

Matthew instinctively grabbed Maria's hand. In seconds, they were across the street and to the wrecker.

Marcos ushered them into the passenger side of the idling truck. He ran around to the driver's side, jumped his slight body in like a gymnast, slammed the door, and pulled forward before stopping between the set of gas pumps. Matthew looked toward the diner and noticed one agent holding his gun with both hands high alongside his cheek, while looking around the far side of the building. The other agent also had his gun drawn in one hand and the other reaching up to take Cracker Jack by the arm to lead him away. Cracker Jack threw his arm up out of the shorter man's grip.

Marcos snapped the manual transmission hard into first gear. It ground and grumbled and protested until it lurched forward. He turned back onto the street in the direction of the diner.

Marcos was leaning up and over the steering wheel to have a better view of both sides of the street. Matthew noticed that Cue Ball and his greasy partner had disappeared.

"¡Dios! ¡Dios mío!"

Chapter Twenty-Six

Flee
March 17, 1995
2:00 a.m.

A BRIEF TIME AGO, their greatest concern was college midterms. In a few hours, their lives had spun out of control with more danger and uncertainty than they could have imagined. Matthew thought of Cracker Jack back in front of the diner, dead or dying.

Marcos muttered under his breath, followed by a whisper, *"¡Si Dios quiere!"* He brushed tears from under his eyes.

They were twenty miles south of Miami before anyone spoke again.

Maria whispered to Matthew, "He was saying, 'We told him it was time to leave Miami, we told him, I told him.'"

"Who is 'we'?"

Matthew closed his eyes for the first time in thirty-six hours. He reminisced about spending time with Maria when she did visitation at the hospital or nursing home. When her father noted that an elderly person had not been to the restaurant, she tracked them down. She also worked with kids at an orphanage near Millinocket. The children loved her, and she knew how to get through to them when nobody else could. That reminded him of another friend, Penelope Thiourea, who he'd met during his Smithsonian competitions in DC. She too worked with disadvantaged children, along with her saintly mother, Annie. Her father, Andrew, was a real estate mogul. He would see them all again in October.

He opened his eyes, feeling a little guilty about mixing the two friends in his mind. He smiled as Maria consoled and interrogated Marcos. Matthew had no doubt that she would one day be a brilliant investigator—her dream job—though he cringed at the idea of her becoming a forensic pathologist. His very own Clarice Starling.

Maria handled the stress so well. Matthew was not really surprised.

Maria explained, "He and Cracker Jack became friends while Cracker Jack was in the FBI's custody. Cracker jack couldn't leave the peninsula, so Marcos made trips for him, passing messages to contacts and getting him the things he needed for his research."

She turned to Marcos again. "Shouldn't we call the police or the FBI or someone?"

"*No, senora. He would not want you to, como se dice, interfiera.* You must trust me. He told me *instrucciones muy especificas.*"

"You warned him. So, you knew something like this might happen?" Matthew said and wondered about Marcos' unusual English. Even *Spanglish* would not describe it.

"Si." Marcos grew quiet again.

Marcos drove the truck and dangling VW bus into the parking lot of a roadside restaurant and gas station.

Inside, Matthew went to the restroom and threw water on his face. He looked in the mirror and swore it was a different person looking back—drawn and serious.

Matthew chose a table near the back wall. He thought of Sean and smiled. He reached up and twisted the bulb off on the hanging lamp over the table. He looked up at the wall clock and noted it was after two in the morning. Maria looked at him inquisitively.

"Something my brother taught me. Sit in a dark corner with your back against the wall. Do you realize that everything has happened in less than three hours?"

"It seems like weeks have gone by," Maria said.

From where they sat, they could see the Shell wrecker and the VW bus. "I wouldn't be surprised if we were followed." Matthew looked for the kitchen, a potential escape route.

After tacos, chips and dip, and draining a pot of thick coffee, they went outside to inspect their bus, which hung off the wrecker like a torn shirt on a clothesline. Matthew examined the bullet holes, one narrowly missing the gas tank.

Matthew climbed up into the driver's seat to get his knapsack and inspect the interior. Someone had folded the back seat down and the pile of their belongings that he had covered with old moving blankets seemed to have grown. Before he crawled into the back to investigate, he rummaged in the glove compartment for his driver's license and found a large manila envelope.

Matthew opened the envelope, and his eyes bulged. Inside were five rubber-banded stacks of twenty, fifty and hundred-dollar bills. There was something else. He reached to the bottom of the envelope and pulled out a leather-bound checkbook. The first line showed a deposit of one hundred thousand dollars. The opening date was January 2, 1990, under the name of Matthew Thaddeus Eaton with the Bank of Boston.

"What the—" Five years ago, Matthew considered.

Tremont Jackson had signed the deposit slip.

"Hey." Maria pulled herself up next to Matthew and looked over his shoulder. "Matthew! Where did you get that?"

"You thought I was holding out on you?"

She punched him in the shoulder. "Stop it. What's going on?"

"I truly don't know. It was in the glove compartment. We'll have to ask Marcos what he knows about this. I'm guessing plenty."

She took the checkbook from Matthew's hand and unfolded a letter clipped to the front inside cover. "That's a wicked bunch of money. It's a joint account with someone named Tremont Jackson. Was that Cracker Jack's name?"

Matthew nodded.

"All you have to do is sign next to Tremont's name, and you have full rights and privileges to the account. I don't understand."

Attached to the bank account letter was a handwritten sticky note. Maria read it aloud. *Matthew. Please take this cash to fix the VW, for traveling money, and to take care of my dad's stuff until we can get together to discuss the future.*

After he helped Maria down from the cab of the wrecker, he looked in the back seat and had an idea as to why their pile of belongings had grown.

The account is insurance in case something goes wrong here in Miami. My people will be in touch when this runs out. Best wishes. CJ

My people? Matthew thought. "I don't feel right taking his money."

He looked out the window and saw Marcos on the payphone in an animated conversation. He rubbed his temples, always remembering one of his crazy dreams when he felt this way; palm trees, a fight, a plane flying low, a dog, an explosion— and bats.

Matthew heard a raspy voice say, "You're a perky thing. Now, why don't you follow old Bubba and check out my Peterbilt deluxe sleeper cab?" Matthew looked out the door to find a hairy, shirtless bull of a man in overalls with his face within an inch of Maria's.

Matthew jumped out of the cab and took four quick strides and tapped the man on the shoulder.

"Beat it, buster, I'm busy," Bubba the trucker said.

Matthew pulled on the bull's shoulder. The man spun and swung. Matthew ducked but not before an anvil-like fist glanced off the side of his head. He heard Maria scream and saw flashing lights in front of his eyes.

Marcos said, "You okay?" Matthew nodded.

Marcos had come over with a gun pulled from his ankle holster. He slammed the larger man against the side of the bus with the barrel of the gun pressed firmly under his chin. Marcos said, "Matthew, take Maria over to the wrecker. Joe Redneck and I will have a little talk."

Matthew took Maria's hand and led her to the passenger side of the wrecker. "I'll go make sure Marcos doesn't need any help."

"Matthew, I don't think he needs help. Stay here. Please?"

A moment later, Marcos pulled himself into the wrecker.

"Thank you, Marcos," Maria said as they cruised out of the parking lot and back onto the highway.

"Yeah, thanks, Marcos," Matthew said. "He caught me off guard—"

"No problem," Marcos said.

The three of them were quiet for a while as Marcos picked up speed. Marcos was surely more than a gas station attendant and casual friend of Cracker Jack's, Matthew determined. He reached into his pocket for the silver pill case and hoped that Marcos would curb his lead foot, so they could make it to Uncle Carl's house in one piece. He voiced his concern.

"It's okay, *amigo. No problemo.*" Just hold on, and we get to *casa de Carl del tio muy rapido!*" Marcos was uncharactaristically talkative. "You know, chicos, I always wanted to be a race car driver like Mario Andretti."

"I can see that. You know, you can cut the Cuban fresh-off-the-boat act if you want to."

Marcos ignored him. "I decided that cars are not fast enough. So, now I fly planes."

Matthew knew from the growing pain caused by Maria's long fingernails digging into his forearm, that she was not enjoying the ride. He was afraid to close his eyes to let the pill take effect, though he needed to.

Maria gasped, "Marcos, there's a stop sign ahead."

The speedometer was pushing over 70 mph. Marcos was going on about *Top Gun,* when he slammed on the brakes and swung the wheel, a 90-degree turn. The VW bus nearly launched off from the back of the wrecker.

Marcos exclaimed in clear, unaccented English, "Why didn't you tell me about that stop sign?"

Marcos spoke about his life in Cuba before his family tried to escape from Cuba on a small sailboat. He was nine. Despite himself, Matthew believed this part of the story.

"Is your last name Estebanez?" Matthew asked.

"Estefan, Estefan." He looked irritated but didn't miss a beat and explained that his father, Jose Estefan, had fallen out of grace with Fidel Castro by voicing his opinion one too many times in public. "My father heard a rumor that Castro was going to confiscate all of his bank accounts, so he transferred all of his money one day and escaped the next with as much as he could carry.

"So, he died in the storm."

"*Si Maria,* along with *mia madre, hermano y dos hermanas.* I was saved by the Coast Guard and adopted by an aunt living in Miami."

Matthew wanted to tell Marcos to cut the Spanglish crap but also wanted to find out more about him. Marcos was fabricating some parts of the story and yet other parts rang true. Sean often said that there's truth in misinformation.

Marcos put the brakes on playing Daytona 500 and Matthew fell asleep. He dreamed about Cracker Jack and the agents falling to the ground; then he was in what looked like a morgue with someone on the autopsy table; then he and Maria were out in a boat in a hurricane; and then … he recognized the girl on the table.

Chapter Twenty-Seven

Arrive
March 17, 1995
3:00 A.M.

THEY ARRIVED AT UNCLE CARL'S HOUSE. Carl Eaton stood at the corner of two large garages—one attached to the house and one off to the right. Late model and specialty cars flanked Uncle Carl on every side. Marcos backed the tattered VW bus into the driveway, and the three exhausted travelers stepped out. Carl took Matthew's hand and pulled him in for hug, shoulder to shoulder.

"So, Matthew's description was an understatement," Carl said to Maria.

"And what did he say?"

"That you were beautiful."

Carl gave her a hug and kissed her on the cheek. While they talked, Matthew led Marcos down the driveway and showed him the money.

"I dunno, I am as shocked as you must be," Marcos said, having completely dropped the *No hablo inglés* act.

"Then at least you can take some money for your trouble."

"No, I cannot accept."

"Can you tell me what happened back in Miami Beach?"

"I wish I could, Matthew but I have to go back and find out for myself."

"Will you call me?"

"Sure."

"Then … you will probably need my number."

"Oh, right, right."

"Are you going to go to the police when you get back?"

"Maybe."

Maria ran down the driveway as Marcos was stepping up into the wrecker. She pulled him down, threw her arms around his neck, and kissed him on the cheek.

"*Gracias por protegernos y por el paseo en rusa* Six Flags," She said, thanking him for protecting them, even though it had been a rollercoaster ride.

Marcos smiled and whispered something in Spanish to Maria, then turned and hugged Matthew like a brother.

"I'm sorry—" Matthew said, with a stutter. "I'm sorry about Cracker Jack. I don't know what else to say—"

"You two know how to make a grown man cry," Marcos said. "We'll be in touch."

As the wrecker sped down the street Matthew looked at the number Marcos had scrawled on the back of the gas receipt. It was the same number as on the side of the wrecker. He turned to see his uncle inspecting the bullet holes in the bus.

Carl led them inside. When they were alone, Maria asked, "Did it seem like Marcos knew your uncle?"

"Yes, and he was waiting for us in the driveway at three in the morning." Matthew scanned through everything that happened since his uncle's first call to him, inviting him to Miami. Puzzle pieces began to fall into place. That was months ago. He rubbed his chin and said aloud, "Damn."

"What?" Maria asked.

"I'm not sure. I'll be right back."

Matthew opened the passenger door of the VW and looked under the seat. Maria came over and quietly asked what he was looking for. He held up an express mail envelope.

"I completely forgot that you were supposed to deliver the envelope," Maria said.

"I know, but I think it was important."

"We can drop it off on the way back home, don't you think?"

"I suppose." And check on Cracker Jack. The thought of returning to the scene of the crime made him cringe.

After Maria turned back toward the house, Matthew tore open the envelope. His jaw dropped as he stared inside.

"It's empty?"

"Empty."

"When did Mr. E give that to you?" She asked, suspiciously.

Before he could think, Matthew said, "South of the Border."

"What? What else have you not told me, mister?"

"I'll explain—" He was about to call Mr. E when he glanced up to see the gray Cadillac down the street. He trotted toward the car and tried to open the front door. "Hey!" he yelled, hitting his palm against the tinted window.

The man who looked like Sarge on the *Gomer Pile show,* saluted with a finger and put the car in gear.

Fuming, Matthew picked up a rock and hurled it, hitting one of the taillights.

Matthew struggled to regain his composure and turned back toward the house. Maria was watching him, hands on her hips.

Carl told the boys that they would share a room for the night. Maria took her things to the unoccupied room, and Matthew laid a blanket on the couch.

After Carl had gone into his room, Maria came out to the sofa. She sat on the floor and put her head on Matthew's shoulder. "You okay?"

Matthew was glad she didn't mention the envelope and South of the Border. But he knew it would come up, sooner than later. "I'm fine. I just can't get out of my mind the pictures of Cracker Jack and the FBI agents covered in blood."

"I'm glad I didn't see that."

"I wonder if I could have done anything to help him. My mind is saying no, but my heart is saying that I should have tried."

"Marcos seemed powerless to do anything, and he obviously has so much more experience than we do. And after watching him handle Bubba, my guess is that he is something far more than a gas station attendant."

Matthew touched the fresh bruise on the side of his face.

She kissed him and crawled onto the couch. Matthew folded one arm to cradle her head and reached the other around her waist, holding her tight against him. Matthew dreamed about the Red Baron and Snoopy both flying Sopwith Camel biplanes, and about Cracker Jack standing at the diner with Uncle Carl, Nick St. Adams and … Matthew's father.

They awoke to the smell of bacon and eggs. Matthew studied the stared at the copper Spanish style tin ceiling tile while trying to make heads or tails out of his dreams. Maria opened her eyes and found herself staring into a pair of big blue eyes. She sat up quickly, buttoned her blouse and ruffled her hair. "Well, hello. You must be Kenneth." She stuck her hand out. "I'm Maria." Kenneth let out a high-pitched giggle and ran into the kitchen.

Matthew stretched, and sat up. "Trying to give the little one some education?"

Maria looked wide-eyed at Matthew. "I didn't mean to fall asleep. What will your family think of me?"

"That you are a hussy from the back woods of Maine that has taken advantage of their defenseless nephew." He put his arms around her.

She pulled away with a laugh and said, "I think I saw a big bottle of Scope in the bathroom, mister."

Bobby lumbered into the room while Matthew dressed. "So, you're the genius?" Bobby asked.

"What kind of genius breaks down in Miami Beach and has to be towed all the way to your house?"

"I saw your bus. 1968, right?"

"67. Are you sure you're only nine?"

Matthew freshened up, which included mouthwash. He joined Maria in the Florida room. Aunt Carol watched him tuck away two large servings and said, "I see the Eaton appetite is hereditary. They say it's because Mainer parents put an ax and a chainsaw in your cribs instead of a baseball and glove."

Maria nibbled on fresh fruit. "We've had two breakfasts since midnight. But you're right, Matthew could eat breakfast three times a day."

Carol said, "I was telling Carl how you two act like a married couple."

Both Matthew and Maria concentrated on their food.

Carl said, "Carol and I were only eighteen when we got hitched."

"He went off with the Air Force, and I barely saw him for the next eight years."

The phone rang, and Carl took it in the foyer. Matthew excused himself to go to the restroom and stepped into the hallway. He heard Carl say, "Yeah, safe and sound. Crazy shit, right?" He listened for a minute and then said, "One way or another. You get somewhere safe, you hear?" He listened again and said, "Yeah, I already called him."

Matthew slipped into the bathroom and turned on the water.

After breakfast, Uncle Carl and Matthew went out to assess the damage on the VW bus. Carl's three-car garage was set up like an auto shop. In the yard were various vintage cars in different stages of repair. He proudly showed off a blue 1958 Biscayne, a lime 1960 Dodge Pioneer, and a red 1952 Packard.

"I can see where Bobby gets his affinity for cars."

"It's a habit I picked up in Maine. Who do you think was my mentor?"

"Ha! Mr. Johnson? He was the one who taught Sean and I, but I didn't know he was that old."

"Hey. Thanks a lot." Carl put his fists up in a mock fighting stance.

Matthew ducked a punch and put his fists up as well.

"Quick reflexes."

While they examined the bus, Matthew asked Carl about his time in the military. Carl told him that a strained relationship with Matthew's grandfather and father was part of his motivation to join the Airforce. "I took to flying like a bird," he said. After eight years and 150 missions, he and Carol moved to Miami, where he bought a commercial plane. He spent the last decade flying cargo to and from Central America.

Matthew thought he was leaving something out. Something major.

Carl said he would still be flying, had guerrilla fighters in Nicaragua not shot him down in 1990—the back injury cut his flight hours in half. He continued to lease his cargo planes to other companies and bought into a hotel investment group.

Though parts of the story were undeniable due to comments that he had overheard his father say to his mother, Matthew was sure that Carl was no ordinary cargo pilot. That he never entirely left government employment.

Matthew said, "You're living the dream, right? Mr. Estebanez always says—"

"Estebanez?"

"He's my … tutor back in Millinocket. Anyhow, he said that the most successful people fail numerous times before making it to the top."

"Sounds like a smart guy."

"He is. One day I hope to take one of my energy inventions all the way to market. I don't want to invent it and let some other company gain all the benefits."

"Know your enemy."

"Determine their strategy."

"Learn what works and what doesn't." Carl chuckled and raised an eyebrow.

"Position yourself to outperform your enemy."

"Beat them before they beat you," Carl said, completing the paraphrase from Sun Tzu's *The Art of War*.

Matthew chuckled and said, "You sound like Mr. E."

"You know, your grandfather built ELF from a two-man sawmill into what it is today. Your father brought it into the twentieth century."

"Dad doesn't talk about it all very much."

"Don't be too hard on him. He went through a lot before you were born."

"The war," Matthew said, and Carl nodded.

"Mr. E says that many inventors never see the fruits of their genius …" Dr. Jackson was case in point, Matthew thought.

Carl said, "I have a feeling you'll find your path sooner rather than later."

Matthew wanted to ask about Cracker Jack, but he decided to wait.

They pushed the bus up on the lift. Carl made some notes, then motioned for Matthew to follow him. Without opening the doors, they climbed into a 1993 Porsche America Roadster Convertible. They zipped out of the driveway and flew up Highway-1 to Sam's Car Cemetery. Matthew was pleased to find that Sam had three beat-up late model VW buses to choose scraps from.

While they were walking across the junkyard, Matthew braced himself and asked, "Uncle Carl, why did you start calling me to come down here? What's really going on?"

"Is there a problem with me wanting to see my favorite nephew?" Carl gave Matthew a playful shove.

"No, it's just your timing."

"I know you kids are under a lot of stress. I've been shot at more times than I can count, in air and on land."

"I didn't tell you about the shooting."

"Seriously? Your machine looks like Swiss cheese."

Matthew wasn't satisfied. His uncle answered every question with a question. Just as Cracker Jack had, at first. Matthew had been a victim of that technique from Sean and Mr. E. He changed direction. "Had you heard of Estebanez before I mentioned him today? Do you know Marcos?"

"Who?"

"The tow truck driver?"

"His name tag said George."

"What about Estebanez?"

He shook his head.

Matthew took out a picture of Mr. E from his wallet—it was from the Smithsonian in D.C.

Carl looked up at the sky. I once knew a Juan Estebanez that ran imports between El Salvador and Miami until the DEA blew him out of the water."

DEA? Matthew tried to remember why his father had mentioned the DEA when he was talking about Carl. Matthew was very young. "So, how about Marcos—George?"

"Never saw him before today."

"What about a guy named Tremont Jackson? His father Cameron was a great scientist and inventor. He was murdered in D.C. back in 1989."

"I think I'd remember them, kid. Nope, didn't know the poor bastards. It sounds like your two scientists were mixed up with some pretty bad characters."

Poor bastards? How does he know the other one is dead? "If you can call the FBI bad characters, then I guess they were."

"The FBI?"

Matthew was angry that Carl was evasive—downright lying. They went back to surveying the junked VWs.

The only available parts were from an earlier model, but their salesman said they would line up just fine. Carl said, "Mr. Johnson would never have allowed us to put anything on an engine that wasn't the exact model and year. He would have said we were inviting disaster."

With the parts wedged in between them, they sped back to the house.

By midday, they had taken the engine apart and had it back together. "Mr. Johnson would be proud," Matthew said.

"He was quite a man. I spent many weekends in the old mechanic's shop. Does he still use that old sawmill barn, the one up against the mountain?"

"Yes!"

"There's some intense Micmac mojo up there."

"Pamola is alive and well," Matthew said.

"It messed with my mind when me and my brothers hiked through the burial grounds and the caves."

"Caves?"

"Oh, yeah. Next time you're up there, head west toward Moosehead Lake and Seboomook. You have to move the brush away along the ridges. But—" he chuckled— "be sure a bear didn't find it first! We walked right in on a half-ton mother and her cubs."

Matthew touched the scar and then the claw. Seboomook.

"Ah. I heard about that. You were lucky."

Matthew nodded and said, "Yeah, as I said, Pamola is alive and well. Trust me. And the barn is where Sean and I put the bus back together—the first time." Matthew thought about how Maria nearly passed out every time they drove over the dike between the lakes. Matthew got up in the front seat with Carl's boys and turned the key in the ignition. She turned over and began humming and backfiring.

"That's air escaping from the manifold. Air cooled engine shit. Hold on." He made a few adjustments. "Try again." The bus turned over and hummed.

"All right!" Matthew said. He took the boys for a spin around the neighborhood.

Over dinner, Matthew asked Carl what he planned to do after the hotel business.

"I don't know what I'll do next."

"Did you ever consider the FBI or maybe the DEA?"

Carl harrumphed and asked, "Why would you ask that?"

Matthew shrugged. "A lot of ex-military go into law enforcement ... and you're in Miami, the cartel's second home."

"You always did read too many spy books. No, I'm thinking, maybe I'll come up there to Maine and get in the lumber business with my big brother."

"You wouldn't last one Maine winter," Carol said.

"You got that right! Maybe you can move down here after college, and I can help you start your business. I can market the product for you, and we'll make millions. That is if your dad doesn't have you chopping down trees up in the Katahdin."

"I think he already knows that's not in my game plan. Not in Sean's either. I think that worries him."

"Sean won't be back, so your dad's going to be looking at you. Just like he did me." He chuckled but stopped when he saw that Matthew wasn't laughing. "Listen, kid. You are your own man. If you stick to what you're doing, and I think you should, you'll have your hands full. The problem with energy isn't going away anytime soon. Look at Venezuela. I fly down there twice a month. The government is unstable, yet we depend upon Latin America for twenty percent of our oil, ten percent from the Persian Gulf. The sooner you can get something viable into the market, the better, and I'm your man for international distribution."

How about near perpetual energy? Matthew thought. Or do you already know?

Carl, the boys, and Matthew gravitated back outside. Matthew and Maria played kickball with the boys and then carried their bags to the bus.

Carl opened the side door of the bus and placed a bag of sandwiches and snacks behind the seat. He lifted one of the heavy moving blankets. "What the hell is all of this, Matt? I thought you said you were packing light." He pulled out a large canvas duffel bag.

Before Matthew could protest, Carl set the heavy duffel bag on the cement driveway and slid the zipper from top to bottom. It was full of files, books, and tapes.

While Matthew examined the files, Carl flipped through a few engineering books and magazines. Matthew began to realize the gravity of what Cracker Jack was entrusting to him. He extracted a leather pouch containing two metal boxes that looked like computer drives, except much smaller than the ones he was familiar with. In the same pouch were three stacks of disks, each labeled and numbered; they were much larger and thicker than standard computer discs.

"What do you think, Matt?"

Too consumed to answer, Matthew examined the white papers attached by a rubber band around each video. He read one of the letters. It was blackmail.

Carl pulled the second duffel bag from the van. Upon examination, they found similar stacks of files, dated from 1970 to 1975. Matthew looked back at the first bag, and the dates on the files ranged from 1964 to 1969. In this bag, there were more computer hard drives in a leather pouch and a box of brown leather-bound books. *Journals!* Matthew's heart raced. He pulled one book dated October 1964 and flipped through the pages. He sat down hard on the pavement. The journals were proof that these bags contained the life work of Cameron Jackson. Cracker Jack's father.

"I don't know about you, Matt, but I think someone cleared out the man's entire office and labs in a flash. There's documentation here from his years at MIT, dating back to the mid-fifties. I'm no scientist, but I think you're carrying the man's life work. My guess is that your friend Cracker Jack stowed this—"

Matthew looked at him squarely. "I never mentioned the name, Cracker Jack."

"Sure you did, Matt. Back at the junkyard."

"No, I didn't." But, he thought, maybe I did.

Matthew let it go for the moment. Instead of arguing, he thought back to Miami Beach and the times he was away from the bus.

Do you suppose this is what they're after? The guys who were shooting at you?" Carl asked.

"I don't know. I just don't know." Matthew wondered if Marcos knew what the bags contained.

While Uncle Carl read, Matthew opened the third bag and marveled at a dozen carefully wrapped ... G-scale model trains.[28] He recalled, there was an old man in Medway, a few miles from town, who had train sets running throughout his house. All the schools scheduled field trips to his home. He carefully replaced the one train. These were quite unique, and he was baffled as to their purpose. The fourth bag

---

[28] Originally the G in G-series comes from German word *Grob*, meaning *big*. They are much larger than the popular HO format (1:29 vs 1:87). "It's possible that Dr. Jackson went through a multitude of permutations to and a process of elimination to find a train sturdy enough to stress the energy cell with a certain level of current, ohms, voltage in relation to the degree and speed of energy drain. To date, I have not found a more suitable vehicle to measure consistent energy expenditure." –*RTS*, p. 114.

held several bulky items including a large hand painted sign, and something heavy, bulging out of a zipped pocket. He reached in and pulled out a black leather pouch. Tucked inside was a gun, bound in an oily leather wrap.

Carl delved into a stack of journals, so Matthew walked around the far side of the bus, opened the passenger side, and placed the pouch on the seat. He wasn't sure why, but he didn't want Carl or anyone else to see it. He unfolded the leather to find a beautiful, black Glock .45 ACP. Inscribed in gold were the initials CJ on each side of the grip. A side pocket of the pouch held four empty magazines and two boxes of ammunition. He stuffed the gun and ammo under the driver's seat. When he turned, Carl was standing behind him.

"What're you doing?" Carl asked.

"Looking for a map."

An uncomfortable pause ensued.

"If you insist on driving instead of flying, we have plenty of maps of Florida in the house." As they walked back to the duffle bags, Carl flipped through a leather book. "This is incredible—it's his journal from 1959."

"We should get all of this back on the bus," Matthew said looking nervously toward the house.

"Tell me, Matt, what are your plans? I mean, if I'm reading this right, you're the man for the job."

"What job?"

Carl hesitated. "I'm assuming … to work on whatever Jackson was working on. I've been reading up on your experiments and research. Your mom is quite proud of you. Well, hell, we all are." Carl flipped through a worn spiral notebook. "This is decades of work. Look here, this entry is from April 4, 1948, about solar-heating a house."

Matthew took the notebook from Carl and read. He smiled. "Dr. Jackson couldn't have been ten years old. I've read about these failed experiments in *Capturing the Sun*. This one was in Dover, Massachusetts. The next notable research was the next year in France where a man created a solar microwave—it only emanated fifty kilowatts, but it was a milestone."

A voice came from the house, and Matthew started loading the bags back in the bus.

Carl straightened the moving blankets over the duffels. "You're not going to show Maria?"

"Not yet."

Carl laughed. "Your funeral." Just as Carl slammed the doors shut, Maria came out of the house followed by two infatuated boys.

Maria, who was well versed in Arabic, German, French and Spanish, was teaching the boys a few words in each language. She had them under her spell. Who could resist her?

"She's pretty special," Carl said, and Matthew nodded.

"I have trouble with one language, let alone five."

Leaning in close to Matthew, Carl said, "If you're over your head, kid, let me know."

"Is there something more you want to tell me?"

Carl shook his head. "Nothing to tell."

"Right," Matthew said sarcastically. "I am just realizing how deep this all goes. But no worries, you've already done too much."

"You know, I could air cargo these to you in Maine. We could list them as grapefruit."

Carl examined a bullet lodged just inside the wheel well. He dug it out, and then another, with a pocket knife and flipped the bullets in his hand. "Thirty-eight and a nine. Looks like someone really didn't want you to leave Miami Beach. You know, I can have the whole damn bus sent up to you by truck and fly you two out of Miami."

Tempting, Matthew thought. He struggled with the promise he made to Cracker Jack, to keep the research safe and secret.

"Let me stew on everything between here and Maine," Matthew said. "I promise to give you a call when I roll back into campus."

"10-4." He slapped Matthew on the back and headed back toward the house.

Matthew was excited to get back to Maine and delve into his new-found treasures. He'd never admit it, but it was a bit overwhelming.

Maria came out, rolling her bag behind her. Matthew put her things in the back while she hugged the boy's goodbye.

Carl refused the money that Matthew offered, and said, "We're family, Matt. If you need anything, anything at all, give me a call. If I can't solve the problem, I'll find someone that can."

Matthew wondered who "someone" might be.

Matthew and Maria drove out of the Homestead area and back onto Highway-1, heading north. They were quiet for a while.

The events of the previous night were like a nightmare. Some parts, that he could not get a handle on, were from a recurring dream. When he opened the duffel bags, reality began to set in.

"What am I going to do?" he mumbled under his breath.

"What?" Maria asked, putting her hand on his shoulder.

"I just can't believe what we've been through these last twenty-four hours. Surreal."

"I think we should drive back to Miami Beach and see if anyone can tell us what happened or stop in to see the police."

Matthew was considering the same thing until his discovery. "What could we tell them? We met a guy named Cracker Jack … who the FBI had in protective custody … and was shot while we escaped in a tow truck."

"Sounds a bit incredible," Maria agreed.

Chapter Twenty-Eight

Chase
March 17, 1995
5:00 p.m.

THE WARM SALTY WIND was soothing, and the bus was purring. Maria slept in the passenger sea t, her head rested in the crook of her arm. Considering they were dodging bullets less than eighteen hours ago, things were going well.

He remembered the windmills and solar panels he drew as a kid. Then his brother gave him a copy of Cameron T. Jackson's *Capturing the Sun*. And now, with the priceless duffels, hidden under the moving blankets, he knew he would not have a moment of peace until they cleared Florida.

They merged onto I-95, and he saluted when he passed the signs for Miami Beach. An elderly woman driving an old minivan passed them like they were standing still. A BMW cut over three lanes and missed them by an inch. The driver honked as if Matthew did something wrong. "Idiot," Matthew said.

"What's that?" Maria asked, stretching, and rubbing her eyes.

"I thought Boston drivers were crazy."

"No, not that," she said, leaning forward, and pointing to the sky. "I mean that!" From his angle, Matthew couldn't see anything but a few wisps of clouds. Then it swooped down in front of him—the plane from his dream!

"We're in an *Indiana Jones* movie," Maria said. A few cars ahead of them, no higher than the palm trees, a WWI Sopwith Camel double-winged airplane complete with twin machine guns under the hump, was set on a collision course with the VW bus.

Maria screamed and covered her eyes with both hands as Matthew swung the wheel and careened off to the side of the highway. Something was hitting the bus, making it shudder. The windshield shattered, and glass spewed into the bus. He could see the pilot's wild eyes through leather goggles—the man was smiling.

Just as the propeller reached within a car's length of the bus, Matthew punched the accelerator to speed under the Sopwith. He heard a crash in the back of the bus.

Maria screamed, "What was that?"

"The engine!" When he looked ahead, the Sopwith had disappeared just as the bus began to lose speed. "I'll be a son of a … how did we get out from under him?"

"I don't know. I had my head down," Maria said as she shook glass out of her hair.

Without warning, he heard a sound like gravel kicking up on all sides of the vehicle. Matthew wished it were gravel. He saw the Sopwith in Maria's mirror. It must have circled around behind them. The plane looked unsteady, dipping its wings from left to right. Bullets whizzed through the bus between him and Maria and out the windowless front.

Matthew forced cars off the road as the bus bounded down an exit ramp into the Liberty Square projects area. At the bottom of the ramp, Matthew took a sharp left and cut under a bridge. The Sopwith Camel kept on his tail a couple of feet off the road.

"He's going to follow us under the bridge!" Maria screamed.

"This guy is nuts!" Matthew floored the accelerator. The entire bus sputtered and shook but kept right on going. He came out from under the bridge with the crazy pilot right behind, putting more bullets into the back of the bus. He turned right onto the first road, between a McDonald's and a BP. Matthew noticed many buildings, homes, and a line of palm trees off to the left. He thought he might be able to lose the plane. He also noticed a small ravine between neighborhoods, so he took a chance the bus's low frame would make it and shot through the field and down into the ravine. It was dry, and they bounced out like a super ball. They sped through some wire fencing, dragging it with them for a hundred yards with wooden posts and wire smacking up against both sides of the bus, then across a field, and finally onto a narrow dirt road. Matthew pulled over to the side and stopped to let the dust settle.

He looked over to Maria as she shook more glass from her hair. He said, "Well, you wanted to add a little excitement to our spring break. I was thinking we could stop in Orlando and swim with the sharks at Sea World for an encore."

"It's dolphins, not sharks," she grumbled.

They were in the middle of a palm tree-lined road, giving them good cover.

"He's not there. I think you lost him, Matt—" then she cried out.

"What? Do you see him?"

"No! It's your head."

Matthew touched his forehead, and blood covered his hand.

Maria dug into his overnight bag and pulled out a shirt. "No, not that one," Matthew protested, "Use the Boston crew shirt."

"You're bleeding, and you're concerned about your precious t-shirts?" Not

finding the Boston shirt, she pulled out another one, which Matthew begrudgingly approved: Harvard Rugby, Ivy League Champions 1979.

"Sean never liked that shirt. Plus, the blood will make a good story."

Maria tried to dab at the wound, and Matthew winced. "We're lost." The thermostat was blinking red, and the engine was sputtering. He looked down a sandy, dead end street. There were a dozen unkempt houses, most of which looked abandoned with grassy front yards and no cars in the driveway.

His mind spun to come up with a plan, then he saw a German Shepherd slumbering on the front steps of a one-story, sun-bleached house. Somehow, he knew he had to turn into that driveway. He pulled up to the garage and sighed with relief. "This palm tree cover is great." On closer review, the house was in good condition, though the grass in the front yard was two feet high, and weeks of newspapers surrounded the mailbox. It all seemed strangely familiar.

"Maria, see if you can open the garage door." She jumped out. Matthew drove in, and they closed the door.

"We've been chased and shot at twice," Maria said. "What should we do?"

Matthew closed the garage door. He didn't know what to say.

"Okay, genius, what's next?" she said, more softly. "Police?"

Matthew tried the door and went into the house, Maria followed. In the kitchen, he lifted the receiver of the wall phone and checked for a dial tone. Dead.

He ran a finger through the thick dust on the counter. There were still dishes piled in the sink. Two Bunsen Burners sat on the counter connected to test tubes. He peered through the swinging door to the next toy infested room. Colorful kid's videos lined the wall behind the television.

Matthew tried the faucets of the sink in the kitchen. The pipes groaned as a stream of rusty water sputtered. He let the tap run as he tried the lights. Nothing. In the garage, he lit the pilot on the water heater. He was surprised that the utility companies had shut off the phone and electricity but not the gas. Imagining a CJ Energy Cell providing energy for everything in the house, he smiled. Matthew went to the bus for his bag when on second thought, he returned to recover the oily pouch he had stowed under the seat of the bus. He loaded fourteen rounds into a magazine, snapped it into place, and double checked the safety. Though his brother had taught him to remove the rounds daily, so they would not compress, he decided he would keep at least one magazine loaded and ready until they were safely home.

He turned off the water in the kitchen.

He could hear Maria exploring. "The water should be hot in an hour or so." He met her in the hallway where she was rummaging through a small closet. Holding gauze, tape, peroxide, she led him into the bathroom.

"Sit."

Matthew obeyed, perching on the edge of the tub. He looked in the mirror. "I think I liked it better with the dried blood."

He gathered blankets and pillows from one of the bedrooms. Judging by the stuffed animals and illustrated books, the child was barely school age. Maria took the blankets from his hands, carried them to the living room, and promptly fell asleep on the couch. Matthew scooted a pillow under her head before sitting on the floor to rest, just for a few minutes.

He woke to noises at the front door. It was dark outside. Slipping Jackson's .45 from under his pillow, he crawled to the window and looked out. He chuckled, "Oh, it's you."

As he opened the door, the black and tan German shepherd pushed her way into the house and ran into the kitchen. Matthew followed her and knelt. Through her coat, he could feel her ribs.

"Got left behind?" Matthew imagined the dog on the front steps day after day, waiting for her family to return. She had shocks of white on her feet, tail, under her chin, and two puffs just above her eyes turned in just enough to give her a sad look. She wagged her tail and licked his face. "Hey, I don't know where that tongue has been. Knock it off." Matthew retrieved some beef jerky and filled a bowl with water. The dog pushed past Matthew and lay down next to the couch.

Maria woke up nose-to-nose with the dog. She scratched the dog's ears and laughed.

"Who is this pretty boy?"

"It's a her, and I like Soledad."

"She doesn't look like a Soledad."

"What would you suggest?"

"What is it they call South Beach?" Maria asked.

"SoBe? I don't know if she looks like a SoBe. Maybe a SoHo. Well, we shouldn't name her. What do you think?"

"My mom always said, give a dog a name, own a dog." Matthew looked into the shepherd's sad brown eyes and thought of his last two dogs, Mr. Pibbs, a chow and pit bull mix, and his beloved bearded collie, Nuke.

After a long, hot shower, Matthew went out to check the engine. He made some adjustments, disengaged a bad cylinder, removed the spark plugs and solenoid, cleaned and replaced them. The engine continued to sputter and backfire as air was still escaping around the carburetor. He rummaged through the tool cabinet and smiled when he found it. What would life be without duct tape, he thought.

The dog trotted out and sniffed his pant leg. "You know," he said, "your master has left a serious collection of tools. Where I'm from, a guy wouldn't leave his tools or his dog." SoBe barked her agreement.

The engine was running, but it wobbled as if it might come unhinged from the engine block. "I'll have to get replacement parts right away, or she won't make it another hundred miles."

"That doesn't sound good. And what about the windshield?" Maria had stepped into the garage. "Are you talking to yourself again?"

"Nope. Talking to the dog."

"Why don't we go back to your Uncle's and fly home?"

"Do you know why they never listed a 0-60 mph time for this baby?" She shook her head. "The top speed was 59." He chuckled and continued taping the fuel line and valve cover. "I thought about heading to the airport, but—" Matthew thought of the research. "I've kind of gotten attached to it."

Maria rolled her eyes. "I know how you are with your toys, but this is serious, Matthew."

"We'll find a mechanic shop or junkyard in the next town." Matthew began to close the door when the shepherd slipped past him and let herself on the bus. SoBe lay down on top of one of the blanket-covered duffel bags and whined.

Maria's left eye narrowed as she pursed her lips. "Now you're in trouble, mister." She laughed and climbed into the passenger seat. "You two were meant for each other, but you can't keep her in the dorm. And I don't think your dad will be too pleased to have another dog at his house."

Matthew figured he would worry about the details later. They took SoBe and left behind their weathered sanctuary. After a few dead ends, they found Highway 7 and drove up the road into the small sunbaked town of Carol City. "One day," he said, "we'll have GPS in the car." He explained how Einstein's theory of relativity would lead to everyone having a personalized, handheld GPS devise one day.

She laughed and said, "If you say so, Einstein."

The sun was rising as they pulled into Paulo's Garage and Junkyard. Matthew stopped in front and opened his punctured back hatch.

A dark, short, middle-aged man with a name tag reading, Paulo, came up beside Matthew. Without waiting for an introduction, he began tinkering with the little engine. He reached in, pried out two large slugs, and stared pointedly at Matthew. Matthew could only shrug his shoulders as Paulo walked into his shop. Before Matthew could consider fleeing, Paulo returned and motioned for Matthew to drive the bus into the mechanic bay. Matthew exhaled a long breath.

Maria went to a nearby store and bought a leash and dog food. SoBe leaped out of the bus and followed her around the corner of the building. Maria nearly stumbled over a sleeping reddish hound dog. As soon as SoBe saw the junkyard dog, her ears lowered, she bared her teeth, and let out a menacing growl while positioning herself between Maria and the beast. "Easy now, SoBe," Maria said. The floppy-eared dog twitched. SoBe stopped growling and cocked her head as she trotted over for a sniff.

Her heart still racing, Maria said, "I don't think a hurricane could upset this old boy, huh, SoBe?" She filled up one of the dog dishes with water and the other with kibble. She filled up the hound dog's dish too.

Matthew felt guilty for using Cracker Jack's money. There was also the bank account to deal with in Boston. I don't even know what equipment I'll need to buy. He wondered if Dr. Jackson had completed at least one CJ Energy Cell that he could reverse engineer, or if the formulae would be enough. So many questions.

He turned to see Paulo running his hand over some bullet holes.

"*Se parece el queso Suizo.*" Matthew said. Paulo shook his head and turned to Maria. She laughed and said something to Paulo. Paulo nodded.

"He said someone could come to replace the windshield."

Matthew tried to ascertain if Paulo may have called the police. He did appear old school. Mind your own business and charge double the price. "*Cuanto dinero estima?*" He knew he could not go wrong with that question, as it was one of the slides in his seventh-grade Spanish class.

Paulo took out a calculator. "*Quinientos dolares, quizas, quizas mas.*" Matthew paid him and told Maria to tell him if it's more, they would settle before they left. On Paulo's recommendation they walked to Loma's Cafe for breakfast.

By the time they got back from consuming Spanish omelets, the bus had a new windshield. Maria went into the office while Matthew started the engine. It was wobble free!

Maria came out of the office followed by Paulo. "He says we don't owe him any more for the work," Maria said. Matthew gave Paulo another fifty dollars. That brought the first smile of the day to the little Columbian's sunbaked face, revealing a few gold-crowned teeth. "*Bueno, senor, bueno. Vayan con cuidado. Dallo con Dios.*"

"May God grant you safe travel," Maria translated.

"Got it," Matthew said. He felt a twinge of compassion for immigrants trying to learn a new language. Thanks to Maria's aunt's, and her mother, when he was little, he understood the gist of most conversations.

Paulo hugged Maria. Matthew was thinking how glad he was that he had trusted the mechanic—when he heard a car drive up. A white sedan, with SHERIFF stenciled in bright gold letters, blocked the VW bus. SoBe sat up in the front seat with her paws on the door and growled. A deputy wearing a smartly pressed tan uniform emerged and spoke to Paulo. "Maybe we misjudged Paulo," Matthew whispered out of the side of his mouth.

"I don't think so."

The deputy approached Matthew. "Your hippie van looks like it was on tour in Vietnam."

"Felt like it," Matthew said. Don't offer up information, his brother would tell him.

The deputy ran a finger into one hole and then another. "And how about the shattered windshield Paulo replaced? And, I'm sure there's a logical explanation for that bandage on your head?"

"It's a long story."

"Something to do with Miami Beach night before last? Or, there was a crazy pilot in the Sopwith Camel shooting up the highway last night. We pulled Vickers 303 Machine Gun slugs out of four cars." He turned to one of the larger holes in the side of the bus. "They make a hole, about that big."[29]

"Both," Matthew admitted, thinking of his dream with Snoopy and the Red Baron. "We got stuck in the middle of both situations."

"What's the chance of that. Did you report either one?"

Matthew shook his head and propped himself up against the bus. He cursed under his breath as he watched the gray Cadillac pass by, and Sergeant Carter saluted.

"Do you have something to hide?"

"No sir. We were just in the wrong place at the wrong time."

"Twice."

"Yes, sir."

The deputy squinted and tucked his thumbs into his holster belt.

Matthew told him most of the story. He left out anything to do with Cracker Jack. He was having a hard time believing that part, himself.

Deputy Alonso nodded and did not interrupt. And he was not taking out his handcuffs. A good sign.

"Do you mind if I look in your van?"

"Bus," Maria said.

"No. Sure, go ahead," Matthew said without confidence.

"Right. Bus." He opened the side door and SoBe barked and bared her teeth. The man smiled but stepped back just the same.

Alonso chuckled. "I know this dog from over on East 9th. What were you doing over there?"

Matthew explained and stopped short of admitting to breaking and entering.

"That's one of the worst crack cocaine neighborhoods in the area. She doesn't like me too much, he said, indicating SoBe. But it's good that you're taking her with you. She's been hanging around that old house since we arrested the owners."

"They are in jail?" Maria asked.

"Yeah, they were running a methamphetamine lab in the house."

The kitchen did look a lot like a chemistry lab, Matthew thought.

"What about the children?" Maria asked.

"Social services."

"Oh, that's terrible," Maria said, and Alonso nodded in agreement.

"We'd been watching the house, hell, the whole neighborhood for quite some time. You could not have picked a street in all of Dade County with more crime." He looked at Paulo and said, "Except maybe over in Miami Gardens—here in Carol City." Paulo agreed.

---

[29] First manufactured in 1910, the Sopwith Aviation Company built over 2,000 planes for Britain during WWI.

Matthew held his breath as the deputy picked up the moving blanket. He unzipped one of the duffel bags and took out a journal. Matthew looked over at Maria who could not see Alonso. The deputy put the journal back, zipped up the duffel. He moved to the back of the bus and opened the engine door. Then he moved to the driver's side door. Matthew sucked in another deep breath. The gun.

The radio in the deputy's cruiser blared. "Alonso, we have a 390 with a possible 417 on 42nd, are you close?"[30]

Alonso walked to his cruiser and reached through the window. He pulled out the mic and said, "Yeah, Jorge, I'm on my way."

"Captain said to let the kids in the VW go, with a warning. Says he'll explain later."

Alonso returned to the bus. "I don't know whether to arrest you two or give you a pat on the back and wish you better luck."

Matthew said, "So, you believe me?"

"I saw the Sopwith myself. We caught up to the nut after he flew under the bridge, which was either good flying or pure damn luck. About thirty cruisers chased him about fifty miles up the coast, and then he disappeared." He frowned. "He caused four accidents and one fatality—"

"Oh no!" Maria gasped.

From the looks of your Volkswagen bug—"

"Bus."

"Right. Right. Okay, I have to go. Be careful."

"Yes, sir, we will, sir," Matthew said.

Once back on the road, Maria said, "Someone else died because of that maniac. Why? Because we saw what happened to Cracker Jack? It makes no sense. We don't know anything, and we could not possibly have anything that they want."

Matthew turned and looked at the blankets covering the duffels.

---

[30] 390 is drunk and disorderly. A 417 indicates that the person might be armed.

Chapter Twenty-Nine

Cornered
March 18, 1995
6:00 p.m.

MATTHEW FOCUSED HIS ATTENTION on getting Maria safely back to Maine. He should have accepted his uncle's offer to fly. The highway was thick with spring breakers.

Maria shook her head and complained that it took all day for her hair to dry.

"What are you thinking about?"

Matthew shrugged his shoulders. Keeping something from Maria weighed a ton. He had a lot of friends but no one like her, his confidant. *In your life, you might be able to count on one hand, your true friends,* his father once said.

"I know you're worried. We're in this together, and we'll be just fine."

In this together, Matthew repeated in his head.

Matthew saw a sign for Daytona—30 miles—and an exit with a large truck stop. Maria went off to the restrooms while he filled the tank. He then went to the payphone and called the number he had for the twins. It was the right thing to do. Their aunt answered, told Matthew that he was irresponsible, and hung up. He visualized smashing a handset to pieces but set it gently back on the receiver.

He turned to see two black SUVs parked near the entrance to the bathrooms. Three grave looking men were standing around the vehicles. The kind you might see flanking a dignitary during a parade. Then two more men came out of the building.

Matthew picked up his pace toward the restrooms and sighed in relief when Maria appeared. They walked together to the bus.

As they drove out of the truck stop Matthew kept an eye on the men by the SUV through the rearview mirror. They seemed completely disengaged from the VW bus. Paranoia, he decided, yet, they seemed out of place.

Thirty miles later, Matthew turned off onto US Route 92, the Daytona Beach and Speedway exit.

"Donna and Darma?"

"No. Thank God. But, I have something to show you."

He pulled off into the huge Speedway parking area and pulled up under a tree. He met Maria by the side door, uncovered the duffels, and waved a hand like a magician uncovering the appearance of a rabbit.

"Where on earth did those things come from?"

"From Cracker Jack. I'm thinking that he had Marcos put them in the bus while we were in the diner."

"How long have you known these were here?" Not waiting for an answer, she added, "And when did you plan to let me in on the big secret?"

"At exit 261A."

"Don't be a smart-ass. What's in them?"

"A life of work."

"Cracker Jack's father," she said, matter-of-factly.

He nodded and shut the door. As they drove out of the parking lot and back onto I-95, he filled her in. "So really, Marcos, you, me, and Uncle Carl are the only ones who know anything about these."

"Nice of you to let me in on your secret," she muttered.

Ouch, he thought.

They drove in silence for a while. The next sign indicated 89 miles to Jacksonville.

"You should feel bad," she scolded.

"Did I say I felt bad?" He looked over at her raised eyebrows.

"Okay. I feel bad."

"So, this is why people are trying to kill us?"

She crawled into the back and unzipped the bag closest to her. They drove in silence for some time while Maria scanned through a few of the journals and diaries. He was glad he had put the pouch holding the gun, under the seat.

"This is a game-changer," she said, as she organized the bags with care and covered them with blankets.

SoBe crawled up on top of the blankets and lay with her head on her paws.

"Now I'll be seeing bad guys at every corner," Matthew said.

"We are seeing bad guys at every corner!"

"Maybe we should turn it over to the authorities."

"This is the chance of a lifetime."

"I know."

They drove in silence and then Maria said something in Spanish about the importance of honesty. "You can do this, can't you?"

"Yes," He said.

"Good!" She threw her arms around his neck as he struggled to keep the bus on the road.

"Let's get back home, so you can get busy saving the world."

Matthew looked one after another into each of the three mirrors. He had a feeling that the paranoia had just begun.

As they headed up the highway, Maria said, "I was sorry that you couldn't work with Cracker Jack, but now, in a macabre sort of way, you can. Tremont Jackson entrusted all this to you, well, it's beyond amazing."

"What about the danger? You heard Deputy Alonso. It's a miracle we're alive."

Maria stretched her arms. "We're alive because it's our destiny. They'll never find us in Millinocket."

Her confidence left him breathless. He liked that word, destiny. She snuggled up to him.

"I've known we were meant to be together since Willow Run," she said.

She rarely mentioned that day and never talked about her mother's death.

"I doubt I could be much help."

"But I feel like I can always talk to you about my research. You keep up with even the most challenging hypotheses."

"I fake it."

Matthew looked at her with raised eyebrows. They both laughed.

"You are always there for me," he said.

"And you, for me."

"Not to mention you make me laugh, and you motivate me when I'm feeling down," he added.

"If that's a proposal, the answer is yes, but you'll have to ask Papa first."

Matthew felt his face heat up.

She said, "You're the only one that understands my interest in forensics. I'm really going to need you when I hit organic chem."

"Ah, now I see the reason you keep me around. Who's going to help me?"

"You could teach the class."

"I hope you get into the internship in Augusta." Secretly, Matthew could not imagine his Maria working in a morgue, but he would never tell her that.

"I'd be the first freshman in the program. Calvin Haybrook is the medical examiner's cousin. He's been bringing Dr. Haybrook to Godello's for years. They love the Pulpo a la Gallega."

"For some reason the coroner loving slimy octopus makes sense."

"¡Oye! ¡Me encanta pulpo también!"

"Okay. Okay. You're first qualification for the profession. But I really had hoped you might still pursue linguistics. It's a gift." Matthew was overly optimistic. There was less chance of him having to smell formaldehyde.

"Well, thank you, kind sir. But it's just a hobby. Did I tell you, I've been learning Farsi from Marjan and Marzieh?"

"Yeah, Marjan told me. Is it much different from Arabic?"

"Completely. Farsi has French influences. Like, thank you is *Merci*."

"Well, Clarice, if … *when* you get into the program, can I opt out on visits to the morgue?" He noted her pout, took his hands off the wheel, and put them to his throat, making a choking sound, and then chuckled."

"Oh, my God, put your hands on the wheel! You are such a drama queen," she said, with a chuckle.

He laughed and said, "I read that the University just started building a molecular forensics lab."

"I know. Otherwise I would have to go to Cal State." She smiled at his shocked expression. "I'll focus my undergraduate studies on criminal psychology and minor in forensic science. I guess I'm not really interested in the medical angle as much as the way forensic investigation relates to the criminal mind."

Matthew grinned.

"What?"

"Nothing," he said, turning onto the exit ramp.

While they waited in the drive-thru for burgers, Matthew caught the eye of a man in a black suit, coming out of the restaurant. Matthew felt sure he was one of the guys he had seen at the Florida rest area. As he drove the VW out of the parking lot, he looked for the black SUVs which he had not mentioned to Maria, yet. He would keep watching his rearview mirror. If he saw them again, he would tell her. As he pulled out into the traffic he saw a white T-Bird with a red roof. "What's the chance of that?"

"What?"

"Look at that car."

"So?"

"It's not just any old car. Do you remember when we first broke down, and I mentioned a mint condition white T-Bird with a red roof that I'd also seen in South Carolina on the way down?"

"Was that before or after your temper tantrum?"

He grumbled. "After. Just before we met Cracker Jack. Anyhow, that's the car. The very same car."

"What makes you think so?"

"Trust me, it's the same."

He watched the T-Bird in his rearview mirror. He got a closer look at one of the two men. It could be one of the Middle Eastern men from the diner in Miami Beach. The T-Bird pulled into traffic a few cars behind them. He cursed. Further back, he could see one black SUV.

Maria studied the map. "We can be in Boston by three tomorrow if we drive all night."

"I'm beat. If I make it another eight hours, I'll be lucky."

"Want me to drive?"

"Sure, if you want to. Maybe we'll stop in little Mexico in South Carolina." As Matthew said it, the thought of Mr. E dragging him out of the shops. You have a lot of 'splainin to do, Mr. E. He frowned and listened to a rattle in the engine and worried. As instructed by Paulo, Matthew had tightened the loose bolts at the last rest stop and would do it again in a few hours.

Deputy Alonso's words rang in Matthew's head: *You have friends in high places.* Matthew said a quiet prayer. Then he thought, what friend was he referring to?

Matthew saw the blue lights coming up from behind just as he heard the siren. He shook his head in disbelief as he looked up and recognized the large green sign. "It can't be." He smacked both hands on the steering wheel, waking Maria.

"What is it?"

"Brunswick-freaking-Georgia! This is the same area we were stopped at on the way down."

"What's the chance of that?" Maria looked at her watch. "It's about the same time too. Wouldn't it be funny if it was—what did you call him?"

"Boss Hog." He maneuvered to the side of the highway. "And no, that would not be funny." The officer ran his hand along the side of the bus as he approached the driver side.

"I don't believe it," Matthew exclaimed.

Boss Hog first peered into the back seat and then over at Maria who waved half-heartedly. That familiar chewing tobacco odor surrounded Matthew's head, and like before, he felt nauseated.

"You hippies on your way back to Woodstock? Where's them twins, and where did-ja get the dog?"

"They decided to fly back, and SoBe's a stowaway."

"Can't say I blame them. And ya can never go wrong with a good hound dog."

Strangely, SoBe lay with her head on her paws without even a growl.

"Sounds like the twins got themselves some sense along with some sunburn." He turned and spat. "You didn't pick up a load of mari-ju-wana for all of your college buddies, did-ja?"

"No, sir." Matthew was going to say that he had seen on *60 Minutes*, a story about Georgia farmers who had converted their cotton and tobacco fields to cannabis.

Hog looked over Matthew's shoulder. Matthew held his breath. Hog said, "Whacha got under them there blankets?"

"Just our luggage and some research materials." Sean had said that Matthew might as well tell the truth, because he could not lie, even if his life depended on it.

"Mind if I take a look?" Boss Hog asked. Without waiting for an answer, he walked around the bus and let himself in through the side door.

Illegal search came to mind as Matthew watched Hog scratch SoBe under the jaw. To their surprise, she slid off, and Hog threw back the blankets and unzipped a couple of the duffel bags. "What did you say you were studying in school?"

"Physics, quantum physics," Matthew replied, and felt like the gun under his seat had caught fire.

As if Matthew had said *hunting and fishing*, Hog said, "That's good, that's good," and closed the side door.

Back at Matthew's window, Hog asked, "What've you done to your head?"

Matthew touched his scratches. "It's nothing. Just something I ran into down in Miami."

"Step out of the van, young fella. I want ya to look at something with me."

Matthew followed the Sheriff's deputy around the bus as he pointed out bullet holes one by one. "Now you want to explain to me what happened here and to your head?"

Matthew sighed. "We literally drove through two shootouts."

"Any other time I would say that's one of the wildest turkey tales I've heard in a long time." He wiped a drip of chew from his face. "But I reckon it could be true. From what I understand, there's a pile of crazy folks with guns down there. Bunch a Cubies runnin' them I-uh-talians and Jews back to New York."

Matthew had to overlook the prejudice and said, "I appreciate you understanding, Sheriff."

The deputy seemed to like the Sheriff tag. He hoisted his belt, but it disappeared again. "Well, son, truth be known, someone from the govuhnuh's office sent out a bulletin from the FBI explaining the whole thing and it said to keep an eye out for you. Since we was already acquainted—you might say—well, here we are."

"What did the bulletin say?"

"Police stuff, but it did mention a shootout in Miami Beach, probably had somethin' to do with drug runners, and a psychotic shooting up the highway.

"I can't see how the two situations are related. You?"

"Yes, sir. I mean no, sir. Just unlucky, I suppose."

"Like runnin' into me twice in one trip?"

He stared at Matthew, squinted, and then nodded to Maria. He touched his wide brimmed hat and said, "Ma'am." As he walked away he muttered, "Damndest thing I've seen in a month of Sundays."

Matthew got back into the bus, but Hog stopped and turned around. He came to the window, pointed with his thumb over his shoulder, and said, "You know those folks?"

Matthew craned his head to look past the deputy. He was pointing to the black

SUVs. "No, but if you don't mind, could you check on them? They've been driving like they're drunk."

"You got it, Dylan," Hog said and walked back to his cruiser.

"I wonder if he knows that Dylan was not at Woodstock," Maria said. "He lived near Yasgur's farm but was in England that week."

"I didn't know that. So, you're a Woodstock expert?"

"I wrote a paper on it. 500,000 in attendance, two died, two babies born, Rockefeller was governor and held back the National Guard when he got a call from Arlo Guthrie, one of his favorite singers, and Stewart Air Force base helped shuttle the bands while the townsfolk made signs saying Hippies Go Home."

"My Uncle Carl was there."

"Well, that was intense."

"Be that a lesson to ya, whippuh-snappuh," she said with a twang.

Matthew pulled back out onto I-95. As the black SUV started to follow, the deputy flagged the driver down and motioned it to pull over.

Once in South Carolina, near Charleston, the traffic thinned, and he did not see either vehicle. They drove into the massive parking lot of South of the Border, and Matthew saw him. "Sit tight, Maria, and keep the doors locked. I'll be right back."

"What is it?" When he didn't answer, she yelled through the closed window, "Be careful!"

Matthew approached the man who had waved to him at the side of the building. He raised his hands and said, "You have a lot of splainin' to do, Lucy."

"You're going to have to trust me, kid. We've been keeping an eye on you and—"

"We?" Matthew asked. "Is my life a script? Who is we? What's going on? What do you know about everything that happened in Miami? What's the deal with the empty express envelope? Who is Marcos? Do you know Cracker Jack? What about the guy in the Cadillac?"

"Whoa, slow down sport," Estebanez said. "We only have a few minutes, and things are going to be dicey for a while."

"Going to be?" Matthew's voice went up a pitch. "Going to be?"

"I've got your back."

"Answer my questions!"

Estebanez crossed his arms and Matthew turned it down a notch. "Please."

"All in good time, son."

"We've nearly been killed! Twice."

Estebanez looked away for a moment, clearly disturbed by this.

"So," Matthew said, "at least tell me, do you know the Jacksons? I don't—"

"They are coming," he said and nodded toward the black SUVs.

"Who are they?"

"I'll know more by the time you get home. Get back on the road. I'll take care of things here."

208 ఆ BRIAN HUEY

Matthew rubbed his face with both hands. "You've got to be kidding, Mr. E. What about the T-Bird?"

"T-Bird?"

"There were these two guys at the diner ... Cracker Jack seemed to—"

"Cracker Jack?"

"Now, don't tell me that you don't know ... his name is Tremont Jackson and—"

"Get back on the road, kid. Everything is going to work out fine from here on out. Trust me."

Matthew hated how lackadaisical Mr. E was acting. Pieces of the puzzle were flying around in his head like bats. Bats, he thought.

"You've attracted a lot of interest, including the FBI—"

"Yeah, how about an Agent Flannigan?" Matthew thought he detected a slight twitch when he mentioned the FBI agent. "How about ... have you heard of the Taliffan's? P7? And, and, and they shot two agents, along with Cracker Jack, I mean Tremont and ... and look at my bus! It's like Swiss Cheese!"

"You're killing me, kid. You've got to get on the road."

"Who do you work for?"

"I don't work for anyone, kid. Trust me."

"I'm having a hard time with that right now."

"Sorry, that's all I can tell you, Matty."

"That's not fair."

"When the time is right."

"Not good enough." The sirens jerked Matthew's attention away from Mr. E. When he looked back, Estebanez was inches away and grabbed Matthew from behind the neck and said, "Everything the Jacksons sacrificed hinges on your success. This is one of the few things I've done in my life that I really care about. Until I met you, I'd done a lousy job, and now Tremont—" He rubbed his eyes and cleared his throat. He let go of Matthew and stepped back.

The doors of the SUV's slammed. Men began heading in their direction. Estebanez took Matthew by the elbow and led him around the building as the sirens grew louder. State patrol cars rushed into the parking lot blocking the path of the men. Someone on a loudspeaker said, "Stay right where you are. Do not move." The man repeated it again and again.

Matthew choked out, "How did ... I mean, where did they ...?"

Estebanez took Matthew's arm firmly and said, "I need you to stay focused; keep your wits about you. Your training will kick in—don't worry."

Matthew wondered what training he was referring to; the month he spent at Quantico with Floyd; or all the training with Sean; or ... all that he had learned from Mr. E over the years. Or, all of it.

"We'll be in touch."

Estebanez gave him a firm push. Matthew made his way back to the bus, the long way around the buildings. Maria was not there, and SoBe was pawing at the window. He stood on the edge of panic. Then Maria, carrying two South of the Border bags, came running up behind him. Matthew had the bus in gear before she closed her door.

"I heard the police sirens and came looking for you. Where were you?"

"I'll tell you in a minute. We've got to get out of here!"

When they were a dozen or more miles up the road, and Matthew didn't see a single car in his mirrors, he said, "You're not going to believe who was there."

"Don't tell me, Mr. E, again?" She said, and Matthew nodded. She continued, "You still owe me an explanation about the envelope."

"I'm still confused about that."

"What did he say?"

Matthew thought of a line from one of his spy books, *You're on a need to know basis and, you don't need to know.* "I really don't know what he knows," Matthew said, truthfully. He did not appreciate Mr. E or anyone using him like a puppet. "I don't know—I mean, he didn't say anything that made any sense, or help to make any sense of it all."

"What do you mean? How is he involved?"

"It's confusing. But just as the SUVs show up, the cavalry comes. Mr. E was not surprised."

She shook her head in disbelief.

"Our best defense will be staying in busy traffic and crowded gas stations." He looked from the desolate tree-lined highway ahead and then in the rearview mirror at the empty road behind. At least they were in the clear. He hoped.

Chapter Thirty

Target
March 19, 1995

IT WAS EARLY MORNING in Vienna when John Lomax, tan and in excellent condition, accompanied Senator Green, fully gray and forty pounds heavier than their last trip from the airport to the OPEC building. Two soldiers escorted Lomax and the Senator into the building, the elevator, and the boardroom. The soldiers, both carrying American made A-4 rifles, took up positions outside the door. Lomax studied the new leader, Bahir bin Taliffan and the bearded man to his right who looked way too familiar.

Lomax scanned the roomful of angry faces. Back in the sixties, their members were visionaries—princes, sheiks, chieftains, and elderly statesmen. The seventies ushered in a conflict of ideas and ideals, but under the leadership of the moderate assistant secretary general, Sheik Mohammed bin Bandar, it remained focused on business, diplomacy, and politics. When the radicals got involved in the early 70's leading to the oil embargo of 1972, Lomax believed the US should have disavowed the non-sanctioned group.

After his service in Vietnam, DOD DIA, Lomax worked as a field agent for the FBI, and then as a Secret Service agent on the presidential detail. It was during his tenure with President Reagan, that he met Senator Green of Texas, and James Seebert, allegedly the leader of P7. Knights of the Round Table or not, Lomax had left the Secret Service and each month made more money than he made in a whole year. Funds arrive like clockwork into his Swiss account from another offshore account.

After Omar bin Taliffan had his uncle killed—Sheik Mohammed bin Bandar, the last moderate member of Hafiz—the new self-appointed leadership of the bin Taliffan brothers gravitated toward radical Islamic fundamentalism. Lomax was sure that Omar and his brothers were capitalists, not fundamentalists. They used the ideology and bin Laden's followers for their own personal gain. In turn, bin Laden used them to further his conquest of the infidels through jihad; however, the holy war had morphed from two armies lining up against each other to strapping bombs onto woman and children and sending them into a building or crowded mall.

A document smuggled out of 93 Obere Donaustrasse Street in 1990 and published by *The Guardian* revealed much about the elite Islamic society and indicted many prominent Middle Eastern families. One line established their mission: *To assure Islamic world dominance and the destruction of western influences.* The non-Muslim OPEC members like Venezuela, the country that initiated the cartel in 1960, along with OPEC and the royal Saudi family, denounced any involvement with any extremist behavior.

Lomax studied the men in the room, noting the menacing looks he received from the new young faces, men half the age of their predecessors. Coming here was a mistake, he considered. Omar bin Taliffan handpicked these men. A car bomb took Omar out last fall in London. CIA or British MI6? Possibly, Lomax thought. Or maybe it was OPEC, trying to weed their own garden. If so, it did not work. Omar's death lead to succession by his extreme younger brother, Bahir who had ties to al-Qaeda. He looked back down the table to Bahir's right. Damn, he thought. Shit. Cousin Osama. Here? He'd seen pictures of the thirty-eight-year-old militant, but he looked like a cleric today.[31]

Lomax did not think Bahir wanted to destroy the West; it was one of their largest customers. But why bring in al-Qaeda?

Senator Green fiddled impatiently with a pen and began to push his chair back. Lomax put a hand on his shoulder and whispered, "You don't want to interrupt Bahir while he's in private conversation with bin Laden.

"bin Laden?" The Senator swore under his breath repeatedly.

Lomax had a passable understanding of Arabic and listened as the young men discussed the fate of Tremont Jackson and the energy research. There was news about a possible Jackson confederate: a college student. Lomax's heart sank at the idea that Tremont might be dead. He thought of their confrontation in the lab and touched the scar on his head where Tremont had walloped him with a basketball trophy. He underestimated the kid. Kid? The highly decorated Special Ops Marine.

Bahir placed his hands on the marble boardroom table and leaned toward his chief lieutenant, the man closest to his left. "So, is it done?" he asked Mahmoud, his head of security and cousin.

"Do we have the research in our possession?" Bahir asked.

---

[31] Bahir's brothers, some born in Yemen and others in Saudi Arabia, schooled in the UK and United States, and many worked in the family construction business. Notably, Prince Ali bin Taliffan, his mother a daughter of the House of Saud, is a tenured professor of international studies at Harvard. bin Laden's father was married 22 times and had 54 children. Bahir's father had six wives and 60 children. Their fathers, both named Mohamed, are credited with building Saudi Arabia and many of the Emirates.

Mahmoud said, "We were not responsible for what happened to Tremont Jackson. We are still not sure of the whereabouts of the research."

"What happened to Tremont?" Lomax asked, excitedly.

"Not sure?" Bahir pounded the table.

"We are following a lead."

"I read your report," Bahir said with a growl. He stood and addressed the full boardroom. "It is preposterous that we can control the price of oil, eliminate competition, and support the largest Islamic freedom fighter networks in the world, but this research still eludes us. Now, am I to understand that we are chasing a boy up the eastern coast of the United States? Who is he?"

Mahmoud, a dangerous character, trained by the Saudi secret police, stood, and walked to the far wall. The projector came to life and broadcast a recent video taken of a young man and woman talking with Tremont Jackson.

"This was before the shooting," Mahmoud said. "The person on the left is Matthew Eaton; the girl in the middle is Maria Valdeorras, both are students at the University of Maine. There is a possible connection between Jackson and a former trained secret service operative. I think our American friends might know more about this?" He looked at Lomax, who shrugged. Mahmoud continued, "His name is Estebanez."

"Just Estebanez?"

"That's all we know, so far. Our cousin, Prince Ali attempted to gain information in northern Maine, in a town called Millinocket, but was attacked in the night. He will continue with his surveillance. Other than that, it is all conjecture."

Lomax knew Ali, an FBI person of interest with no criminal record. So, he thought, that's who went into Fazio's office before me. Lomax would have stumbled into Ali, had Estebanez not got to him first and smacked him with that bat. The word *shooting* kept ringing in his ears. God, I hope Tremont is okay.

To Mahmoud, Bahir said, "Please proceed, cousin."

"Ali and I were in the Mabahith[32] together. He's capable. He thinks he knows Estebanez. If it's the same man, then he is a ghost. Killed years ago, by a KGB agent. His CIA code name was Zebo; one of the most dangerous operatives in the field, along with the Wolf and Ivan Mikhailovich with the KGB and Israel Samuels with Mossad."

"They bleed the same as any man," bin Laden said, contemptuously.

"Ali has located a detective in Millinocket. Joe Fazio has been looking into this Estebanez. If Estebanez is Zebo and the one who hit Ali over the head … regardless who he is, he said he had a message for you."

"He did?" Bahir asked.

---

[32] Like the FBI, the Mabahith controlled domestic security and counter-intelligence. In Saudi Arabia, the General Intelligence Presidency resembles the CIA.

"He said to tell you that it was his town and next time he would be coming for us."

Lomax almost chuckled aloud.

"So, now he's a CIA spook and a comedian," Bahir said.

Mahmoud turned and glared at Lomax and the Senator. "Anything you would like to add, Mr. Smith? Senator? I find it hard to believe that you know nothing about this."

Lomax raised his hands and said, "I know about Estebanez. I'm sending one of my men, Domenic DelGercio, up there to keep an eye on things."

Mahmoud's eyes narrowed and said, "What do your friends James Seebert and the P7 know about this?"

Lomax shrugged.

Mahmoud continued, "It is even more interesting, Mr. Lomax, that the boy is Sean Eaton's brother." He crossed his arms in satisfaction.

The room hushed.

Again, Lomax was surprised. If there were a top ten most wanted list from Afghanistan to Baghdad, Sean Eaton would be public enemy number one. He leaned back and clasped his hands behind his Cowboys baseball cap. "Now that, my Mabahith friend, is interesting."

Senator Green leaned over and whispered, "Eaton, the Marine sniper?"

Lomax nodded.

"It's time to leave," the senator said.

bin Laden spoke. "I know Sean Eaton. *Majnūn fi lraas jundiin.*[33] We fought together near Kandahar. This is no coincidence."

Bahir interrupted them. "How could you not know this, Senator? How is Sean's brother involved in all of this? Is Eaton working with Estebanez?"

Senator Green shifted his weight. "I really don't know."

Lomax gave the Senator a long stare and said, "My guess is that when Sean is not on a mission. Sean works for Sean, your eminence."

The Senator cleared his throat and shuffled some papers. "We'll have to investigate this further when we return to the States. I don't mind telling you this is all going outside of what my constituents and I would deem appropriate. I do not wish to have anything more to do with your obsession with eliminating competition … You, you … you bring a terrorist into—"

"It is too late, Senator," Mahmoud said. "As we speak, we are all in a race to retrieve the research."

"Who do we have in the U.S.?" Bahir asked.

"Our very best." Mahmoud exhibited the hint of a grin.

---

[33] Depending upon the dialect, monikers for Sean translated to crazy or insane Marine, or soldier.

"Our cousins, Ahmed and Saleh? Ah, I should have known that was Ahmed charging my American Express. Tell me of their progress."

"They have followed Eaton into the Carolinas." Mahmoud's face showed his satisfaction. "It appears your friend DelGercio and his team are also in pursuit along with others, feasibly the FBI."

Lomax cursed under his breath. Perhaps he did not give Mahmoud enough credit.

Senator Green cursed and said, "Taliffan, this is unacceptable. If something happens to these young people, the FBI will be all over it. That would be detrimental to our relationship, not to mention it would compromise my position in the Senate."

Mahmoud responded, "We will clean up your mess. Saleh and Ahmed are most capable and well trained. You might remember, they were the two Cobra guards you met during your last meeting here."

"We agree on one thing. Letting the research fall into the wrong hands is not an option," Senator Green said. Lomax raised an eyebrow because many of the wrong hands were sitting at this table. It was time to leave.

Someone turned the lights up, and Bahir waved a dismissive hand at Lomax and the Senator. "Thank you for your visit." The doors opened, and two Cobra guards stood at attention.

Senator Green did not get up. He finally said, "You have gone too far, Prince Taliffan. I will have to report this to the Department of Justice."

John Lomax and bin Laden locked eyes. Lomax shuddered, but he kept his seat.

"We will reconsider our relationship, and if charges against you and your group are the result, then so be it!" the politician continued.

Lomax put a hand on the Senator's shoulder and said, "Wayne," but the Senator brushed it off.

The Senator raised his voice. "You have plainly admitted to conspiring with known terrorists!" He avoided bin Laden's eyes. "Are you mad? You have admitted to two of your agents chasing down U.S. citizens."

Mahmoud was now standing behind the Senator. He pulled a small gun from his robe and twisted a silencer onto the end while the politician talked.

Lomax clicked his tongue, slid his chair back and stepped away from the Senator. He had two choices: disarm Mahmoud and never leave this room alive, or let the cards fall as they may. The men closest to the assassin had already stood and moved toward the corners of the room.

The Senator appeared oblivious. Mahmoud placed the muzzle against the bottom of his neck under the occipital bone; Lomax knew this was to minimize bone and blood dispersal. With his other hand, Mahmoud threw a bag over the Senator's head and pulled the trigger. A small amount of blood splattered like a sunburst across the marble table.

Bahir looked disgusted. "Clean up this mess." He shifted his attention. "Mr. Smith?"

"This will be hard to explain. As for me, I wasn't here. This will not change the course for my associates or me." He paused and looked around the room. He knew his life was as fragile as a caterpillar under foot.

Tremont, dead? Wayne, dead. Lomax had to force his emotions in check. He continued, "I trust our arrangement has not changed? When we obtain Jackson's research, your people will assist in financing product development, and we will share equally in the profits."

His mouth twisted into a grin. "In the meantime, together we will continue to control prices and maintain the demand for both oil and whatever this is that Dr. Jackson discovered. Are we good?" Lomax stood, adjusted his baseball cap, and picked up his worn satchel. "I'll contact Sean when I get back and talk to him about the connection with his brother. I'm as perplexed as you are. And don't worry about DelGercio and his men, they will do what I tell them."

Bahir waved a hand in dismissal. Lomax did not look at either *bin*. The Cobra guards escorted him to the elevator. Lomax said, "I hear there's a high probability of rain." They did not respond. At the front of the lobby, the guards stopped, and Lomax stepped aside as the Wiener Rettung unit, Austrian EMTs, carried a gurney down the steps. Lomax held the door for them. He regretted losing the Senator on his watch.

If he hadn't played his cards right, there would be two gurneys headed for the basement.

After Lomax departed, Bahir turned his back to the group.

Bahir didn't look at the Senator's body when he asked Mahmoud, "You are sure our cousins didn't pull the trigger in Miami?"

"I am sure. They would not have hesitated if we had obtained the research, but no, we had nothing to do with the hit on this Jackson."

Bahir flipped through some notes. "I had a charge on March 14 to my American Express for 131,000 Riyal, that's 35,000 U.S. dollars. Calvin's Classic Cars?"

Mahmoud shrugged. Bahir shook his head. "Ahmed."

Mahmoud said, "He felt that a vintage car would seem less suspect. You know Ahmed."

Bahir turned to Osama and said, "Is this how you are training our family members?"

Bin Laden smiled and said, "As you know, cousin, Ahmed schooled at Princeton. Since then, he has had a propensity toward Western ideas. Insha'Allah. Saleh, he is a true soldier of Jihad." Everyone in the room repeated, insha'Allah.

"I must admit, their EKO Cobra training seemed paradoxical. Now I see where Allah's greater plan exceeds our earthly understanding."

Mahmoud said, "Ahmed keeps a collection of automobiles at his family home in Salzburg—" He stopped speaking when he realized he had interrupted. "My apologies, please continue."

After a pregnant pause, Osama said, "That is all. Saleh will keep Ahmed focused."

"And perhaps Ahmed will keep Saleh from doing something reckless," Bahir said.

Bahir turned to the Hafiz members, and lowered his voice, and his eyes seemed to turn to fire as he presented his benediction. "Allah is with us. Failure is not an option. Islam depends upon control of energy—all energy resources." He bowed slightly and said, *"Assalamu alaikum."* Peace be upon you.

Two women, wearing full black Niqab coverings, with only their eyes showing, began cleaning up the blood, while the two EMT's from the Wiener Rettung unit, nervously placed the Senator on the gurney and rolled him out of the room.

Chapter Thirty-One

Fail
March 19, 1995

"WHAT THE HELL HAPPENED?" Flannigan said as he paced at the far end of the seventh-floor FBI conference room. He frowned at the life-sized picture of J. Edgar Hoover staring back at him with disgust. What was left of the team of the Miami Beach detail sat either hunched down in their seats or leaned over the table, resigned to their failure.

Agent Sven Stevens said, "These kids showed up and—"

"I know what happened! And I've listened to excuses for the past—"

Stevens rubbed his eyes. By the looks of him, he could have played on the line in the NFL. He stammered, and said, "I'm s-s-sorry—I was up getting forty-winks—I should have—"

"Hold on, Patrick," said Juan Cerraro. "I sidelined my men to moonlight as Tremont Jackson bodyguards as a favor to you. The guys are still reeling, so go easy. Twenty-two raids and stings, and we have not lost an agent. In one night, we lose two."

"Ah, hell, I know," Flannigan said and threw a wad of paper at the wall. "Shit."

Cerraro put on his reading glasses and looked down at a file. "We know the kids are between Dillon, South Carolina, and Richmond, assuming they are still headed north. That's where we lost them." He looked over his glasses at the over-sized agent and asked, "Stevens, who's on the list of suspects?"

"From what we've gathered at the South of the Border, those kids are up against some heavy hitters," Agent Stevens said. "Someone has hired professionals."

"Could be NSA?" another agent suggested.

"No, these guys were all independent contractors, retired government security or mercenaries. We've tracked four black SUVs pursuing the VW bus. We got two of them, but the other two bypassed our trap."

"What trap?" Flannigan asked.

"We got an anonymous call," said Stevens.

"Zebo," Flannigan said.

"Who?" Cerraro asked; Flannigan waved him off, so he said, "Who else, Stevens?"

"We have identified two EKO Cobras."

"Two what?" Flannigan asked.

"Austrian antiterrorist soldiers," Stevens said.

"You are not going to believe the jacket on these two jokers," Cerraro said. "They are sons of the Yemen consulate to Austria. One schooled and boxed at Princeton, and the other attended the Saudi's war school until they kicked him out. He's suspected of running with al-Qaeda."

"What's their angle?" Flannigan asked.

Stevens interjected, "They are related to both bin Taliffan and bin Laden."

That drew a whistle and exclamations from everyone in the room.

"Bahir is twice the shithead his brother was. We need to take him out next, and Osama, while we're at it."

"Did we take out Omar?" Agent Diaz asked.

Cerraro answered, "Could have been MI6, but my bet is on Mossad. Anyway, that's above both our pay grades, let's stick to the situation at hand."

Stevens continued, "Everyone is after the same thing: whatever Tremont entrusted to the kids. We had the highway patrol stop them in Florida, but their passports came up clear. They're driving a late model T-Bird and claim they're road tripping to visit a cousin that teaches at Harvard."

"Bullshit!" Flannigan yelled. "That's too much of a coincidence."

"We agree," said Cerraro, "especially since they were in Miami Beach on the seventeenth. When Agent Alaron—" He paused at the mention of one of the two agents shot and killed while protecting Cracker Jack, "when Ricardo checked in, he said they parked near the Executive Clubs. He said he would kill to have that T-Bird in his driveway."

"Yeah," Stevens added, "you know how Ricardo is—how he—was."

"Bring them in for questioning. Austrian Cobras or Yemeni rattlesnakes, I'll get them to talk," Flannigan said.

"On what charge?" Cerraro asked.

"Jaywalking or picking their noses, I don't care!" Flannigan rolled up the sleeves of his wrinkled shirt. Turning to the wall, he said, "If anything happens to those kids—"

"Who were you talking about earlier? Zebo?"

"Estebanez," Flannigan said. He didn't want to cross this bridge yet. He was getting the idea that Jackson's friend, Tremont's godfather, was one in the same.

"Right, Estebanez. What's his status?"

"Don't know," Flannigan said. He ran his hands through his greying hair, and

his face softened. He said to Cerraro, "I'll go meet with Ricardo Alaron's wife and Hector Paya's parents."

Cerraro put his glasses on the table and lifted a hand. "I'll handle that, Patrick."

Ignoring his friend, Flannigan looked to Mildred and asked, "Get me a copy of their employee files?" Then looking at Cerraro, he added, "You wouldn't have had them there if it weren't for me. It's my responsibility."

"I'll go with you," Cerraro said.

Someone knocked and entered. "Fey," Cerraro said, "What do you have?"

"Here's the files on the men in Dillon at the Mexican place—"

"South of the Border," Stevens offered.

Cerraro read through the two pages of typed notes. "They were former secret service agents. We have them in custody in our Raleigh field office, detained on weapons charges, some registered, some not. So far, ballistics has not been able to link them to Miami Beach. We'll either have to let them go or risk this becoming an incident."

"What about the Sopwith Camel?" Agent Diaz asked.

"The what?" Flannigan asked.

Cerraro told him what he knew about the pilot firing at cars on the highway, killing one and injuring others. "Eaton would have been in the vicinity when that happened." He handed a page of notes to Flannigan.

After he read a few paragraphs he said, "Someone borrowed a plane that should be in a museum, shot up the highway, and then returned the plane to its hanger. Nobody saw the pilot. If it's related, then my name is Placido Domingo."

"Then, you were a good composer," Cerraro said, "because if you read further, you'll see that Deputy Alonso verified that a 1967 VW was in for repairs in Carol City, and there were .50 cal and 9mm bullet holes in the side of the bus."

"That's bizarre," Stevens said.

Flannigan began to pace again. "We can't afford the press picking this up. Wait twenty-four hours and let the guys in Charleston go, but find the other two SUVs."

Assistant Director Harrington burst into the boardroom. "What the hell is going on? Are you running a covert action behind my back again?" He waved a file. "I will bust you so far down, you'll be working at Dunkin' Donuts and wondering what happened to your pension—if I don't have you locked up instead. Two good men dead! With your name on their blood."

Flannigan started towards the Assistant Director. But Stevens pushed his chair back, stood up, and wrapped his arms around Flannigan. Only after Harrington made a quick exit did Stevens let go of his grip.

"I'm sorry, boss," Stevens said, "but I thought you were going to hit the AD."

Coughing up a storm, Flannigan patted Stevens on the shoulder. "You really should have been an NFL draft." He returned to the end of the room. "Let *me* worry about Harrington. You focus on finding the kids. Unless they changed vehicles, that van can't be too hard to find."

"True," Diaz said, "It looks like Kent State met Woodstock on wheels."

"I have no idea what that means, Diaz." Cerraro dismissed the rest of the team. When the last agent closed the door, they both leaned back in their chairs as Flannigan offered Cerraro a cigarette. After they lit up, Cerraro said, "This is a fine mess you've gotten me into this time, Ollie."

"It sure is, Stanley." They both took long drags on their Marlboros and, clearly not for the first time, blew smoke at the no smoking sign next to J. Edgar.

"Thanks, Juan."

"No problem. I want to get all these bastards as much as you do. They've been making us look like fools, we might as well be Laurel and Hardy."

Flannigan closed his eyes and thought about Tremont. His heart sank. Again.

"What's your take on the Austrian and Middle Eastern connection?" Flannigan asked.

"This is the State Department's or the CIA's area, but if these guys are in the USA, then it's our problem too. What do you know about this Hafiz group?" Cerraro asked.

"Just what I read in the papers," he said. "I think they use OPEC as a cover to coordinate terrorism and assassinations across the globe. My guy at spook central, says they killed their own Secretary General—Band-Aid or Bandar or something like that. If it were me, I'd send a few Sidewinders into their building and anywhere they sleep. That goes for Osama bin Laden too. If we don't stop him now, he'll be running al-Qaeda from a cave, and we'll never get him."

"We still use those heat-seeking Sidewinders?"

"They just came out with an updated version, the Aim 9X Sidewinder. That baby can find an ant in the middle of a parking lot."

"Those newspapers you read are keeping you well informed." Cerraro pulled out some black and white photographs and slid them over to Flannigan. "These are the two EKO Cobras with the T-Bird. They passed through customs in Miami two days ago. This morning we confirmed their ties to Prince Bahir bin Taliffan. They're cousins raised in Austria. Ahmed Jobrani Maher is just a cowboy wannabe, but he's the smart one. Saleh, the other one, is known in the Arab world as *koshrakan*—the shadow of death. He's insane. Saleh's trail has been difficult to follow. I wouldn't doubt he spent years in the Yemeni desert training with his Bedouin relatives—and bin Laden." Cerraro leaned on the back legs of his chair.

Flannigan put his head down. After just two hours of restless sleep, the call came in about Miami and he rushed to the office. He was going to fly down to see Tremont today. Karen and Cameron's deaths flashed like a digital sign in his head. He looked up. "Why?"

"Jackson's research must be in that van."

"That's what I was thinking. So, where the hell is the T-Bird now?"

"We lost track of it in North Carolina."

"The shooter?" Flannigan asked.

"Shooters. The waitress at the diner, Juanita Florez, was hysterical. She says that she saw these two," he tapped pictures in the file, "across the street before the shooting started."

Cerraro pushed over a file. Flannigan picked up the first picture of a wide-faced, bald-headed man. "Cue Ball?"

"Alfonse D'Amato, aka Cue Ball, just finished a nickel in Leavenworth." Cerraro added, "D'Amato is suspected to have been involved in at least ten mob-related hits over the last twenty years, but like Capone, all we could get him on was tax evasion."

"He was top dollar," Flannigan said, "put out an APB on Mr. D'Amato."

"No need. Cue Ball and Clayton—"

"Clayton the Carver? The sick bastard who finishes his contract by—"

"The same. Both demons are at the gates of hell. They were both crushed in their sedan while chasing the wrecker."

Flannigan picked up a stack of files and walked to the door. "Let's find those kids. Or we're going to have more funerals to attend."

Chapter Thirty-Two

Hide
March 19, 1995
3:00 a.m.

THE WEARY COUPLE looked for the green highway signs for a place to stop.

"There. Turners Crossroads," Maria exclaimed. The first sign indicated two hotels, the next showed one restaurant and the last featured two gas stations.

"Compared to the last five exits, Wilson is a booming town," Matthew said.

Both hotels had seen better days. Maria said, "Eeny-meeny-mini-mo, let's take the one with the picture of the funny-looking man drinking that oversized cup of coffee."

"Done. At least we can get coffee and eggs before we leave."

After parking, they dragged themselves up three flights of rusty wrought iron steps to their corner room. Maria went straight to the shower, and Matthew went back to the bus. He and SoBe walked around the entire building twice. Multiple pairs of shiny eyes stared at him from the dumpster and woods. SoBe pounced, and the feral felines scattered. Other than the night clerk and the cats, they could not be more alone. He returned to the room to find Maria on the bed, wrapped in a white towel. He smiled, sat down, kicked off his shoes, and lay his head on her lap.

"You should take a shower," she said.

"Maybe later."

"Now."

"That bad, huh?"

"That bad."

She laughed and pushed him away. He dropped his clothes at the door to the tiny bathroom. A roach, something you never see in Maine, ran across the floor. It was out of sight behind the toilet before he could do anything. If Maria had seen it he would have surely known about it.

When he came out, Maria was under the covers and fast asleep. Matthew removed Dr. Jackson's gun from his overnight bag and placed it under his pillow. Despite the roaches, the place was not half bad. Before long he was asleep.

Matthew woke and stared at the dirty ceiling, illuminated by streaks of sunlight emanating through tattered red curtains. His dreams were disturbing, and he tried to piece the fragmented images: the storm, a swarm of bats, his Micmac friend Kyle, Chief Tanner, Sean, and the last vision which caused him to wake up, Maria in a lab with dead bodies all around. A morgue. Looks like, he determined, it's something I'll have to accept.

SoBe's eyes followed Matthew as he slid out of bed and went to the sink where he rinsed with mouthwash. "I'm trainable," Matthew whispered to SoBe, "how about you?" He crawled back into bed and kissed Maria awake.

Maria went to the window and pushed open the curtains. He waited for Maria to go into the bathroom before retrieving the gun. A church bell rang.

In Cup O' Joe's they had opted out of the full breakfast, settling on coffee and prepackaged pastries.

"At least the cup-o-joe is hot," Maria said with a grin.

"The blue tinted eggs did me in."

As Matthew backed out of the parking space on the east side of the hotel, a gray U.S. government-tagged sedan pulled in on the west side. Two men exited the car and entered the manager's office.

Amused, a man in a gray Cadillac sipped his coffee and waited. He watched the kids pull into the parking lot, while the Crown Victoria pulled in on the other side. Two FBI agents bolted from the coffee shop and started the engine. The man in the Cadillac cut in front of them causing the sedan to hit the Caddy. He got out of the car, strutted over to the flustered young agents, and feigned a tirade.

He insisted that the local police come to write a report. When one of the young agents showed his FBI identification, the Cadillac owner said, "I don't care if you are J. Edgar Hoover's ghost! We'll wait."

After the city of Wilson police officer finished his report, and the angry agents raced out of the parking lot, the Cadillac owner approached the pay telephone next to the coffee shop and made two calls. He went in for a refill of what he thought was damn good coffee—thick and black; he ordered eggs which also turned out to be excellent. He was not in a hurry, figuring it would not be hard to catch up with the cavalcade. Though he had not seen the two black SUVs or the T-Bird for the past twelve hours, he figured they wouldn't be far behind. What a circus, he thought.

As soon as Matthew pulled off the highway at the border of North Carolina and Virginia, he realized his mistake. Construction signs dotted the desolate area. Besides a couple of trucks in the back-parking lot, his was the only passenger vehicle. Not a problem, he thought, I'll just keep going. He looked in the mirror and cursed. The white T-Bird was approaching. Matthew tried to accelerate, but his bus was toast against the 292-horsepower V-8 engine under the T-Bird's hood. The T-Bird swung wide around the bus and cut them off.

"Matthew!" Maria yelled.

Matthew stopped just short of ramming the antique. One of the two men from the diner smiled and waved. Matthew didn't know what to think, but he reached under the seat, lifted the snap on the leather pouch, and closed his hand around the butt of Jackson's gun. SoBe growled.

"Matthew, where did you get that?" Maria asked. "You're scaring me."

"Trust me, I don't want to have to use it. If anything happens to me, keep your head down, drive right through their car, and go for help. Don't stay here." He stepped out, with the engine running, and walked away from the bus with the gun held behind his back.

Both men were now out of the T-Bird. The man closest to him spoke first. "Mr. Eaton, we're sorry to stop you this way, but this—" He seemed to be struggling for the right word. "Charade? Yes, this charade has gone on long enough. We have had quite a time trying to get your attention. Fortunately, those who meant to do you harm, have been detained."

That's strange, Matthew thought, the man had a Germanic accent.

"We mean you no harm, Mr. Eaton. Allow my brother to inspect your Volkswagen, which I am sad to see has taken quite a beating since Miami. I want you to know, we had nothing to do with all of that." He reached his hand out to shake. "I am Ahmed."

Matthew did not take Ahmed's hand. The other man was moving toward the bus on Maria's side. SoBe barked a warning. "Please stop," Matthew said. "What are you looking for?" The man stopped, folded his arms and leaned on the hood. Matthew did not detect any firearms, but they could have them tucked behind their backs.

"An honest question deserves an honest answer. We believe you may have something of ours, that a new acquaintance of yours may have had in his possession. We would like it back and will pay you handsomely … as a reward, of course … for its safe return."

"I have no idea what you're talking about."

"Then you have nothing to fear. That is a gun you are holding?" The man raised his hands. "Keep it trained on me while my brother looks. If what we are searching for is not in your Volkswagen, we will leave you to your travels and not bother you further."

If Matthew said no, there might be a fight. If he agreed, he might have to turn over the duffel bags to get Maria out of here safely. *Now*, where is Mr. E? And where is the highway patrol when you need them? He looked toward the semi-trucks. "Neither of you move. I'll show you, but then you have to leave before any of us have to resort to violence."

Both men kept their hands halfway up and walked to the bus's side door.

Matthew said, "Please stand up on the grass." He then motioned to Maria to open the doors.

"Matthew," she said in a whisper.

"Please, just do it, and hold onto SoBe."

Matthew kept his eyes and the gun on the two men. The man called Ahmed was still smiling.

SoBe broke away from Maria, both men jumped back, and Matthew grabbed her collar just in time while she growled and barked.

Maria peeled back the blankets to reveal mesh bags of oranges and grapefruit as well as boxes of fireworks and enough roasted peanuts to feed an army.

"*Ya ibn el kalb!*" the other man said, followed by a guttural growl. He continued to mutter in Arabic as the two men lowered their arms. Ahmed was not smiling.

Matthew was sure that if he were not holding SoBe, the second man would have attacked him. He made eye contact with Maria; she was about to say something, and he shook his head.

"Is this what you are willing to pay me a lot of money for?" Matthew asked, his voice cracking ever so slightly. "Fruit and fireworks?"

Ahmed craned his neck to look deeper into the bus. He started to laugh. "You really have no idea what we're looking for, do you?" he asked.

"Whatever it is, it must be valuable because people have been trying to kill us … I think because they think we have it."

"Have you seen or heard from your friend Estebanez since you left Maine?"

Before Matthew could speak, someone from the semi-trucks yelled, "What's going on over there? Is everything all right?"

"Well, is it, Matthew? Is everything all right?"

Matthew lowered the gun, slightly. "If we never see you again, sure."

"*Kama law 'anana humqaa,*" the other man said.

"My brother says you must think we are fools."

"I don't know what else I can say," Matthew said.

"We have caused you enough worry." He turned and tried to take the other man by the arm, but he shook Ahmed off and glared at Matthew. He looked at Maria and spoke in Arabic. He then spat on the ground at Matthew's feet.

SoBe was pulling on her collar, still growling. Matthew considered letting her go.

The men returned to the T-Bird. Ahmed started the engine. The other man stood by his door and mimicked firing a gun with his right hand, before getting in the car and slamming his door.

The trucker yelled again. Matthew set the gun inside the bus and waved. "Everything is fine, thanks." Matthew got into the bus as the T-Bird drove away.

"They knew our names, Matthew."

They also knew about Mr. E, Matthew considered. Where the hell are the duffel bags? Where did all this fruit and stuff come from?

"What did the crazy one say?"

"A lot of cursing, that you were a son of a dog, I think, and then he said some very nasty things about what he would do to your princess—that's me—if you don't give them what they want."

He felt dizzy, stuffed the .45 in his belt behind his back, and rubbed his temples. He reached into his pocket and found nothing but change.

"Here." Maria handed him the backup silver pill case she kept in her purse. She had been carrying spares for him ever since he could remember. "Maybe you should lie down for a few minutes and let the medicine take effect."

"We really should get out of here. The trucker might have called the cops, and I don't want to have to have to try to explain any of this." He swallowed the pill, thought for a moment, and then took another.

"Where is the research?"

Matthew just shook his head in disbelief.

He placed the gun under the seat.

I've known Mr. E since I was six. But, do I really know him at all?

Chapter Thirty-Three

Escape
March 19, 1995
11:00 p.m.

THEY HAD NOT SEEN the black SUVs since South Carolina, and the T-Bird seemed to be off their trail. They passed through Delaware and drove up the New Jersey Turnpike into New York.

Halfway across the George Washington Bridge, Matthew glanced at the fuel gauge. "I should have filled up at the last Turnpike service center."

"Maybe we can make it to Greenwich. I'd feel a lot safer if we were past New York City."

"We're riding on fumes."

"What could be worse than what we've been through already?"

"Escape from New York?"

"I remember!"

"Kurt Russell and Adrienne whatshername with Ernest Borgnine?"

"Adrienne Barbeau," she said.

"Like swimming in the ocean after watching *Jaws.*"

"Matthew Thaddeus Eaton, you have a phobia, or should I say, another phobia."

"I do not, and that wasn't my point," he protested, while he boarded the Dr. Maria psychoanalysis train. Anyways—" He suddenly realized he had no idea which way to turn. They found themselves amidst the Cross-Bronx Expressway cloverleaf. He remembered his father's colorful language when passing through the same junctures, especially when he missed signs or ended up on the wrong highway.

"There's a sign for Getty." He pulled off the Tremont Avenue exit—appropriate, he thought—and landed square in the middle of a road construction site with blinding halogen lights, jackhammers, and front-end loaders dumping concrete. He couldn't go back up the ramp, and as he maneuvered around the cavernous site, he came to the blocked ramp.

"I hate to be superstitious, but did this happen in the movie?" Maria asked.

"You're not helping," he snapped and regretted it as soon as he said it.

Maria gave him *that* look. "Just get us out of here, Matthew."

Lights filled the rear-view mirror and then a large silver grill with the Chevrolet symbol came into focus. Couldn't be. He could not go forward, he could not go left because of the median toward what appeared to be a retail center, so he made a right toward the city. He turned into the pitch black. He rubbed his eyes and tried to focus on the street ahead.

"I don't like this, Matthew. We really should stop for directions."

After less than a mile, he took a left at the first major intersection. He expected signs for an access road to I-95. Block after block, he drove farther and farther into the city. He got excited when he pulled back onto Tremont Avenue, then then the road became the Bronx River Parkway.

Bright lights reflecting in his rearview mirror caught his attention. "Damn. There it is, the black SUV!"

Maria looked out the back and caught her breath. "There's two of them!"

He picked up speed. There wasn't another car in sight. He didn't bother stopping for the light and made a sharp left under the large bridge.

Just as he was about to enter the Bronx Parkway, one of the trucks swung wide and cut him off.

Maria screamed.

Matthew tried to regain control without hitting the SUV and went the only way he could—straight into the Bronx Park. "There's got to be cops around here. There have to be."

Thunder boomed. Matthew flinched, and a flash of lightning lit up the park. SoBe whined, pushing her way up front and onto Maria's lap. Maria read the nearest sign and said, "Jungle World Road? We're on Jungle World Road. This can't be good."

They passed over the Bronx River as the road took them deeper into the park. The narrow, winding street had intermittent lamp posts casting a dim light. He was hoping there was a way out at the bottom of the park. After taking a left, he realized too late that it took him away from their escape route. The river was ahead between a copse of pines and picnic tables. He turned left to backtrack. Wrong again. "We're trapped!"

Matthew reached beside his seat for Jackson's .45 as the SUVs flanked the bus, forcing him to stop in a cul-de-sac. They faced two maintenance buildings, with the river to the right, and woods to the left. Thunder crashed and rolled. He snapped at Maria, "Get in the back with SoBe!"

Maria was about to protest when someone jerked her door open and pulled her from the bus. Matthew yelled, but SoBe was ahead of him, diving on the back of the man. Matthew heard a thud and a horribly sick whine from SoBe. He raised the pistol, when his door swung open. Someone had him by the shoulder. Matthew brought the gun under his left arm and pulled the trigger. The sound reverberated through the bus as Matthew and the man he'd shot, fell together to the ground. Matthew rolled away, but the man lay motionless.

The heavens expelled all its rain at once. Blinded, he stepped forward as another man came around the back of the bus with one arm around Maria. In his other hand, he held a gun pointed at Matthew. Matthew raised his hands. From behind, someone took his gun and then thumped him in the kidneys. Matthew fell to his knees and gasped for breath.

The man holding Maria said, "That's enough, Frank. There's nothing in the VW. Nothing but fruit and shit."

"Shit? What you mean *shit*, DelGercio?" the man behind Matthew yelled. Torrential rain muffled their voices.

"Not literally." He threw something down in front of Matthew. "We'll take them with us, and we'll have the bus picked up later. Hurry up."

Frank moved to pick up the black plastic bindings.

Once tied up in the SUV, Matthew surmised, it would be the end of them. What would Sean do? He launched himself at the man's knees, grabbed his gun wrist, and brought a knee to the groin. The man buckled but still managed to drive an elbow into Matthew's gut.

DelGercio reappeared, and Maria screamed, "He's going to shoot!" Matthew turned his opponent as the gun sounded. The bullet hit Frank square in the back, an inch from Matthew's hands. Matthew fell into a puddle as the gun roared again. He pried Frank's gun out of his hand and brought it level with DelGercio. Matthew yelled, "Now!" Maria dropped to the ground, just as Sean had taught them. Matthew thought he had shot high, well over the man's head, yet DelGercio grabbed his shoulder and dropped his gun.

Maria had disappeared, and Matthew braced himself for a bullet. A speeding car arrived, hydroplaning to a stop.

Instead of firing, DelGercio staggered away, holding his shoulder. Matthew blinked hard and raised his gun. DelGercio said, "Looks like your lucky day, kids. Tell your guardian angel thanks for not planting a double tap between my eyes."

The other SUV started forward with a roar and came close to hitting the park ranger.

Matthew looked at the gun in his hand and the men at his feet, blood and water mixing and flowing into the gutter.

The ranger yelled, "Hands in the air; I've got you covered." When Matthew didn't respond, the man shouted another warning. "Drop your weapon, or so help me God, I will shoot. I will."

A familiar voice said, "Matthew, don't turn around. Let go of the gun." A hand was on his wrist, another on the gun. "I wasn't here. Just answer their questions. I thought I was going to lose you both for a minute there. How would I explain that?"

"What ... how did ... who are—"

"I'm sorry I didn't get here sooner," Estebanez said. "We lost you guys back at the construction site. Thank God for that tracking device."

"Tracking device?" Matthew repeated, his voice sounding hollow. He turned to look for Estebanez, but all he saw through the rain were eerie silhouettes. He studied the men at his feet and felt sick.

With his voice cracking, he yelled, "Maria!"

"I'm under here. I think I'm stuck."

"Thank God!"

"That I'm stuck?"

"That you're okay. Stay right there."

"Like I have any choice. Are those men dead? Was that Mr. E?"

"I think so, and yes, it was."

Maria whispered,"*El hombre está destinado a morir una vez y después de eso para enfrentar el juicio.*"[34]

The rain had subsided, and the moon was peeking out between fast-moving clouds. Matthew and Maria sat in separate squad cars as ambulances and television crews arrived. The park area turned into a different kind zoo, Matthew thought. He looked over at the park ranger who was telling his story to a Channel 5 reporter. He pointed their way. Earlier he had helped dislodge Maria while Matthew power lifted the side of the bus off its axle an inch or two. As the ranger cut Maria's bindings, he said he had worked in the park ten years and had never seen anything like it. The only time he had ever pulled his weapon was to clean it or place it in the bureau drawer when he got home.

When questioned Matthew and Maria agreed to say that after the wrong turn, they found themselves in the middle of a shootout. Again.

NYPD officer Coleman opened Matthew's door and led him over to where Maria and a man were leaning against the other patrol car. In between them was SoBe, with a bloodstained bandage on her head.

The detective—handsome, rugged, and wearing a dark suit with a badge hanging off his lapel pocket—laughed at something Maria said. Past the detective Matthew watched a man who smiled, touched the brim of his Dallas Cowboys cap, walked away, and got into a cab.

SoBe barked and pulled on the leash. When Maria saw Matthew, she threw her arms around him. SoBe nearly knocked them to the pavement.

---

[34] Paraphrase of: And as it is appointed unto men once to die, but after this the judgment. –Hebrews 9:27 (KJV)

Officer Coleman said to the detective, "I checked on the kids, and they're who they say they are—wrong place at the wrong time, is my guess." She then turned to Matthew and whispered, "Your friend said to stay out of trouble for the next 500 miles."

The detective said, "You two must have the worst luck of any spring break college kids in history. There's a trail of police reports tracking back to Dade County." He handed Maria his card. "Call me if you think of anything else that might help."

Officer Coleman winked at Matthew and walked toward the ranger. The detective got in his car and drove away.

"That's it?"

"We better get on the road before they change their minds," Matthew whispered.

Once they left the Bronx Zoo and media circus, Matthew pulled into the first Getty station for gas. Maria told him what the detective told her about the dead men. One of the men had a long file of military, police, and U.S. government intelligence work. The one the others called Serg, had no identification. The remaining SUV had US government license plates.

Taking a deep breath, Maria asked, "What was Mr. E doing there?"

"I don't know. But he showed up just in time to save our lives."

Maria laid her fingers along Matthew's cheek. "Are you going to be okay?"

"You look as if it was just a day in the park."

"A night in the park."

He rubbed his sore shoulder. It hurt slightly worse than everything else. "I have to admit, I'm still shaken."

"It'll take a while before the shock wears off. Even trained professionals go through a period of post-trauma after something like this."

My Dr. Maria, Matthew thought.

"So, you k—, pulled the trigger ... twice. How do you feel?"

"Really, Doc?" Matthew added, "I didn't kill them both. The guy holding you shot the second guy. Frank was his name."

He wished he could talk to Sean. Or a shrink. He looked at Maria. Another shrink. Or, maybe Chief Tanner. For months his dreams included crazy images that had played out in real time over the last few days.

He was gripping the steering wheel so tight his knuckles had gone white. "I'm sorry to get you into this."

"*Estoy donde Dios quiere que yo sea.* I wouldn't want to be anywhere else, *mi amor.*"

As they turned onto I-95 and saw the big green sign for New England, he opened his window and drew in a long breath of fresh air.

"Let's go home."

Chapter Thirty-Four

Safety
March 20, 1995
3:00 a.m.

TAKING BACK ROADS Matthew navigated the tree-lined Merritt Parkway as Maria dozed. He turned on talk radio, and a familiar name caught his attention. The talk show host was discussing Senator Green from Texas, head of the Senate Committee on Energy. Apparently, children had discovered the Senator's body along the Danube River near Nuremberg, Germany.

Matthew switched the channel to light jazz. The world was going crazy. People were ready to kill over some research which most believed to be speculative.

How did I get involved in all this? He thought about Uncle Carl, Marcos, and Mr. E. They all seemed to be in on a game he didn't know he was playing.

Maria woke with a start and looked over at him. "I was dreaming about that plane! That did not happen, did it?"

"I don't know which is worse."

"I know, right?" She shook her hair with both hands, flipped it all forward and wrapped a hair tie around a ponytail, and then pinned it on top of her head.

He loved that five second action.

"You look tired. Why don't we take a break? Or I can drive," she said.

He took the next exit, a few miles from New Haven, and into a roadside rest area.

He took a pill and lay on a bench with his UMaine Crew cap covering his face. SoBe licked his dangling hand before settling at his feet.

Suddenly he was running after two men, Dennis Weaver, the sporting lodge proprietor, and the man with the Cowboys cap. Both men turned to him and had six-guns strapped around their waists. Weaver said, "Draw!" Mr. E had taken his gun, so Matthew reached into the duffels and threw Dr. Jackson's books as a storm kicked up, bats swarmed, and Pamola threw lightning bolts at them all.

Boom! Matthew sat up, choking like he swallowed water in the swimming pool. The sky was dark with storm clouds and thunder boomed off in the distance. He looked left and right; it was just the three of them.

"That's what they call a power nap," Maria said.

"I couldn't fall asleep."

"You were asleep for nearly an hour." She handed him a half-peeled orange. "Dreaming?"

He told her what he could remember while he scratched behind the dog's ears, careful to avoid her wound. "You did good, girl. You did really good."

"Pamola again. I dreamt of him a lot this week, and the storms from the Micmac legends. I wish the old chief had not told us those stories. I always feel like I'm drowning.

"Me too.

They picked up Maria's car on the UMaine campus. Following Maria, Matthew nearly drove off the road while watching for trouble in the mirrors. In Millinocket, the first stop was Godello's Restaurant where Matthew gave Mr. Valdeorras a huge bag of oranges. Mr. V asked him about the cut on his head and Matthew told him that he fell on the beach.

At Maria's house, Matthew carried in all of Maria's luggage. "I think you doubled what you brought," he chided. She laughed and didn't seem to be interested in unpacking.

"Papa won't be home until tonight, you know," Maria said, grabbing his shirt, and pushing him down on the couch. SoBe stretched out on the oriental rug and lay her head on her paws with a long sigh.

In a while, they both fell into a deep slumber, and after a few hours, Matthew rolled off the couch, kissed her, and stumbled out of the house. He drove the bus straight to the old ELF sawmill compound. Everything looked normal so after turning off the security he parked the shot-up VW bus in the barn.

Matthew closed the barn doors, cracked open a Sea Dog Old Gollywobbler Ale, and sat on the stool at the mechanic's desk staring at Mr. Johnson's latest projects—Sean's blue Jeep Grand Cherokee which had needed a new timing chain and transmission, a '64 Mustang, and a '74 Charger. He signed deeply. It would take more than a few engine parts to fix the bus.

Where is the research?

He remembered Chief Tanner's last words to him, a few weeks earlier. "Only after you look into the sun can you reason about what it is." Matthew first wondered

234 OF RIAN HUEY

if the chief had read Plato. [35] Have I been staring at the sun? Or at a cave wall. He wondered if the chief's words, and the recurring dreams could be relevant to everything that had happened, and something that is going to happen. "It's all anything but scientific," he said, in conclusion.

He left the barn with SoBe on his heels, fired up Sean's blue Jeep Grand Cherokee, and headed for the Eaton estate.

In the Eaton kitchen, Matthew's mother hugged and kissed him. She ran her fingers over the cut on Matthew's head. "What on earth happened?" She asked. Matthew expanded on the fall on the beach story while his mother studied SoBe's injury.

"And who is this? Was she surfing too?" She lifted the bandage and caught her breath. Matthew told her an abridged version of finding SoBe.

"I didn't even know I should have been worrying. I suffer enough with your brother's exploits, you know."

Matthew nodded and felt relieved that news of their exploits had not made it this far north. He sat at the table and inhaled biscuits, sausage gravy, and scalloped potatoes while his mother became acquainted with SoBe.

His mother made a project out of folding a dishtowel and asked about Maria.

His face was hot, so he ducked his head and grinned.

"Sweetheart, you need to get through college before thinking of having a family."

"Mom!" He said and laughed.

"Well, someone has to say it. And things happen, and I hope it's not too late." She placed her hand on his and smiled. I suppose if something ... well, you didn't have to go all the way to Miami. Just remember, I'm too young to be a grandmother." And they both laughed.

"No worries, Mom. Besides, there's Sean."

"I hope he meets a nice girl. I know he's lonely."

Matthew thought of some of his brother's stories. Sean was anything but lonely. But he too wondered if his brother would, or could, ever settle down and raise a family. It was hard to imagine.

"How are your headaches, sweetheart?"

"Manageable," he lied. In fact, he realized, they had become much more severe and frequent.

"Should I set up an appointment for you?"

"I like Dr. Greco, but she thinks narcotics are a solution. I don't need all the side effects. I'm okay, Mom, really."

They heard his father's truck. He came through the front door and said, "Well, if it isn't good-times Charlie." As if he had not seen SoBe, he poured himself a glass

---

[35] Plato's *Alegory of the Cave.*

of Scotch whiskey. He turned to his wife, gave her a kiss, and looked inquiringly at his son.

"Hi, Pop. How are things at the mills?"

"With all this free time, I have plenty of work at one of the sawmills," Parker said. He looked down. "What are you looking at?"

SoBe cocked her head.

He turned to Matthew and said, "We could use a German Shepherd watchdog up at the Oxbow sawmill. I could use your help up there too."

"It's nice to see you too, Dad."

His father grunted, but Matthew thought he saw a hint of a smile. He took a bottle of olives out of the fridge and headed back toward the great room where he switched on the news.

"I'm sorry, honey," his mother said.

Matthew waved it away.

"When I met your father, he was gentle and laughed all the time."

He found *that* picture of his father hard to imagine. He kissed his mother and took SoBe to his room. He fell onto the bed without removing his shoes. Soon into a deep sleep, he battled a horrific storm on a lake surrounded by pagodas and Micmac burial structures made of logs and tree limbs. Pamola was angry as ever and began throwing lightning bolts from atop Mount Katahdin, and Cracker Jack was trying to toss Matthew a life preserver. Then, the man with the Cowboy's star on his cap held a gun to Matthew's temple as up on a hill Kyle Gespasian drew his bow back and let an arrow fly.

Church bells rang the next morning as Maria met Matthew at the AT Café, packed with hikers getting ready to attack the Appalachian Trail. They ordered tomato soup and grilled cheese, while Maria suggested that they confide in Johnny Fazio's father, as he had been a cop. Matthew trusted Joe Fazio, but in the end, the fewer that knew, the better. "Besides, there's bad blood between Mr. Fazio and Mr. E."

Maria looked at her watch, kissed Matthew, and rushed out the door. She had to catch up with her father at St. Martin of Tours, on Colby Street. Until spring break, she had never missed Mass. Her two aunts often gave Matthew the *evil eye*, and he had learned to expertly avoid the subject. Matthew's family attended St. Andrews Episcopal, or the Presbyterian Congregational church, but only on holidays. He could not remember the last time his father had joined him and his mother. Like Matthew, he preferred to meet God in the outdoors.

That afternoon they pushed off onto Millinocket Lake in a black cherry all wood canoe that he and Kyle built when they were sixteen.

"Incredulous."

"What?" Maria asked, as she laid back against him.

Matthew steered with his paddle as the current pushed them along. "That's the word that comes to mind when I consider this contrast to our tumultuous spring break."

"I think when Mr. E gets back, he'll have some answers."

Matthew hoped so. It was going to be difficult to go back to Orono and leave Maria behind; and his poor bus. So many questions unanswered, he mused.

Matthew wrote Monday, March 26, 1995 on the top of one of a dozen yellow pads. He stuffed them all into his backpack and hiked down to Fogler Library where he settled into his favorite corner of the fourth floor. He positioned a tall empty garbage can in the corner, about ten feet away. He began to plan how he was going to attack the future, with or without the research. He filled the first pad with everything he could remember from the journals, and every word Tremont had said. On the next pad, and the next, he drew graph after graph, chart after chart, and formula after formula. After a few hours there were dozens of crumpled balls of yellow lined paper in the corner trash can. The puzzle pieces did not connect. On the first page of the last yellow pad he wrote in bold letters, something Tremont had said which he also read in the last entry of Dr. Jackson's last journal dated August 2, 1989:

The prize in the box
CJ Energy Cells
the 3/3 formula

Mentally exhausted and starving, he leaned back and stared out at the students milling onto the courtyard between Grove Street and Moosehead Road.

Miami Beach seemed like a hundred years ago.

He turned to his worn copy of *Capturing the Sun* and thought, what a tragic waste it was to lose not one, but two Jacksons.

A tap on the shoulder startled him from a dream about chasing the man in the gray Caddy. "Hello, Matty. I'm still mad at you for dumping us off in Daytona without even a goodbye kiss."

He turned to see Donna and Darma smiling over his shoulder. "I would have picked you girls up but—"

Donna interrupted, "I'm just teasing. My aunt told me you called when you got to our exit. Why did you leave Florida so soon? Well, never mind. I've been carrying this thing around for days." She dropped a fat envelope on the desk. "Some guy paid me two hundred dollars to deliver it to you."

"What did he look like?"

"Probably close to my father's age," Donna said, "But in better shape, tan, a cleft chin. Does he sound familiar?"

Matthew shook his head.

"Dallas hat," Darma said. "And handsome in a rough sort of way. Like Redford."

"A Dallas Cowboys hat? With a silver star on the front? he asked, and they nodded.

"He sure could have saved a few bucks by giving it to you himself, don't you think?" Darma said. She kissed him on the cheek and whispered, "If Maria ever gets tired of you—"

Donna kissed him on the other cheek and said, "That goes double for me; even though I totally have a girl crush on her. I wish I had her confidence."

When they were gone, he tore open the envelope and found photographs. There were pictures of him and Maria with Cracker Jack in Miami Beach, and later with Marcos at the truck stop, then a few of them in the driveway with Uncle Carl's family. There were also pictures of him and Maria in Millinocket just this past weekend, a picture of his mother hanging clothes on the line, and one of Mr. V at the restaurant. There was no note. There didn't have to be.

Matthew packed up his books. "I wonder when the bloody horse's head is going to show up in my bed."

Spring passed. Matthew did his best to concentrate on his classes and his MIT program. He talked to Maria each night. Nearly every morning before the sun rose, he wore out his anxiety on the river with his rowing crew or in the pool.

One day Erich stopped by the pool on his way to the track and after their usual banter, commented on how serious he had become. "What the hell happened on spring break, man?"

Matthew almost confided in him, but Tremont's warning held him back.

At the very least, Matthew expected to hear from the authorities, but by finals' time, he had still heard nothing. Somehow, he knew Mr. E had intervened. Where the hell was Mr. E? Most of all, he wondered and worried about the precious cargo Cracker Jack had entrusted to him.

He finished his semester finals and express mailed his revised MIT project. He now specialized in quantum physics, as it related to energy storage. That was also Dr. Jackson's concentration in the 50's.

Today was his last morning on the river until September. Instead of rowing, he pushed out into the choppy water of the Penobscot in a seven-foot kayak. As his muscles strained and swelled, he thought of how he and his brother had spent many summers racing in kayaks and hoped Sean would soon be back. The last postcard had a Kuwait postmark and said, "Study hard, I'll see you soon." He so wanted to tell Sean about spring break, but could he? Should he?

Each night since Miami, he sat in the Fogler Library, devouring everything he could find on the physics of chemical, metallic, fission, atomic and neutronic reactions. And when not competing on the river, he drove to Cambridge, where his enthusiastic MIT professors set aside articles and books on his new core subjects. He also researched the biographies and whereabouts of Dr. Jackson's former teammates, the Fraternal Order of Alternative Energy. He hoped he would meet them one day.

His MIT advisor, Dr. Hessen, was a strange bird. Matthew hoped that when he attended MIT full time for his PhD, he could request another advisor. The man was … what's the word, sinister. Yes, he decided, sinister.

Matthew packed up Sean's blue Jeep, strapped his kayak and single skull on the top, and latched his road and mountain bikes to the back.

He was now satisfied that he could study, work in labs, and submit his research, all the while skirting wide around CJ Energy Cells, an entirely new and renewable energy source. Nobody would ever guess that he was preparing himself for the time when he'd receive the duffel bags full of miracles.

"If I receive them," he said out loud.

Chapter Thirty-Five

Riddle
June 2, 1995

A LOGGING TRUCK FLIPPED over on I-95. Matthew had allowed plenty of time to get from campus to Maria's graduation. He thought.

He drove up to Stearns High School, past the "Class of 1995 Graduation" sign, parked and ran into the building, down the hall, and into the auditorium. The packed room seated no more than two hundred, with families lining the walls and kids sitting in the aisles. He heard a familiar voice greet the audience. Maria was at the podium delivering her valedictorian message. She looked up, and there was a different version of *that look*. He spotted his parents and Mr. V, sitting together in the front row. He plunged through the crowd of Moms, Dads, and siblings.

After the graduation, most of the senior class and their families gravitated a few miles east to Godello's. An awful local band played to the crowd as the party lasted late into the night.

Matthew sat on the front stoop of the restaurant as Maria said goodbye to the last guests.

"Hey, Matt. Did I tell you I heard from Sean last week?"

Matthew turned to see Nick St. Adams holding the last case of booze to take back to his truck. He leaned on a deck post and was more than a little drunk.

"Mom and Mr. V were just talking about not hearing from him. Sean had planned to be here, but his orders must have changed, last minute. Did he say where he was?"

"I don't know. Bosnia or Afghanistan, I suspect. But he could be in DC. Who knows? He can't say, you know. So, he wanted me to check on you and ask if you saw your Uncle Carl when you were in Miami? And if you had any trouble on your trip?"

"Uncle Carl?" Matthew thought of an old show his mother loved, *Lost in Space*.

Danger Matthew Eaton. "Yeah, Maria and I stopped in to see Uncle Carl, and no, we had a great trip. No trouble."

"Oh. Huh." He seemed to struggle for his next words. "Well, that's good. How is Carl? Love that guy, you know."

"He's good, Mr. St. Adams," Matthew said.

"Nick. You should always call me Nick. Okay, well then, I'm going to get my ass back to the Sailor Son. That Cockney witch will run out all my regulars if I let her," he said, referring to his cook and barmaid, Val Hare. A most peculiar woman.

It was midnight. Matthew and Maria watched St. Adams drive away.

"Sorry I was late, there was a logging truck—"

"You made it; that's what's important. I'll help my dad close. Let's get breakfast and catch up?"

Matthew kissed her just as he heard Mr. V clear his throat and open the door.

"G-great dinner, sir," Matthew said and Maria chuckled.

At home, he joined his mother in the kitchen as his father had long since gone to bed. Matthew swore that the dishes in the sink were rattling from his snoring. He sat down in his usual chair.

"That was such a great night. Hmm? Maria's speech was so natural, so full of hope for the future. She was the most beautiful valedictorian imaginable, don't you think?"

"Gorgeous."

His mother dried her hands and gave him a stack of mail. The letter on top had a return address of Destin, Florida. He noted that there was no postage or postage cancellation stamp.

"When did this come?"

She turned to the dishes in the sink. "Felix," she started, "Mr. Estebanez brought it by, yesterday morning."

Matthew's chair nearly fell over as he stood. "He was here? Is he still in town?"

"No, honey." She looked down the hall and they both waited to hear his father snoring again. She continued, "He said he had business to attend to, and all he left was that envelope."

Bewildered, he looked at his mother. "Was he here long?"

Oh, maybe an hour, or two."

As he tore open the letter, he asked, "Did you tell him I'd be home today?"

"Yes dear, but he said he had business overseas and couldn't wait. He told me you would understand."

Matthew scanned the hand-written page. The one man who possibly had answers, visited his mother instead of him, and only left him a one-page note bearing the latest riddle.

"Goodnight, honey." She kissed him goodnight and retreated to the living room.

Matthew gathered up the mail and his luggage and went up to his room. He tossed everything on the bed and sat at his desk. A riddle. Great.

He and Mr. E had stumped each other on puzzles and riddles since meeting at the cemetery twelve years ago. But this one was different. He paced and wrestled over the content until falling asleep with the letter on his chest. His mind continued to analyze each line as he slept. Strange images danced in his mind of a pirate and his treasure, space missions, European architecture, like the London Bridge and the Eifel Tower, monks, and those damn bats.

> *Within this year, the mortar set, and now the treasure lies: The Clementine lunar probe launches an old bottle vertically from the moon's surface. Four hundred thirty milliseconds after launch, the bottle is exactly 2,222 millimeters from the moon's surface, and 5 seconds after release, the bottle is moving towards the moon's surface at exactly 5 meters per second. The time in milliseconds tells the cornerstone year when the object is exactly 4 meters from the moon's surface. Once inside, the only yarn, one who spins has to sell, is to tell. Your destiny lies four paces south of that which was made in the oldest of the largest in Europe by mass. You are over a barrel as the seller has lodged high prices.*

The next morning, Maria and Matthew sat at Danny's Nook in the center of town. They held hands across the table until Sister Madeline walked by and cleared her throat. They let go, laughed, and busied themselves with studying Mr. E's riddle.

"Did you sleep at all?" Maria asked.

"Not a wink."

"I slept like a hibernating bear."

"That's a picture. So, I have the math portion figured out, but I think that was a ruse to throw me off. I don't know what his game is now. My mother was acting weird last night. She called Mr. E, Felix. He never told me his first name."

"You don't think—"

Matthew held up his hand. "I wouldn't put anything past him, especially now, but my mother would never. So ... don't go there."

"I'm not saying they did anything, but it's possible there's some chemistry between them. Mr. E is charming, and your mom is high class and beautiful. He's been part of your family's life for more than a decade, so—"

"Which parts of don't go there don't you understand?"

She took a bite out of her egg and jalapeno cheese biscuit and mumbled, "I'm just saying."

He flattened out the riddle and read it aloud yet again.

"What else could a spinner be? Maybe it's a silkworm or a spider? And notice, he indicates the spinner doesn't have any yarn? So maybe instead of yarn, it's thread."

"Or a tale."

"A tail?"

"A yarn can be a story or a tale."

"Oh, right," she said laughing.

They tried to dissect each word, but as the morning lapsed, every five minutes they were fielding interruptions to congratulate Maria and welcome Matthew back to town.

Mr. Baker asked his usual question on his way to the door, "When you two gunna stop shacking up and get married?"

Maria rarely blushed. Matthew noticed the red tinge to her olive skin. He only saw that when she was about to punch him in the arm for talking out of school.

Ignoring the shacking up part, Maria answered, as she always did, "I'm too young to get married, Mr. Baker."

And Mr. Baker replied, as he always did, "Me 'n Margaret, we was only fifteen, but things were different back then."

On the way out the door, they ran into Joe Fazio, who had an office above the restaurant.

Joe bear hugged them, one in each huge arm. "Is that your mutt sitting by the door?" Matthew nodded, and Joe continued, "Johnny will be back from college on Monday, and the wife insists that you two join us for eggplant *parmigiana e molto bene!*" They assured him they would not miss it for the world.

"Hey," Joe said, "where's that Cuban? When you left for college, he disappeared."

"I really don't know," Matthew replied.

SoBe followed them into the Jeep and jumped in the back seat, as they drove to the barn. Inside, they paid their respects to the VW bus.

"I keep thinking about Cracker Jack, and those men in the Bronx," Maria said.

Me too, he thought. He held her tight, still thinking of the riddle. But Maria had other things on her mind.

Later, they sat on a blanket covering a couple bales of hay, laughing at SoBe, who was now fast asleep with her forepaws covering her eyes.

"Every time I look at her, I think of those poor kids living with drug dealer parents."

"Maybe we should have picked them up too?"

She hit him in the shoulder. "Don't make fun of me. Can you imagine how much those children miss SoBe and how much she must miss them?"

"Maybe one day we'll go back and look for them," he said.

"Okay, back to business."

He read the riddle over a few times, then lay back staring at the beams in the ceiling. After a few minutes he cried, "I've got it!" He jumped to his feet. "The treasure is in the cellar of the Katahdin Sporting Lodge!"

She hit her hand against her forehead. "Weaver? Mr. Weaver! The spinner is a weaver!"

"Exactly. Mr. E spent more time at that lodge than anywhere, and he talked about forbidden wine down in the cellar more than anything."

He engaged the security system, and the three of them ran out of the barn, jumped in the Jeep, and sped out onto Fire Road 13 toward the Golden Road.

"While I was studying at the lodge, I listened to Estebanez play on Weaver's eccentricities. They debated everything—the history of a bottle of wine, the value and year of a rare edition of Walt Whitman's *Leaves of Grass,* or Thoreau's writings about the woods of Maine. When Weaver wasn't there, I just know that Mr. E would go into the cellar on his own, which meant he either had a key or broke in."

Maria asked, "The equation?"

"The answer is 1776. That's the date on the cornerstone. Mr. E said that Weaver often lived in that era—in his mind."

"What about the largest land mass in Europe?"

"France."

"Over a barrel?"

"I don't know—maybe a wine keg?" "Are you going to be okay, driving over the dike?"

"It's been a long time, I don't know."

They reached the narrow pass the locals call *the dike,* between Millinocket Lake and Ambajejus Lake. Matthew was deep in his thoughts about what he hoped to find at the lodge when he realized Maria was unusually quiet. He turned to find her hyperventilating. The Jeep screeched to a halt. "It's happening?"

"I don't know. I mean, I know, but I," she struggled to talk and held her hands to her chest, choking between breaths. SoBe whined and licked her face.

"I think I should take you back to town. I'll bet Doc Malone would see you on short notice."

"No! I mean no, let's go ahead, it will pass."

Matthew wasn't convinced.

"Really. Let's just get out of here."

Reluctantly, Matthew put the Jeep in gear, and took Baxter Park Road, ten miles toward the bottom western side of Baxter State Park. Minutes later he turned off at the Katahdin Sporting Lodge sign and drove up the steep gravel drive to the front of the two-hundred-year-old rustic building.

He studied her.

"I'm fine. Really. It's beautiful, and the views are stunning!"

"You've never been here?"

"Um, no. I've been waiting for you to invite me."

SoBe bounded out and ran after a snowshoe hare, high tailing it to the woods. "SoBe!" Maria called.

"She hasn't caught one yet. She'll come back. The exercise is good for her." Matthew looked at the parking area. Winter is the busy season for Weaver, but there's typically a lot of year-round activity. There were four trucks and two SUVs in the lot, as well as Weaver's '56 XK-140 Jaguar Roadster, exactly like one that his actor hero drove.

"The visitors are probably hunters," he noted.

They walked up the granite steps into a massive porch and through thick solid oak doors, hung in the late nineteenth century.

"How are you going to get into the cellar?"

"I have no idea. Maybe he'll just let us in."

Maria laughed. "Even my father has never been allowed in the wine shrine, and he has tried many times."

He pointed a finger at SoBe and said, "Stay in the Jeep. We'll be right back."

They approached the front desk where Mr. Weaver stood with his back to them. He was adjusting an autographed picture of the actor Dennis Weaver. Signed in person well before the actor filed a restraining order on the lodge proprietor. Satisfied, Weaver slapped his hands together and turned to his guests. He raised his eyebrows comically as he asked, "Have I ever told you about the other Dennis Weaver?"

"Yes, sir, you have," and before Weaver could ask Maria, "I've told Maria as well," Matthew said. With that small lie, he aimed to save an hour or more.

"Then I will save you the boring details. Did you know he and I are the same age? Born on June 4, 1924, we're both 6'4, and my wife's name was also Geraldine, God rest her soul. I think he will come to visit one of these days soon, don't you think?"

"Absolutely, Mr. Weaver. My father was saying something about that the other day," he said, knowing how much Mr. Weaver respected his father. What his father had said had more to do with the crazy side of the story. Weaver smiled and pushed the brim of his cowboy hat up a bit.

Weaver walked along the front desk that spanned the width of the room. Mounted heads of big game decorated the walls, along with Native American relics. He reached behind the picture and took out the key Matthew had seen him hide many times. "It's about time you kids got here."

Surprised, Matthew said, "You were expecting us?"

"I said it would take you a week to figure out the riddle." He looked at his watch. "I figured you got the letter after the graduation—by the way, congratulations, Miss Valdeorras—so, it's been less than twelve hours. You've cost me a 1947 Australian Torbreck Shiraz. A rare bottle indeed." He sighed.

Matthew and Maria smiled at each other.

"You will be the first Eaton in over a hundred years to visit the Weaver cellars.

And you, the first Valdeorras ever." He walked to the end of the desk before saying, "And the last."

"No photography, ladies and gentlemen, and please do not touch anything. You break it, you buy it."

Matthew wanted to ask about the Eaton who visited the cellar a hundred years ago.

They followed Weaver into the lodge library full of lounge chairs, small tables with chess sets ready for play, and thousands of books, of which many were first editions, some preceding the American Revolution. Maria's eyes widened as Weaver pulled a nine-foot-by-four-foot false bookshelf away from the wall to reveal a rounded black door with crisscrossing steel bars. It creaked and groaned under its own weight as the musty air blew their hair back. Weaver motioned for them to go ahead as he pulled the library shelves and then the medieval door behind him.

"Maria said, "I can't see in front of me." There was a clicking sound as Weaver lit an oil lamp with a fireplace lighter. "This is spooky," she said. "I love it."

At the bottom of the steps was a larger door that took a Herculean effort to open. Even cooler, damper air rushed to meet them. Weaver reached past Matthew and lit another oil lamp.

The cavernous cellar became illuminated in front of them, revealing aisles of wine racks as far as they could see. They heard another click behind them. When Matthew turned, Weaver—who in the flickering lamplight, resembled a killer out of a Hitchcock movie—was closing the door. "I like to keep the doors closed when I'm down here. Watch your step, children."

When they reached the bottom, Matthew asked, "Mr. Weaver, do you know what we are looking for?"

"Go down to the end of the third aisle and turn right."

"Near the oldest French wines, Sherlock?" Maria asked.

"Elementary, my dear Watson," Matthew confirmed.

They found, stacked against the far wall, Jackson's duffel bags. Matthew leaped forward and caressed them reverently. "I've been thinking about you guys for quite some time."

"More like obsessing," Maria said, laughing. "Me too!" Matthew turned around expecting to see Weaver, but he was gone. He walked around the corner and looked down the aisle. He called out, "Mr. Weaver?" When he got to the base of the stairs, he was just in time to see the door shut and hear the key turning in the padlock. He ran up and tried the black iron handle. It would not budge.

Matthew returned to Maria and rummaged through the four bags and was satisfied the contents were all intact. He removed a large faded hand painted sign: Jackson's Place. He visualized Cracker Jack reaching up and unlatching the sign for the last time. In his dreams he saw Tremont, the two rottweilers, and two empty rocking chairs. It was a sad vision. He dug down deep into one of the bags and pulled out the gun from its oily rags.

"I sure hope you won't need that again," Maria said.

"Me too, but it's nice to know we have it. As far as I can tell, there's no other way out of here except up."

"Why would Weaver lock us in down here? Mr. E wouldn't put him up to this."

"Why would he go through all this trouble when he obviously is the one that took the duffel bags out of the bus down at South of the Border? He's the only one who could have put the gun back in the bag. Right? If he planned for Weaver to lock us down here, he wouldn't have left us a weapon."

"Then who put him up to this?"

"Maybe Weaver is working with the guys in Bronx Zoo, or the Arabs. He's a greedy bastard, not to mention nuts, so if someone got to him after Mr. E delivered the bags, they're either in Millinocket or on their way. I trust Mr. E."

Though, Matthew thought, it seems that somehow, he is the mastermind behind all of this.

Matthew said, "Then again—"

"What?"

"Nothing." I feel like such a damn puppet, Matthew thought. Mr. E *has to be* one of the good guys. He's worked with me all these years. He patted the duffel bag under him. "Even if he isn't who he said he is, it's clear he's always been watching out for me—for us."

"007, huh," she said with a smile.

"Now it does not seem quite as far-fetched."

Maria sat down beside him.

"He devoted a decade to working with you. Even if under false pretenses. Were you able to reach him?"

"I called the number I had. It clicks five or six times like it's being forwarded, then a woman answers; she says, 'Destin Sailboat and Wine Sales.'"

"Really?"

"Yeah, and then she takes a message. I called the Shell station in Miami Beach. I told the guy who answered that I was a reporter doing a story on the shootout. He had never had anyone working for him by the name of Marcos, Estebanez, Estefan, or anyone meeting that description. He did have a wrecker stolen off his lot that same night, and the employee, George, who was supposed to be on call that night, never showed up again. But the shot-up wrecker did."

They sat in silence for a while, and then Maria chuckled.

"What's funny?"

"I just had a picture in my mind of Clarice stuck down in the cellar with a serial killer!"

"You, my dear, are insane, but there's not another woman in the world, besides Clarice, who I'd rather be with."

She threw one knee across his lap and straddled him. "I know." She kissed him. "We're going to get out of this mess. We have the research, and you're going to get busy saving the world."

Maria pushed off Matthew and began exploring the cellar. Matthew loaded twelve rounds into a magazine and snapped the clip into Cameron Jackson's .45. He wondered how many times over the years, Cameron or Tremont had held this same gun, expecting someone to come through the door.

When he caught up with Maria, she had a bottle of 1988 Canon La Gaffeliere in one hand and 1973 Chateau Montelena Chardonna in the other. She said, "White or red?"

Matthew took a deep breath and let it out slowly. He looked down a long dark row of racks. Thanks for the riddle, Mr. E, he thought. *You are over a barrel as the seller has lodged high prices.* Over a barrel indeed, he thought.[36]

---

[36] *Over a barrel* is a phrase that has little to no etymology. It's origin and meaning are left to pure speculation but may have to do with the practice of putting a man over a barrel to expunge water from his lungs. The interpretation is much clearer, to put someone in a grim situation, to leave them high and dry. That idiom is easier to track. When a ship was stuck in the mud, it was high and dry. The first indication of print usage was in the *London Times*, circa late 1700s, That [boat] was left high and dry. That [person] was left high and dry. The juxtaposition of Mr. E using this idiom, is ironic at best.

Chapter Thirty-Six

Lost
June 3, 1995

THE NEXT DAY, everyone in the town buzzed about the disappearance of their Matthew and Maria. The *Katahdin Times* moved their front-page story about a controversy over the new owners of the Great Northwestern Paper Mill property. Before this, the biggest story in the area was the train crash of 1979, heard two counties away. Today's headline read, "MISSING! Jeep Found Abandoned." The article, complete with a picture, reported that a Great Northern Paper Mill employee was heading toward Millinocket for work and noticed a Jeep on the side of the Golden Road between Ambajejus and Millinocket Lakes. "It just seemed out of place," he told the reporter. The Mill guard called the Millinocket police.

As the first squad car drove up, the Ranger, Pete Cartier Marks, a Millinocket-born Native American met Officer Franklin Dubois. "Hey Frank, I was heading up to Baxter when I heard your call over the radio. So, with Sean gone, I guessed it must have been Matthew driving the Jeep?"

"I hate to think anyone would do them harm. They're like my own kids. Maybe they went for a hike and got lost."

"That don't make much sense, Frank. Why would they park here, leave the doors open, and the keys inside?"

"Thanks, Pete. I'll radio Harry that we need search and rescue."

Colonel Harry K-9 Williams held the top post in Maine's Department of Inland Fisheries and Wildlife. The Colonel was best known for upgrading the bureau's search and rescue equipment to high technology, and for drilling his wardens on techniques until they dropped. Harry came to the Bureau of Warden Services fresh out of UMaine's School of Forest Resources as a K-9 specialist in the early eighties.

"I'll hang here. I called in, and we have four off-duty Rangers on their way. I also called my mother," Pete said, "and she's going to call Chief Tanner. If anyone has seen anything up here, he'll know, or find out."

"Don't start telling me this has to do with that damn granola spirit on the mountain, Pete. I really don't have time for it."

"Pamola. And I know you're not a believer, Frank, but I've seen too much crazy stuff up here."

Officer Dubois spat and shook his head. "You and that wolfhound cousin of yours are close to Matthew, right?"

"Kyle Gespasian, and yeah, he is already north of here looking for sign."

Dubois nodded and reached into his cruiser for his mic. He told dispatch that this was definitely a Code-2 10-57, an urgent missing person case, and requested to be connected with Maine Fish and Game.

While they waited, Pete said, "I graduated with Sean."

Parker Eaton sped into the area in a truck labeled with the letters ELF.

Dubois briefed him on what little he knew while they hiked the Ambajejus side of the dike and then hiked toward Millinocket Lake, on the eastern side of the dike. They crossed over the Golden Road, pressed between thick rows of bushes, and then crossed over the Baxter Park Road. Stopping to rest between The North Woods Trading Post and Big Moose Inn, Parker said, "Someone had to have seen something. This is a busy time of year up here."

As they climbed down a steep embankment toward Millinocket Lake, Dubois said, "Pete and I have questioned a few. So far … we have no leads."

Breathing hard, they hiked the rest of the way through a thicket of pine trees. They stood for a long time staring out into the vast Millinocket Lake and off toward the smaller eastern mountains.

"Nothing here but trout, perch, and bass," Dubois said, but he yelled Matthew's name as loud as he could, waited, then yelled again. Sound carried for miles down there.

They hiked the quarter mile back to Matthew's Jeep, down through the white birch trees, and then to the Ambajejus shore below where a man crouched at the water's edge. Sergeant Allen Willis, a game warden, had a muscular build despite the gray at his temples under a black cap. He appeared to be in his fifties, but some said that he was well over seventy. He wore the bureau's forest-green military-type fatigues with red insignia and patches above the pockets and shoulders.

Willis reached out, shook Parker's hand, then gave Dubois a friendly nod. "Hell of a situation, Parker. The colonel has made this our top priority. The chances of finding them are much higher in the first few days, so we'll waste no time."

"Thanks, Al, it means a lot to me that Harry sent you."

"I was only a few miles north, checking on a crazy drunk harassed by a moose. I was about to arrest *him* for harassing the moose! But this was more important."

"Do you have all three airboats at your disposal?"

"Only two, but they are on the way. Harry, I mean Colonel Williams has also

dedicated our K-9 teams. And you know we have the best dive team in the country—"
He paused and looked away from Parker's shocked expression.

The men stood on the beach, looking north toward the floatplane base. Dubois
interjected, "Jean LeVasseur will have two floatplanes up in the air within the
hour." To the south was a boat launch and several seasonal cottages, and off to the
southwest, they could see a few small islands and Jo-Mary Mountain, part of the
hundred-mile wilderness. "There are already a couple dozen locals out on their
boats searching the shore area of all eight lakes. The off-duty Baxter Park rangers
are getting them organized."

Parker sighed deeply and said, "We got a hundred thousand acres to cover and
half of that is water; beyond that, we have over half a million acres of wilderness."

Warden Willis encouraged. "We'll find 'em."

Parker's lined and weathered face softened, briefly. "I know you guys will pull
out all the stops. All my employees will be up here within the hour to help search."
He looked over at four men huddled over a map spread out on the hood of a truck.
"Those Rangers coming in is sure appreciated. That looks like Pete. He knows these
parts even better than Matthew and Sean. Other than Kyle, he's the best. Kyle's a
pain in the ass, protecting those wolves, but the best Micmac tracker in the north
country." He rubbed his forehead as Dubois told him that Kyle had been out tracking
Matthew and Maria within minutes of seeing the abandoned Jeep.

Parker nodded, and said, "Nothing makes sense here, Frank. What do you really
think? And don't give me the canned cop version."

"You're right, Parker. It's like they vanished. I called Augusta, and they're
sending a forensics team to dust the Jeep. Right now, it's all we've got. Joe Fazio
seems to be the last to see them at the cafe. I only hope there's a simple explanation,
like when you misplace your wallet or keys. They're always somewhere close by."

"Matt's an expert woodsman, Sean taught him well."

"Do you think the dog was with them?" Dubois asked.

"What dog?"

"The kids had a shepherd mix with them in town."

"Oh, right, I don't know, I'll ask Kate," Parker said. He watched as Phil Valdeorras
approached with Kate.

"Honey, Sean is on his way. I was able to reach his CO this morning."

Parker nodded, and they embraced. He then shook Phil's hand whose
countenance looked like a strong wind could snap him in two.

It had been forty-eight hours since Matthew and Maria disappeared. Dozens of cars
and trucks lined the one-mile stretch of parallel roads. Ranger Pete had called in
every ATV owner and boater in the area, official or civilian. Search parties were

underway on land and by water and Pete helped the agitated wardens coordinate a makeshift command center on the Ambajejus shoreline.

Someone hailed Warden Willis from up on the Golden Road. "That's Warden Donnie Leighton," Willis said. He's setting up a large tent and some tables down here." The warden jogged up the hill to meet Lieutenant Leighton.

A square-jawed, blonde, college-aged man approached Parker Eaton. "Mr. Eaton, I recognized you from the picture in Matthew's room." He shook Mr. Eaton's hand. "I'm Erich Schmidt. Matthew and I go to school together."

"Right, the carver," Parker said.

"Matthew showed us pictures of your eagles. I agree with Matthew, forget about engineering."

"Trying to tell that to my dad. So, I heard the news on the radio."

All eyes focused on two large colorful vans, clad with large satellite dishes, as they raced up the Golden Road from Millinocket.

A well-known reporter was speaking into the lens. "We are here in the North Woods of Maine where science savant, Matthew Eaton and his friend Maria Valdeorras, disappeared two days ago."

In seconds, Matthew and Maria had become national news.

A burly crew-cut stranger wrote down notes on a spiral pad while leaning against a gray Cadillac Seville. Kip Ackerman, the *New York Times* reporter who had written extensively about Dr. Jackson for many years, hurried toward the man.

Estebanez arrived that morning from Bahrain. He and Marcos lay on thick-cushioned lounge chairs, soaking in the sun at their Catamaran office and home, moored off the coast of Destin, Florida. A guard, wearing a shoulder-holstered .45 approached to hand Estebanez a portable telephone. The man returned to his post on the port side where he stood staring toward the shore. Across the boat stood another man of similar height and build, a cigarette hanging from his lips as he stared at his side of the ocean.

Estebanez said, "I've been away. Slow down. What are you talking about?" He listened for a moment before he dropped his cigar on the deck and leaped to his feet. "Bruno, Marty, get the dinghy." They ran mid-ship and down in the galley to change and pack overnight bags. They both slipped extra magazines and boxes of ammunition in with their gear. Marcos and Estebanez, then rushed to a dinghy attached to the stern of the yacht. To Bruno, he yelled, "Call ahead to have my plane pulled out of the hanger. We're going back to Maine."

Four hours later, the Cessna Citation V landed a hundred miles north of Millinocket at the Presque Isle Regional Airport. He considered flying into the Millinocket Regional Airport to save time but didn't want to bring the media down on top of him.

"Are you going to call him? What time is it there?"

"Late. He probably already knows." Estebanez cursed and hiked up to the air traffic controller's office where he borrowed the phone. "Hey, kid. I'm in Maine and will be on the scene in a few hours." He listened for a minute. "I'm not sure what to think." He listened for another moment. "Son of a—I'll call you as soon as I get there. I'm sorry, kid."

"He's upset?" Marcos asked.

"Damn right he is. I can't believe nobody called me."

"I'm sure nobody knew how to reach you—and nobody knows about me."

He placed both hands on his head and ran them down his face, stopping to massage his temples. *How could I have been so stupid?*

Twenty-seven feet above Matthew and Maria, two news crews camped out in the lobby of the Katahdin Sporting Lodge. Stacy Stossel, broadcasting live, interviewed the proprietor.

"Yes, I knew the kids well," Weaver said, "and it will be a tragedy if they aren't found. Why it wasn't long ago, young Matthew was studying chemistry or astronomy right over there." He pointed a bony finger in the direction of the library. "Of course, I had not seen him or Miss Valdeorras ... Would you like to see the library? Or perhaps my collection of Dennis Weaver memorabilia?" With that, the cameraman panned back to Stacy who, through a small receiver in her ear and a tiny microphone on her lapel, was in conversation with the Atlanta news anchor.

"Yes John, the people of the small mill town of Millinocket are in shock." She said into the camera, "There has been no word from the authorities that they have a lead." She listened before replying, "That's right, John. He is the very same young man who amazed the science community as a child. His high school science teacher told me this morning that Eaton won the Smithsonian Youth Inventors Award, six times. Matthew is currently a student at the University of Maine." She listened again. "Thank you, John. We'll be getting information to you as the story unfolds." She pulled the tiny microphone from her collar and handed it to her assistant. "Send Rick and Landon to town and get some interviews with the locals, see if they can find the paper mill employee who first reported the abandoned Jeep. Carlos. You and Sheila, stop at the picnic grounds where they set up the search and rescue command center. Linda, if you come across their parents, call me."

Back in Millinocket, reporters camped in front of the Eaton's home. Godello's closed. The ELF office and mills ran on skeleton crews.

Parker, Phil, and Kate had barely slept since their children went missing. Sean had arrived and led a team northwest of the search party camp.

Maria shivered and looked at her watch while repositioning her head on one of the duffel bags. "It's nearly noon. It'll be three days. Papa will be sick, and I'm worried about SoBe." She watched as Matthew pulled a dusty bottle out of a wine rack.

"How about a 1962 Chablis Grand Cru?" He stumbled on the pronunciation of Vaudesir Billaud-Simon and sat down next to her to dig out the cork with his pocketknife. "I'm worried about SoBe too." He looked at the empty wine bottles lined up in front of them. "Want another potato?"

"I don't think I want to see another potato as long as I live."

"My ancestors survived on potatoes, beans, and oats before the famine."

"Good for them. I want a steak." She sat up and held her head with both hands. "But I'll take another carrot."

"If we only had some oil, salt, pepper, foil, and a camping stove, I could make us a great hiker's stew. A few pounds of beef wouldn't hurt." He went over to the crates of carrots, potatoes, and onions. With his pocketknife, he peeled the skin off a carrot before handing it to Maria.

"Eh, what's up, doc?" she said with a wine-enhanced grin.

Matthew looked up from reading the last of more than forty journals. "You're a cute carrot-eating lush, Bugs."

"I'm worried about SoBe. You don't think Weaver would hurt her. And there are a lot Linx and wolves up here—"

"She can take care of herself," Matthew said, unconvincingly. SoBe was a Florida dog; not bred in the North Maine Woods like the dogs he grew up with.

She took the new bottle from Matthew to wash it down. "At least we're discerning drunks." She put a hand to her temple. "Oh, my head hurts. Speaking of headaches, you haven't needed your pills since we've been down here."

"That's true. Maybe it's the expensive wine?" Matthew removed a small notebook from his back pocket and made notations about the environment, humidity, barometric pressure, carrots, potatoes, and wine. Strange, he concluded. He had been in correspondence with Dr. Sacks in New York City, and hoped to meet him one day.

"I guess we are going to have to keep you drunk in a dungeon. Don't worry, we can set up your energy lab, and I'll allow you conjugal visits."

"Really? With who?"

Maria's jaw dropped, and she gave him that look. He knew what was coming as she knuckle-punched his shoulder. He could not control his laughing, which made her even more infuriated.

After the spar, and some afternoon makeup romance, Matthew leaned back against the cold wall and stared at one of the lamps. "The flames are flickering."

"So?"

"There has to be a breeze coming from somewhere."

Maria picked up the bottle and followed as he walked the outer perimeter of the cellar. Matthew found that the cool air was strongest along the floor. They walked to the far corner where crates of bottles and boxes of antique winemaking equipment blocked the back corner. The breeze came from between the rustic items.

Maria climbed unsteadily onto one of the barrels. She handed down crates and unusual iron and wood tools, as Matthew piled them up against another wall. When they finally cleared it all from the black wall, a door materialized, identical to the one leading from the library to the cellar. A rusted padlock with a skeleton keyhole on the handle, hung from the latch on a steel bar spanning the width of the door. The breeze was coming from where the dirt and rock floor had eroded to reveal a four-inch space.

Matthew went back to the pile where he'd thrown an iron pole. He slid it into the padlock and leveraged one end against the rock wall. "Let's just hope the old lock has weakened with time." With his foot against the wall, he pulled on the other end with all his might. It wouldn't budge. Then, he heard a heavy door creak.

"Someone's coming, Matthew."

"Hide," he said, running to retrieve Cameron Jackson's pistol.

Chapter Thirty-Seven

Search
June 6, 1995
11:00 a.m.

WHEN THEY GOT TO THE CRIME SCENE, Estebanez and Marcos saw the Jeep surrounded by four CSI officers surrounded by yellow crime tape. CSI had sprayed evidence squares on the grass around the vehicle. Cars, trucks, and vans of every kind lined the road.

Estebanez and Marcos joined the locals and law enforcement. Estebanez tried to avoid Flannigan. Shirt untucked, tie hanging wrinkled just below a day or two of stubble, the agent looked up and nodded. Estebanez turned away to look for Kate. He looked over at the square man leaning against the gray Cadillac Seville. The two saluted each other.

Marcos followed his uncle and said, "Mr. Kerr is a reliable friend."

"He's always willing to take time away from his retirement to help out," he said, and then thought, oh, shit, when Flannigan cut him off. "Hey, kid," he said to Marcos, "give me a few minutes."

"Hello, Estebanez, or is it Zebo today, or Smith?"

The men stared at each other. Flannigan chose his next words carefully. "The Jackson's meant a lot to me as well. You are here for them? Otherwise, a guy with your creds, shadowing a kid in Maine—makes no sense."

Estebanez squinted.

"A word of warning." Flannigan flipped his thumb over his shoulder. "There might be a few guys here that reek of paid mercenaries. I think they followed your boy from Miami to Maine."

"You got any names on these guys?"

"Lomax and DelGercio." He looked for a reaction and when he didn't get one, he asked, "You know anything about them?" Estebanez shook his head. Flannigan pointed toward the shore. "Do you see the guy over by the water—the one talking to Sean Eaton? His name is Kip Ackerman, he is with the *New York Times*."

That name rings a bell, Estebanez thought. Cameron mentioned him a few times. And ... something Cameron had said the week before—

"He says he can connect your Matthew with Cameron and Tremont Jackson and plans to release the story, once the kids are found." Flannigan held a long pause again. "If I were you, I would keep the press as far away from Matthew as possible."

Estebanez shook his head and said, "Thanks for the heads up."

Flannigan nodded, then reluctantly turned away.

Near one of the shelters, Estebanez spotted Joe Fazio, Sean Eaton, and Matthew's German friend. Flannigan walked over to them and handed his card to Erich while Estebanez struck up a conversation with Officer Dubois. He learned that Sean's search party had just returned from working their way north of the lakes around the base of Mount Katahdin.

Fazio said, "What the hell is he doing here?"

Estebanez glanced towards a man wearing a Dallas Cowboys cap. He began walking toward him when Fazio cut him off.

Officer Dubois finished writing in a notebook and said, "I'll let you know as soon as I know. You'll do the same?"

"Absolutely, Frank. Good to see you again," Estebanez said. He then turned to Joe Fazio and smiled. "I came as soon as I could." He reached his hand out to shake, but Fazio folded his arms and turned away. Sean stepped up and accepted the handshake and held it tight.

"It's good to see you again, Sean, though I wish it were under better circumstances. I hear you've had some serious tours—Iraq, Afghanistan, DC." Estebanez nodded at Erich.

Sean's shoulders relaxed. "Thanks for coming," he said, "We combed the north side of the lakes. My dad's going up in a helicopter right now. Mom is around here somewhere, but you knew that." He grinned. "You know Erich Schmidt, one of Matthew's buddies from UMaine." Estebanez nodded and introduced Marcos, and then Sean retreated to the tent.

"Sean is quite the guy," Erich said absently. "Matthew talked about him all the time. You too. I'd like to talk to you about getting into your line of work. I'm talking to Agent Flannigan as well."

"You are into boats and wine?" Estebanez asked. Erich stared blankly, then laughed. "Right, right. Got it." He winked.

"Your father is the well-known auto industrialist with BMW?" Estebanez had read a file on Erich's father and found it interesting that Erich and Matthew had become chums in college. Wilhelm Schmidt's file starts as a young engineer, working in the Führerbunker in Berlin, Germany, head of the Hitler motor pool. And later, as a co-conspirator with Claus von Stauffenberg in the East Prussia FHQ

Wolfsschanze, on the operation known as Valkyrie. Schmidt fled to Sweden and migrated to the United States after WWII.

"Yes, that's right," Erich said nervously. "I, um, I hope we find them soon." Erich went back to the shelter where Sean was filling packs with provisions for another day in the mountains.

Estebanez's heart began to race as he saw Kate Eaton approaching. Marcos grinned, and Estebanez lifted a finger as a warning. Marcos lowered his head and covered his grin with a hand.

"Kate, I got here as quick as I could. This is my nephew, Marcos."

"Thank you, Felix, it's all so bizarre. They have to find them." She struggled to hold back the tears. Regaining her composure, Kate looked at Marcos. "It's nice to meet you. I was beginning to think Felix had no family and was beamed down here from an alien ship."

"Well, that still may be true."

Kate gave him a half-hearted smile and asked, "Do you mind if I talk to your uncle alone?" She took Estebanez by the arm, and they walked away from all the commotion.

"I've missed you, Kate. And Matthew."

"I can't tell you how upset Matthew was that you came and went without seeing him."

"Things got crazy with my other businesses and—" He noticed something other than worry in her eyes. "What is it, Kate?"

"I have to ask you something, Felix."

"Sure."

"Do you know anything about all of this?"

"How could you even think such a thing?" Estebanez pulled away from Kate in a show of indignation.

Kate seemed embarrassed. "I've never pressed you about your past, but Joe Fazio—"

"You don't have to say more. Old Colombo Joe has been on my ass for years. I have nothing but Matthew's best interest at heart." That part was real, he thought.

"I know. Joe's also looking out for our family." She hesitated. "But this all happened after Matthew read your note."

"That was nothing but a game, you know, the word game we've been playing for years. I'm still trying to figure out the last one he gave to me to solve."

"I must admit I thought the riddle a bit strange."

Estebanez frowned. "You read it?"

"Of course," she said.

The sound of trucks arriving got their attention. She retreated to greet the latest search party coming from the north. Estebanez wanted to say something to dispel all her worries when he noticed that the arriving search party included Parker Eaton.

He said to Marcos, "This would be a good time to check out the lodge and see what Weaver knows."

"You don't want to face the other man, Uncle?" he asked.

"Keep your thoughts to yourself, or there'll be another missing person around here."

As they walked toward the rental car, Marcos couldn't resist. "She's close to your age. That's a first."

No exactly the first, he thought. As always, when he thought of Kate, Karen came to mind.

Marcos ducked as Estebanez tried to smack him alongside the head. "You are misconstruing concern among friends. Let's find young Eaton, shall we?" They withdrew as the other four-wheel drive vehicles arrived.

Estebanez sped up Baxter Park Road. He looked in his rearview mirror to see a familiar Land Rover spin through the dirt and onto the road behind him. At first, he thought he should lose the tail, but he had to find Matthew and check on Jackson's research. He wondered which was more important. His professional training said the research, but his heart said the kid. Maybe they were one and the same.

They turned up the gravel driveway to the Katahdin Sporting Lodge.

"You trust this guy? Dennis something?"

"Dennis Weaver. You know, like the actor?"

"Don't know him."

"McCloud?"

"Nope."

"*Seven Angry Men?*"

"Nope."

"*Gentle Ben?*"

"Never was much for television."

"Well, don't mention that to him."

"Gotcha."

After a long silence, Estebanez said, "What is it?"

"Agent Flannigan had some interesting things to say."

"Yeah, well every time he's involved, someone gets hurt. He should stay the hell away."

"I was there in Miami," Marcos said. "I didn't—"

"You did exactly what Tremont told you to do. You got those kids out of there safely. As I've said before, there was nothing else you could do. Tremont knew the risks."

"I know but—"

"Let's focus on finding Matthew." The truth was, Estebanez blamed himself. He should have been down there, watching Marcos's and Tremont's back. If, he thought,

I had made as many mistakes as an operative, as I've made with the Jacksons, and Matthew, I'd have been dead a long time ago.

They pulled into the parking lot in front of the lodge. Four hunters in full camouflage were stowing gear into their truck. They looked out of place. But this was a tourist area where people came from all over the world to hunt, fish, and hike. He studied the men again.

Estebanez was glad to see that the media had departed. An elderly couple walked on a path along the cliff overlooking the valley and Mount Katahdin. A peregrine falcon, white with black speckles, and a black-hooded face, screamed and swooped within a few feet of the hunters. The Micmac would call that a sign, and not a good one. A dog barked nearby. He wondered where SoBe was.

"Wow," Marcos said, "You don't see that in Florida."

"On second thought, why don't you stay out here? Try to stall Joe Fazio."

"The big Sicilian? No problem," Marcos replied.

"And keep an eye on those hunters; the Arab—"

"Arab?"

"He has put the same bag in and out of the truck twice. I'll only be a few minutes."

A Land Rover sped into the parking lot and came to an abrupt halt next to Marcos. Joe Fazio struggled out of the vehicle. "All this hiking is more than I'm used to," he said to Marcos. He tried to step aside Marcos, but Marcos continued to bar his path. "It's Joe, isn't it?"

"What are you and your uncle doing up here?"

"He thought they might know something."

Marcos grabbed Fazio's beefy arm as he pushed.

"You really don't want to be touching me, kid," Fazio said. "I snap bread sticks bigger than you."

"My uncle wanted to talk to the owner alone, first. Less threatening."

"I'll tell you what I know. Your uncle is up to something and knows a whole hell of a lot more than he's letting on. I'm betting he's been up to no good ever since he showed up in the region." Fazio lifted the snap off his shoulder holster and checked the load of his old police-issue model .38-caliber revolver. He was about to head up the stairs when he heard the grating sound of a magazine seated in the frame of a gun. He turned around to see Marcos holding a 9mm Beretta.

Marcos smiled. "Let's just wait and see what my uncle comes up with."

Before Fazio could reply, a gunshot went off inside the lodge, then another, and another. Without looking at each other, the two ran up the steps. Marcos put a hand on the door and waited for Fazio's nod to push the huge door open. They both kept their guns in ready position when they entered the foyer.

Weaver and another man lay on the floor in pools of blood. In Weaver's hand was a nineteenth century long-barrel Colt pistol from his antique collection. Blood seeped out of a wound in his neck. Fazio knelt, checked Weaver's pulse, then closed the innkeeper's eyes. He picked up his gun to waist height, then disappeared around the corner.

Marcos kept his gun on the other victim while he kicked the gun out of his hand. He checked for a pulse. "Dead," he announced.

The sound of people at the top of the stairs brought Fazio back into the foyer. Marcos aimed his gun up the stairs. "It's okay." Lodge guests stood staring over the catwalk above. One woman screamed when she saw the bodies.

"Get back to your rooms, folks," Marcos said. "There's been a shooting."

A maid came down the hallway behind Marcos and screamed when she saw Weaver's body. Marcos told her to go back to somewhere safe.

Fazio left again to check the rest of the lodge. He met up with Marcos in the lobby. "There's no sign of your uncle and the first floor is clear." He looked at the gun and said, "I'll bet that relic backfired. Where the hell is Estebanez?"

Estebanez came from the east hall of the lodge. "There was at least one more in the hotel. He went out the back, and I lost him." Kneeling over the unidentified body, he whispered "Domenick, you idiot." He laid a hand over the dead man's eyes. *"Que Dios lo tenga en la gloria,"* he whispered.

"You know him, Uncle Z?"

"We worked together in Havana back in the day. It was just before the Gipper signed Executive Order 12333.[37] That was the last time we *legally* tried to take out Castro. Domenick DelGercio," he said, "had the highest CIA security clearance. Last I heard, he was a NOC in Europe."

"Z? Is that what you are, Estebanez?" Fazio pressed. "NOC? CIA? I figured something like that when your records came up cleaner than Mother Teresa."

Estebanez did not pay attention to Fazio. He rubbed his eyes. "Domenick was a good man, but he must have become a gun for hire after the Cold War went warm."

Marcos asked, "Was he the one at the Bronx Park? You put a bullet in his shoulder."

"I winged him before he shot the kid."

"What?" Fazio said and raised his .38 toward Estebanez.

"We're the good guys, Fazio." Estebanez said.

"I'm not so sure. That guy in the Dallas Cowboy's cap was talking about the kids caught in the middle of a shooting in the Bronx. You've got some explaining to do."

Estebanez noted the familiar quip and looked at Fazio strangely. "Let's put our differences aside until we find them, okay?"

"Drop the act," Fazio said. "Where are the kids, you bastard? You may have

---

[37] Executive Order 12333: Part 2.11 No person employed by or acting on behalf of the United States Government shall engage in, or conspire to engage in, political assassination.

fooled the people of Millinocket, but in Chicago, we would have run you out on a rail years ago."

"Joe, put down the gun," Marcos said. He had slipped behind Fazio and was aiming his 9mm at his back.

"For Matthew's sake, you're going to have to trust me," Estebanez said. "Do you really think I intended to hurt these kids?"

Joe lowered his gun. "Go on."

"It appears Weaver was holding them for ransom," Estebanez said, altering the truth somewhat. He explained to Fazio that seconds before Weaver was shot by DelGercio, the old man had confessed that he had been offered a sizable sum by two interested parties: DelGercio and an Arab man.

"Why would people like them be interested in Matthew?"

"I haven't a clue."

"You're lying. DelGercio might have shot Weaver, but don't tell me Weaver shot DelGercio."

"When I stepped into the foyer, they were arguing. Weaver had his gun on DelGercio."

"So, what did they want with the kids?"

"We might never know," Estebanez lied. "Before Weaver tried to take a shot at Domenick, he told me all he had to do was hold the kids for a few hours. When hours turned into days, he must have mentally shut down. The Weaver I knew was eccentric and maybe a bit greedy, but he wouldn't have hurt the kids. I've seen him shut down like this a few times. Just before Dom shot him, Weaver corrected me by saying his name was McCloud, not Weaver, that Weaver was an alias, and he was undercover."

"Nutcase," Fazio said. "So, where are they?"

"If you can keep the hunters distracted, I can look for Matthew and Maria. We need to buy some time until the cavalry arrives."

"What hunters?"

Marcos went to the front door and looked out. "They are moving toward us."

Fazio stepped next to Marcos. "If those are game hunters, then I'm Princess Di."

"I called the command center and spoke to Flannigan." Estebanez lied. The last thing he needed was the FBI and the media up here.

Fazio lowered his gun. "Why don't *you* watch the Arabs, and I'll look for Matthew and Maria?"

Marcos lowered his gun as well and went to the front windows.

Estebanez said, "I know this lodge. Hopefully, I can find Matthew and Maria before someone else does. With your help."

"If you're playing me," Fazio added while going through the front door, "I will make sure you never step foot in Maine again, never talk to *any* of the Eatons ever again."

Marcos said. "I'll watch the back."

Fazio walked out onto the porch, whistling. He sat down in one of the rocking chairs with his gun tucked to his side. Marcos looked at his uncle waiting for an explanation. When none came, he hustled to guard the back doors of the lodge.

Estebanez ran to the front desk and retrieved a flashlight and matches. Back in the foyer, he peered out front. The alleged hunters were milling around the parking lot with marked professional caution. He wondered what was holding them back from storming into the lodge.

When Estebanez was sure it was only him and the two dead bodies, he went to the library and searched along a shelf next to the false bookcase. He found the book he was looking for, the first edition of Noah Webster's *The American Spelling Book*, 1801. He figured this book had been off the shelf no more than a dozen times in the last two hundred years, and each time due to him. He retrieved the duplicate key taped behind it.

He then turned off the lights and waited. Thunder rolled in the distance. While turning the skeleton key in his hand, he thought about New York City ten years ago, when he had a locksmith duplicate the original key. While he waited for the key, he had made a detour to Sotheby's, where he put the first of Weaver's wines up for auction. He might have felt guilty but considering all the international laws he had broken over his career, this little venture was the easiest to forget. He deposited half of the money in his Swiss bank account, and the other half in what he liked to refer to as MEET, Matthew Eaton's Energy Trust, also a Swiss account. Before the sniper killed Cameron, Estebanez had promised the scientist to continue to keep an eye on Tremont and Matthew, and to help them bring CJ Energy to fruition, should anything happen to him. Estebanez also made the same promise to Karen about Cameron and their unborn baby. He was also to make sure they never needed to go to the government or the public for funds. Weaver provided the perfect vessels to pump up the savings, to add to his collection of mission targets' ill-gotten gains. He never killed or stole from anyone that didn't have it coming to them. Estebanez justified Weaver's donations due to the way he hoarded wines that belonged to the world. Okay, he thought, that's a bit of a stretch.

As he opened the false bookshelf and unlocked the first door, he smiled at the memory of that first bottle. He chose one of five rare old bottles from the cellar that none of the experts at Sotheby's London thought existed. He didn't tell them there were more. He sold the bottle in a private auction for $314,000. Soon, after their acquaintance, Estebanez had realized that Weaver had long since lost track of the expansive inventory in the cellar. Over ten years, Estebanez had sold fifty-three bottles. Each Swiss account now had more than five million dollars. With interest and good investing, there should be enough for Matthew to launch the greatest world-changing invention since electricity. His smile turned to a frown as he wondered if Matthew was still alive. Weaver, if you weren't already dead, I'd kill you.

He pulled the doors behind him and hustled down the steps to the next door.

"What the hell is this?" He lifted a heavy padlock, like the one at the top of the stairs. He cursed and hoped that the same key would fit. He dropped the key in his haste, but when he finally got it in the skeleton keyhole, he heaved a sigh of relief.

He stepped into the cellar and called out. He drew his gun and walked to the far-right side where he'd stored the duffel bags. When he got to the back, the bags were gone. He bent down and pushed over a pile of carrot and potato shavings. Behind him, he noticed a lot of empty wine bottles sitting in neat rows and smiled. Judging by the labels, they'd consumed a small fortune. He knelt, picked up a few corks that were in perfect condition. He studied the slits in the top. Smart, he thought. Estebanez knew ten ways to remove a cork without a corkscrew, and it seems that Matthew used the serrated knife method.[38]

Backtracking through the maze, he got to the other side and found stacks of crates and winemaking equipment. He worked his way to a door. He kicked something and knelt to find a busted padlock and a long pipe. He pushed on the door, and it leaned open. Dusk was settling in. He could see plenty of lush vegetation, but nothing more. He put his full weight against the door and it flew open. He grabbed at the doorframe and his fingers latched on as he dangled over the sheer cliff. He swung his legs forward, and his body passed vertically on the way back. No luck. He tried again, and again. On the fourth try he let go and landed on the edge of the cellar floor, wobbled … and got his balance.

While on the floor catching his breath, he noticed a splotch of crimson.

As he retreated to the steps, he studied the floor. He found what he was looking for: stains of blood along the wall where someone stumbled toward the stairs. The picture was becoming clear. He ran up the steps. More blood. He pushed the shelves out and peered into the library. He could hear Fazio talking, or more accurately, arguing. He left the door unlocked and closed the bookshelves.

He looked at Weaver's hands. One was covered in dry blood. His blue blazer revealed a tear where a bullet had grazed his arm. The blood had flowed down his arm where it dripped from his hand.

"What have you done, Weaver?" he hissed. "Marcos!"

Marcos came around the corner. "One of the Arabs was out back. He won't wake up for a while. What did you find in the wine cellar?"

"Nada. But the kids were down there. I want to look out back and to the left, toward the valley and the lake. Either someone took them out of the cellar, or they went over the cliff. It's a straight drop to the bottom."

---

[38] Matthew apparently used the serrated knife method, pushing the point of his knife in as far as possible and then screwing and pulling the cork out. He could also have pounded the butt of the bottle against a wall; pushed a knotted string through a hole; pushed the cork into the bottle; screwed a large screw into the cork (but he would need pliers); or pushed a ball inflation needle into the cork, with a bike pump, and the cork will pop out.

"The research?"

"Gone."

"That can't be good."

Marcos moved to the window and Estebanez to the door. With a glance to the sky, Marcos said, "That storm is coming in fast."

One of the hunters growled at Fazio. "Look, Capone, you are what, a private dick? No authority here. So, I think you will let us into the lodge, yes?"

"Don't think so, Saddam," Fazio replied.

Marcos whispered to Estebanez, "There's one to the right of the porch. Can't see to the left. There's at least one over there, and there's one by the truck. That leaves one more Arab and DelGercio's man unaccounted for."

Tucking his gun out of sight, Estebanez stepped outside. "We got a problem here, Joe?"

A light rain was falling. Thunder cracked. "I don't think these guys are hunting rabbit or elk."

"What is your business up here, sir?" Estebanez asked, though he recognized the leader. The family resemblance was uncanny.

The Arab relaxed his shoulders. "We do not want any problems, Mr. Estebanez. We are vacationing in this beautiful land and concerned about the shots we heard inside the lodge. I assure you, we mean no harm. We would like to check in and dine."

Estebanez reasoned, if they had the research, they would already be gone. Weaver must have thought he could benefit from a bidding war between Dom and these men.

"Ali bin Taliffan," Estebanez asserted.

The man straightened his shoulders and said, "Prince Ali Mohamed Sharif bin Taliffan, at your service."

"I'm familiar with your family. Particularly your brothers, Omar and Bahir."

"Cousins. *Qad yastarih eumar alrruh mae Allah*," May Omar's soul rest with God.

"Omar *rruhih mae lashshaytan*," Omar's soul, Estebanez said in perfect Sunni Arabic, is with Satan.

"If I did not know you were an ignorant Westerner, I might be insulted and forced to take revenge."

"It's a good thing that I'm ignorant, then," Estebanez said. "Well, Prince, here's the situation. I believe you had business with Weaver. He's dead." Bin Taliffan didn't blink. "From the way I see it, old Weaver was playing you against another interested party, and now there are two bodies in the foyer."

Bin Taliffan's smile disappeared. "I would like to see this for myself."

Fazio was about to object. Estebanez raised a hand to cut him off and opened the door for bin Taliffan. He signaled Fazio to continue keeping guard outside. Looking

confused and miffed, Fazio settled into the rocking chair. "If you guys are game hunters, I'm the Sultan of Arabia."

Inside, Ali bin Taliffan looked at Marcos. "I don't suppose there's a price I could offer you for the merchandise Mr. Weaver was kindly holding for us?"

"I don't know what merchandise you're referring to, Prince Ali. How is your Harvard Crimson Rowing team doing? I understand you led quite a crew there."

"You went to Harvard?" Marcos stated. "Man, I'm all for emigration, but we sure educate our competition, don't we? You and your family go back and play with supply and demand and increase per barrel prices using economic models you learned at Harvard."

Estebanez gave Marcos a look that said, "Not now."

Bin Taliffan's eyes narrowed. "I believe this country has been good to Cuban dissidents." He revealed a bright white smile.

Marcos pushed away from the wall to respond, but his uncle put up a hand. Marcos leaned back, crossed his arms in a way such that his 9mm gun was more visible.

"Let us not dance around the subject. My sponsors are willing to offer you a seven-digit sum, negotiable."

"Whatever you're looking for, must be quite a threat to your sponsors. But I can't help you. Before this place is swarming with police, FBI, and media, you should get on your way. And make a call to Austria. Let cousin Bahir know what he's looking for—if it did exist, is gone."

"And what assurance do I have of that, Mr. Estebanez?"

"My word."

"The word of an international spy?"

"You flatter me, Ali. I am but a teacher and mild-mannered, rare wine and sailboat merchant," Estebanez said.

Marcos could not quite stifle a snicker.

As the rain came down harder and he heard sirens in the distance, Estebanez put a hand on Ali's back and escorted him out the door. The sirens got louder.

Ali stopped and turned; his eyes seemed to change color as they burned into Estebanez. "We will meet again."

"Fabulous. I'll bring my catalogs to the meeting." He moved his hand to Ali's wrist and squeezed. "If you or anyone comes near Millinocket again, you'll endure more than a few swings of a bat. And then, you will join Omar. *Hal Tefahome?*" Do you understand?

Ali's eyes burned brighter.

Fazio, pointing to a seven-foot totem pole, said, "And I will send you all to what the natives here call *the happy hunting ground.*"

Bin Taliffan pinched Fazio's cheek. He pulled away in time to miss a punch from the angry detective. Ali backed down the steps, looked up into the rain and thickening black clouds, then back up at Fazio. "By the way, Capone, there is no Sultan of Arabia. But if there were, you could not shine the rubies on his robes."

Thunder crashed, and the rain blew in waves. Fazio stood and lifted his revolver. Estebanez put his hand on the cold steel. "Let's turn our attention to finding the kids."

The alleged hunters, including one who stumbled into the lot from the back of the lodge, retreated to their dual cab pick-up truck, and headed down the driveway.

Lights glistening in the rain and with sirens blaring, a cavalcade of vehicles roared into the parking lot of the lodge.

Chapter Thirty-Eight

Storm
June 6, 1995
9:00 p.m.

KATE LEANED AGAINST THE POST that made up the center of the large tent—the command center. She watched as Parker, Sean, and Erich scanned a topographical map with two game wardens. Sean marked off all the areas combed by the three search parties and took out a yellow highlighter to mark unsearched areas.

A man approached Parker. He said, "Hello, big brother."

Everyone turned their heads to look at the newcomer. Kate ran over and threw her arms around her brother-in-law. "I'm so glad you are here."

Parker walked over to his brother. "So, it takes this to get you home?"

"No. If you were in a pine box, I'd come for that too."

They were like two black bears facing off over a bee hive, Kate thought, as they stared each other down. You could hear the water lapping against the beach. After a long moment, Parker put his hand out, and they shook. She shook her head but smiled. It was tough to get Mainer men to hug at a funeral.

"What did you fly, the Phenom?" Sean asked, referring to one of Carl's smaller jets.

"No, we have a new Piper Cheyenne; I thought I'd break her in."

"How did you know about this mess?" Parker asked.

Carl hesitated and glanced quickly toward St. Adams who turned away. "I heard it on the radio and flipped on the TV."

Parker stared at his prodigal brother for a minute longer, then returned to studying the maps.

Kate watched as Maria's father withdrew toward the dark sky. He said, "That storm is moving in fast. Chief Tanner says it's a bad omen, that the mountain is angry. We have a similar mythological god in the Basque country, *El monstruo de Bibao.*

If they're out there—" he choked back his tears. "Kate. If I lost Maria—"

Kate put a hand on his shoulder. "We'll find them soon, Phil. I would know in my heart if anything happened to Matthew."

"Yes. Salina always knew … even before Maria caught a cold." Kate put her arm on his shoulder and led him toward the shelter, away from the wind and rain.

Deputy Dubois and a ranger approach at a run. The ranger said, "A call came in from the Lodge. There were gunshots, and the guest said that two men were dead. The innkeeper, was one of them."

They watched as reporters and their teams rushed to their vans.

"Vultures!" Parker sniped. "They smell blood, and they're off."

Sean folded the maps. He and Erich edged towards the tent entrance.

"How could that be related to all of this?" Erich asked.

"I doubt that it is," Sean said. "I'm sure we'll get details once that pack of reporter wolves gets up there."

"Where the hell do you think you're going?" Parker barked.

Erich replied, "Mr. Eaton, we were studying the map, and there's one area on the north side of—something Jesus lake."

"Ambajejus."

"Right," Erich said, "Both search crews missed it. It's pretty rough ground, but we thought the two of us could handle it better than a large group."

"Take the mule," Parker said, handing Erich the keys to the six-wheel company truck.

Kate jumped as thunder cracked, and it began to rain harder.

Pete came over the hill with a soaked dog at his heels. Two much larger German Shepherds from the K-9 unit rushed out of the tent barking at the new dog.

"Mrs. Eaton, Mr. Eaton!" Pete said breathlessly. "Pamola may be changing his mind. I think you'll want to come across to the Millinocket Lake beach." He was holding a pair of binoculars. "I was accounting for the search boats when this dog comes out of nowhere," he leaned over to catch his breath. "She kept running to the water, and then back to me."

"You're making no sense, Pete!" Parker said.

Kate threw her arms around the dog's neck. "SoBe! What a good girl!"

"Mom, do you know this dog?" Sean asked incredulously.

"She's Matthew's … and Maria's! It's SoBe!"

"Matthew has a dog?" Sean said, and looked at his father. Parker Eaton raised his eyebrows and nodded.

Sean grabbed Pete by the shirt and jerked him. "What else, Pete? Spit it out."

"Well, after the dog came out of the water, I ran to my truck and got my infrared binocs out, and I got to tell you—" He stopped and bent over. "I knew Pamola was behind all of this. My mother said it took its prisoners."

"Prisoners? What prisoners?" Erich asked.

"Matthew and Maria, he must have taken them to Alomkik, but, then a few hours ago, Chief Tanner said he saw in a vision that they were on the water. I knew—"

Sean still had Pete by the arm and shook him again. "Damn it, Pete, we know all about the God of Thunder! Why is everything such a production for you? What is it, man?"

"It could be Matthew and Maria!"

As the rain intensified, SoBe barked, ran ahead, then back to the crowd, and then back up the hill. Like a scene out of Frankenstein, the group pushed Pete up across the dike, toward the other lakeshore.

At the water's edge, it was impossible to see anything with the moon behind clouds.

"Everyone quiet for a minute," Parker yelled. "Listen."

They heard the faint sound of a small motor. Parker snatched the infrared binoculars from Pete. No one breathed. "I see them! By God, it's them!"

Sean grabbed the glasses. "I'll be damned."

There was a collective cheer. "They must be a couple miles out," Parker said. "Pete, what the hell are you waiting for? Let's get in a boat and go get them."

Sean put down the binoculars. "There's a slight problem, Dad."

It was the first time in a long-time, that Sean had referred to him as anything other than sir or something with an obscenity attached to it.

"What, son? What?"

"I've never seen waves like that on any of the lakes."

Erich said, "The waves are kicking that little boat around like a Styrofoam cup."

"Let's get out there, or they'll be taking a swim," Pete said.

"Nobody's better on the water than Matthew," Kate said, but her voice lacked her usual confidence.

Thunder pounded in the heavens, followed by lightning bolts that seemed to stretch all the way to the water. In the brief light, the group could make out the small craft, about the size of a quarter, as it lifted above the waves and then disappeared.

"Let's go!" Pete stood on the back of a boat tied up to a tree. Thunder muted the outboard motors when the Eatons, Erich, and Maria's father, climbed into the boat. They bounced out into the choppy water. "I've radioed to the Wardens and Rangers. Hopefully, we won't need them." Pete flipped on a searchlight as the clouds released a violent rage of stinging rain. Navigation was impossible.

"Why are you slowing down, Pete?" Kate yelled over the sound of the rain and the boat motor.

"I don't want to run them down."

Sean stood at the helm with the infrared binoculars. "There's no sign of them."

"They couldn't just have disappeared," Erich said.

"If they went over—" Pete's thought escaped into the wind.

"I see the boat!" Kate yelled and pointed. Pete turned the spotlight on the rowboat. It was floating upside down. The small motor sputtered faintly.

Sean handed the binoculars to his father and flipped off his shoes and socks. He dove into the rising waves. Pete guided the cruiser in the direction of the rowboat, which had now vanished. He pulled the spotlight off the rack to shine it in slow arcs.

They had lost sight of Sean.

Parker held a ringed buoy in his hand. Sean's head broke the surface. He caught the ring buoy his father casted. Phil and Parker braced and pulled. Phil yelled, "Maria!" and nearly dropped the rope. "Hang on, Phil," Parker shouted.

Sean swan towards the boat and held up Maria's arms. Her father took her hands and, with Parker, pulled her onto the boat. Kate checked her vital signs.

"She's not breathing!" Kate said and began performing CPR.

While Kate tried to revive Maria, Pete yelled at Sean. "Did you see Matthew?"

"I'm going back! Get the light on me." Pete pulled himself on board, helped Erich up, while Sean swam back into the darkness.

"I thought you couldn't swim, Erich!" Pete yelled.

"I can't!" Erich replied. It's a long story. Matthew and I—"

While Pete maneuvered the boat, Parker held the light on Sean. Still, there was no sign of Matthew.

Maria coughed from behind him.

Kate choked on a sob and rolled Maria on her side as she coughed up lake water. She opened her eyes to see Mrs. Eaton and her father looking down at her. She mouthed, *Matthew.*

Off toward shore, they could see three, four, now five lights. Small fishing boats moved toward them. Pete got on the bullhorn. "Slow down! Slow down!" He blinked the searchlight in Morse code: *slow, slow, slow.* He followed with *Man overboard. Man overboard.* The boat captains slowed and spread out, their searchlights scanning the water in all directions.

Sean dove in a controlled pattern, knowing the chance of finding his baby brother in the dark lake water was slim. He held to the rowboat to catch his breath. "Matthew!" He dove and resurfaced. "Matthew, damn it, we need you," he gasped. He dove again. Everything depended on his brother.

Under the dark waves, he saw flashes of light, and the indistinguishable faces of his victims. Six faces were clear. One he had seen often in the tent with Tremont. He kicked to the surface gasping for air. "If Tremont hadn't just walked away from it." He was close to screaming. A wave hit him hard and he went under. When he came up, he sputtered and coughed. "Tremont. If it wasn't for him—." He reached for the rowboat and clung to the side. "I'm sorry," he screamed, "I did what I had to do, bro." Then he laughed, a crazy laugh. "But, it was a hell of a shot; 1,823 meters. One hell of a shot. If the old scientist had lived—"

The sound of metal against metal. He skulled the water; turning; a light blinded him. Pete held onto the other side of the overturned rowboat.

"What the hell, Sean? That old scientist in DC?"

"Just talking bullshit, Pete, that's all. Damn, PSTD. The shrinks want to take me out of action, but the boys at the Pentagon know they need me. But I'm fine. Just talking crazy. Put out that light … just need a second to breath."

Pete smacked a hand against the boat. "Jackson! A day after the murder, you showed up in town. Nick had just opened the Sailor Son. You were spouting off about all the crazy radical Islamics you killed and how you could take out a terrorist at 1,800 meters."

"You never knew when to keep your mouth shut."

"What's all that got to do with Matthew?"

"Pete!" Sean snapped. "Let's focus on finding Matthew."

Sean took a deep breath and went under the water.

After a dozen more dives, Sean cursed and began to swim toward the fishing boat. Something in the water out into the open water caught his attention. It was more of a sense of something, like the way he knew a Mujahideen warrior approached his camp. He stopped and stared into the distance. He turned out to the wide-open lake.

The exhausted crew strained to see through the stinging wind and rain. "Where's Sean going?" Erich yelled.

Parker turned the boat in the direction Sean was swimming and pushed its throttle. Everyone saw his target—a red and white metal cage on top of a white buoy, bouncing on the waves.

Erich asked, "What is it, Mr. Eaton?"

"It's a warning beacon. The light is burnt out.

Sean grabbed onto the buoy. "Damn good thinking." Matthew had tied himself to the beacon. Blood was seeping from the old headwound. He was unconscious but alive.

Erich jumped in the water with Sean. It was all everyone could do to get Matthew's limp body onto the boat.

Parker signaled the other boats by blinking his searchlight in Morse Code: *Success. Alive.* The other boats soon converged upon the Eaton crew.

The news went out from radio to radio that the kids from Millinocket were alive. The crowd from shore watched as the searchlights headed toward shore. Fifty yards above the beach, media, medics and search teams began to congregate on the dike between the North Woods Trading Post and Big Moose Inn.

Parker and Sean stood on one side of the ambulance, Kate and SoBe on the other. The EMT's pulled the ambulance doors shut. It sped off and disappeared into a curtain of rain. Sean turned his head and saw Chief Tanner. Their eyes locked. Sean looked away.

Down on Millinocket Lake, the last boat limped into shore.

The news was grave. Pete's body lay on a gurney. The med tech covered his head with the white blanket and tightened the buckles on four straps across his body.

Chief Tanner shook his gray head. He turned and looked up just before thunder boomed. Everyone looked in the same direction to see a long flash of lightning that seemed to touch and linger at the peak of Mount Katahdin, outlining Pamola.

Epilogue

Genesis
The Summer of 1995

THE BALANCE OF SUMMER PASSED. After three days in intensive care, and another three recuperating, Matthew stood on the front steps of Millinocket Regional Hospital. He had ten stitches in his scalp.

Matthew leaned against a pillar on the steps of the hospital. A man kept glancing up from his tennis magazine and smiling. He was short, younger than middle-aged, with wiry black hair, wearing an ugly patterned sweater, a yarmulke on the back of his head, khakis, and topsiders. Another reporter, Matthew surmised.

He said, "Hello, Matthew, I'm Kip Ackerman, from—"

"Oh. I know who you are," Matthew said bluntly. Mr. E had warned him about Ackerman, and there were references to him in Dr. Jackson's journals.

"You must be getting tired of reporters. I know things are touch and go with Maria, so I just wanted to give you my card. When things settle down, I'd like to fly you to New York. I know some things that you need to know." He trotted down the steps without looking back.

"What kind of things?" Matthew hollered after him. The reporter waved without turning back around. He seemed genuinely concerned, Matthew thought.

Matthew trotted down the steps and out to the Jeep. At Rideout's AG Market he saw a late model white Thunderbird—with a red convertible top. He spun the Jeep around and sped down Poplar Street but lost the T-Bird in town. He returned to the grocery and then back to the hospital. He touched the tender wound on his head. "I know what I saw," he said, trying to convince himself.

Matthew stopped at the nurse's station and asked for Dr. Nancy Fielding.

"When do you think Maria will wake up?"

"Honey, her hypothermia was severe. It could be a while."

Matthew stayed with Maria and slept in the waiting room after visiting hours, sneaking back in after Nurse Clara would kick him out.

One night after he left the hospital, he sat in his Jeep and perused through a stack of mail his mother had given him. One envelope caught his attention; the return address was the Federal Bureau of Investigation. He tore it open and inside was a business card with the name of Patrick R. Flannigan, Special Investigator. On the back of the card: *Call me if you need me.*

As he walked toward the hospital and put the card in his wallet, he bumped into a man who pulled his baseball cap down over his eyes. Darma's description. The star on his cap and the cleft chin was enough to send his mind into high alert. The man jogged up the steps to the hospital. Matthew followed. While he walked he slipped off his backpack, reached in and carefully unfolded a black leather pouch, loaded a magazine, and snapped it into Jackson's .45. He looked up and the man was gone. Skating past the nurse's station, he stayed the entire night in Maria's room.

Matthew tried Sean at their house, but his mother said he had been staying in town. He knew Nick St. Adam had a room over the Sailor Son Saloon and tried calling. Bingo. Nick said Sean was sleeping off a four—or five-day drinking bender. Nick would not let him drive home, and said Sean repeated something about the angry spirits.

"Did your Uncle Carl say anything?"

"About what?"

"I'll have Sean call you at the hospital, Matt," Nick said and hung up.

The call came through to the hospital an hour later. Matthew took it at the nurse's station and was surprised to find Sean coherent. He thought seriously about telling Sean about the T-bird, and the man in the Cowboys cap and didn't know why he hesitated. After a long silence, Sean suggest that they should meet a couple of hours a day at the ELF barn. It would be good for Matthew.

Reluctantly, with the urging of Mr. V and his mother, Matthew left the hospital and took the Golden Road up to the barn. He and Sean started working together on the bus and the distraction seemed to help. It appeared that Sean was sober. But it was hard to tell for sure.

Sean informed Matthew he'd received orders to report to the Pentagon in a week. His superiors said he had to take a desk job for a while.

"DIA?" Matthew asked.

"I'm attached to three agencies, DIA, NRO, and TID.[39] No wonder I'm a mess," Sean joked.

"What do you mean?"

"They say its PTSD. But that's a label used to get out of a soldier's duty, in my opinion. Hand me that wrench."

---

[39] Defense Intelligence Agency (DIA) is a section of the Department of Defense, (DoD). National Reconnaissance Office (NRO) is one of the big five intelligence agencies. Terrorist Intelligence Division (TID). No information is currently available on the TID.

Matthew thought it explained a lot and wondered if he should tell his parents. He rubbed his eyes. "I'll be right back." He and SoBe went out into the bright sunlight. He was afraid he might have his own breakdown, his own PSTD. He had held it together in front of everyone. When he was alone, he was surprised to find out how religious he had become. Not that it was a bad thing, he considered. He had once called his mother and grandmother, professional prayers. Something that he was not very good at. He looked up to see a golden eagle contrasting against a single white cloud. The Micmac's believe they are a good sign, especially after a storm. He needed a good sign. Tears welled up in his eyes.

The day before the biggest day of the summer, Sean picked up Matthew at the hospital in the mule, their father's GMC Dooley six-wheel truck. They drove northwest on Millinocket Road, took a left onto Fire Road 13, a right to Fire Road 15, then soon turned north into a dirt road, taking them through a copse of pines. The woods opened to a clearing where the abandoned mechanic's shop sat between other ELF buildings.

They ate sandwiches their mother made, drank cold Sea Dog Old Gollywobbler Ale, painted, and repaired the barn. The next day they began to patch the war-torn VW bus with Bondo, *lots* of Bondo. Matthew told Sean, he was thinking about setting the barn up as a place to work on his research. But he didn't say anything about the extent of the research, just that he needed to keep it secure and secret.

Sean liked the idea: "Let's make this as tight as the Cheyenne Mountain Complex."[40]

"Have you been there?"

"Me and ... Yeah, I trained there for three months."

When they weren't working on the VW bus or stringing wire for the security system, Sean seemed content to just sit, drink ale, and talk. "So now you're battle trained." He took out a smoke and leaned against the VW. "Most folks in the military train, but never engage in an actual firefight. As a civilian, you survived a pretty dangerous mission."

"I don't know about that." Matthew sat on the stool at Mr. Johnson's workbench. "Can you call spring break a mission?"

"It was more than a field trip."

Matthew wondered how much Sean knew. "How do you get used to it?"

"You just do."

"I can't believe Pete drowned. When Maria gets out, we are going to go to the

---

[40] The Cheyenne Mountain Complex is a military defensive bunker south of Colorado Springs and Peterson Air Force Base which also includes the North American Aerospace Defense Command (NORAD) and United States Northern Command (USNORTHCOM) headquarters.

mountain, over by Sandy Stream Pond, and put out more rocks for Pete. The Micmac say it will appease the great spirit—"

"Put a couple out for me too, bro," Sean said quietly.

Matthew shook his head and said, "In high school, he used to kick your butt in the summer mile swim on Millinocket Lake. How could he have drowned?"

"When a man's number is up, there's nothing anyone can do about it."

It was a cold response; an unfortunate statistic. Is this what the years on the front line had done to his brother?

Sean walked over to the VW. He ran his hand along the sanded Bondo. "This would make for a backdrop in a painting. They hit you with .50 caliber and small caliber."

Matthew checked his phone for messages. Nothing. He wanted to be there when Maria woke. He studied his brother and wanted to talk to Sean about what happened that week. But something held him back. So, he asked, "You're painting again? Great."

"Calms my demons," he grumbled. "They caught the guy with the Sopwith Camel."

Matthew could not hide his surprise. He hadn't mentioned the biplane to anyone. Uncle Carl?

"What do you expect from military intelligence, little bro?" He went to the fridge for another beer. "How this joyride stayed out of the media, I'll never know. I'm impressed. One report said that a wealthy aviation collector escaped the psych hospital. I don't buy it. He said someone stole the plane and then returned it to his Boca airstrip. If he can't prove it, or prove his alibi, they'll book him for murder."

Matthew doubted an old man was flying that plane. "What else have you heard?"

"The shootout in Miami has a tight lid on it. Whoever was there—wasn't there. There's another report where this bus was involved in a sting in South Carolina. And how about two homicides at the Bronx Park Zoo?"

"Coincidences? Wrong place at the wrong time."

"Nice try, junior. You know what I always say about coincidences."

"There's no such thing."

"Exactly. Then there's the whole Katahdin Sporting Lodge episode. I don't care what the papers say; Weaver was crazy but not that crazy. He locked you down there because of something you knew or something you had. I can't say I trust your buddy, Estebanez, for a lot of reasons, but he and Fazio took care of business at the lodge." He sat on the floor and leaned against the '60 Corvair. "How did you get out, and onto the lake?"

"There was a door in the back of the cellar. We broke the lock only to find it opened to a cliff. We were about to give up, but Maria noticed a rabbit run along the side of the mountain, suspended in air. There was a trail off to the side. When we were out, I jammed a few tree limbs against the door, in case Weaver came back. The trail led us around to the south side of the lodge and down to the lake; there's a boat dock there with small boats and canoes." He decided not to mention putting a bullet in Weaver's shoulder as they escaped.

He didn't know what to say next to his brother. Cracker Jack made him promise to keep his secret. From everyone. Even family.

"What's so damn valuable in those bags that someone is willing to kill you over it?"

There it is, Matthew thought with a cringe. "What bags?"

"Don't treat me like an idiot, kid. I can find out what Clinton is having for breakfast and change the menu before he takes his first bite. You have some serious characters on your trail. Your guardian angel knows it; that's why he's been watching over you all these years."

"My angel?"

"I can offer you protection, security and help with whatever you are doing—plus, I'm your brother—but you have to level with me."

Matthew made his decision.

Matthew began, "I don't think they intended to kill me. Just wanted to scare me and steal this scientific work I came across. It was entrusted to me." Matthew thought he detected a sparkle of satisfaction in his brother's eyes.

"Well, it's got the Saudis, U.S. government, and crime lords all zeroed in on Millinocket. You're quite a celebrity."

"I would prefer it to all go away. I could get down to going to school and working on my own research … now that the other research is gone. Gone forever."

His brother barked. "What?"

"I had everything in the boat. There's no use trying to retrieve it. It was all computer drives, journals, and well, paper. Most of it was paper."

Sean cursed under his breath and began pacing. "Do you think you can replicate the research? If anyone can, you can, right?"

Matthew knew he was winging it now and decided a half-truth would be better at this point. "I think so, Sean."

"We are going to help you do just that!"

"We?"

"You have more friends than you know." Sean walked around the shop. "Like I said, I can help you turn this place into a fort."

"That would be great," Matthew said, lightheaded. "I figure I can get up here every other weekend. I'll probably have to quit the swimming and rowing teams. They don't seem as important."

Sean said, "Don't quit. Work them in. I gave everything up to serve my country, and I have no regrets, but you—" He stopped pacing. "I've seen more kids your age take a bullet before they even had the chance to enjoy a good cigar, expensive whiskey, and the bed of a passionate woman." This was the Sean that Matthew remembered.

The things Sean wasn't saying rang loudest in his head. "Sean?"

"Yeah?"

"Back when you were finishing your masters at Yale, you brought a friend with you to the house. What was his name?"

"Tree."

"I know, but what was his real name?"

"John Imbrognio," Sean lied. "We called him Tree, and sometimes, Little John. Why?"

"I remember his visit and how interested he was in my drawings. That's all. He's the one who gave me the books on solar energy, right?"

"No, that was another guy I knew. He's dead now."

"What's he doing now?"

"Who?" Sean popped the hood of the Corvair. He went to the ignition and tried to turn it over.

"Your friend, Tree. John Imbrognio."

"He was killed in the Middle East."

"I'm sorry."

Matthew thought his brother didn't sound very sorry. The word *misinformation* came to mind. He frowned.

"Do you have a picture of him?"

"Who? Imbrognio? I might. I'll look around. Hand me that oil rag over there."

The day after Sean left for Washington, Nurse Reed called, and Matthew rushed to the hospital. She was awake. Matthew rushed to her side. When she heard about Pete, she cried.

"What about ...?"

Matthew shook his head and she let it go.

The next day, Dr. Fielding announced that Maria would be out of the hospital earlier than expected. Matthew had not seen anyone suspicious in a week, but before he would leave the hospital he made sure Maria had at least her father or Officer Dubois watching over her.

He drove to the ELF storage shed and retrieved a kayak, strapped it to the top of the Jeep and headed to the south end of Millinocket Lake. He knelt on the water's edge, only half in his wetsuit and thought he might be sick. Knowing what was coming next, he cursed, realizing he hadn't brought his pillbox. He held out his hands, and they were shaking.

He could hear his crew coach in his head and he repeated aloud, "Got to face your demons, got to get back in the boat."

"I haven't been called a demon since my third wife filed a restraining order against me."

Someone clicked their tongue. Matthew turned to find a 9mm pointed at his head, held by the man with the sharp cleft in his chin, and the Dallas Cowboys cap. Matthew raised his hands half-mast.

"Where is the research, kid?"

"At the bottom of the lake—lost in the storm."

"You're lying," Lomax said calmly, taking a step toward him, and placing the muzzle against Matthew's temple. "Turn around."

Matthew closed his eyes and said, "Look, I'm tired of this crap!" The man was quiet. "It's at the bottom of the lake!" With a deep breath, Matthew opened his eyes. The man was gone.

He sat down hard cross-legged into the tall grass and buried his head between his knees. Then he let himself fall to his back, arms spread. Looking up into the white-puffed blue sky, he watched a large "V" of Canadian geese pass overhead. "God. Is this ever going to end?"

Up on a hill overlooking the lake, Estebanez, in full camouflage gear, prone with the crosshairs of the sniper rifle zeroed in on Lomax, took his eye off the scope and removed his finger from the trigger. He was 174 meters from the target. He would not miss. Lomax walked away. Too bad, he thought.

He removed the scope from his rifle, and put it to his eye. He looked past Matthew and studied the young Micmac—Matthew's pal—Kyle Gespasian. Kyle, bookended by wolfhounds, was about a hundred meters north of Estebanez, but less than 30 meters from where Lomax had stood. He had had an arrow loaded in his bow and was about to put it through Lomax's right eye. A good friend, Estebanez mused.

He and Marcos, had taken turns these last weeks following Ahmed, Saleh, and Lomax. Estebanez was looking for a reason to eliminate them all.

He sat up and took out a cigar, but did not light it. Instead, he watched Matthew fall onto his back, then, after a while, get up, finish putting on the wetsuit, and push out onto the water.

He disasembled the M-40 Marine Sniper rifle, and thought of Kate Eaton.

On the day the hospital released Maria, the reporters swept in like a three-alarm fire. Where had they been hiding all this time, Matthew could not imagine.

"Before I take you home, I have something to show you," Matthew whispered. Nurse Reed helped her out of her wheelchair at the top of the front steps of the hospital. Matthew had convinced Maria's father to let him drive her home. First, they had to deal with the reporters, then they were on their way.

Twenty minutes later, Matthew parked in the Willow Run Cemetery. He looked around to make sure the old caretaker was gone and shot up the steep hill along the cobblestone path.

Maria gave him a quizzical look. They had not been to her mother's gravesite together since that dismal rainy funeral night.

Matthew reached into the back seat and picked up an old book and bouquets of flowers. They walked hand in hand over to the western end of the hill and knelt at a bright white marble gravestone. He laid the flowers below the headstone and began clearing branches from her grave as Maria said a prayer and spoke to her mother.

Matthew left her alone and leaned up against a tall, thin poplar about ten feet away. Maria came over, put her hands around his waist, and lay her head on his chest.

She was sniffling, so he took a handkerchief out of his pocket. They both laughed when she blew her nose. She attempted to stuff it back in his pocket.

"You can keep it," he said.

"Who carries handkerchiefs anymore," she stated.

"My grandfather had—"

She interrupted and asked, "You told me you wanted to show me something?"

He smiled and led her over toward the northeastern corner of the hill where stood the largest and perhaps the oldest oak tree in the area.

"On a sunshiny day, the old mill doesn't look as ominous, does it?" Maria asked. "I used to think it looked like a huge monster."

They held hands and stared north over the lakes and on toward Mount Katahdin. Matthew said, "I thought of the mill as a great big bear looking out for its cubs. Now that the big bear is dying, I fear for the people of this region. Maybe one day we can come back and start businesses that will help revive the area."

"When you finish CJ Energy Cells, you can bring a new form of industry, like manufacturing energy-efficient products," she said.

"I will, when I can safely get back to the research. With all this attention, I don't imagine it will be anytime soon." They sat on one of the large oak tree roots.

They were quiet for some time. Matthew stood up and said, "Close your eyes." He took out his old pocketknife. When he stepped back, the newly carved bark gleamed next to his old inscription.

M&M Were Here 1984 -1995

"Hmm. I always wondered what you were up to that night. You knew, didn't you?"

"Knew?"

"That we would be together."

He opened the book and handed it to Maria. Pressed into the very center page, in a chapter on Quantum Secrets of Photosynthesis, was a flattened, once yellow, rose. Maria looked at Matthew with wide tear-filled eyes. Matthew took her hand, and they walked back to the Jeep.

"*Eres el amor de mi vida,*" Maria said. She pushed him up against the Jeep, and up on her tip toes, kissed him passionately.

A few minutes later, the Jeep bounded down the cobblestone walkway and out onto the Golden Road. Around the first bend, Matthew had to swerve to miss an oncoming white sedan. He frowned, noticing the *Channel 9* emblazoned on the door. While he was studying the car, he barely missed hitting a large news van complete with satellite dishes and more *Channel 9* decals.

"They won't find us up here," Matthew said. He stared across the loft at the wall—it seemed to vibrate. Monks in robes. A hawk. Kyle. He rubbed his eyes. What was it? Something from his dreams—

"Let's hope not," Maria said. They lay together on a Micmac-made wool blanket in the hayloft inside the barn.

"In just a few weeks we'll be worrying about tests, instead of people shooting at us. I'm not sure I'm ready to go back."

Maria sighed, then said, "I'm excited, and it looks like I can intern at the Augusta Medical Examiners' office on the weekends."

"Dang, Clarice, the morgue?"

"You don't have to visit," she said with a pout.

"Sounds like we'll be too busy for long trips."

"I think we'll spend the break on campus or here. It'll be a lot safer."

"You think I'm safe?" He tickled her. They rolled over twice. Covered in straw Maria ended up on top.

"I'm the one to be afraid of. Very afraid." She sat up and began pulling hay out of her coiled hair.

He studied her movements. She made him feel delirious. He wondered when their relationship changed from friendship into something so much deeper. Perhaps his enlightenment unfolded as she lay comatose in the hospital. It was then that he had to consider a world without her. A world he did not want to live in.

Before he could stop himself, he said, "We love the things we love for what they are. An irresistible desire to be irresistibly desired."

She stopped unwinding straw from her hair. "You trying to rip off Robert Frost?"

He chuckled, and said, "So what? I read."

"And what are you trying to say?"

He stood up, and brushed straw off himself while displaying a sheepish grin.

She let the subject drop. "You should be excited to get going on your research."

"If they'll let me." He thought about the photographs Donna and Darma had delivered to him in the library, then recalled seeing the T-Bird at the hospital. And then there was Lomax. Where was Mr. E? He has a lot of splainin' to do. One thing was clear: the danger was far from over.

"They don't know you have the research. Do they?"

"That's the thing. We won't know unless someone attacks us again. I don't know if I can subject you to a world where we'll be looking over our shoulders every minute of every day."

"I choose to be subjected," she said stubbornly. "I'm in your world to stay, mister. And don't you forget it." She twisted the skin on his side until he yelped.

"At the very least, we'll leave the research where we hid it. I have enough information in the journals to keep me busy. When we feel that the fervor has died down, then we can plan how to keep CJ Energy safe. That's about as far out as I can think. Especially since we don't know who we can trust."

"There's Mr. E."

"If we knew where he was."

"He'll get in touch with you."

"Yeah."

"And then there's Sean. If it wasn't for him—and poor Pete—we wouldn't be here today."

"True," Matthew said slowly.

"My father said that after Weaver was killed, his oldest son returned from California, on an extended leave from his teaching position at Stanford. Did you know that?"

Matthew nodded and said, "He's running the lodge, and putting it up for sale. The wine and antiques are up for auction."

"You said you and Sean were working on this barn. What were you doing?"

"We replaced rotted boards, painted and had only finished the wiring and the basic security system when Sean was called back to Washington. He had some ideas on how I could set up a lab, but I don't know. I think I talked him out of hiding booby-traps around the perimeter. Mr. Johnson or someone else could get blown to smithereens."

"What is a smithereen?"

"It's Gaelic from smidirīn, tiny fragments."

"How did I known that you would know that," she said, and rapped his head with her knuckles.

He ducked, shrugged and said, "I have a lot of useless knowledge."

"You have a lot of useful knowledge."

Matthew remembered something his mother had handed him this morning. "I'll be right back." He left the loft and found it in the front seat of the Jeep. He studied the small cardboard box. It had no return address. He took out his knife and cut through the thick tape. Styrofoam peanuts fell out and blew away in the wind. They really need to outlaw those, he thought. He caught his breath. He unfolded the bubble wrap and held a beautiful multicolored ceramic flask engraved with the name *Wolfgang Pauli*. The note inside read:

I'd like you to have this. The rest of the story is in the journals. He always felt that this was charmed.

The note was not signed. He studied the flask. Wolfgang Pauli died in 1958. For the briefest of moments, Matthew thought it could have been from Mr. E. Or … he thought of how Tremont had opened an account in both of their names, years before meeting him. He looked back at the note. *I'd like?* In the present?

He tried to shake away the theory forming in his mind. It would be impossible. Absolutely impossible. I saw it happen. Didn't I?

Matthew now had three personal mementos from Cracker Jack's father; the gun, the flask, and a signed copy of *Capturing the Sun*. And of course, the *complete* life work of one of the greatest minds in quantum physics.

Maria called from the barn, snapping him out of his reverie. "Did you tell me at the hospital that Sean asked where the research was stored?" She came out and put the trash from their picnic into the back of the Jeep.

"You could hear me? What else do you remember me saying."

She laughed. "You'll never know. At least until I need to use it against you."

"No, but I told him it was lost in the storm. I'm not sure why I lied about it, but it seemed the right thing to do."

They returned to the barn. Matthew went up to the loft to retrieve their backpacks, and she followed him up. He wrapped her in his arms, and they fell onto the blanket.

"I agree."

"Agree to what?" He pushed back a flock of curls and kissed her neck.

"I agree—everything else can wait."

"Good thinking," Matthew said.

She put her hands on his chest and pushed him back down. Her left eye closed slightly.

This time Matthew thought, *that* look took on a new dimension.

"Then you're going to focus on saving the world, right?"

"Absolutely."

Excerpt from

PERPETUAL Book II
Assassins

The SUVs hit them from both sides.

Sean fumbled among broken glass and felt for his Glock. No luck. He reached for the switchblade and cut his seatbelt away.

He said, "I'll have to thank your neighbor, the assassin, for trying to stick me with this. Last time I saw her … Matty?"

Sean shook Matthew, and his head rolled to the side. Blood trickled from a head wound. Sean felt for a pulse and muttered, "Hang tight, sport." He reached for Jackson's .45. One of the assailants in the passenger seat was slumped over, less than a foot away. The driver lifted his head from the steering wheel, turned to Sean, and raised an Uzi. Sean fired a double tap. The first bullet shattered the window. The second shot caught the driver between the eyes.

He looked ahead, squinting at the harsh lights spinning from a dozen police cruisers in front of the OCME.

Sean looked for the other large SUV. Less damaged, it had pulled away and had spun about twenty feet toward the Hampton Inn before coming to a stop. Two Asian men were pulling themselves free from the wreckage. One was carrying an Uzi micro pistol capable of firing six hundred rounds per minute. The other lifted a much heavier Type 73 machine gun, unique to the North Koreans. Sean crawled to the backseat, hoping to draw them away from Matthew. His door jammed up against the other SUV, so he only had one choice, to go out in the direct line of fire of the assault team.

Sean threw the door open and hit the ground rolling. Bullets kicked up all around. He thought one caught him in the side, and one in the shoulder. He scrambled to the back of his Lincoln sedan, around to the back of the adjacent SUV, and then to the front, where he reached in and took the Uzi from the driver. Sean shoved Matthew's .45 Glock into his belt and looked over the hoods of the two vehicles, drawing a dozen shots from each of the attackers. He dropped to the ground at the front tire, blindly pointing the Uzi toward the perps, firing off a burst. The man carrying the Type 73 rifle went down, grabbing his leg. The other ran out of Sean's line of sight.

The four attackers were indistinguishable, wearing non-marked navy-blue fatigues. He cursed himself for letting his guard down but marveled at the boldness of this incursion. The men were Yong-ui Baen, from the secret order of the Dragon Serpent. The North Korean secret police, the SSD—or from special operations. The SOF, chose each soldier carefully. The Yong-ui Baen trained eighteen hours a day, seven days a week.

How could I be so stupid and not realize they were tracking me? How the hell did they get into this country undetected?

Sean knew this attack had nothing to do with Colonel Xi or with whatever had happened to Maria.

Sean had been proud of the intel report suggesting that the young new leader of North Korea had it out for him. Kim Jong-il had purportedly labeled Sean the number one enemy of the state. The chairman's generals had deduced that Sean was responsible for wreaking chaos across North Korea. They had pinned on Sean the assassinations of their four top scientists, who were allegedly involved in developing an underground nuclear facility in Kumchang-ri.

Sean had to admit it had been difficult to hide as a 6'2" sandy blonde Caucasian in a country where everyone looked and dressed the same—their average height less than five feet.

A crunch of glass, and Sean turned. The passenger of the first SUV was raising a handgun. Sean heard the Korean's gun fire, but his own bullet lodged in the man's throat.

He rolled out from behind the vehicles, and firing two rounds, ended the career of the Yong-ui Baen man on the ground.

Warm blood ran down Sean's side, and he felt light headed. He blinked as two women exited the Hampton, shook his head, and cursed. What did they think was going on out here? Fireworks?

One last assailant with an Uzi was one too many. The last thing the attacker would expect was a direct assault. So, that's exactly what he did, while firing in the direction he had seen the last man disappear.

The last Korean soldier had circled around and was waiting. He grabbed one of the women and held her in front of him. The other woman fell to the ground screaming. Sean dropped and lost the Uzi as the man fired. He rolled behind the SUV and reached for the .45, rested it on his forearm, and waited.

Beginning to lose consciousness, his last thought was, how would he get Matthew out of this.

PERPETUAL *Assassins* – Book 2 in the series
Now available wherever books are sold
Visit the Perpetual Writer at *www.BrianHuey.com*

And he shall separate them one from another, as a shepherd divideth his sheep from the goats: And he shall set the sheep on his right hand, but the goats on the left.

– Matthew 25: 32, 33 (KJ Version)

Acknowledgments

To my father.

James E. Huey (1930–2016) was born and raised in the mining towns of Pennsylvania. Pop contributed sixty years of service to other veterans. He was an avid reader. When Dad liked *Perpetual,* I knew there was hope.

And my mother.

Darlee Anderson Huey is a southern bell, born in Petal, Mississippi. She met Dad in 1954 while visiting Aunt Alice in Cleveland, Ohio. It was part of a family conspiracy. Mom is a faith filled woman, tremendously creative, an avid photographer, and an amateur botanist and ornithologist.

In gathering the details to tell the tale of the Jackson's and Eaton's, and their quest to make the world a better place, any mistakes remain my own.

Regarding debts that cannot be repaid, thank you to my family, friends, and associates who have contributed their wisdom, expertise, patience, and time to deliver the *Perpetual* series of novels to you.

Please find a comprehensive list of appreciation on my website.

Above all, I thank my Lord, the *author* and finisher of my faith. —*Hebrews 12:2 NKJV*

About Brian

Born and raised in Ohio, Brian graduated from UNC where he competed in swimming and diving. Having owned businesses in advertising, manufacturing, and finance, he often paraphrases Mark Twain, saying that reality truly is stranger than fiction. *Perpetual*, he says, is the story of dreamers and inventors on a quest to accomplish the impossible, while pitted against tremendous obstacles, not the least of which are naysayers and the status quo. He has worked as a trade magazine writer and editor, and written short stories, screenplays, and TV pilots. He lives in North Carolina and is working on additional *Perpetual* novels and a new adventure suspense series based in the Adirondacks. When asked about Cracker Jack, he replied, "Stay tuned."

Brian loves to hear from readers.
Visit the Perpetual Writer: *http://www.BrianHuey.com* ...
... and your favorite bookseller, for more novels in the *Perpetual Series*.